'After her glorious first novel, *The Gifts*, Hyder has
returned with another beautiful slice of historical fiction.
The Illusions is charming and intriguing, sparkling with
magic and romance.' – Jennifer Saint

'For a truly immersive, can't-put-it-down read, *The Illusions* will
whisk you to the late Victorian age with this story of two young
women, Cecily, a con artist's assistant and Eadie, a photographer
and early film maker trying to make it in a man's world. Cecily
and Eadie's paths will soon collide in a kaleidoscope of magic,
theatrics, illusion and love.' – *Red* magazine

'Hyder is a wonderfully accomplished storyteller. *The Illusions*
is a magical tale of innovation, darkness and delight.
A book to disappear into – I devoured it greedily.'
– Joanne Burn, author of *The Hemlock Cure*

'With clever storytelling and a magpie's eye for shine and
enchantment, Hyder takes us to a world where magic, moving
pictures and illusion mix – and where all are made better
by human kindness.' – Annie Garthwaite, author of *Cecily*

'Captivating and fascinating . . . A fabulous second novel (for adults),
firmly cementing Liz Hyder as an author to watch. Beautifully
crafted, *The Illusions* steps into a world of trickery and deception,
while shining a light on the importance of friendship and love.'
– LoveReading Star Book

'Filled with wonders in all forms, in real life and in the theatre,
this is a story that will mesmerise and cast its spell.
I loved it.' – Essie Fox

'Spellbinding storytelling, wonderfully drawn characters and the
thrill of the theatre make this book unputdownable.' – Louise Hare

THE
ILLUSIONS

AUTHOR BIO

Liz Hyder has been making up stories for as long she can remember. *Bearmouth*, her debut young adult novel, won a Waterstones Children's Book Prize, the Branford Boase Award and was chosen as the Children's Book of the Year by *The Times*. *The Gifts*, her acclaimed debut novel for grown-ups, was published in 2022. She has a BA in drama from the University of Bristol and was, once upon a time, a member of the National Youth Theatre. Originally from London, she has lived in Shropshire for over a decade.

THE ILLUSIONS

LIZ HYDER

AN ASTONISHING STORY OF WOMEN
AND TALENT, MAGIC AND POWER

MANILLA
PRESS

First published in the UK in 2023 by
MANILLA PRESS
An imprint of Zaffre Publishing Group
A Bonnier Books UK company
4th Floor, Victoria House, Bloomsbury Square,
London, England, WC1B 4DA
Owned by Bonnier Books
Sveavägen 56, Stockholm, Sweden

A CIP catalogue record for this book is
available from the British Library.

Paperback: 978-1-78658-189-1

Also available as an ebook and an audiobook

1 3 5 7 9 10 8 6 4 2

Typeset by Palimpsest Book Production Ltd, Falkirk, Stirlingshire
Printed and bound in Great Britain by Clays Ltd, Elcograf S.p.A.

Manilla Press is an imprint of Zaffre Publishing Group
A Bonnier Books UK company
www.bonnierbooks.co.uk

For in and out, above, about, below,
'Tis nothing but a Magic Shadow-show,
Play'd in a Box whose Candle is the Sun,
Round which we Phantom Figures come and go.

The Rubaiyat of Omar Khayyam
translated by Edward Fitzgerald

Any budding conjuror must start at the beginning.

I have learned, through my own experience and years of practice, that, in essence, all magical effects come under one of only six headings.

I should say, whilst I have chosen six, there may be others who might argue for seven or ten. Perhaps you yourself may even invent a new one for, however much one knows, I assure you, one can never learn all there is to know about magic.

The first of my six headings is 'Production'.

Examples for an amateur conjuror might include producing an endless number of articles from a hat, catching money from mid-air, or plucking a string of coloured handkerchiefs from an apparently 'empty' hand.

Through the use of palming, sleight-of-hand and employing some item that serves as a 'cover,' the conjuror may secretly produce the article he wants to show. This must be already concealed, and attention should not be drawn to it until the grand 'reveal'.

Extract from *The Secrets of Magic* by George Perris
(published by Saxon Press, 1895)

PRODUCTION

March 1896
BRISTOL

A storm is coming. It lingers in the air, dances in the trees, and blows at the roof tiles, trying to prise them from their holds. The rusting weathervane at the top of St Andrew's rattles, swinging in circles at the sudden gusts and gales that make the church's resident barn owls hide in the bell tower, huddled together for warmth.

Beneath them, a small crowd of men and women gather in the midst of the graveyard, holding tightly on to their hats and bonnets as the wind tries to cast them off into the black of the night. Arter Evans, an ageing con artist with a knack for the theatrical, tries his best to hold both their attention and his lantern, a battle he is in danger of losing. The deep and often empty pockets of Arter's frayed woollen coat carry a smattering of coins from his audience, and they clink faintly as he picks up a small bell from the top of an old headstone.

His accomplice, sixteen-year-old Cecily Marsden, barely hears the bell ring from where she hides, crouched behind a large, moss-covered gravestone in the far corner of the dank churchyard. The wind is doing its best to steal the sound away, but Cec, as she prefers to be called, is focused entirely on something else. *Something impossible . . .*

The wind blows around her as her mouth falls open. Her left palm faces outward, empty. Leaves and white petals from early blossom circle her like a tiny tornado in the dark. In front of her, about a foot away, and stubbornly resisting the wind's power, a playing card is held up without her even touching it.

The four of diamonds, freshly plucked from her pack, hangs suspended in mid-air. Held up with – well, she is not entirely sure.

Over the past eight months or so, ever since a chance encounter in a room above a tavern in a grubby corner of London, Cec has developed a serious interest in card tricks – an obsession, almost. Since then, she has practised, secretly, at every spare moment, sewing hidden pockets into her dresses so her two dog-eared packs are accessible whenever she chooses. She has practised in narrow beds in empty rooms, when Arter was out on drunken sprees, lost to the bottom of the bottle in the darkest alleyways of whichever town they found themselves in. She has practised, as she does tonight, whilst waiting for a show to start. She has even, although she would never admit it, practised in rare, quiet moments whilst sitting on the privy, dress hitched up above her knees.

She had swiftly mastered the basics – switching cards, marking a deck, fanning and shuffling – and is confident now in all manner of tricks, begging and borrowing from card sharps in the many taverns they passed through on their way to Bristol. But she has never dared share it, not with Arter, nor anyone else. It's the only thing she has that is *all hers.*

And never before has young Cecily Marsden achieved *this.*

It is impossible. Just as she witnessed that night in London, months ago. A wrong turn into an empty room with a stage. An awkward young magician still learning his craft, a rehearsal without witnesses − until Cec silently stepped in. Gossamer threads, thin as a spider's web, strung high across the stage. Concealed paper hooks on the back of the cards floating in mid-air. Nothing but a clever trick.

Tonight though, there is no thread, no hidden hooks; nothing, except Cec and her impossible card . . .

Cec gasps and the card falls to the ground like a dead weight. She pounces on it, tucking it back into her hidden pocket. Her mind whirls, full of questions, as she tries to steady herself for her performance, wrestling her thoughts back to Arter.

'Ladies and gentlemen!' he bellows throatily as the audience shiver, nudging each other. 'Prepare yourselves! For tonight, you will witness a genuine spectre − the famed ghost of St Andrew's! The Lady in White herself! Tonight, ladies and gentlemen, at the stroke of midnight . . .' He pauses for effect. '*She will walk again!*'

There is a collective intake of breath from the audience and Arter nods, pleased, before continuing in his booming voice. 'Hers is a story of tragedy. An echo from the past of an exquisite young beauty who fell in love with a handsome, dangerous—'

The wind steals Arter's words away and Cec struggles to focus. She puts a hand to the pocket of her stiffly starched dress, feeling the cards underneath. It must have been her imagination. A vision caused by an empty stomach. But it wasn't. She *knows* it wasn't . . .

'The Lady in White, now abandoned by her lover, lost and alone,' Arter annunciates, as clearly as any actor in the West End. 'She came to this very church, in the heart of Clifton, to pray for her soul. She knelt on the cold flagstones, hands clasped together, and when she was done, she rose, and entered the tower. She climbed every one of the stone steps to the very top and looked out upon her last night on earth.'

The first chime for midnight rings out – Cec's cue to begin her part in tonight's charade – and the barn owls take flight from the bell tower, scattering across the graveyard, before disappearing into the dark.

'Hark!' cries Arter theatrically, a hand cupped to his ear. 'The Lady in White will soon appear!'

Cec concentrates, trying to wipe the impossible card from her mind. Candles are no good in weather such as this, so she must make do with a small oil lamp. The wind snatches the flame away as she tries to light it and she curses quietly, adjusting a veil over her face before trying again.

The fifth chime already echoes around the graveyard by the time the Lady in White finally emerges. Her ghostly lamp reflects the luminous paint of her costume as Cec glides smoothly, silently, around the front of the church to gasps of astonishment.

'Three times she will encircle the church! Three times she will search for her lost lover!' Arter cries, trying to make himself heard above the clanging bells.

Cec walks slowly, each foot placed purposefully on the uneven path in front. The starched veil draped over her bonnet hides her intricate make-up: a semi-skeletal face, carefully drawn on with a stick of charcoal to her own design. After her final circuit of the church, she is to remove her veil and reveal her face. She has been hoping someone might faint tonight when they see it – by far her favourite reaction – but as she disappears into the darkness on the far side of the church, her mind slips back to her impossible four of diamonds . . .

'Here she comes again!' cries Arter, moments later, as the Lady in White re-emerges, somewhat out of breath, for Cec has pelted around the back of the church as fast as she can. 'See how she *glides*!'

Cec focuses on her feet as she once more reaches the far end of the church. She turns the corner, lifts her skirts, and starts to run around the back of St Andrew's – but her haste makes her careless.

She trips, crying out as her ankle twists beneath her. A large branch from a nearby oak, loosened by the wind, has caught her off-guard. Crumpled on the ground, Cec feels her foot to check no bones are broken. She forces herself to stand, but her smooth glide, practised to perfection, is impossible without just a little rest. She leans on the cold stone walls of the church, knowing both Arter and the audience will be impatient for the Lady in White's third and final appearance.

Cec grimaces, grinding her teeth and trying not to hobble, as she comes back into view. Thunder rumbles above and the wind picks up speed. In full sight of the audience, it snatches her ghostly bonnet and loosens it, carrying it away, the veil trailing in its wake.

'Her head! The Lady in White's head!' screams one woman before she flees, certain for the rest of her days that she saw the decapitated head of a spirit flying over the church. The hysteria spreads and the crowd scatters. One man spies Cec as she turns towards him, and all *he* sees is a rotting, skeletal face. He shrieks as he pelts off, his wife running to catch up with him.

Arter holds his hands out, begs for money from those who haven't already paid – but it is too late. The entire audience, like the owls of St Andrew's, have vanished into the night.

'What on earth happened?' Arter snaps, cuffing Cec around the ear, too fast for her to dodge.

'*Ow!*' she cries, glaring at him. 'It wasn't my fault! I *told* you the storm was coming but *you* were the one who still insisted we do it tonight.'

'Ah, well . . .' He grumbles at the reprimand. 'Sorry, Cec. Shouldn't 'a hit you.'

She purses her lips and he shrugs, holding out his hand to show that half the coins he collected were simply buttons and badges. The perils of collecting money in the dark. He slips the few coins into his coat pocket.

'Not enough for a decent meal,' he says, sorrowfully. 'Not for both of us, anyway. Ah, I'm getting too old for this.' He sighs mournfully. 'I coulda been one of the greats of the stage, Cec. And instead, here we are . . .'

Cec rolls her eyes for she's heard this a hundred times and more.

'I tell you, Cec, I coulda been!' Arter says insistently. 'And I tell you somethin' else for nothin' too, if an opportunity comes your way, grab it with both hands, girl! Don't end up like me . . .'

'What now?' Cec asks wearily as her stomach rumbles, drowned out by the thunder echoing around the churchyard.

'Home,' he replies. 'Sleep it off. Hope tomorrow brings better luck.' He sighs and shuffles his feet. 'Come on then,' he says. ''fore the rain comes.' And with that he marches off in great loping strides, his coat flapping out behind him.

For a fleeting moment, Cec hates him. Loathes him with every inch of her being. Five years since this old trickster with his grey-streaked hair and sallow cheeks plucked her from the streets, the small girl with a loud voice and a knack for fast learning. Five years of Arter's broken prom-ises. Of scratching a living, of half-empty bellies, of famines rather than feasts. She forgets for a moment how much fun he can be, how generous and silly, how he can transform himself in the blink of an eye. She forgets how much she's learned from him, how he's used more and more of her ideas in their little shows over the years, how she'd be lost without him. All she can think of is her hunger, her resent-ment and fury. She *knows* he'll drink it. The money. That once again she'll fall asleep, blanket wrapped tightly around, only to wake and find Arter gone or already half-cut in his bed, a stench of beer and gin hovering above him like a cloud.

Cec reluctantly follows him onto Clifton Hill as Arter disappears ahead, underneath a tower of scaffolding. She lags behind, her ankle still niggling her. Another house being painted and preened. All these grand terraced houses, filled with folk who never know what it is to go hungry. Cec hates them too. She clenches her fists as she thinks of it.

'Come on!' Arter bellows over his shoulder, not bothering to look behind, and Cec growls, glaring daggers at him, fingernails digging hard into her palms as she struggles to contain her temper.

She sees it happen almost before it does. A sense of inevitability like a cup too close to the edge of a table. Time seems to stretch and expand as the wind roars across the whole of the city. The house's wooden scaffolding turns towards her. A twist in its legs. A lean to one side as if all three storeys of it are curious to see her.

She sees Arter, underneath, the scaffolding forming a tunnel around him, the moon peeping out from the clouds above, bright for a moment. His distinctive silhouette, the top hat that had seen better days, his long coat fanning out behind him. A glimpse, in black and white, before the scaffolding groans and splinters, collapsing in on itself like a tower of cards, swallowing him up.

Cec stands, frozen to the spot in horror, as the storm whips away the cloud of dust and she sees the damage left behind. Huge planks of wood snapped like matchsticks, piled up like a small mountain. And there is Arter. Trapped in the midst like a broken bird. One corner of his coat flapping, black and useless, like a snapped wing.

'Arter!'

Cec runs to him, forgetting the pain in her ankle, forgetting everything. Her breath comes hard and fast as she clambers over the broken timbers to reach him, splinters of wood digging into her hands and knees, sharp as needles. But it's too late. Arter stares into nothingness, a puzzled look on his face, a frown of bewilderment.

Arter.

The wind whistles triumphantly as rain starts to patter down, light at first and then heavier, harder. Cec's hair comes loose from its pins, whipping across her face as she stares at Arter. His crushed hat. His torn coat. In the outstretched palm of his right hand lie the buttons from earlier; after a moment, Cec reaches out and takes them. She rolls them in her own hand like rosary beads before putting them in her pocket, next to her beloved cards.

She is all alone now.

Soaking wet and shivering, Cec pummels with her fists at the front door of the house on Dowry Square, her face still streaked with make-up despite both the rain and her tears. Her feet had developed a mind of their own, taking her to the one person in all of Bristol that might be able to help, to a house that, if you had asked her earlier, she would have denied she could even have found again.

The door opens and she stands, dripping pools of water in a dark hallway. Then there is light and warmth, soft carpet underfoot, and a panelled room with large sash windows. Unfamiliar faces are sat around a table – half-drunk glasses of port, plates with scatterings of crumbs – and there, in the heart of the gathering, is Mr Roderick Skarratt himself. A fire crackles in the hearth and a clock ticks.

Skarratt stands. He is shorter and yet more imposing than she remembers. 'What is the meaning of this?' he asks, sharply. He comes closer, his face fuzzy at the edges somehow, black ink bleeding around her vision. 'You're Arter's girl? That's right, isn't it?'

He glances back at his companions as Cec nods, trying to remain steady on her feet as the shock of it finally hits her. Arter's staring eye, his outstretched palm . . .

She nods as a sob starts to rise up. 'It's Arter, sir. It's about Arter—' She feels Skarratt's hand on her arm, fingers tight, holding her up as her legs start to feel less solid. 'It's . . . he's . . .' The words elude her for a moment before she howls them out, a wail of disbelief. 'He's dead, sir. *Arter's dead!*'

The blackness around Skarratt's face spreads slowly inwards and all Cec can think about is her impossible four of diamonds, suspended in mid-air. Her searing anger with Arter moments before his death. Her fists tight with rage. The way time had stretched. The scaffolding turning towards her, as if it were looking at her, before collapsing, crushing both Arter and her whole world in a moment.

Her last thought as she feels herself falling into darkness, her vision vanishing to a pinhole, is that somehow *she* did it. The scaffolding. Her fury. Her clenched fists . . .

I killed him, Cec thinks. *I killed him.*

And the words dance inside her head, pattering like the rain on the window outside.

Eadie Carleton picks, nervously, at a loose thread on her dress. This is the first séance she has ever attended and, if all goes to plan, will almost certainly be her last. She shivers, reassuring herself it is just the chill of last night's storm still lingering in the air.

Mrs Carnesky's drawing room feels oppressive, with its maroon flock wallpaper and dark furniture. A plaster bust of a bearded man sits on a plinth in the far corner and Eadie wonders who it might be of, before her foot, tapping impatiently, nudges against the Gladstone bag that used to belong to her brother, Louis. The touch of it reminds her of why she is really here. Inside is a small mechanism, an item brought to the Carletons' shop for repair, and which she had puzzled over for some time before realising its true purpose.

Eadie glances around at the four other women seated at the circular table: mother and daughter, Mrs and Miss McDonald, the elder a tall woman with a shelf-like bosom, the younger pinch-faced with sadness; Mrs Beattie, a silent lady with hair as white as snow; and finally, Miss Everett, a nervous young woman with dark circles under her eyes. Only two seats remain as their host closes the heavy velvet curtains with a flourish and the doorbell rings.

'Our last member for tonight's proceedings,' Mrs Carnesky announces in her husky voice, as she gently places a large pillar candle in the centre of the table.

Moments later, a young man bursts in, followed closely by Mrs Carnesky's maid. Grey-haired despite a youthful face, he is of medium height with a boyish, eager energy and a neat little moustache. *Perhaps grief has made him prematurely grey*, thinks Eadie, noting that, unlike the other attendees, he is not dressed in mourning but is instead in a well-cut pinstripe.

'Terribly sorry I'm late,' he says, breathlessly, smiling apologetically and catching Eadie's eye. Mrs Carnesky indicates for him to take a seat, and he nods as the maid leaves, closing the door behind her.

'You are just in time, Mr——?'

'Er, Ferris. George Ferris,' says the man, pausing for a moment as Eadie racks her brain. *Ferris . . .* She's sure she's heard that name before.

'Ferris? Like the American engineer? Of the great wheel?' Eadie finds herself asking, and Mr Ferris smiles.

'That's it, exactly!' he replies, not taking his eyes off her as he pulls out the empty chair opposite. 'Alas, I am not him, though. Engineering's not *quite* my forte.'

He grins as he sits, and she smiles back, puzzled for a moment. She cannot quite place him; the faint London lilt, the grey moustache on a young man's face, his confident charm strangely at odds with the sombre air of expectation in the room.

Mrs Carnesky leans forward to light the large candle on the table before slowly circling the drawing room, extinguishing the gas lamps and plunging them into darkness. Shadows dance around the walls as the candlelight flickers.

Eadie swallows. She firmly believes those that have passed can no more communicate from the 'other side' than a pig can fly – particularly as she now knows the truth behind at least one of their host's secrets. Still, she cannot help but give a quiver of anticipation as Mrs Carnesky joins them at the table. Eadie's beloved Papa died well over a year ago and she misses him dreadfully. Then her brother Louis disappeared just three months after that. Even though Eadie doesn't believe in the spirit realm, she can see the appeal for those, like her, left behind.

'Now that we are all present, we may begin,' Mrs Carnesky says, her voice full of warmth and honey. 'I have communicated with the spirits since I was a small child, as my mother and grandmother did before me. This evening, I will act as a bridge between this world and the spirit realm. I assure you, whatever happens tonight, whatever you witness, you are perfectly safe. There is nothing to fear.' She nods reassuringly. 'It is time. Please, may I ask each of you to take the hands of the person either side? We must form an unbroken circle for the spirits to come.'

Eadie glances at Mr Ferris across the table as she reaches out to the women either side of her. The golden light of the candle flickers across his face and she is sure she sees the side of his mouth twitch.

'I ask now that you close your eyes,' Mrs Carnesky says, soothingly. 'Do not be concerned if you find yourself breathing more deeply. It's perfectly natural.'

Eadie listens to her own breath, feels her chest moving up and down. She opens her right eye a crack and, to her surprise, Mr Ferris is looking directly at her. Caught out, he gives a slight murmur, screwing his eyes up as Eadie, puzzled, once again closes hers.

'Tonight, we gather, oh spirits, to seek guidance from your world,' intones Mrs Carnesky. 'Come, spirits! We invite you into this house, to join us. Come, spirits! *Come!*'

She pauses and the candle splutters. Eadie sneaks another peek as shadows flicker around the room, wisps of darkness that form inky shapes of figures and forms in the corners and curtains.

It's only my imagination, Eadie tells herself, forcing her eyes closed as her heart and breath quicken.

'Come, spirits! Give us a sign that you are here!' Mrs Carnesky cries.

A loud knock comes from somewhere indeterminate, as if emanating from both within the table and inside the walls themselves. Once, twice, three times. Eadie jumps. Murmurings of disquiet rumble around the room as everyone opens their eyes, faces full of alarm and surprise.

'Do not be afraid, friends!' Mrs Carnesky implores. 'I ask that you keep hold of each other's hands. The circle *must* be complete if the spirits are to remain. And they are here! I feel them! Speak spirits, speak! Use me as your vessel!'

Ridiculous, thinks Eadie, reassuring herself as her heart continues to race. She glances at Mr Ferris, who frowns at Mrs Carnesky.

Mrs McDonald, to Eadie's left, lets out a sob, and their host leans her head back, her body spasming. Just as Eadie thinks perhaps Mrs Carnesky really *is* having a fit, she stops, motionless, before turning towards Mrs McDonald.

'My darling wife,' says Mrs Carnesky in a strange, low voice with a hint of Glaswegian. '*How I have missed you!*'

Mrs McDonald gasps. 'Jeremy . . .?'

'Cora!' Mrs Carnesky continues in the same, low voice. 'And Bettina! My dearest daughter!'

'Oh, Jeremy! We miss you so very much!'

'My darlings! Know that I miss you in return; know, too, the other side is as *wonderful* as anyone might wish.'

'Oh, Jeremy! Is Mother there with you? And Father? And Aunt Joan?'

'I cannot stay, Cora; I am fading already but we are *all* here, I promise you. Farewell, my darlings! Until we meet again! Until . . .'

The voice fades as Mrs Carnesky's head falls onto her chest. The McDonalds sob as the rest of those in the room hold their breath.

After a while, Mrs Carnesky raises her head, speaking again in her normal voice, although she seems drained by her experience. 'The spirits are with us this evening, friends. One has already spoken but there are others who wish to converse with you. Show yourselves, spirits! *Show yourselves!*'

The candle goes out – to a gasp of surprise – throwing them into darkness. Eadie squints, trying to see, as an icy finger of fear rolls down her spine.

A faint, pale face appears in the dark, floating in space. As it climbs higher, towards the ceiling, a christening robe rises beneath it. 'Mama . . .?' says a small child's flute-like voice. 'Mama . . .?'

To her right, Eadie hears Miss Everett draw a sharp breath, and she finds her own hand suddenly gripped tighter by the young woman.

'Mama?' the little voice asks. 'Do you miss me, Mama? I'm here, on the other side. Waiting for you to join me . . .'

There is a scrape of a chair and the scratch of a match as George Ferris's furious face is illuminated, his eyes blazing.

'*No!* This goes no further! This woman is a fraud and an imposter!' he proclaims loudly. 'And I'll prove it!' He brings the lit match towards the child's head to illuminate a chalky, crude face that looks nothing like a real human – and far more like the balloon it actually is. There's barely a second for Eadie to try and process this startling revelation before the child's face explodes in a loud bang.

Screams of shock reverberate around the room as little pieces of glowing rubber float down, settling onto the hair and hands of those present.

George Ferris marches around the room, lighting the gas lamps and bringing the world back into view. 'It's nothing but a balloon on a rod!' he says, angrily. 'Japanese silk, luminous paint . . . nothing but tricks and lies!'

Eadie, stunned into silence, looks around her, at the tear stains on the pale cheeks of the McDonalds, at the distress on Miss Everett's face.

Mrs Carnesky's eyes are wide with surprise.

'The knocking sounds were easily done,' George continues. 'An inflatable bulb concealed in one of the table legs or a hidden pole, operated by Mrs Carnesky's foot. Perhaps even a false hand hidden in plain sight as her real hand raps sharply beneath the table. And the voices – I'm sorry, ladies, believe me, but it's nothing more than a ventriloquist's trick. Mrs Carnesky would be better onstage than deceiving the innocent people of Bristol!'

'Enough!' says Eadie, finding her voice as she stands. 'Enough, Mr Ferris. Please. You have made your point. Everyone, perhaps it's time we took our leave?'

'The spirits did come,' says Mrs Carnesky softly but defiantly. 'They did . . .'

'Then why the balloon?' asks George, sharply. 'Why the rod and the christening robe? If the spirits *were* here, what need have you of a conjuror's tricks?'

He reaches forward, grabs the christening robe, and shakes out the metal rod underneath. Mrs Carnesky sits motionless and diminished, unable to defend herself, as George leans toward her right hand and grabs it, pulling it until it comes loose.

He holds up the disembodied hand and raps it on the centre of the table. 'Nothing but painted wood!' he says, with disgust.

'Mr Ferris!' says Eadie. '*Please* . . .' She motions around the room to the shocked faces as Miss Everett rises, clutching a handkerchief to her mouth. Mrs Beattie follows her, an arm around the young woman, as they quietly exit.

'Mrs McDonald?' Eadie ventures, softly. 'Miss McDonald?'

The mother and daughter slowly stand, their grief writ large upon their fallen faces as they lean upon each other.

'I'm sorry. Truly,' George says, as the McDonalds make their way toward the door. He offers his arm, but Miss McDonald shakes her head.

'No, Mr Ferris. You have done *quite* enough,' she replies, as she and her mother leave.

Eadie moves to follow them, to help in some way, but instead remembers her Gladstone bag. She lifts it up onto the table and opens it, extracting the strange-looking instrument, all metal rods and leather straps, which she places next to the false hand.

'Not a surgical device at all,' she says, quietly. 'Is it, Mrs Carnesky?'

'You were in this with him then, Miss Carleton?' Mrs Carnesky glares at her.

'No!' Eadie replies, bemused, for she has never even seen Mr Ferris before.

'I know who you are now,' Mrs Carnesky continues, sourly, turning towards George. 'I know *exactly* who you are, Mr Perris!' She emphasises the 'P' in his surname. 'George *Perris*. I should have seen through you right away. The upstart magician, scouring the land to crush people's dreams!'

George gives a slight nod of acknowledgement before reaching up to his moustache, pulling it off in a single swift move. He ruffles his hair and white powder falls out of it in a faint cloud, revealing his true, dark hair underneath.

He is not prematurely aged at all, thinks Eadie, her mouth agape, as George reveals himself to be roughly the same age as herself, no older than his mid-twenties.

'I don't *crush* people's dreams, Mrs Carnesky!' says George, sharply. 'I don't give them false hope or lie to them as you do. You use the same tricks as any stage conjuror but when we magicians perform, our audience *knows* it's an illusion. You pretend it is *spirits*, the ghosts of those who are gone. You're a fraud and an imposter preying on the bereaved and vulnerable. Offering false hope, destroying lives, and all in the name of profit.'

He looks at Eadie and she cannot, in truth, disagree with anything he has said, but is still fuming at him for what she sees as his extraordinary lack of tact.

He reaches out his hand. 'Miss Carleton?'

'I shall see myself out, thank you, Mr Ferris. Perris. Whatever your name *really* is.' She nods at Mrs Carnesky before leaving, hand clasped tightly around Louis's now empty bag.

The wind is picking up again and the temperature has dropped but Eadie's anger is more than enough to keep her warm as she stamps westwards. The streets are quiet this late at night being, as they are, some distance from the city centre, and the sound of footsteps behind her makes her turn as George Perris rushes to catch up with her.

'Forgive me, Miss Carleton, I have offended you and—'

'It is not *me* who you should be worried about, Mr Ferris, Perris,' snaps Eadie as she marches along, George keeping pace alongside. 'The poor McDonalds – did you not stop to think how hurt they would be? And, worst of all, someone in that room had undoubtedly *lost a child*! Can you imagine how dreadful that must be? And you exploded it! Blew up its face in front of us!'

'Yes, well, I hadn't intended the flame to get that close . . .' he says, sheepishly. 'But Carnesky was preying on you all! You don't know what hold people like her can have over someone, what damage they can do. I've seen it, Miss Carleton. Witnessed frauds like her drive the vulnerable and grieving to acts of desperation.'

Eadie stops and faces him. 'Mr Perris, I cannot deny your *intentions* were worthy, but really! In a single swoop, you upset every single person in the room, writing yourself in as the hero before thinking through the consequences. Could you *truly* not think of a better way to have achieved the same end?'

George looks crestfallen. He frowns to himself, deep in thought, before looking back at her. 'I understand now, Miss Carleton,' he says, slowly. 'I see why you're so furious with me. You are, perhaps, right to reprimand me for being somewhat insensitive to the situation—'

'Yes!' she says, firmly. 'I am.'

'But *you* had her table-rapping device, did you not? Perhaps *you* wished to expose her? Perhaps, Miss Carleton, you are so very angry with me not because, in revealing the truth, I caused undeniable upset, but because I stole your thunder?'

Eadie boils over. 'How dare you, Mr Perris? Good Lord, how *dare* you?'

She glares at him furiously as he raises a questioning eyebrow, a faint smile lifting the corners of his mouth. She trembles with anger, lost for words.

A horse-drawn tram rattles up the incline towards them and Eadie dashes to it, George following, before she turns. 'You're allergic to moustache glue, by the way, Mr Perris,' she says, eyes glinting, as George reaches up to the faint red mark on his upper lip. 'I hope it gives you a *terrible* rash.'

To Eadie's surprise, he laughs, which only serves to infuriate her more. She swings herself up onto the tram, determined not to look back, yet something makes her do so.

George Perris, conjuror extraordinaire, exposer of mediums, and undeniably one of the most handsome men she's ever seen, doffs his hat, bows elegantly and gives her a wave before the tram rattles around the corner, removing him from view.

When Eadie finally arrives home to 5 Regent Street, a handsome Georgian terrace deep in the lofty environs of Clifton, her anger has cooled. She peers in through the window of E. D. Carleton Photographic to check all is well before heading through the door to the left of the shop that leads straight upstairs to her rooms above. They are quiet and still as Jenny, her young maid-of-all-work, has long since left and Eadie has lived alone since her brother vanished.

Slipping off her coat, Eadie puts the kettle on the range for a warming cup of tea but when she heads into the sitting room, she's surprised to see a huge bouquet on the side table. No one sends her flowers these days. *Not since Max* . . . she swallows at the thought of his name – the man who broke her heart – even as she picks up the envelope beside the vase.

A note from Bill, her second cousin, and co-owner of E. D. Carleton Photographic since the death of Eadie's father.

Dearest Eadie,

I could not resist sending you these and I hope they serve as a form of apology too. An incredibly exciting opportunity has arisen. I'll explain all in due course but I'm afraid I'll be away for two days. I'm sure, as always, you will manage admirably. The future looks bright, Eadie, very bright, and I cannot wait to reveal all – I'm certain you will be as enthusiastic as I!

Yours truly,

Bill

Eadie groans. They're already short-staffed, having lost their last assistant to the bright lights of London some months ago. Bill's absence means she'll have to man the shop on her own *and* try to finish work on her latest living pictures projector.

What on earth is he up to? Bill has never given her flowers before. Why didn't he warn her he was going away? Questions bubble up in Eadie's head, a rash of irritation that somehow leads her thoughts straight back to Mr George Perris.

PARIS

She is in the audience again. More impossible than even the strangest of illusions Valentin will perform tonight. He feels her presence from where he stands onstage in his black tailcoat, short white hair slicked back, wand in hand.

Olivia . . .

The second night in a row her distinctive shadow has appeared beyond the back row of the stalls. Not a one-off trick of his imagination after all.

Ever the professional, Valentin masks his unease with a smile as he tries to ignore her. He bows at the sound of applause, continuing as if nothing were amiss. The bright limelight illuminates him as the eyes of the packed auditorium in the Théâtre de Cluny follow his every move – and yet, he cannot help the unease welling up, the prickle of discomfort, as the hairs on his arms stand on end. *Come, Valentin!* he rebukes himself. In all his long career, The Great Valentini has never left a show unfinished, and he is determined tonight will not be the first.

From his pocket, Valentin pulls out a large white handkerchief, embroidered around the edges with red hearts and black spades. He casts it into the air and over a glass bowl of dark, murky ink atop a tall wooden stand. Once, twice and a third, final time, the conjuror taps the covered bowl with his wand, before removing the handkerchief with a flourish.

'*Et voila!*' he says, a wry grin across his face, as a squadron of orange goldfish circle in clean water to a round of applause. Valentin bows elegantly before continuing, hands working automatically, wand flicking at objects as he effortlessly transforms them in an instant, words spilling from his mouth in formal yet fluent French; his routine polished to perfection over decades.

He smiles at the audience as he makes omelettes in a top hat, then pours an unlikely range of drinks – wine, water, hot coffee and gin – from a single large teapot, handing them to the front rows as they cheer him on.

All the while, she waits beyond the stalls, watching him from the darkness. *Olivia* . . .

As Valentin pours the final drink from his impossible teapot, a flicker of black and white zigzags across his left eye, lingering in the corner of his vision. He blinks slowly as if to dispel it, but he knows only too well what it is, and the pain that will soon follow. There are just three more illusions before The Great Valentini's finale, but it is now a race against time; a sprint to beat the migraine before it snatches away his sight, rendering him silent with bone-splitting pain.

Valentin tries to concentrate on his next trick, a demonstration of mind-reading using members of the audience but, as he goes to select his first volunteer, the silhouette moves from the stalls and heads towards him. It *is* Olivia, he is sure of it. She comes up the aisle, hidden behind the flicker of his migraine, and he imagines her just as she was that dreadful night when all became lost. A muddle of images fills his mind. A milk bottle glowing in the dark. The swoosh of the theatre's heavy curtains. The weight of her in his arms.

'*No!*' he cries, swaying on the spot. A murmur of disquiet amongst the audience as The Great Valentini moans in pain, hands to his head. The audience are on their feet, voices calling for a doctor, as Valentin feels himself go limp, falling sideways to the floor and colliding with the warm, polished boards of the stage.

Faces swim in and out of view as he shivers, forcing himself to look up. Auguste, his assistant, forehead creased with worry. Monsieur Deschamps, the theatre manager, with his shock of red hair and a look of concern.

And there *she* is, right behind where the migraine's aura flickers and sputters in monochrome shards. *Olivia*. A strong smell of the perfume she used to wear as he feels a gentle brush of her hand on his shoulder – the touch of a ghost.

Sharp darts of pain stab at him and with a last, nauseous groan, The Great Valentini closes his eyes.

Later that evening, after the audience has dispersed and the theatre on Boulevard Saint-Germain has fallen silent, Valentin sits in his cramped dressing room. The migraine now defeated – thanks to a generous shake of opium powder – his head feels strange, both heavy and clear.

He turns on the lights around the mirror and looks at his gaunt reflection: short white hair clipped close to his scalp; cheekbones prominent; his usually sparkling blue eyes dulled. In the brightness of the light, it seems impossible that any phantom might exist, but The Great Valentini knows only too well that certain things are beyond the realms of easy definition.

'When did I get *old*?' he mutters to himself, running a hand over his neatly trimmed beard, the last of his stage make-up long since removed.

Oz, more formally known as Oswald the Great, and the laziest dog known to humanity, growls gently at his feet, and Valentin sighs as he spots a newspaper in the jaws of his beloved Border terrier. He gently extracts it, Oz being far too indolent to indulge in a game of Tug.

Auguste must have put the paper to one side for him, for Valentin sees that an article has been circled. He reads it, at first with a quick scan and then slowly, letting each word sink in.

LE MATIN, Friday 6 March, 1896

ILL-HEALTH OF FAMED MAGICIAN, THE PROFESSOR

The many who were delighted and puzzled by the extraordinary feats of The Professor, the renowned English magician, on his previous tours to France, will be saddened to know of his declining health. The conjuror, known widely in England as 'The Greatest Living Magician', is approaching his sixty-first year but is said to be perilously ill and unlikely to recover. A favourite of Le Matin's *representatives, The Professor has often credited the magicians of our country as a key influence. A native of the city of Bristol in the west of England where he still resides, the celebrated conjuror was widely expected to name his successor in a grand retirement show, but no further details have been announced. The Professor's first choice is rumoured to be Mr George Perris, a conjuror with a less formal style and yet to perform in France. The other contender, we are led to believe, is Mr Roderick Skarratt, who appeared in Paris last year to great acclaim.*

The Professor is dying.

Valentin's dearest friend and bitterest foe. His old rival and the finest, most audacious conjuror Valentin had ever worked alongside.

First his vision of Olivia, now this. Valentin's chest tightens as memories clutter his head, falling through time. Little vignettes of love, laughter and loss; joy and sorrow intertwined as tightly as the three of them had once lived. The Professor's last words to him still cut at his heart: 'But how *can* I forgive you? How can I forgive the unforgivable?'

It would have been her birthday today.

Valentin sighs, tapping the article with the tip of his finger and looking back at his reflection in the mirror. 'The Professor,' he murmurs softly. 'The Professor and The Great Valentini.' The brightest magicians of their generation. Wizards of wonder. Masters of illusion. The greatest of friends before they were torn asunder. He hadn't heard The Professor's name for so long and it tugs at him, reincarnating the painful past to the present in an instant. And now The Professor is dying . . . Perhaps that is why Olivia returned?

A reminder of unfinished business, a past littered with ghosts that Valentin has spent decades running from.

Valentin cannot bear to think without his hands being active. He reaches for a pack of cards and begins to cut and shuffle. He fans them out on his dressing table, a perfect arc of reds and blacks, diamonds and spades, queens and kings, all the while his mind a whirl. A rush of clarity. He looks up at the mirror, inhales deeply, and breathes a short, sharp *puff* at the deck.

As glorious as it is impossible, each and every one of the symbols flies off and up into the air, leaving white, empty card behind. Spades and hearts, diamonds and clubs, all suspended like glittering dust as Valentin holds his left hand up. He tilts his palm a little and the markings gently rotate, as if nudged by a light breeze. Valentin sees through them to his own reflection beyond and knows what he must do – what he should, in fact, have done many years ago.

'Well, Oz,' Valentin says, quietly. 'It's time we went home. Back to England.'

He drops his hand, and the symbols fall silently, like coloured rain.

BRISTOL

Cec doesn't remember much about the past few days. They flew by in a sort of feverish daze, part dream, part nightmare, memories and imaginings merging into one. A policeman, a ruddy-faced young man with an oily moustache, sits next to Cec's bed and she gives him a statement.

Arter. She sees it, again and again: the scaffolding falling, his black coat flapping in the wind, his blank eyes staring through the rain . . .

Gasping for air, she sits up as a scream forces itself out of her, only to find something warm and soothing pushed to her lips, a blanket of blackness enveloping her once again.

She is elsewhere. In a tavern on the edge of London, reliving an evening from months ago. Her feet take her towards a green door, her palm warm upon the cool brass handle. A creak as she steps into the empty room, a stage in one corner, a faded red curtain pulled to one side. Above the boards, floating in mid-air, are two playing cards. The ace of spades and the queen of diamonds. Cec walks towards them, close enough to see the truth: a thin web of threads concealed by clever lighting. Then Arter steps out from behind the curtain, blank-eyed, and she knows he is dead.

★

Cec sits bolt upright and finds herself in a narrow bed in an attic room. It is nowhere she recognises and yet its white-washed walls, clean linen and skylight feel comforting somehow. A jug and bowl of clean water sit on a table.

Arter . . .

The thought of him pierces her heart. She remembers her clenched fists, her rage just before the scaffolding fell . . . *Did I really do that?*

Cec reaches for her playing cards, automatically, only to realise she's wearing a nightdress, crisp and fresh. Someone else's. She throws the covers back in a panic before spotting her old dress and coat, and her Lady in White costume draped over a chair in the corner. She goes to them, her ankle twinging a little. A sigh of relief as she finds her cards tucked inside. Only then does she notice her hairbrush by the jug, her small case of belongings under the chair. Someone must have gone to her lodgings. Someone is looking after her. *But who?*

There are footsteps outside and Cec leaps back into bed, pulling the covers up and hiding her cards under the pillow. A young maid comes in, a few years older than her, dark-haired and with a warm smile. She places a plate with a bun on it by Cec's bedside.

'You're finally awake then!' she says, cheerfully. 'You must be hungry. Get that down you whilst I fetch the master. He wanted a word as soon as you were up. Oh, and in case you don't remember, from before, I'm Mabel.'

Cec nods an acknowledgement and tears straight into the bun, stuffing it into her mouth, as Mabel leaves. The sweetness of the currants makes Cec sigh with pleasure but as soon as she's done, the weight of it sits in her stomach like a rock.

She doesn't deserve kindness. Not after what she did.

When the door next opens, Cec is surprised to see Roderick Skarratt standing next to Mabel.

'How are you feeling?' Skarratt asks, stepping in and sitting on her bed. He glances back at Mabel and she smiles at him fondly before leaving the two of them alone.

'It must have been overwhelming, the shock of it,' Skarratt says, tilting his head to one side. 'Marsden, isn't it? Cecily? Have I remembered correctly?'

He smiles sympathetically as she takes a good look at him. He's slighter than she remembers, more handsome too, with high cheekbones and golden hair. His eyes are such a dark brown they appear almost black. At a guess, Cec would put him in his early thirties.

'Arter will be laid to rest here in Bristol,' Skarratt says, solemnly. 'A discreet ceremony to see him on his way, as he would have wished.'

Cec tries to read his expression but finds she cannot. *Arter would have wanted horses and carriages, plumes and wreaths, and as much fuss as possible*, she thinks wryly, before the thought of him overwhelms her.

'I know I was only a distant relative, but I'll do the right thing,' Skarratt adds. 'And you – may I ask what your plans might be, Cecily?'

'I don't know, sir,' Cec replies, her voice suddenly small. 'But I thank you for taking me in, after . . . all that's happened. I'm very grateful.'

'You worked for Arter, yes?'

She nods, unsure what to say. Skarratt's weight uncomfortably close, pinning her legs down underneath the blankets.

'I remember you coming here, some months back. Arter after a favour, as always. You intrigued me even then. Arter's little urchin. May I ask, what did he tell you about me?'

'That you were a magician, sir,' Cec says, her hand reaching for the comfort of her cards under her pillow. 'Is it true?'

Skarratt smiles knowingly. 'Some call me the greatest of my generation.'

Without thinking, Cec pulls out her playing cards, regretting it even as she does so. Skarratt laughs merrily at the sight of them as she shrinks inside.

'Mabel told me. Two packs hidden in your dress. Card tricks, is it?' He wags his finger, a look of amusement on his face. 'No, no. Stage magic is for *men*, little Cecily. *For men*. Oh, dear, the face of disappointment!'

He smiles, touching her cheek for a moment, his fingers cold as she flinches away. 'But magic isn't always for the stage, little urchin. Besides, I'm in need of a new recruit. Another maid. One left recently, for a bigger establishment, and I have thus far been unable to find a suitable replacement. Someone trustworthy, loyal, to work alongside Mabel and

Mrs Jamieson, my cook. Able to be discreet at all times, to turn their hand to a range of duties.'

He adjusts his position on the bed before asking about Arter: how long they worked together, details of what they did; but Cec chooses her replies carefully. She doesn't know how much Skarratt really knew about Arter's scams, and she is wary too. Arter didn't regard his cousin terribly highly — she remembers that much — but they had been short of coin when they first came to Bristol and Skarratt had lent them money. *And he's looked after me since the storm so it stands to reason he must be a good man. Doesn't it?*

'I know full well who and what Arter really was.' Skarratt smiles as Cec falls silent. 'Please. There's no need to conceal the truth from me, but I like that you remain loyal to him, for loyalty is something I prize most highly. If you are as loyal to me, Cecily Marsden, I'm certain other, more *exciting* opportunities will arise in no time.' He grins and his teeth are white and shiny. 'How old are you?'

'Sixteen, sir.'

'*Sixteen?* Well, well. You look younger.' He reaches out, tilts her chin up to the skylight and examines her. 'What a pretty child you must have been,' he murmurs, releasing her. 'Sweet Cecily, that's a flower isn't it? A rather lovely one if memory serves. Then the role is yours if you want it. Bed and board, this room as your own, uniform provided. Other duties as and when required. And, as I say, *opportunities* . . .'

He picks up her pack of cards, turning them over in his hands, before handing them back to her. 'Opportunities, sweet Cecily. To assist in certain *aspects* of my work. Discretion at all times. A magician must keep his secrets.'

Cec's heart thumps as he smiles charmingly at her. Regular food *and* a bed, this whole room as her own! An opportunity to live with a *real* magician. A professional, not a con artist like Arter. And a chance to help Mr Skarratt with 'aspects' of his 'work'. To learn from him. Not just a maid then, but more. Much more.

She's landed on her feet, hasn't she? And Arter had said on their last night together, that if an opportunity came your way, you had to grab it with both hands. Cec pushes aside her misgivings.

She nods slowly at him and he grins with satisfaction, his eyes bright.

Guilt twinges in Cec's heart. *I don't deserve this . . . Not after what happened.*

'One last thing,' Skarratt says. 'Anything you see or hear in this house is not to be shared outside of it. Under *any* circumstance. Understand?'

'I understand, sir,' she says, softly. He holds out his hand and she goes to shake it but, to her surprise, he lifts it to his lips instead.

'Welcome then, sweet Cecily!' He laughs, kissing her hand. 'Welcome to my little family!'

George Perris is distracted. He waits, in the entrance hall of The Professor's apartment on Lansdown Place, plans for a brand new illusion tucked under his arm, but his thoughts keep returning to the intriguing young woman from the séance. Her sharp tongue and turn of phrase, her curls of blondes and browns desperately trying to escape the pins that held them in position. Her blazing dark eyes and the smattering of freckles across her nose. *Oh, Miss Carleton . . .*

He wonders if their paths might cross again but Bristol, whilst nowhere near as big as the capital, still has a population of some 300,000 or so. If only he could have talked to her for longer, explained a little more. *How else am I to expose these people?*

He has tried so many methods already but whatever he does, it seems to backfire somehow. Last year, when he presented an onstage exposé of a séance in London, not long before he moved to Bristol, it even led some to claim George himself was possessed of special powers.

He sighs, wondering again what Miss Carleton's own plans had been for the strange apparatus she was returning to Mrs Carnesky. Surely she had been planning to expose her too? And if not in the way he had, then how?

'Mr Perris?' says Mrs Gray, The Professor's formidable housekeeper, as George snaps to attention. 'He's just getting dressed. Would you like to wait in the morning room? I'll bring some tea through.'

'Of course,' George says, following Mrs Gray. 'Thank you.'

Playbills from The Professor's glory days stare down at him from the walls; trophies and medals lined up like soldiers on the mantelpiece. The room is a veritable museum to a living legend, this brilliant conjuror who had performed for the great and good across the globe for decades, playing to packed-out auditoriums all the way up to royalty. George had admired him ever since he was a child. Now, The Professor had become not only his friend, but his mentor too, and soon George will be named as his successor.

Sometimes, though, George thinks, *it all feels rather overwhelming.*

After a while, The Professor is ready to receive him and George follows Mrs Gray into the conjuror's bedroom, where the man himself sits up in his wheelchair, glasses on, nose in a book, as Mrs Gray pours tea for them.

'Ah, Perris! How are we today?' The Professor rasps in his distinctively gravelly voice, placing his book to one side. He is a tall, unusual-looking man, grey-haired and, recently, grey-skinned, with an angular face centred around a large nose as sharp as his wit. At certain angles, he appears distinguished, handsome even; at others plain odd, yet there is something strangely compelling about him.

'It's good to see you, sir,' says George, as Mrs Gray plumps up a cushion behind the older conjuror.

'Pish, pish,' says The Professor, waving his hand. 'Now, young man, how are you getting on with your finale?'

'I have it here!' George says, excitedly, smiling to conceal his nerves as he unrolls his plans over a desk near The Professor's wheelchair.

'Aha!' says The Professor, pushing up his glasses and squinting at the paper.

'Imagine if you will,' says George, setting the scene, 'lights up onstage. A huge shining copper tank, smooth and curved, ribbed with rivets. A single door with a large window cut into it, facing the audience. No other visible exits or entrances. The tank itself will be on wheels so it can be spun around.'

'Mm-hmm.' The Professor nods.

'The door is opened, and the audience is shown the inside – empty of course. A member of the audience, perhaps a handful, is invited onstage to inspect it.'

'Stooges?'

'No, there'll be nothing to hide and you know I don't like using them.' George looks at The Professor for his approval but the older man is frowning at his plans. A knot of doubt forms in George's stomach as he continues. 'Having shown the tank is empty, I step inside. The door is chained and padlocked behind me. One spin of the tank – I've vanished but a woman is now inside, dressed in the *exact* same clothes I was wearing.'

'And then?' says The Professor.

'A bit of business – "Where could he have gone?" and so on. The woman is released, the tank examined. Then the door is relocked, the whole thing spun again only this time, a gorilla is inside. Well, a man dressed as a gorilla.'

'Hm . . .'

George senses he's losing his audience and makes a final push. 'The third and final time, a bowl of goldfish is put on a plinth so it can be viewed through the window. The tank is spun and—'

The Professor cuts him off. 'The tank is empty. Then you appear at the back of the audience holding the same bowl of goldfish. Round of applause, standing ovation. That the idea?'

George deflates.

'It's not *bad*, Perris.' The Professor sighs. 'Just not a finale. After all, isn't the tank merely a glorified sealed cabinet? The copper will look impressive, I grant you, but the content is not quite there yet. Is it?'

The Professor's words hit hard. George has worked for so long puzzling out the technicalities, the staging and present-ation, only for this to be the response.

'Perhaps this is one of the tricks leading up to the finale?' The Professor suggests. 'Don't be disheartened, dear boy. You'll work it out.'

Will I? George thinks, having tried numerous ideas already, all of which The Professor has dismissed. And so much is riding on it: the Professor's retirement show, the stage shared jointly with him – George must prove that he is worthy of The Professor's patronage, the right choice as successor. The pressure is on. Not just to impress the audience, but the wider magic world too.

'My only proviso is that you come up with your finale *soon*,' the Professor says, coughing into a handkerchief. 'I'll be back on my feet in no time, and we must crack on!'

Mrs Gray and George catch each other's eye, for The Professor has not left his bedroom for well over a week now. His mind as bright as ever, his body seems increasingly to defy its owner's wishes.

'I wish I could borrow your wand, and make you better in an instant,' George says warmly, and The Professor snorts.

'But you, young fellow, have no need for a wand! So old-fashioned, so passé.'

'I don't believe I phrased it *quite* like that.'

'Perhaps. But, alas, there is no wand in existence that might make me young again. And it is right that that is so. An older man cannot live a young man's life again.' The Professor wheels himself forward to better look out of the window at the trees lining the square outside. 'I've made many mistakes over the years, Perris, some of them very grave, but I accept them as my own. You won't understand, not yet. Perhaps you never will, for you are far kinder than I was at your age. "All done by kindness," yes? Your motto. You live by it still?'

'I try to.'

'Good.' The Professor sighs and takes his glasses off, tired suddenly as Mrs Gray places a blanket over his knees.

'I'll be away now for a few days,' George says, taking his cue to leave. 'In London for meetings, hoping to view those animated pictures I've heard so much about. I'll be sure to pick up those orange biscuits you like – the ones from Fortnum's.'

The Professor nods, closing his eyes, as George rolls up his plans, trying not to show his disappointment.

'I'll show myself out,' George says. 'Thank you for the tea, Mrs Gray.'

'George,' The Professor says, eyes still closed, 'I have faith in you for good reason. Don't forget that.'

The Professor waits until the door closes before opening his eyes to find Mrs Gray rearranging a vase of marjolettii tulips on his desk. His favourites: they are lemon coloured with pink feathering around the edges.

'You could have been kinder to the boy.' Mrs Gray
tuts. 'Oh, I nearly forgot,' she says, reaching into her apron.
'A telegram.'

'Ah! What would I do without you, Nellie?'

'You'd be lost, that's what,' Mrs Gray says as The Professor
reaches for his glasses again and reads the telegram.

'Well, well, well . . .' The Professor says slowly, before handing
it back to her. Mrs Gray's eyes widen as she reads it too.

'What perfect timing!' The Professor exclaims, his bark of
laughter echoing around the room. 'You know, Nellie' – he
grins mischievously – 'I rather think this calls for a brandy!'

When the bell above the shop door of E. D. Carleton
Photographic rings, and Bill bursts in, Eadie is busy in the
studio out the back, setting up for a session later that day.
She has already placed the chairs and plants in front of the
painted backdrop and will raise the blinds later, when her
clients arrive, to avoid it getting too hot.

It takes all of Eadie's effort to bite her tongue when Bill
comes in, full of eager energy, but she decides to let him
put his case first. Last night, she had stayed up late, tidying
the shop specially as if to prove a point. The cameras, tripods
and other equipment all gleam with polish, her finest photographs neatly framed and displayed. Both the counter and
the door behind it, that leads first to the studio and then
into Eadie's workshop, have been freshly rubbed with
beeswax, and the scent of industry lingers in the air.

'Did you like the flowers?' Bill asks, beaming, and she nods.

'Thank you.'

'I bet you cannot wait to hear what I have to say!' he says, rubbing his hands together.

'That's certainly true. Shall we go upstairs, talk about it over tea? We've got a bit of time before we open.'

'Ha! I knew you wouldn't be able to resist talking about it straightaway! I thought to myself, "If I know Eadie Carleton as well as I think, she'll be onto this right away. *Right* away."'

His face is so shiny when he's pleased, Eadie thinks, frowning as she locks the shop up before heading upstairs to the rooms above. Bill follows her into the sitting room, a long, high-ceilinged place with tall sash windows that let in plenty of light at the far end. On the left is a fireplace, on the right a long sofa, and the room is cluttered with a handful of mismatched armchairs, piles of books and a few small tables. Much like the other two floors of the teetering terrace house, the walls are covered with art of all kinds, a legacy of Eadie's father's passion for collecting.

'I wanted it to be a surprise,' Bill says, fidgeting, as Jenny, Eadie's maid, puts the tray of tea things down, a discreet nod at Eadie before she leaves.

'It was certainly that,' Eadie replies, drily.

'You're cross with me? I thought you might be, at first. But, Eadie, listen – I wanted to have it all ready, everything lined up to make it as easy as possible.'

'To make what easy?'

'An offer. To buy out the company. A once-in-a-lifetime offer. The shop, the contents, everything—'

Eadie stands, her face suddenly hot. 'What do you mean?'

'Travers and Company, in London. They want to buy us out. And they're offering – my word, Eadie! – they're offering at least *twice* the market value. We'd be debt free. More than that, we'd have money! Lots of it.'

Eadie stares at him, outraged. '*No, Bill!* Absolutely not.'

'Eadie! Please. Sit down. Think! No more pressures, no more worries about annual turnover, profit and loss. You'd be free! *Free to invent.* More money than either of us could have dreamed of. Imagine! You could have your own cottage in the countryside; your *own* studio, a bigger one! Space, fresh air, a garden even. Time *and* money! Freedom to do what you want.'

Eadie is struck dumb. But this *is* what she wants! And Bill has dared go off and talk about *her* business with other people without even consulting her!

'I knew you'd like it when you knew more!' Bill smiles. 'But that's not all.' He glances down at the rug before looking back at her. 'You know I'm fond of you, Eadie. Very fond. I thought this could be a way of solving everything. The financial worries around the business, the troubles we've had with staffing, the demands I feel you've struggled to cope with . . .'

Eadie drifts, only half listening, her anger rising. *If only Papa hadn't died, if only Louis hadn't vanished, I would never have been forced into this partnership with Bill. If only . . .*

Her brain jolts to a stop. Bill is looking at her expectantly, for he has said something her ears registered but her mind did not.

An unanswered question that makes her palms unpleasantly damp.

'I'm terribly sorry,' she finds her mouth saying. 'Could you say that again?'

'I was saying if we took Travers up on his offer, we'd be even better off *together*. If we were married, I mean,' Bill says, as her stomach churns. 'Eadie, I'm serious. We've worked closely together for over a year now, and I hope you would agree it's worked excellently. The business has expanded – our reputation stronger than ever. We've been business partners all this time. Why not partners in another sense too?'

Eadie is horrified. Since Max, she has never thought of *anyone* proposing – and certainly not Bill!

He looks at her hopefully.

'But . . . but, Bill,' she says. 'I can't say I'd ever thought—'

He interrupts. 'Well, think about it now. It makes perfect sense. And you know I'm fond of you. Very fond, in fact.'

Fond! Eadie is aghast. Fondness isn't love! Fondness is what you feel for someone else's dog or cat. Fondness isn't the raw burn in your chest and skin, catching your breath, heart racing, when the person you long for is near. Where's the passion? The *craving*? The sheer yearning to give yourself entirely to another? To look into their eyes and see whole other worlds within? She thinks of Max. His perfect lips on hers. His arms pulling her closer. The cascade of cherry blossom falling around them in the sunshine.

And now this. *Bill.* Fondness isn't *love*. Fondness is *nothing* . . .

Eadie looks at Bill and cannot, in that moment, think of any person she would feel less inclined to share her life with.

'No,' she says, firmly. 'I'm sorry, Bill. No.'

'Think about it,' he says again, with a smile. 'You always say you don't know what you'd do without me.'

Eadie resists the scream building up within her. How can he misunderstand her so? She *loves* it here, with her messy old workshop full of experiments, right in the heart of Clifton. She loves the view from the back of the tall terraced house, the city curving down to the docks, the tall ships gracing the harbour below, the hills in the distance. This place is everything. Her home, her work, her *life*.

'*No!*' she says, adamantly.

'I understand,' Bill says. 'You'll want to think about it. Of course.' He smiles again, stretching on the sofa, arms wide out as if he owned it – and it pushes her over the edge.

'No, Bill! Damn it! I could never even contemplate marrying you!'

Bill is shocked. 'Eadie! You can't possibly mean that!'

But now her tongue is loosened, she cannot stop it. 'You assume too much, Bill. You assume I want to live in the countryside when that is *your* dream, not mine. You assume I wish to marry you because – what? I've not had any other offers? You assume I'll agree to this half-baked idea about selling the business, *my* business, without even *talking* to me beforehand. *How dare you?* This is my *home*! Have you even stopped to think about why Travers might want to buy us out? We're at the forefront of moving pictures – not just in Bristol, but the whole of the south-west! Of *course* he wants to buy us out! But you've not thought about any of that! You've only thought of *yourself*!'

He stands up, moving towards her, but she steps away. 'You don't mean it, Eadie! Please!'

'Oh, I *do* mean it, Bill. Every word. You mean to take away my freedom, to put me in some cottage in the countryside, far from my friends, from my *real* home? To take away the work that is my *life*. How could you think I would agree to such an idiotic scheme? How *could* you?'

This time it is Bill who is rendered silent, the colour draining from his face. 'You think I'd take you away from your friends?' he snaps. 'What friends, Eadie? Tell me, *what friends*? When your father was still alive and Louis was here – all those suppers, everyone crammed into this room, Max at the piano – it's all gone! Tell me, honestly. When was the last conversation you had with someone you consider a friend that wasn't about lenses or tripods?'

Eadie trembles where she stands. She does have friends, *she does*. So what if she talks to them about her passions?

'You always were ungrateful,' he says, quietly. 'All the times you've left me to run the shop because something more exciting has come up. You've treated me as a boot boy, not a partner.'

A stab of truth hits Eadie in the chest. 'I'm sorry you think that's the case. Believe me, I—'

But he interrupts her. 'Well, as you're so keen to do everything exactly how you wish, why not give it a go? You can do the exhibition in London on your own. How about that?'

'Bill—!'

'*No!* If you're so keen to go it alone, then your wish is granted. Run this place, go to the exhibition on your own.

Do it, Eadie! Let's see how long you last before you come running back to me for help.'

Eadie grinds her teeth. Running to him for help, indeed – *he* was the one who *offered* to help! 'All right then,' she says haughtily, glaring at him. 'I will.'

'I'll show myself out,' Bill says sharply, pausing in the doorway. 'I'm not much, I know, but I *do* care about you, Eadie, more than perhaps any other fool might. So determined to be independent at all costs, so headstrong! Oh, and Travers wants an answer within the month. I'll leave you to think on that.'

Eadie hears him go downstairs, the slam of the heavy front door before she dares let it out: the loudest scream she has done in years. One long furious howl of anger and frustration. It's so loud she feels as if the sash windows rattle. She takes a deep breath to calm herself as Jenny comes running in.

'Everything all right, miss?' her young maid asks, concerned as Eadie brushes down her dress.

'Nothing to worry about,' Eadie replies, catching a glimpse of herself in the mirror, jaw set even as her heart beats furiously. 'Everything's in hand.'

Barely a handful of people are present for Arter's funeral. *But*, Cec thinks, *he would at least have approved of the grandiose setting.* The high dome, the tall pillars, wide galleries and airy pews of Holy Trinity in Hotwells. The organ at the far end booms mournfully, echoing around the empty church, as Cec fidgets. Her black dress, borrowed from Mabel, is too big and pinned together in a way that makes it wildly uncomfortable. She stares at the wooden coffin, knowing that Arter is inside. *It's my fault*, she thinks to herself. *All my fault.*

Skarratt leans in. 'It's as he would have wanted, little urchin,' he says, handing Cec a black-bordered pocket handkerchief.

She blows her nose, lost in her thoughts. Skarratt has been so kind to her, so generous, and yet this service feels to her rather like a show: in his house there is no black draping, no crepe over the mirrors, none of the clocks have been stopped, and there's not even a wreath on the front door. He is not, it seems to Cec, in mourning as a gentleman should be, and yet he had paid for this service, hadn't he? Taken her under his wing too. And it was true that Arter and he were distant relatives, not close by blood or even geography until recently . . .

She looks up at Skarratt, catching his eye as he smiles benevolently at her, and she feels guilty for being ungrateful.

Later, as they stand together in Arnos Vale cemetery, Skarratt whispers in her ear: 'I'll be your family now, sweet Cecily.' And, as Arter's coffin is slowly lowered into the ground on creaking ropes, Skarratt's arm snakes around Cec's shoulders.

When they return to Skarratt's house on Dowry Square, Cec finds the buttons she took from Arter's hand still in her old dress. She had meant to throw them in after the coffin but was so overwhelmed by everything that she forgot to even take them with her. She rolls them in her palm, imagining the rattling sound they might have made as they scattered across the wooden lid of Arter's coffin.

Another dress waits for her on her bed now, laid out as if the person inside it had vanished in an instant. A maid's outfit, a cast-off from the last girl to hold the job. Cec knows from the size and shape of it that it'll be a near perfect fit. She runs a finger over the material. Skarratt had mentioned something earlier, about needing her help that evening. A soirée, a service for others.

'I wouldn't ask if it weren't absolutely necessary,' he had said, with a charming smile. 'And I know you'll do what I ask. Won't you?'

She had smiled and nodded – for what choice did she have? What choice did someone like her ever have? Cec looks around her room – *her very own room!* – and thinks back to when the scarlet fever struck, rampaging through the crowded tenements of Bethnal Green like a river of death. She was six at the time. Only fragments remain from before then. Her mother's warmth. Fighting over the last piece of bread with her brother. Beetles and bugs hiding in the cracks of the plaster that she would trace with her finger before squashing them. The smell of piss and worse. After the fever abated, a dozen and more children, like her, were left orphaned and few grown-ups were prepared to take on more hungry mouths. She shakes the memory away but Arter slips into her mind instead.

Arter.

Cec wills herself not to cry.

My fault. It was my fault!

Her secret eats away at her, her precious playing cards now tucked underneath her mattress, untouched.

A deep breath as she starts undoing the buttons on the maid's uniform. Cec had never thought to become a maid, not after so many years of Arter's cons and shows, but she knew better than most that anything was better than the streets. Reliable work, a comfortable bed, hot food – her stomach rumbles at the thought – she was grateful for the opportunity, truly she was.

She won't let Skarratt down.

LONDON

George Perris will never again look at the world the same way. He sits, a changed man, as for the third time, a dozen films are projected onto a sheet in front of him in a theatre on Leicester Square. His fingers tingle as he watches the impossible become possible. Life captured, mortals immortalised, repeated again and again in front of him.

He watches the same set of moving images once more, greedily gulping them up. Glimpses into factory life at the end of a working day. Streams of people coming out of wide wooden doors. Hats and bonnets, smiles and laughter. A train pulls into a station, a hustle and bustle of travellers amongst silent clouds of steam. A fierce sea with a storm rising on the horizon. More scenes fill his hungry eyes. Flickering images in black and white, reels of real people in real time, brim-full of life. An outside picnic with a giggling, plump baby, leaves silently rustling in the trees behind. *So lifelike! So real!* An old wall is demolished, smashed down by men with mallets only to be miraculously rebuilt, brick by brick, to cheers from the audience, as the projectionist cranks the footage in reverse.

George sits, dumbfounded and bewitched, as the auditorium empties around him.

By the time he finally emerges into daylight, stumbling into the crowds outside, he's certain he has seen the future. He resists the urge to grab everyone on the way, to shake them by the shoulders, tell them what he has seen, and demand they go and experience it for themselves. His mind fills with possibilities as he makes his way to a restaurant in the heart of Bloomsbury, a lightness in his step.

'Animated photographs!' George cries, his eyes sparkling, as he throws the programme down onto the table where his business partner, Hugh Greenhouse, a tall, serious man with gold spectacles, already sits. 'Animated photographs! They're *the future*, Hugh! I've seen the future!'

'A nine-day wonder.' Hugh snorts. 'A novelty act – it won't last.'

'Ha!' says George, fidgeting with energy. 'That's where you're wrong! You should have *seen* the faces of those around me! They were *spellbound*!'

Hugh sighs, motioning to a waiter to bring them the day's menu, the soft clatter of cutlery and the burble of hushed voices bouncing off the panelled walls around them.

George rarely feels at home in Hugh's choice of restaurant filled, as they so often are, with politicians and City men. But today he is so full of excitement he barely notices their surroundings. 'Hugh, the potential of animated photographs – it's *incredible*! Think! Is it not a form of magic in itself? A series of still images, projected at just the right speed, in just the right quantity, so our eyes and brains interpret it as movement? Come, if that's not the greatest of illusions, what is? Think of all the ways in which we could use it! We might even interact with it somehow, onstage. The possibilities are endless!'

'We don't *need* it,' says Hugh calmly, as a half-bottle of claret is delivered to the table. 'What does it add apart from novelty? I can see it's excited you, but to me, it's simply a distraction.' He leans forward. 'If we are to set up a new home of magic in Bristol, what we already have is enough! We must give audiences what we *know* they want, not fiddle around with new formats. The risks are too high.'

George sits back in his chair, frowning at his partner. 'I'm sorry to disagree, Hugh, but it's the future, really. Have you actually seen living pictures?'

'Yes, and frankly I cannot see what all the fuss is about. What use a replica of life when I am living myself? What interest a train coming into a platform when I can stand at Paddington or a dozen other stations and see the real thing?'

'But we need ingenuity and inventiveness in our shows! And what are living pictures if not that?'

'We'll agree to disagree. Besides, what of The Professor? Is the plan still on?'

George sighs. 'I don't know. He took to his bed over a week ago, but he's been out of it and in his wheelchair a few times. He's on the mend, I'm sure of it.'

'Then you must *make* him name you as his successor. Publicly and as soon as possible. Quash the rumours. You know a paper in Paris reported he was practically on his deathbed? We can't have that same story running here!'

Someone catches Hugh's eye, and he stands and smiles, as Harriet, George's sister, joins them.

'Harry!' Hugh says, kissing her on the cheek. 'Delightful as ever!'

'Oh, honestly, Hugh,' Harry says, pleased. 'Sorry I'm late.'

'George has been telling me all about animated pictures,' Hugh says, as they sit down. Harry shoots a dark look at her brother.

'I thought we were going to go together, this evening?' she says.

'Sorry, Harry. I found I had a bit of spare time and couldn't resist.'

'Were they as good as you hoped?'

'More than I could have imagined!' he replies, dreamily. 'You'll see this evening, Harry. You'll understand then.'

'Forgive me both for returning the conversation to work,' Hugh says, lowering his voice in case a newspaper man might overhear. 'But I must get this straight. The Professor. You think he's not *seriously* unwell then, George?'

'Hugh, I assure you he's far from his deathbed – but, yes, he is rather unwell. I can't push him, not until his health improves. What sort of person would I be?'

Hugh looks over his glasses at him. 'George, that's not all that's concerning me. Skarratt is putting his name out as a contender for The Professor's successor, and the papers are lapping it up.'

'Roderick Skarratt is a two-bit conjuror who blurs the lines between magician and medium and has stolen far more than he's ever invented,' George says, fiercely.

'We know that, but does the public? Does the press? He's a rival, George. Whether you like it or not, the world takes him seriously and you'd do well to do so too. He's not a bad performer, but he's a truly excellent self-promoter.'

'The Professor knows what he's doing. He's waiting for the right time, that's all.'

'We have to trust him, Hugh,' Harry pleads. 'George knows him far better than us.'

'Very well.' Hugh sighs. 'But if The Professor doesn't name you soon, George, then I shall have to think seriously about the level of investment we're putting into this. You understand? My contacts want to invest in The Professor's successor, along with everything that comes with that – the value of the endorsement, the *publicity*. And the longer this drags on, the more Skarratt puts his name about, the harder my job is in convincing them that man is you.'

George nods, crestfallen. It's the first time Hugh has said anything like this. As they order lunch, George finds his appetite has vanished, like one of his tricks, and has instead been replaced by a stitch.

BRISTOL

It is the dead of night and Cec, costumed and bewigged with long, flowing dark hair, is balanced on top of a spindly ladder leaning against the back wall of Skarratt's house.

She isn't quite sure what she expected to be doing this evening as part of Skarratt's 'service to others' but she certainly hadn't expected this. Inside, a small séance takes place in Skarratt's first-floor parlour and Cec waits outside for her cue. Her role is to appear, briefly, at the window, the face of a loved one recently lost. A trick, that's all. No worse than many of the scams she did with Arter – but then, why does she feel so uneasy?

She has no time to ponder it further as the curtains swoosh open to reveal the room within, dimly lit with flickering candles. Skarratt points towards her, and a woman she doesn't know looks at her with such joy and wonder that it makes her want to run away and hide. Instead, as instructed, Cec holds her hand up, almost touching the windowpane as the woman stands, tears streaming from her eyes. Skarratt gives Cec an almost imperceptible nod before he pulls the curtains closed.

She descends, removing her wig as soon as her feet touch the ground, before heading inside to the warmth of the small, well-equipped kitchen. Supper was eaten some time ago and Cec busies herself with helping Cook and Mabel put the now clean pots away.

At the sound of a woman's voice on the stairs, high with happiness, Cec hides behind the door to listen.

'I'm so glad to have seen her. To know my girl is safe on the other side!'

There, Cec reassures herself, *I've offered comfort, just as Mr Skarratt said.*

Not long after the slam of the front door, Skarratt comes into the kitchen and releases Cook from her duties for the night, sending Mabel upstairs to clean the drawing room. He holds his hand up for Cec to wait, not taking his eyes from her, until they're alone.

'You did well tonight, little urchin,' he says. 'I'm sorry to have asked this of you, today of all days. I know it must've been hard, after Arter's funeral.'

Cec nods. 'Why d'you do it, sir?' she asks, suddenly. 'This sort of thing. It's not what I expected. From a magician, I mean.'

He looks at her coolly for a moment, before motioning for her to sit at the kitchen table.

'You're thinking it's wrong,' Skarratt says smoothly. 'What we did this evening. Come, sit. I owe you an explanation, now you're part of my little family.'

Cec sits silently, watching Skarratt as he joins her at the table. He sits for a while before sighing and running his hands over his face, and when he speaks, he looks away, avoiding her eye.

'My wife died.'

He lets the silence fill the room, the words visibly hard for him to say.

'Some years ago now. She killed herself. We were very young and lived in Devon at the time. A snug cottage with a long flower-filled garden that reached all the way down to the river at the far end. Her family had not approved of the match, but we were happy there, amongst the gentle hills. Or so I thought. And then one night . . .' He shakes his head, his voice cracking. 'After the rains, one spring, I was working late in my study, and the water was high, the river threatening to go over the banks. I saw her from my desk through the window, a flickering candle in her hand, clad only in a thin nightdress. A bright light in the dark, heading towards the raging river. I ran down the stairs, out into the garden to stop her – but she was already gone. Swept away into the black waters. She drowned herself rather than live with her restless mind. And it haunts me. Her lungs filling with water, the distress she must have felt.' Skarratt looks her in the eye, his face drawn. 'It was *my fault*, Cecily.'

Cec swallows.

'She always was a delicate creature, and I failed to protect her. I didn't listen, didn't address her fears and worries – and then it was too late. *But she speaks to me, Cecily!* At night. Whispers in my ear when I'm asleep, and I'm comforted by it. I realised I could offer solace to others too. That's why I do what we did tonight.' He sighs. 'I'm sorry I couldn't find time to explain this to you earlier. I know I've asked a lot after our farewell to Arter. But, Cecily, life goes on, and the dead, they are with us still.' He looks down, frowning a little. 'Sometimes those who have passed come to me, visible and insistent, and I listen and pass their messages on to those left behind. But I cannot always ask them to do my bidding. Sometimes they don't appear, no matter how much I would wish them to. Then there are times, like tonight, when I need a little more assistance.'

Skarratt smiles sadly at her before standing to take his leave. 'Goodnight, Cecily,' he says from the doorway. 'I'm so glad you're here. Despite the circumstances that led to it.'

When Cec goes up, a while later, she lies in bed and thinks of Arter, of his coffin being lowered, and the small service. It's so quiet at night without his snoring and hiccups, without him chuckling away in his sleep in a nearby bed.

She fidgets, thinking of the woman's face from earlier as the curtains were pulled, the look of joy at believing she saw her dead daughter. She goes over Skarratt's speech again in her mind. *His poor wife with her restless mind. His fault. Just as Arter is mine.*

It *was* a kindness that he was offering. Wasn't it?

Valentin steps off the train, emerging into a cloud of steam and memories at Temple Meads. After days of travelling, he is finally back in Bristol.

So many years since I was last here.

As the cab takes him up Park Street, Valentin rests his head against the cold glass of the window, his past around him wherever he looks. He clasps Oz for comfort, but when he steps out of the cab at The Professor's home on Lansdown Place, he waits outside, looking up at the windows. He has only been here once before and his memory of that meeting was made fuzzy owing to the drink he had consumed before-hand. A few swigs too many to embolden his final attempt to make peace, he only remembers how he wept afterwards, a trail of tears that took him to the Channel and beyond, never to return. Until now.

He taps his walking stick on the ground, the bronze handle of a creature – part dog, part dragon – smooth in his palm. The words of The Professor haunt him as he taps them out on the flagstones. Each one like a dagger. '*How can I forgive the unforgivable?*' It takes him some effort to pluck up the courage to ring the bell.

When Mrs Gray opens the door, his breath falls out of him. She looks the same. A little softer around the edges perhaps, her blonde hair turning silver, and yet, still the same. 'It's been a while . . .' she says, arching an eyebrow.

'It has.' Valentin bows, taking his hat off as she beckons him in. 'Yet you don't look a day older, Mrs Gray.'

She tuts, pleased, before throwing her arms around him, embracing him tightly. *So long since anyone held me like this*, he thinks.

'I know my visit may come as a surprise,' he says, when she releases him.

Mrs Gray smiles softly at him. 'I'll take you through,' she says as he hands over his hat and walking stick.

Valentin follows her along the hallway, steeling himself, for he has no idea what reception he might face. Anger, resentment, a much-hoped-for forgiveness: he has gone through so many permutations in his mind.

A deep breath and Valentin steps into The Professor's bedroom, Oz trailing behind. The man himself sits up in bed, hidden by a newspaper, which he slams down as Mrs Gray departs, shutting the door behind her.

'Well, well, well . . .' rasps The Professor slowly, as he eyes Valentin. 'Look what the cat dragged in.'

The last time Valentin saw him, they were both in their early thirties. He gazes at his old friend, noting how the years have altered The Professor too: his cheekbones sharper, the grey hair flat on his scalp.

Valentin looks deep into The Professor's bright eyes, still full of mischief, the curve of a wry grin forming on his old friend's face. So much to say, yet where to begin?

'I thought you were *dead*,' The Professor says, after a prolonged silence.

'No,' says Valentin. 'Quite alive. I have been overseas, that's all. Mainly in France.'

'Might as well have been dead then. You look *awful*,' says The Professor, sharply.

'You don't look too good yourself. Your skin has as much colour as your hair,' Valentin retorts. He glances at a chair next to the bed. 'May I?' and The Professor shrugs. 'I've come to make amends,' Valentin says as he sits. 'To extend the olive branch of peace.'

The Professor groans, theatrically. 'Funny how *everyone* comes out of the woodwork when they think you're off to meet your maker. Friends, relatives . . .'

'Well, I have no relatives to care, as you know,' retorts Valentin. 'So, in some ways, you might count yourself fortunate.'

The Professor snorts before narrowing his eyes. 'I suppose you already know that I am dying?'

Valentin's heart twinges. 'You always were over-dramatic, Henry.'

'I knew you'd return, Valentin. I knew you'd come back. To Bristol. To me.'

'You just said you thought I was dead!'

'No, no. I *knew* you'd come back. A feeling. Deep down.' The Professor solemnly puts his hand to his chest. 'That – and the telegram from Auguste telling me you were on your way.'

Valentin laughs – he can't help himself. 'I'll be damned! You old—'

'Come now! You're not far off as old as me,' The Professor retorts, before launching into a coughing fit. 'Tell me that's not the same bloody mongrel you always had,' he adds, clearing his throat and pointing towards Oz, already prostrate on a small rug.

'Why?'

'He'd be older than Methuselah if he were.' The Professor sighs, a wheeziness rattling through his chest. 'Valentin, truly, I'm glad you are returned, for there is something I would ask of you. Would you grant a dying man one last wish?'

Valentin edges forward on his chair. This man, who had known him so well, who he had trusted and adored, who he had let down so badly . . . he would grant him anything if he could. *Anything.*

'I know it's too late, Henry, but whatever you ask of me, I'll do it,' Valentin says, sincerely. 'Only name it and I'm at your command. I owe you that much – I owe *her* that much, too. Anything.'

Valentin cannot bring himself to say her name for it hurts too much. *Olivia.* He closes his eyes a moment, remembering his old lodgings and how happy they were in those last few weeks. *Before.* His hands around her waist, slowly waltzing, gazing at them both with eyes full of wonder. The baby so soft and warm, his downy head fluffy like a chick's, fast asleep as she hummed and Valentin led the three of them in a dance.

He opens his eyes, a lump in his throat, to see The Professor watching him closely.

'You'd really do anything for me?' The Professor rasps. 'I must look dead already.'

'What is it, Henry? Your wish?'

'I need your help. You see, I always thought I would meet my maker in the theatre, Valentin. Onstage, where I belong, clutching at the curtain as I toppled into the audience. A dramatic end. Headlines in the papers. A night to remember.' He chuckles. 'But these past few years . . . Look at me. The applause I get now is for *longevity.* But I want them to remember me for brilliant shows, for impossible *magic.* I want to be applauded for who I am now, not out of nostalgia or pity. My retirement show approaches – the last time I will perform onstage, and I am to share the limelight with my successor, a young man by the name of George Perris. He's brilliant, Valentin – quite brilliant.'

Valentin reads him like a book, even after all these years. 'You are worried the young man will outshine you?'

'Oh, come now! I want Perris to shine, very much so. He reminds me of you in some ways. So many ideas . . .'

'But you wish to shine too?'

The Professor nods.

'How on earth can I help with that?'

'Oh, Valentin. Because you are the best, of course! The Greatest Living Magician—? A title I never should have earned! A ridiculous nickname dreamed up by some newspaper boy. Pish and piffle. And now, finally, I can hand the responsibility to another, but I need that brain of yours first. That flair for showmanship! You are a more natural magician than I ever was. Perris has no finale yet – but, in truth, neither do I.' He grins mischievously as he reaches for his glass of water. 'One last show, Valentin. Together. Go out with a bang. What do you say?'

Valentin scratches his head, wondering for a moment if this is all a trap in some way, a chance for The Professor to enact his revenge. All these years, so much to say, yet never had he imagined this. An offer of collaboration. One last chance to work with his old partner in mischief. One last chance to make amends.

'Come back tomorrow, Valentin. Take me out of this damned house, outside somewhere so I can feel the breeze on my face. We'll talk on it then. If you wish, that is?'

Valentin looks closely at him, the brilliant young man he once knew so well still there. Those same eyes. That persuasive smile.

'Please, Valentin,' The Professor says, sincerely. 'For old times' sake. Don't make me beg further, for you know I cannot abide a grovelling.'

'Tomorrow then.' Valentin relents as he stands. 'We'll see what might be done and, if I can help, know that I will.'

The Professor smiles, a nod of gratitude, as Valentin goes to the door. He turns back, his eyes going to a small painting by the window that he has avoided looking at. A young blonde woman looks out of the canvas at him, a smile upon her face. Valentin's heart twinges.

'I loved them, Henry,' Valentin says, slowly. 'Not a day passes that I don't think of them, that I don't miss them. Not a day when I don't regret what happened. The multitudes of "if onlys" that have plagued me ever since. And I've wanted to tell you that for so long. Because I can never apologise enough for what happened. Never. A curse I must bear until my last day.'

The weight of grief sits heavy between them. Memories of the long dead, the past just out of reach.

'Valentin. It was not your fault,' says The Professor, quietly. 'Truly. It was never your fault, and I am so very sorry I ever made you feel that it was.'

It's an apology Valentin never even hoped he would get. He waits until he is outside before he lets the tears come, his chest tight with love and loss, even after all these years.

LONDON

Eadie is desperately trying to put on a brave face. She stands by her display in the corner of the Royal Agricultural Hall, a grand, red-bricked building in the heart of Islington, plastering on a smile as a group of attendees passes by. They continue around the corner without even pausing to look, and part of her crumbles inside.

She had woken at the crack of dawn after a terrible night's sleep, then embarked on a hair-raising cab journey to Temple Meads, only to discover that her train was seriously delayed. By the time she arrived at the exhibition hall, the doors were already opening and, because of her tardiness, she had been relegated to a corner spot despite having paid a premium for a more prominent position. She'd argued her case, but nothing was to be done and, in truth, the fight had gone out of her.

Her stand feels bare compared to the rest of the exhibitors. The echo of conversation reverberates around the brick walls, yet her little corner of the hall remains sparsely attended. A gentleman who walked past earlier, as she was setting up, sneered at her: 'You should have brought more with you if you want us to take you seriously, Miss Carleton!'

Damn him – and damn Bill too! Eadie had worked so hard to keep her father's business going. Today should have been all about showcasing her wares, making more sales of her new projector and improved lightweight tripod – but her plans were hampered by how much she could carry without Bill's assistance.

She blinks back her tears for a moment before pinching her cheeks to put some colour in them, forcing herself to smile. *Come on, Eadie. Pull yourself together.*

'Damn,' mutters George despondently, another stitch forming as he sits on a bench in Leicester Square. The morning had already been filled with frustration and it was not yet ten o'clock. Despite Greenhouse's warning about animated pictures being a novelty, George had returned to where he'd seen them, enquired as to practicalities and costs, and been rendered speechless by the response. An extortionate £100 a week to rent the projector, plus two authorised personnel and the films themselves on top of that!

His new idea – his plan to show living pictures as part of his big Bristol show – vanishes into the ether. He simply cannot afford them.

At a loose end, for Harry is meeting with some of her music hall friends this morning, George wanders the streets, chancing upon a stationer in Covent Garden. He picks up a copy of *The English Mechanic*, a publication he occasionally buys to keep up with new developments. He absent-mindedly flicks through it until an article catches his eye.

THE ENGLISH MECHANIC, March 1896

Anyone who has missed the wonders of 'living photographs' has decidedly missed a sensational thing. Alongside the London and Bradford companies featured in our last issue, a Bristol photographic company is now expanding their business by turning their hand to animated pictures.

In E. D. Carleton's patented apparatus, prints no bigger than a postage-stamp are projected onto a ten or twelve-foot screen. Plainly, such high magnification calls for perfection in the tiny originals, something the company's owners, Miss Edith Carleton and Mr William Waterfield, renowned for their photographic expertise, are well versed in. The mechanism, like the lady inventor Miss Carleton herself, is wonderfully delicate. Both camera and projector machines are identical in principle and contain an aluminium sprocket-wheel, a presser pad, a cam and a steel finger.

(article continues overleaf)

George blinks, not believing his luck. He returns to the start of the article, reading every word slowly, hope rising. *E. D. Carleton Photographic.* Miss Carleton and a Mr Waterfield. *Bristol.* Living pictures might still be within his grasp then – and in his new home city too! And Miss Carleton at the séance, she had heard of Ferris, the engineer, had she not? Dare he hope *this* Miss Carleton might be the same intriguing young woman?

He scans the rest of the article, only to find the company is part of a photographic exhibition in London today. Then he must get to Islington as soon as possible.

Please let it be her! Please!

The vast, echoey hall is filled with stand after stand of tripods and cameras from all over England, with very little to tell them apart. Not only does the apparatus look almost exactly the same, the men look near-identical too: the same hats and suits, the same formality – it all reminds George of Hugh Greenhouse's gentlemen's club.

It takes him some time to find E.D Carleton Photographic in the far corner. *It is her!* George thinks, delighted, as he catches sight of Eadie in a navy dress, one of only a handful of women in the entire hall. He notices, with a smile, as he quickly makes his way towards her, weaving between the crowds, that her curls are as wayward as before. He stands in front of her, rendered quite dumb for a moment before he recalls the powers of speech.

'Miss Carleton, I must speak with you! Mr Perris. You may not remember—'

'I remember you *perfectly* well, thank you, Mr Perris! Although I must say I'm surprised to see you here.'

'It's of great importance.' He holds up his copy of *The English Mechanic*. 'About your projector . . .'

'You read the piece?' she asks, looking at him closely.

'The entire article, numerous times.'

'Even the line, "The mechanism, like the lady inventor Miss Carleton, is wonderfully delicate"?' Eadie asks, hotly. 'They wouldn't have talked about Mr Waterfield like that.'

George represses a grin. 'I had no idea you were the same Carleton as the establishment in Clifton! Or that you were developing a Bristol version of moving pictures.'

He reaches out to the camera nearest Eadie, runs a finger gently along the brass cranking handle. *Imagine. A wooden box that can hold such magic within.* 'It's beautiful,' he says, as Eadie looks at him, puzzled.

'Mr Perris, I had no idea you were the least bit interested in cameras. I thought your interest lay only in stage magic, with a side hobby of exposing mediums.'

'Miss Carleton. About living pictures,' George says, ignoring her sarcasm and feeling suddenly shy. 'I, er—' He glances back at the far end of the hall, at the people and traffic on Upper Street, the frame of the window shaping his view as if it were a screen with the outside projected onto it. The miracle of film – of everyday movement captured forever on celluloid. The immortality of bodies in motion.

He looks back at Eadie and wonders how to put it into words. 'I saw them yesterday,' he says, hesitantly. 'Animated photographs. I saw them for the first time and, in truth, I haven't looked at the world the same way since. See, Miss Carleton, it's almost like a magic trick. The recreation of real movement, real people, but reproduced in a sort of kingdom of shadows. I believe, most sincerely, it will change the world.'

'And what might a conjuror want with such a thing?'

'To embrace it as part of my act. To interact with it, perhaps, create something new. To bring it to a wider audience, explore its potential. Look, Miss Carleton, I know we got off on the wrong foot, and I'm sorry for it. I know from my enquiries elsewhere that I'm in no position to buy a projector, certainly not at London prices. But I wondered if—'

'Might you show moving pictures at this grand show that has the whole of Bristol talking?' she asks, interrupting him. 'Assuming the rumours are true about you being The Professor's successor?'

'It's not public as yet but yes, I would hope so. If it were possible, I should like that very much.' George's cheeks flush. 'Miss Carleton, forgive me. The other night, at Mrs Carnesky's, sometimes I'm not as good at explaining myself as I would wish.' He gazes at her, trying to guess what she is thinking. 'You might help me, Miss Carleton. Perhaps you're the only person who can. And perhaps I might help you, in exchange? After all, your stand doesn't appear to be as busy as the others, hidden away as it is.'

'And how exactly might you help with that?' she asks, and he grins before turning away to face the groups passing by.

'Roll up, roll up!' he cries, waving his magazine with a flourish. 'Come and see the impossible! The star of the latest edition of *The English Mechanic*! E. D. Carleton Photographic, all the way from Bristol! Animated photographs! Lenses and tripods! Innovation and ingenuity! Roll up, roll up!'

A small crowd is already gathering by the time George turns back to Eadie.

'You'll have to tell them the technical side of things,' he says. 'But I can at least get them here, so you have an audience. How about it? Will you help me? To get animated pictures on the stage, in Bristol?'

He smiles hopefully and, despite her misgivings, Eadie cannot help but smile back. 'The thing is, Mr Perris, there are many elements you'll need to consider. The films themselves. A projectionist. A suitable screen.'

'But we can sort that out, can't we?' He holds out his hand. 'Can't we, Miss Carleton? *Please?*'

Eadie looks over George's shoulder at the small crowd behind him, remembering when she first saw living pictures herself, last year, as part of a photographic society outing. The excitement she had felt then bubbled up in her like champagne. She feels it again now. *He is right*, she thinks. *Living pictures* do *change the way one looks at the world*. Like the apple of knowledge: once bitten, there can be no going back.

She looks at George closely, the first time she's seen him in daylight and without remnants of powder in his hair. She takes in his well-cut brown suit, the dimples in his cheeks, and she cannot deny she still finds him extremely handsome. And yet, performers are never good people to trust. *He was so tactless at the séance, and isn't his behaviour today somewhat rash too?* Yet, if she is to prove herself to Bill, she must take every opportunity that presents itself — even if it is far from ideal.

'Then I look forward to doing business with you, Mr Perris,' she says formally, as they shake hands. He chuckles happily, and Eadie hopes that she won't come to regret her own moment of rashness.

BRISTOL

Cec is busy cleaning, lost in a maze of her own thoughts, when a box on a shelf above falls down, glancing off her shoulder.

She has never done a regular job like this before and is surprised to find how exhausting it is. Scrubbing floors, cleaning windows and mirrors, polishing ornaments – she's found it all utterly mind-numbing, yet has never ached so much in her life.

Even before Arter, when she had been scraping by as a messenger, Cec had been out and about all the time, her job taking her to all sorts of interesting places across the capital. She had cut her hair short and wore patched-up boys' clothes for safety, fortunate to be nimble and a fast runner. Alas, it couldn't last forever, and when the lure of opium became too much to resist for the older members of the gang, the whole group crumbled away.

And then came Arter. A crisp October morning, blue skies and a chill in the air. Cec had targeted a corner of the market near a confluence of narrow passages and lanes for a quick escape if need be. She borrowed a wooden crate from the fruit stall for a small stage and laid her shawl out in the hope of coins. She'd performed dozens of times and more in front of the gang, but doing it like this, so very publicly, was still new to her. The day before she'd made enough for a pie and a bun and the fruit stall woman had given her an apple too.

She'd started with 'Where Did You Get That Hat?' followed by a handful of other music hall hits. It was only when she was singing 'Ask a Policeman', some of her small audience joining in, that she realised the gaunt man leaning against the doorway over the road was watching her, a smile on his thin lips.

When she was finished, he came over and deliberately placed a whole penny on her shawl before looking up at her.

'There's another if you can sing that in a Scottish accent,' he said as Cec eyed him up.

'Edinburgh or Glaswegian?' she asked, hands on her hips, and he laughed at her cheek.

'Watch a bobby in a fight, in a tick he's out of sight, for advice on rapid flight, ask a p'liceman!' she trilled and he clapped, delightedly, before paying her to sing it in three other accents too, Yorkshire, West Country and she'd forgotten the third now.

'Can you look sad for me?' he asked, his eyes full of laughter, and Cec obliged, even producing a solitary tear that ran down her cheek.

'Arter Evans,' he said, offering her his hand. 'And I am *very* pleased to make your acquaintance.'

And so it began. Arter had offered her security and protection, a chance to learn all manner of new things, reading and writing, an opportunity to travel too.

He would laugh if he could see me now, Cec thinks, ashamed, as she bends down to retrieve the box that had fallen down. Arter had always extolled the virtues of the open road, the chance to move from city to city, exploring and adventuring. And now here Cec is, at someone else's beck and call, trapped by brick walls. A house of secrets and tricks as befits a magician, but not in the way she imagined: the dining table with hollow legs; the secret door in the wall, concealed so well she only came across it by accident . . .

The lid has fallen off the box to reveal its contents within. A number of small raggedy dolls with eerily real faces. Cec picks one up and drops it immediately when it pricks her, sharply. Gingerly she tries again, taking a closer look. A boy in a brown suit with a blue necktie, dark hair, and a wide smile. A long pin runs right through the doll's midriff and out the other side.

What kind of a man keeps dolls? she wonders, frowning as she replaces the box on the shelf. There's a small wooden cabinet to one side and, her curiosity piqued, she opens that too. Rows of hooks filled with keys of all different shapes and sizes, a paper tag attached to each with a string of numbers on it. She closes it before looking around at the other boxes and choosing another. The inside is packed tight with little black books filled with names and dates and what look like codes. *How strange!* Cec thinks, intrigued, as she reaches up to put the box back.

A hiss behind her and she turns to see Mabel staring.

'You're not supposed to be in here!' Mabel whispers, grabbing Cec by the arm and pulling her out. 'If he saw you in there!' She shakes her head. 'It don't bear thinking about! You must never go in. *Never*. It's the master's private study and he don't like us in there.'

'But the grate was dusty and the door was ajar!' Cec says, in her defence.

'Word of advice,' Mabel says firmly. 'He's a good master with a good heart and you can trust him with your life. But he needs to trust you too, see? The loss of his wife – I know he told you – it hit him very hard. He was broken when he moved here, when he first took me and Cook on. It's our duty to look after him, keep things as he needs so he can help others.'

Cec nods, wondering what other secrets might hide within these walls, as Mabel firmly shuts the door of the study.

That night, Cec lies in bed, moonlight streaming in through the skylight. She misses her life with Arter. How, on the rare occasions when they were flush, they'd blow their money on good food and cheap music-hall, splash it on cabs and clothes before times got tough and they had to pawn it again.

A memory comes to her and Cec gets out of bed, reaching underneath her mattress to retrieve her cards. She hasn't dared open them since that stormy night, but she does now, the pack solid and reassuring. For Cec has finally remembered what Arter said about Skarratt, not long after they first came to Bristol.

'He's got proper money all right; talent too, but he don't want to share it with the likes of us. Still, I wouldn't do what he does, Cec. Dabbling in the unknown.'

The words go around her head as she clambers back into bed. She thinks of the séance and of Skarratt's dead wife who talks to him at night . . . and she thinks of Arter too, of his staring eyes in the rain.

Dabbling in the unknown.

Cec fans the cards out, left to right across her lap, selects one and holds it up in front of her, left arm outstretched. She breathes slowly as she takes her hand away.

For a brief heart-stopping moment, the seven of hearts stays exactly where it is, suspended in mid-air, before falling onto her blanket beneath. A gasp escapes Cec's lips and she swiftly puts her cards under her pillow, scared by what she's done.

Perhaps this is what I deserve, Cec thinks, pulling her blankets up. *After what I did to Arter. A house full of secrets. Then I should fit in admirably.*

The suspension bridge is much higher than Valentin remembers, the sides of the gorge steeper too. He stands on the Clifton side, behind The Professor's wheelchair, pausing as the ground plummets away to the Avon below.

'At this rate, I'll be dead before we've got there,' The Professor says, drily. 'You never were good with heights . . .'

Valentin remains silent as he pushes him forward, not daring to look up at the view. *Such a beautiful city*, he thinks, remembering how he had first fallen in love with Bristol: the elegant terraces, brick factories and busy docks; the theatres and restaurants, tall ships and narrow barges, leafy squares and medieval inns. He had fallen in love with Olivia at the same time.

The Professor had called in a favour from the family who owned Burwalls, a grand house on the Somerset side of the gorge, whose grounds encompassed an old cave that both magicians were familiar with.

They are shown through the side gate and Valentin helps The Professor out of his wheelchair, walking slowly with him, arm in arm, down a small green path to the cave itself. A hole in the roof lets in light and an earth bank curves around the back.

The Professor sits, reaching into his pocket and pulling out a flask. 'For old times' sake!' he says, taking a swig and offering it to Valentin, who shakes his head. 'Do you remember how we used to come here?' The Professor asks, gleefully. 'A perfect little auditorium for new ideas.'

'I remember,' Valentin says. A memory of Olivia sitting where The Professor is now, giggling at a new trick he'd invented, fills his heart. He loved to make her laugh. She had walked back with him across the bridge that same day, guiding him safely over, and he had dared hope. Until that weekend, when he had seen the two of them through the restaurant window. Olivia with *that man*. Ernest Harding. His hand on hers. Proprietorial. Yet she did not move it away.

'Did you ever make it to India in the end, Valentin?' The Professor asks. 'That long-held dream of yours. You said you were in France, but I wondered . . .'

'The rope trick was always hokum,' says Valentin.

'And the vanishing? The man said to have perfected it, in the far south, the tip of the continent?'

'A tale told by idiots. You cannot find what doesn't exist.'

'Perhaps,' says The Professor, thoughtfully. 'Yet we cannot know everything. We are in a new age of invention and understanding, are we not? A new enlightenment. Living pictures, motorised tricycles, electric trams. None of those used to exist. Someone had to imagine them first.' He looks at Valentin. 'You see, Valentin, I *do* have an idea,' he says, gently. 'Perhaps my best yet. But I cannot for the life of me work out how to enact it.'

By the time Valentin and The Professor emerge from the cave, the light is going. They have spent the day lost in conversation, plotting and inventing, chuckling and laughing. They have pondered on the present and relived memories from the past.

'Come, I must get you back, or Mrs Gray will have my guts for garters,' says Valentin, as he helps The Professor up the slope and back to his wheelchair.

'Nellie won't be cross with *you*,' he answers, sinking into it. 'She always was very fond of you.' He coughs as a gentle breeze picks up, a rustle of leaves surrounding them. 'Spring!' he sighs. 'Ah, a time to be by the sea. Those coastal winds blow away the cobwebs like nothing else. What I wouldn't give to—' He breaks off, and both he and Valentin remember the same place and time. A heavenly summer by a hidden cove to the far west of Wales, the golden sands and rockpools of Druidston. The grand stone house they had rented, perched on the cliffs above, its winding path curling down to the beach. They had explored the little cave and waterfall to the south, searched for shells and sea urchins. They had swum in the sea, the three of them – The Professor, Olivia, and Valentin – played cricket on the beach as ponies cantered by. They had lazed in the shade under gnarled oaks, cooling themselves with lemonade as peregrines danced overhead. Footprints in the sand the foamy waves had long since washed away.

'It came up for sale once,' The Professor says. '*That* house. You remember.'

'You should have bought it then,' Valentin says, and The Professor chuckles as Valentin turns the wheelchair around.

'I saw her, Henry,' Valentin says softly, as they reach the bridge. '*Olivia*. Impossible, of course. But I saw her. In Paris. At the back of the stalls, two nights running. And on the last night she stepped out of the shadows, towards me, as a migraine came. The first time I have ever been unable to finish a show. Then I saw the article about you, in *Le Matin* . . .'

'I know,' The Professor says. 'Auguste told me. It reminded me of that man you saw, at the back of the stalls at the Old Vic. Do you remember? The theatre ghost.'

'But it *was* her, Henry. I'm sure of it. Even her perfume. But no one else saw a thing. Unless . . .'

The Professor shakes his head. 'It was not me, Valentin. I would not be so cruel as to do such a thing. Perhaps it was simply your own mind, your own extraordinary self . . .'

He turns his head to look at Valentin over his shoulder, clearing his throat as he does so.

'You know, she told me about you,' The Professor says slowly. 'Olivia. All those years ago. She made me promise never to say anything, least of all to you.' He smiles gently at him. 'She told me all about that night, when you made the pictures in her book come alive. How you filled the room with butterflies, dancing in the air . . .'

Valentin's eyes fill with tears. '*She told you?*' he whispers. And he understands then that The Professor knows, has in fact known for a long time, that Valentin has a touch of the impossible about him.

'I have no idea how you did it,' The Professor says, slowly. 'But I wish I'd seen it too.' He reaches up and rests his hand on Valentin's on the back of his wheelchair. 'I missed you,' he says, quietly, gently squeezing his friend's hand.

'Henry, I never thought you would forgive me. For what I did.' The words still so hard for Valentin to say.

'Oh, Valentin. The dreadful things I said. I never thought *you* would forgive *me*,' says The Professor. 'All this time. We've left it so late, old friend. So much we should have said, years ago.'

They head back, over the suspension bridge, in silence. And this time, Valentin looks up and out towards the bright lights of the city, his tears blurring and smudging the view as the Avon flows far beneath his feet.

Eadie sits, with a cup of tea, in her father's old armchair in the sitting room, flicking through the newspaper before placing it to one side. She still looks, occasionally, to see if there is news of her brother but, as ever, there is none. She reprimands herself every time for the faint flicker of hope it gives her. It had been so hard, losing Papa first, then Louis just months later.

Papa had been everything to Eadie and Louis. Their mother died not long after Louis was born and so it was Papa who took responsibility for bringing them up. He had schooled them, played with them, teased them, encouraged and entertained them. A tall, elegant man with gentle hands and a clever mind, he had a talent for invention and the delight of a child.

The two siblings had reacted so differently to the news of his death. Whilst Eadie had thrown her energy into saving the business, Louis had crumbled. He had grown pale and thin, taking to his bed for long hours. A crack opened up between them, Louis unable to articulate his grief as Eadie tried to paper over her own.

And then there was Max . . . *Oh, Max!* Eadie sighs, glancing up at the mantelpiece and remembering the photograph that used to sit there. She and Louis and, between them, a wide grin across his handsome face, Max. *The terrible trio*, Papa used to call them. Eadie wishes, not for the first time, that Max had died too, because wouldn't that be easier?

She had wanted him ever since Louis first brought him home, quick-witted and golden-haired, with mischief in his green eyes. He fitted in with the Carletons so well, their lives entangled since Louis's first weeks at Clifton College. And, as time went on, and they grew into adults, everyone expected Max and Eadie to marry, *everyone*. Max's mother, Mrs Habington, even used to jest about it whenever Eadie and Louis went to stay with them on their small estate in Herefordshire. A running joke with a seam of truth within.

It was Max who first suggested it. The pact. That they would marry when Eadie turned twenty-five. And then, on her twentieth, newly returned from the capital after her studies, they had gone on a seaside trip to Weston-super-Mare. And in his card: *To my future wife, on her birthday*. He had pressed it into her hand, gazing into her eyes. Eadie had known then that he was serious. And all the little notes he sent, the true meaning concealed in the spaces between the words. *That kiss underneath the cherry tree!* They had eyes only for each other. Or so Eadie thought.

The row between him and Louis came out of the blue. Already exhausted by grief at the death of her beloved Papa, and desperate to stop his business unravelling, Eadie tried to intervene, but to no avail. For the first time in their long friendship, Max and Louis refused to even speak and neither of them would tell her why they'd rowed in the first place.

Just days later, the arrow to Eadie's heart came: news of Max's engagement to Miss Trelawney, a young and wealthy heiress in Cornwall. An announcement in the *Times* that Eadie read in bewilderment, her tears blurring the words. Max's letter arrived the following day, a short formal note apologising for not having forewarned her, wishing both her and Louis well.

She had thrown it into the fire in a rage.

It was the money. It must have been. Max always was rather reckless with his finances, keen to make a bet or raise the stakes in a card game. It *was* the money, she remained convinced of that.

The following day, Eadie had moved the photo of the three of them and put the piano up for sale. The thought of Max's hands dancing over the keys was too much to bear, standing as it was in the corner of the sitting room.

And then Louis had left. An overseas trip to restore his health and humour. Eadie had encouraged it, then came to regret it, for he never returned. The Paris hotel he'd been staying in confirmed his departure but then the trail went cold. No note, no letter, nothing. Eadie had tried to find him: a trip to the French capital herself, a photograph of him in her hand, advertisements in the newspapers. But, perhaps Louis had not wished to be found.

Eadie closes her eyes, rebukes herself for dwelling on the past. She has enough to think about now, with the business, with Bill. She's not heard a peep from him since he walked out and she'll be damned if she's the one to break the silence. Her preferred option is to buy out his half of the business, but despite doing a roaring trade in London – thanks in large part to Mr Perris – she doesn't have anywhere near the funds to do so.

She opens her eyes and reaches for her tea, only to find she's already finished it.

Later, after a long day in the shop and studio, managing customers and clients, doing her best to be both herself and

Bill, Eadie heads, determinedly, to her workshop to continue work on her new projector.

It's late by the time she finally climbs the stairs to her rooms and finds the plate of cold meats and cheese that Jenny has left. Eadie has lost her appetite though, and instead heads to bed with a cup of cocoa.

The sash window in her bedroom rattles in the wind and she rolls over, struggling to sleep. Max comes to her again. This time, they are hand in hand, laughing with joy, waltzing like whirlwinds. As she dozes off, still dancing in her dreams, Max's face shifts, merges like a double exposure in a photograph, to that of George Perris.

She jerks awake, startled. There is so much she needs to do if she is to triumph over Bill; she cannot allow herself to get side-tracked. Not by memories of Max, and certainly not by thoughts of Mr George Perris.

Cec isn't supposed to be anywhere near Arnos Vale. She should be running an errand at St Nicholas Market, but instead has taken a detour to the cemetery to pay her respects to Arter – and to give back something she took from him.

'I'm sorry,' she whispers, standing by his brand new grave-stone, dwarfed by the larger monuments and statues surrounding it. 'I miss you,' she says, laying her hand on the cold stone. 'I didn't mean for any of this to happen. I never meant to hurt you, Arter, honest.'

Cec takes out the buttons she extracted from his palm and, one by one, she places them in a line on top of his measly headstone. Different colours and sizes. Browns and oranges, blues and blacks, greens and greys. An offering to the dead.

A pigeon flaps its wings noisily, and Cec feels someone's eyes bore through her, a prickle on the back of her neck. She turns.

Valentin is puzzled by the fresh flowers he finds on Olivia's monument. They cannot be from The Professor as he's barely left his home of late. From whom then? He places his own offering – a bunch of narcissi – at the base of her headstone. *In Loving Memory. Never To Be Forgotten.* The smaller letters underneath tug at his heart.

He blinks his tears away, surprised to find the cemetery quiet on such a bright day: only an elderly woman, grey-haired and bent over, and a small, young girl with flaxen hair, fresh-faced and thin in a maid's outfit. She turns towards him, just as a movement catches the corner of his eye.

The elderly woman shuffles slowly along past the chapel but Valentin's attention is drawn above, by the clatter of a loose tile, dislodged by the scrabbling feet of a pigeon. It plummets, falling straight towards the woman's head and Valentin instinctively holds his left hand up, palm out.

The tile hovers in the air, its descent briefly halted, as Valentin realises the young girl holds her hand up too. He stares at her, wordlessly, as she looks back at him in astonishment. Their bodies mirror each other, half crouching, left palms facing out. A moment of absolute stillness.

The tile falls, smashing on the path behind the elderly woman, seemingly oblivious to the near disaster as she shuffles onward and away.

Valentin cannot tear his eyes away from the girl. A halo of colour circles her head: what appear to be buttons hanging, impossibly, in mid-air.

She is like me.

The thought rings in Valentin's head like a bell as a look of panic comes over the girl. He struggles to his feet as she leaps to hers and runs.

'Please!' he cries, as he pelts after her. He is fit but not as fast as he once was and despite her skirts, she is small and nimble. He follows her, desperate to catch up, but she is too quick for him. They twist and turn along paths until they reach a dead-end by a locked metal gate. The girl pulls at it hopelessly, rattling the padlock before glancing back with a look of terror.

Valentin holds his hands up and walks slowly towards her, hoping not to frighten but to reassure. 'Please . . .' he says — but it's too late. She grabs at the gate, pulling herself up and over the top, dropping softly down on the other side. She looks back at him through the bars.

'Please,' he repeats, as he approaches. 'I won't hurt you; I promise I can help. *Please.* Let me help you . . .'

She stares at him a moment longer before running off, the sound of her boots fading as she disappears around the corner, back onto the streets.

Valentin wraps his hands around the bars of the gate, the iron cold against his palms. *All these years of searching.*

The only other one like him he has ever found, and she's vanished.

Mr Hodges is Eadie's last customer of the day, dashing in just as she is about to lock up. She smiles as she welcomes him in. Always cheerful and interesting, he is a few years older than her, with a neatly trimmed beard, thick black hair and a passion for photography. He also, she knows, has a deep purse, thanks to his salary at the bank.

'A pleasure as always, Miss Carleton,' he says, as he finalises his purchase of a new camera, his second of the year. 'Thank you for allowing me to keep you a little later than usual.' He glances at the wad of envelopes the postman delivered earlier and that Eadie hasn't had time to move from the counter. 'No Mr Waterfield?' Mr Hodges enquires.

'He's away at the moment,' Eadie says, avoiding his eye.

'I see. Well, if I were lucky enough to work here, I'd never go away! But I suppose one must venture out to see what the competition is up to, eh?'

He grins as he taps his hat back on, the bell ringing as he leaves.

Eadie goes to the window, fastening to it the notice she has drafted, an advertisement for an experienced shop assistant.

The light has been perfect all afternoon and she feels resentful in having missed it. If she had an assistant, she could have gone out and made the most of it to record a new living picture . . .

As Eadie locks up, tired and overwhelmed, her mind turns once again to the money Bill offered and the easy life it could buy her.

Jenny, Eadie's young maid, is still in the kitchen, busying herself with the last piece of cleaning, when Eadie enters. Jenny looks up and smiles and Eadie finds herself smiling back, despite her worries. Her little maid has been a godsend. Hard-working and cheerful, despite, to Eadie, a baffling lack of interest in photography. Eadie had taken her on after Papa died and their old maid moved away and she had taken to running the odd idea past her. She does so again now.

'Jenny. Do you think I should sell the business?' Eadie asks, suddenly, and her maid looks at her, startled.

'No, miss! *Why?* You've worked so hard for it. Why would you do that?'

'Sometimes I think it would be easier. Simpler. And what if there was a good offer, someone wanting to buy me out?'

Jenny frowns. 'Is that what you want? But wouldn't they be making profit off the back of your hard work? Don't give it up, not when you fought so hard for it, miss. It'd be a waste if you ask me. Really it would!'

Later, when Eadie goes up to bed, she takes her father's old notebook with her. If she holds it close as she turns the pages, there's still a faint whiff of him: a mix of his cologne alongside the oils and inks of the workshop – all faded now. She holds it gently in her hands, its worn red leather binding soft with age, rough leather strap wrapped around as a fastener. Inside, each page is packed with drawings and sketches, inventions and tricks; his magpie mind etched onto the pages in graphite and ink. Scratchy sketches of incomplete inventions, phrases he'd overheard, and rude jokes that made Eadie's eyes water with laughter. When she reads it, she can still hear him, his voice singing out from within the loops of his handwriting. Her last connection to him. She cannot even visit his grave, for he died so far away, on the other side of the globe. A visit to his old friend, an overdue reunion from which he never returned. *India.* A word that, for her, drums up images of colour and spice, heat and tea, saris and stories. The country that stole her father.

Eadie looks through the final pages, at the last words her father wrote, far away when the fever had already struck. Strange symbols and equations that make no sense. A puzzle she has yet to solve.

She closes it softly, knots the fastener around to keep the words safe within. *Papa never gave up*, Eadie thinks, as she tucks the notebook under her pillow. *He would have fought for the business, no matter what. I'll simply have to find a way to buy Bill out, no matter how hard it is.*

George is never entirely sure if The Professor is joking or not, but this time, alas, it seems he is most definitely serious.

'I'm afraid I booked the Prince's Theatre some while ago and thought it was high time I came clean,' The Professor says, a glint in his eyes. 'More tea, George?'

'But the twenty-fourth of April is barely six weeks away!' George protests, a headache beginning to pound in his temples.

'Well, perhaps a deadline will chivvy you along? One last grand illusion to add to your plans. Your finale, Perris. What will it be, eh?'

'Please, sir, I need more time!' George begs. 'Not just the finale, but the technical side of things too. The mechanics, the props, the costumes! *Please.*'

'There is no more time,' The Professor says, coughing dramatically. 'We are running out of time, dear boy.'

Afterwards, George paces the Downs, his mind a soup of images and ideas, none of which can be extricated as anything useful. He walks fast and faster still, as if he might walk himself into a world in which his show will be ready in such a short space of time.

He'd thrown himself into work with his mechanicians, the Hogarth twins, at their workshop earlier, trying to resolve various technical issues without success. Now the afternoon was almost gone and time was slipping through his fingers. Less than six weeks until the show! He feels sick at the thought of it.

As George wanders back into Clifton, he passes a grand house with equally grand railings, the sunlight shining through them creating a flickering effect as he walks, similar to that of moving images. His mind shoots straight to Miss Carleton.

Of course! She hadn't yet replied to his letter requesting a meeting to discuss the projector but now he has a confirmed date for the show, he has the perfect excuse to drop in. Perhaps film might yet prove to be part of his finale? Certainly he is still keen to include it, despite Greenhouse's reservations.

George walks purposefully to Regent Street, only to find E. D. Carleton Photographic closed for the day. He glances at his pocket watch, realising that it's even later than he thought. An advertisement is posted in the window and he scans it.

SHOP ASSISTANT. Wanted immediately. None but experienced need apply. Particulars with testimonials addressed to Miss Carleton, 5 Regent Street or apply within. Excellent prospects.

George goes to ring the bell of 5 Regent Street, to the left of the shop, only to find Eadie's young maid opening the door at the same time.

'She's in the dark room upstairs,' Jenny says, helpfully, after George tries to explain why he's there. 'Oh, Mr Perris, really, I should take you up and introduce you, I know I should but I can't stay, I'm running so very late! And Miss Carleton's always willing to talk about living pictures. I'd just go up if I were you, given you're a client. When you get to the landing, just call out her name and she'll know you're there.'

And with that, she's gone. George enters, gingerly closing Eadie's front door behind him before treading quietly up the stairs, feeling like an intruder. Paintings, photographs and framed sketches of all sorts and subjects clutter the walls.

Charcoals and pencils, inks and oils, flora and fauna, bucolic views and street-scenes.

When he reaches the first floor landing, he glances in at the room to his left. A small square kitchen with a sparkling hearth and a spectacular view over roofs and buildings down to the docks, the watery heart of the city, and further still, to distant hills framing the horizon. He peeps through the opposite doorway into a long sitting room. Still no Eadie. He knows he should call out, as Jenny had told him, but there is such a stillness in the house that he doesn't want to break it. Instead he continues up to the next floor, one foot in front of the other, feeling his way up as he ascends into darkness.

The door to the room on his left is ajar and through it, George can see a flickering light and hear a rattling sound. He gently nudges the door open and sees Eadie cranking a projector, her hair in a loose, curly plait, and on the screen in front of her – *oh!*

He is transported, in an instant, to the suspension bridge: the tall towers of the bridge shadow-like behind a flock of pigeons who feed, pecking and fluttering, as a small figure runs towards them. A little girl gets closer, bigger and bigger on screen, until the birds take fright, scattering in a cloud of silent wings. Tiny feathers float down as the girl pelts through them, grinning as she disappears to the left of the screen, and the film, all too brief, reaches its end.

An empty clacking for a moment before Eadie turns. She jumps as she sees George, her hand to her heart.

'I'm so sorry to startle you, Miss Carleton,' says George, eyes full of wonder. 'Your maid let me in. I . . .'

He is lost for words. The beauty of the film, the smooth movement, the clarity of the image. Every shade of black and grey and white. The girl's fierce determination, the wings of the pigeons moving as one. It is like breath and heartbeat; a dream that slips away even as you watch. It's one of the most beautiful things he has ever seen. And there *she* is too, the magnificent Miss Carleton, her curls trying to escape the heavy plait that lies down her back.

'It's extraordinary!' he says, regaining the power of speech. 'Miss Carleton, it's *extraordinary*. Would you play it again? Please? For me?' and she flushes before resetting the coil of celluloid, cranking it again so the little girl, endlessly energetic, runs toward George in an exact repeat. The pigeons flutter and the girl smiles as she pelts past the camera, looking briefly into the lens, straight at George, for one delightful, heart-stopping moment.

'Miss Carleton!' George breathes, his eyes lit up. 'I had high hopes, but my goodness! I've never seen the like! That beats anything I saw in the capital, hands down. If that isn't *true* magic, I don't know what is.'

Eadie blinks with surprise, flattered and embarrassed in equal measure, and they stand awkwardly for a moment until George breaks the silence. 'I don't suppose I might be able to see your other living pictures too? The ones mentioned in *The English Mechanic*?' he asks, hopefully.

'If you like,' Eadie says, shyly, her lips curving into a genuine smile that warms George's heart.

'How many do you have?'

'Not as many as I'd wish. But more than are featured in the article.'

'And can I see them all?'

'How long do you have?'

'Miss Carleton, for *this*, I have all the time in the world.'

She pulls up the blackout blind, the light from outside shining in, and George sees the flush behind her freckles.

'After all, this is the future, is it not?' George says.

'Yes, Mr Perris,' she says, looking at him, and George feels she's seeing him, the *real* him, perhaps for the first time. 'I believe so too . . .'

Cec sleeps fitfully, the man from the graveyard falling into her dreams, his blue eyes sparkling like jewels. She runs from him just as she had at Arnos Vale, dry-mouthed and panicked until she wakes with a gasp. That man. He saw what she did. Stopping that tile from crashing onto the woman. He saw it all! He even held his hand up, in mockery of hers!

She *was* right to think she killed Arter.

What else am I capable of?

She remembers the buttons, a coloured ring around the edge of her vision, and clasps her hands tightly under her blankets. Whatever strange powers she might be possessed of, she cannot control them. There is only one thing to do and that is to confess, to the only person she knows who understands the unknown.

Cec dresses slowly, her feet feeling like lead weights as she ties her boots on. The last set of stairs to the ground floor feels endless as she drags herself down, building up her courage, step by step.

Skarratt sits in the dining room, buttering his breakfast toast, the scratch of his knife sounding to Cec like nails on a blackboard.

He looks at her questioningly as she knocks on the already open door. Her heart thuds as he beckons her in and she stands there silently, fighting a wave of nausea and nerves.

'I killed him,' she says quietly as Skarratt frowns, puzzled.

'Arter . . .' Cec says, forcing the words out as the tears start to come 'It was my fault, sir. *It was my fault, Mr Skarratt!*'

He pushes his chair back and comes to her, arms tight around her, and Cec feels as if it's the only thing holding her together.

'It wasn't your fault,' he says, his mouth by her ear. 'You must not blame yourself!'

'It was!' she sobs. 'It was, sir! The scaffolding! The—'

'Come, come!' he says, firmly. 'The worst storm in years, that is all! We must be strong! Resilient in the face of grief!'

Mabel comes in with hot coffee and puts the pot down with a clatter as she sees the two of them embracing. She frowns at Cec as Skarratt releases her, holding her by the shoulders for a moment.

'Arter was always going to die in some act of misfortune, Cecily! It's how he lived his life! Come, wipe your tears, and join me for breakfast.'

He sits back down and she joins him, her cheeks still wet.

'You must put it out of your mind, little urchin!' He smiles. 'The only person responsible for Arter was his own self. But I'm glad you shared this with me. Now here, have some coffee to bolster you.'

Cec sniffs sadly as she pours coffee for them both. *He doesn't understand*, she thinks. *But I tried, I did.*

'Now, my dear, I have an excellent distraction for you,' Skarratt says, tucking his napkin back in. 'I've been pondering whether you might be ready for something new, to assist in another of my gatherings. Waiting duties. Tea, coffee, the odd glass of something stronger. Mabel will instruct you, of course. For a little soirée in a few days. You'll say yes, won't you? We all have our part to play, sweet Cecily. All equal in this household.'

And yet I don't see you *cleaning the fireplaces*, Cec thinks, before reprimanding herself for being ungrateful. She sips at her coffee, wincing at the bitterness.

After breakfast, Mabel is off-hand with Cec, until she explains that she was upset about Arter and the maid's sunny smile soon returns.

'The maid before me, Mabel,' Cec asks. 'Where did she go again?'

'Oh, she weren't up to it,' Mabel says. 'That's the truth. Too young and silly if you ask me. But she found a job elsewhere and bless her for it. She won't be back to steal your job if that's what's worrying you. Not everyone's suited to this line of work, but I know a good master when I see one. He may be a little peculiar in some ways but aren't we all? He's got a good heart and that's what matters.' She rubs Cec's arm. 'Now come, that hearth won't clean itself now, will it?'

That night, Cec moves her playing cards, putting them safely back underneath the mattress. Skarratt didn't believe her and so she must face this alone. She holds her hands out, remembering the tile in the cemetery and the elderly woman. She had saved her, she was certain of it, but how can she forgive herself for Arter? And who exactly *was* that man in the cemetery?

Cec lies on her back, her mind churning and tumbling as she watches the stars slowly move across the firmament, pinpricks of white framed by the skylight.

Not a single soul has responded to Eadie's advertisement for a shop assistant and she's already had to cancel several bookings for the studio — male clients who refuse to be photographed by a woman. Then there's a seemingly endless stream of correspondence as a result of *The English Mechanic* article, the day-to-day running of the shop, the knowledge that she should really paint a new photographic backdrop for spring, and, on top of it all, she's promised George Perris two specially commissioned living pictures.

George Perris. He slips into her thoughts again and she frowns. Such an energy about him, a sort of human firework who might whizz off in any direction. He burns so brightly, and she finds it hard to look away. Yet in the next moment, he can be so quiet and thoughtful, eager to listen and learn.

He reminds her of Max, and it frightens her.

She glances over at her wastepaper bin, filled with that evening's failed attempts at a note to Bill. She cannot get the wording right. The temptation to call him back, to make amends, is strong. So much to do on her own! Yet she's managed thus far, hasn't she? She looks down at her latest half-written note, before throwing it in the bin to join the rest. Let Bill be the one to break the silence. She will stay strong. And at least Jenny can use the wasted paper as firelighters.

The doorbell rings, interrupting her thoughts, and Eadie glances at the clock, puzzled that anyone might call this late. She heads downstairs as it trills again. She has no idea who she might find on the doorstep, but whatever possibilities run through her head, none included the tall young man standing before her.

His mop of black hair is longer than before he disappeared a year ago. Before the tears and paperwork, the newspaper advertisements and endless questions. His face is a little thinner, but it is unquestionably him. He holds up a copy of *The English Mechanic*, the issue with her interview in, an apologetic look on his face.

Louis.

Eadie is not the fainting type, nor is she prone to violence – but there are so many emotions that rise up, volcano-like, within her that it's inevitable an eruption of some sort will follow.

'Eadie—' Louis doesn't manage any more than that before his older sister, full of fury and love, relief and resentment, slaps him hard around the face.

Shocked, Louis reaches up to feel his cheek smarting underneath his hand. Then, to the great surprise of both of them, it is *he* who faints.

The second of my headings is 'Mental Phenomena', perhaps more widely known as 'thought-reading' or 'second sight'. The performer may, apparently, transfer his own thoughts to another person, or 'read' the mind of another.

This might take place in the form of being able to accurately predict something an audience member secretly writes down. My personal favourite is a trick in which I go into the auditorium and am handed a random, personal item from a member of the audience. My sister, Harriet, blindfolded onstage, then describes said object in immense detail. The trick is repeated several times to prove the audience member is not a 'plant' or 'stooge' – a collaborator pretending to be an ordinary member of the public. I should say I never use these in my performances.

There are those by the name of mediums who claim to be genuinely possessed of 'second sight' and other 'magical powers'. Yet, somehow, they can never prove this, and are invariably found to be making use of the methods well known to conjurors. I have little regard for magicians who blur the lines between magic and mediumship – I believe them unworthy of holding the title of 'conjuror.'

Extract from *The Secrets of Magic* by George Perris
(published by Saxon Press, 1895)

MENTAL PHENOMENA

Skarratt is mesmerising. He stands in the corner of his parlour, candlelight flickering, his hair shining gold, commanding everyone's attention. Cec's heart races as she tries to stay calm, a lit candlestick clutched tightly in her hands, her back to the door.

Skarratt faces the small audience gathered around the table: a middle-aged man; three young women in their early twenties; and a plump, grand woman in her late thirties who Cec knows to be Skarratt's sister, Marianne.

'A spirit is trying to communicate,' Skarratt says, tilting his head. 'A letter G, I think . . . possibly a J.' He waits, the atmosphere electric as he looks at his audience one by one, taking his time. 'It is a J. I am certain of it. John, I think, or is it, Joan? Ah, *John*!' he says, decisively. 'I can hear you more clearly now, John. You recently passed, you say? An accident, no one was to blame.'

One of the women lets out an involuntary sob and Skarratt's eyes go straight to her.

'It is to you whom John wishes to speak,' he says, softly, looking over her shoulder as if he sees something behind her. 'He stands beside you. Tall, with dark hair, swept back over his brow, and a warm smile. He is putting his hand on your right shoulder. Can you feel it?'

The woman reaches up to her own shoulder, eyes wide, as Skarratt continues.

'He says he felt no pain when he passed, only a sense of falling upwards, of being drawn towards the sky. John says the train carriage turned swiftly, a screech of brakes, and his last thought was for you. Sarah-Jane.'

Cec doesn't dare breathe. She squints at the spot above the woman's shoulder but all she sees is darkness.

'He says . . .' Skarratt listens again, nods as if he's having a conversation. 'He asks me to give you a message. To tell you that he regrets not having asked for your hand. He says he visited a jeweller, in Birmingham, a commission for a ring, but it was not yet ready.'

The young woman stares at Skarratt, hands now clutched to her heart as tears flow down her cheeks.

'He asks me . . .' Skarratt leans his head to one side. 'He asks me to tell you that he loves you. That he will always love you, Sarah-Jane. He says there is a tree, an old oak that is meaningful to your family.'

The woman sobs as she nods. 'Yes!' she whispers. 'Yes!'

'That is where John planned to ask for your hand. He wishes most sincerely he had been able to do so.'

Cec's mouth falls open. *How could he know such a thing?* She stares again into the empty darkness by the woman's shoulder. Might Skarratt be able to make impossible things happen too? Just as she can . . .

'John says it has taken him great effort to talk to you tonight, but he couldn't leave without telling you how much he loves you. He says you will understand.'

'I do! I do . . .' cries the young woman.

'His tears fall for you too,' Skarratt says. 'But now he has passed his message on, he is free. He loves you very much, Sarah-Jane . . . and he bids you farewell.'

Cec has never seen anything like this before. Her heart continues to race and she feels as if she stands on the brink of something dangerous.

'There is another here tonight too,' Skarratt says, turning towards Cec as the others follow the direction of his gaze. 'Arter Evans. I know his name, for I also knew the man.'

Cec's mouth is suddenly dry. She tears her eyes from Skarratt's and scans the room, as if half-expecting Arter to step out of the shadows. 'Arter?' she ventures, her voice no more than a whisper.

'I am here,' Arter's voice says, and she's startled to hear him – even more so when she realises it comes from Skarratt. She gasps and the group gathered around the table murmurs too, their hands still tightly held in a circle.

'I'm here, Cecily. Right here,' he says, as she stares at Skarratt, the voice of an older man emerging from that of a far younger one. *Arter.* It *is* his voice – she'd know it anywhere! But it's impossible! Yet what is and isn't possible seems increasingly to her to be a blurred line.

'I'm here, Cecily. And I bring a message from the other side.'

She holds her breath, frozen to the spot. *Does he know? What she did?*

'It weren't your fault, little one,' Arter says. 'Don't blame yourself. What a lovely send-off it was. The perfect farewell. I see you've found a new family now too. It's as I would've wished, Cecily. God bless you!'

Skarratt smiles – and it's at that moment the lit candle in Cec's hands burns itself out. A drop of hot wax on her thumb. A sharp intake of breath as it scalds her skin, returning her to her senses. The candlestick slips from her grasp and thuds onto the carpet, a splash of molten wax.

A trick. That's what this is. Arter never once called her Cecily, always Cec! And the funeral wasn't how he'd have wished it, not at all.

Cec knows then that she is being played, just as she and Arter had played their own marks over the years. She feels foolish as Skarratt comes to her, his arm around her shoulder as he opens the door to the hallway.

'It's all right, Cecily,' Skarratt says, softly. 'I'm sorry if it troubled you. It rather surprised me to have Arter here tonight too. One never knows which spirits may come. Please, you're released from your duties. I hope Arter's words brought you some comfort.'

Cec casts a look behind, at the group around the table, their circle of hands unbroken. She's certain it wasn't Arter speaking, only Skarratt's impressive mimicry. But what then of John, the young lady's beau? The detail of the oak tree, the jeweller in Birmingham? Was any of that real or was it simply telling Sarah-Jane what she wanted to hear? And yet, hadn't Skarratt's version of Arter told Cec what she most wished to hear too? That his death was not her fault . . .

Perhaps Skarratt really was trying to offer solace, but why then does she feel so uneasy?

Reluctant to go to bed and be alone, Cec helps Cook in the kitchen, lost in thought as she mechanically puts away the cutlery and teacups, uncertain of whether she is cross or comforted, furious or forgiving.

It is late by the time everyone leaves, and on Cec's way up to bed, she passes the open door of the first-floor parlour.

Skarratt sits at the table, a lone figure, counting out a pile of coins. He looks up at her. 'An excellent evening! Success all round!'

'And Arter?' she asks, seeing a sudden glimmer of uncertainty in his eyes.

'Oh, little urchin, I'm sorry,' he says, softening. 'I hope his appearance didn't startle you too much . . .'

'No,' she lies. 'I found it reassuring. But sir, may I ask, how did you do it? Arter's voice?'

He stares at her a moment before his face falls. 'I'm sorry, Cecily, but it was no trick. I hear them, the spirits, on the other side. Faintly, as if they are far away, as I told you before. Like my wife. Like Arter tonight. They come when they're called to our world by the strong emotions of those left behind. A gift I am blessed with – cursed with, too.'

'Then I might talk with him again?' Cec ventures.

'It's . . . unlikely I'm afraid, not now he's passed his message on. But I'm glad you found it reassuring. Now, good night. It's been a long evening.'

Cec turns to the stairs, slowly making her way up to the top floor and the solace of her small bedroom. *He is a liar*, she thinks, as she undresses herself for bed, a sense of unease lingering.

She is finally drifting off to sleep when she hears a strange sound emanating from Skarratt's bedroom, directly beneath hers. The squeak of springs accompanied by a range of animalistic grunts and cries. Cec puts her thin pillow over her head to block it out. She knows full well what it is, for she has spent many nights over the years in thin-walled lodging houses. She wonders who might be in there for Skarratt has not had any female callers outside of his little gatherings. Her thoughts go to Mabel and she shivers at the thought of his cold hands over the friendly young maid . . .

Eadie doesn't know whether to laugh or cry. It seems impossible that Louis has returned, and yet here he is. The faint silver scar above his right eyebrow, the same unruly black hair. She watches him in the flicker of firelight, unable to take her eyes off him, rendered silent by the sheer number of questions within her.

He hadn't eaten since breakfast for he'd been travelling all day and there's a thin and hungry look about him. *No wonder he fainted*, she thinks. He sits on the rug close to the fire, curled up in front of it like a cat, his hands around a warming cup of cocoa. He's already devoured the crumpets Eadie was planning to have for breakfast, and the cheese and bread she'd found in the kitchen too.

'What happened?' she asks, and he looks at her, dark eyes swimming with stories he isn't yet ready to share.

'I was unwell,' he says, slowly, looking away. 'I'm sorry, Eadie. Truly.'

'I thought you were dead.'

'Sorry . . .'

'If I'd known you were unwell, I could have helped. I would have come and fetched you. Brought you home.'

'It wasn't like that. It wasn't a chill or a sprain. I wasn't in my right mind, Eadie. I thought it would be simpler, easier if I disappeared. Stopped being a burden to everyone. When Papa died . . .'

Eadie's chest aches at the mention of their father. The black hole of sorrow she clawed her way out of by throwing herself into work. She had saved the business, but had the business not saved her too?

'I felt untethered,' Louis says, softly. 'I lost myself. I thought, perhaps, this world would be better without me in it. So, I stepped out of my life for a while. I'm sorry, really I am, but I wasn't in my right mind.'

'"Wasn't in my right mind"?' Eadie says, gulping her cocoa down. 'Over a year of me thinking you were probably dead, and that's the best you can come up with?' She frowns at him, torn between wanting to throw her arms around him, and pummelling him with her fists. Instead, she sighs. 'We should both get some rest. It's very late and I've got work in the morning. Your old room is — well, I've been using it for storage.'

'Eadie . . .' He looks at her imploringly.

'*I don't know what to say to you, Louis!*' She turns on him, eyes full of fire. 'I didn't know if you were dead or alive. Papa was already gone. The business on the verge of collapse. I felt I had lost everything! No note. *Nothing!*'

'I understand why you're cross—'

'Oh, Louis! I'm not *cross*, I'm *furious!*' She glares at him before sighing. 'Whatever the truth of it, wherever you've been, I'm glad you're back. More than anything. Now go to bed. You've got a *lot* more explaining to do tomorrow.'

They walk up the stairs together. Out of the corner of Eadie's eye, Louis resembles their father as he was when she was a child. The same height and broad shoulders, the mop of hair, even the way he walks. It hurts her to look at him.

They reach the door of his old bedroom at the top of the house, a garret room with a sloped ceiling overlooking the street. Eadie steels herself to open it for she has put many of Papa's old things in here. Louis had left for France before they finished sorting out Papa's belongings, and two more cases had arrived subsequently, from India. Most of it was still in there, for Eadie hadn't the heart to go through it alone.

Louis opens the door and looks at the clutter. 'You kept all my things?'

Eadie nods, not meeting his eye.

'Thank you,' he says, softly.

'Get some rest,' she says, turning away even as he reaches to embrace her.

In the early morning, when Eadie wakes, she convinces herself it was all a dream. So much so that she makes herself pad across the landing from her own, larger bedroom at the back of the house, and knock gently on Louis's door before opening it. The shock of seeing him fast asleep, long legs sticking out, unruly hair over the pillow, tugs at her heart.

He really is back, she thinks, shutting the door. So many emotions fly around her head, so many questions, too, as she sits quietly with a cup of tea on her own in the kitchen, for it is Jenny's half-day today. Eadie is fearful of leaving the house in case Louis vanishes again, but she knows he was never a lark like her, so she takes a quick stroll on Clifton Down to try and settle her mind, leaving a note behind on the off-chance he wakes before her return.

She is deep in her thoughts when something odd catches her eye, beyond the observatory that dominates this lower part of the Down. By the edge of the gorge, a girl with her arms outstretched. Eadie's eyes widen.

My word! She's going to jump!

Eadie is already running towards her.

Last night had left Cec feeling sullied, hearing Arter's voice from Skarratt's mouth, words she knows he would never say. The walls of the house feel as if they are closing in on her, and so she takes a roundabout route to the clothiers in Clifton, a wander along the cliffs for fresh air.

She knows, in theory, that it's possible to leave Skarratt's – but where might she go? There's no one else in Bristol she can ask a favour of and she can hardly enact Arter's scams by herself. As a young woman without references in a city she is still familiarising herself with, she knows full well that her options, as always, are rather limited.

The wind is strong where Cec stands, overlooking the bridge strung across the gorge. She looks at the birds dancing in the sky and wonders what it might be like to join them, what it might feel like to fly . . .

Cec reaches out her arms, balancing on the tip of her toes for a moment, allowing the wind to hold her. She closes her eyes, and then – she falls.

Her breath is knocked out of her.

Stunned, Cec finds herself flat on her back, with someone beneath her. The stranger's arms are wrapped around her middle and Cec prises them off.

'I thought you were going to jump!' the stranger says, panting a little, before rolling out from under Cec and standing, brushing her dress down.

'I wasn't, miss. I wasn't!' Cec says, indignantly, as she sizes the woman up. She has long, curly hair of every shade between blonde and dark brown, freckles over her nose and cheeks, and dark eyes that stare at her. Her dress is smart but frayed at the cuffs and her boots are clean and not patched like Cec is used to.

'Eadie Carleton,' the stranger says, offering a hand.

'Marsden, Cecily. I prefer Cec though, or Cecil.'

'Are you all right, Miss Marsden?' Eadie asks, as she helps Cec to her feet.

'Honest, miss, I'm fine.' Cec sees the concern across Eadie's face. *She really did think I was going to jump!*

'Well, it seems as if we've both had rather a shock. Might I interest you in a cup of tea with lots of sugar in, and possibly a bun? It's rather good for such things. And you can tell me all about walking along cliff edges,' Eadie says, wryly.

Cec sees that Eadie wants to get her away from the edge of the gorge so she agrees to a quick cup of tea. Besides, Miss Carleton seems rather hard to say no to.

Alas, when they reach the tea rooms on Princess Victoria Street, Eadie realises she has left her purse at home. Instead, Cec finds herself, somewhat reluctantly, following her new acquaintance through the door of 5 Regent Street and up the stairs above E. D. Carleton Photographic.

'We can have tea in here,' Eadie says, showing her into the sitting room with its tatty-looking sofa. A pile of intriguing books, cloth- and leather-bound, sits on a table beside it.

'I'm only a maid, miss,' Cec says, feeling uncomfortable, for she's already been gone from Skarratt's house longer than she intended.

'There's nothing "only" about a maid,' Eadie says, firmly. 'Jenny who works with me is a godsend. May I ask where you work? I could ask them to come and collect you.'

'No, miss, please! I'm fine, honest. And I don't want to disturb my master. He's got a lot on, you see.'

'What does he do?' Eadie asks, and Cec hesitates.

'He's a magician.'

'Not Mr Perris . . .?' Eadie ventures, and Cec shakes her head.

'No, miss. I don't know any Mr Perris. There's nothing you can do, miss. I'm fine, really. It was just – I wanted to see what it might be like. To feel free. You wouldn't understand . . .'

'I think I might,' Eadie says, quietly. 'More than you would imagine.'

Cec looks around, at the large mirror above the fireplace, at all the books and paintings. Their worlds are so different. How could Eadie possibly understand?

'Wait here,' Eadie says, getting up and heading to the kitchen. 'I'll bring the tea in if you don't object to me making it. Jenny won't be here until later I'm afraid.'

Cec fidgets, looking closely at the nearest pile of books. A red cover draws her to it and she picks it up, feeling the soft leather under her fingertips. There's a noise at the sitting-room door as Eadie wrestles with the handle and Cec is embarrassed to think she might be seen prying. She quickly slides the book underneath her.

As Eadie comes in, the tea things balanced on a tray, Cec notices the newspaper lying on the arm of the sofa. An advertisement is circled, and she reads it, her heart leaping as she does so. An assistant, for the shop downstairs, the very one that Eadie lives above. A lifeline! A way out of Skarratt's house with its shadows and secrets!

'Are you the same Miss Carleton?' Cec asks eagerly, pointing at the advert, and Eadie smiles as she nods.

'Might I apply, miss?' Cec asks hopefully.

'Do you have experience as a shop assistant?'

'No, but I'm a fast learner. And it can't be harder than juggling a hundred and more things as a maid. Please, miss. *Please.*'

'I'm sorry,' Eadie says, reluctantly, as she pours the tea. 'Really I am, but I'm afraid I need a boy or a young man.'

'*Why?*'

'Because I would lose custom if only women work here. My business partner, Mr Waterfield, is currently absent and I'm already losing customers because of it. I have male clients who will not deign to be photographed by a woman. Others who won't even speak to me if Mr Waterfield is present in the room, despite the fact I'm far more experienced. I'm sorry, Miss Marsden, but I have to be practical. I can't change the world on my own. No matter how much I might wish to.'

'But you can at least *try*!' Cec cries. 'Please, miss! I need this, really I do!'

'I'm sorry,' Eadie says, again. 'Perhaps I might help in some other way?'

'How?' Cec says, resentfully, as her escape route disappears in front of her. 'You think *you* can't change the world, Miss Carleton? Imagine how the likes of me feel.'

Eadie is stunned into silence as Cec stands, knocking over her cup, the hot tea dripping onto the rug below. As Eadie runs for a cloth, Cec slips the red book under her apron.

'I'm sorry!' Cec says, a quick glance behind at Eadie's hurt face, before she pelts down the stairs and out onto the street, the stolen book clasped tightly under her arm.

Valentin is lost in thought as he wanders through Leigh Woods. He takes the path towards the old hillfort but instead finds himself near the bottom of the gorge, the river flowing swiftly past. *The impossible girl at the cemetery.* His mind returns to her again. Her left palm raised, the buttons, filled with colour, arching around her head. The look of fear on her face when she saw him . . .

A paddle steamer going past rouses him and Valentin glances back at the suspension bridge high above, clinging on to either side of the steep gorge like a limpet. Gulls circle in the sunshine overhead. Rivulets of water like veins in the estuary mud. Olivia had liked it here. A place of contrasts. The harsh rock-face, the soft foliage of the trees. Birds of all varieties. He turns and heads uphill amongst the primroses and snowdrops, the first shoots of wild garlic emerging. He smiles, allowing the memories to flood back in.

The first time he met her. All those years ago. Her nose in a book, curled up in the window seat of The Professor's family home in Westbury. She eyed him suspiciously, suppressing a smile, before returning to her book. Even then, he had been fascinated by her.

'You must be the one my brother keeps talking about. The Great Valentini,' she had said suddenly, and Valentin bowed elegantly.

'You don't *look* very great,' she said drily, and he laughed.

'Magicians aren't all that they seem,' he replied, and it was her turn to chuckle.

'Shall I ask you to show me a trick?' she said archly. 'Or do you refuse to do them on command?'

He had felt shy suddenly, awkward in his own skin.

'Come on,' she said, stretching as she stood. 'Let us find Henry and then he can introduce you properly. With a fanfare and a parade.'

She stepped towards him, closer and closer – before leaning forward to pull a flower out from behind his ear.

'Impressive,' Valentin said softly, as she grinned.

An animal cries out in Leigh Woods, a piercing sound like a hungry infant, and in a flash Valentin is transported elsewhere. To another time. To his small parlour. To the look of shock on Olivia's face as her waters had broken, cascading down onto the rug. It all happened so fast. Hands trembling, he had cut the cord himself, dazed by it all even as the midwife arrived, too late to help. And Valentin held him for the first time. This tiny fragile creature, this beautiful baby boy with an ancient face. He had laughed with delight as the face frowned and turned puce, filling the air with wails louder than a siren. They had been so happy.

And he destroyed it all . . .

He shakes the memory from his head, focusing back on the girl at the cemetery, her blonde hair and wide eyes, and he remembers now who she reminded him of. That portrait of Olivia on the wall of The Professor's apartment. Painted years before Valentin met her. All that potential contained within. Her whole life ahead of her . . .

An idea strikes him and he is annoyed with himself for not thinking of it earlier. The girl at the cemetery, she had been crouching beside a grave, perhaps the name on it might provide a clue? When he reaches the road, Valentin hails the first cab he sees and heads straight to Arnos Vale.

'Arter Evans, you say?' the vicar asks, pulling out a register as thick as his arm as Valentin nods.

'I might be a while,' the vicar says apologetically, opening the giant book and leafing through its pages as Valentin glances around, taking in the small chapel he finds himself in.

'Ah, yes,' the vicar says, clearing his throat and tapping the register. 'Arter Evans. A man with a somewhat *unusual* reputation.'

'Unusual?' Valentin repeats, and the vicar pointedly looks at the donations box. Valentin sighs, slipping some coins in, and only then does the vicar answer.

'Some sort of petty criminal, I'm led to believe. A con man.'

'One who did well enough to pay for a gravestone.'

'No, no. He didn't pay for it . . .' The vicar runs a finger down the register. 'It was paid for by Mr Roderick Skarratt. A benefactor, perhaps?'

Valentin frowns. *Skarratt*. Now, where does he know that name from?

Cec is still in her thin undergarments when Skarratt bursts in and she is reminded there is no lock on her door. He looks her up and down, his eyes lingering.

'Get dressed!' he says. 'Visitors are on their way, and Mabel already has her hands full. I need you to run some errands, little urchin, and I'm afraid it'll be a long day for all of us. Now hurry. There's no shortage of things to be done.' And with that he's gone and Cec finds herself staring at the empty doorway.

She closes the door and tucks the chair under the handle, making it impossible for anyone else to burst in.

Almost a week has passed since the incident at the gorge and it has played heavily on Cec's mind. The tale of Skarratt's poor drowned wife had resurfaced in her thoughts too. *A restless mind*. Cec wondered if that's what she had before forcing herself to dismiss it. After all, she hadn't meant to throw herself off the cliff. She simply hadn't thought about how dangerous it was. If that woman, Miss Carleton, hadn't saved her . . . No. It didn't bear thinking about. *Better alive and fighting than dead and dust.*

It was a shame about what happened afterwards, though: that shop job, tantalisingly out of reach.

Cec reaches under her mattress and pulls out the book she stole from Eadie. *Serves her right*, Cec thinks, guiltily, as she runs her hand over the red leather cover, loosening the fastening.

She had been disappointed to discover it didn't contain a story, for she had been hoping for a novel, a tale she could lose herself in. Instead, the book is filled with notes and diagrams, the contents of someone's mind turned inside out, let loose in ink and scribbles.

Cec has gone through every page, laughed quietly at the rude jokes, puzzled over the diagrams, and been baffled by the equations and symbols. But although she isn't averse to a bit of thievery, the guilt has slowly gnawed away at her. After all, Miss Carleton had helped her, offering friendship as well as tea. And this wasn't a mass-produced novel she might never notice missing, but something personal. *The Property of Edward David Carleton* is emblazoned on the inside cover.

Cec decides that today is the day she will return it.

Less than an hour later, when she is out on some errands for Skarratt, Cec stands outside Eadie's shop. She looks through the window to see Eadie herself behind the polished wooden counter with a bearded young man, laughing and smiling.

A nugget of resentment builds, perhaps that is the very man who has taken the job she might have had, if only Miss Carleton had been braver.

Cec resolves to keep the red book a little longer but is so absorbed in feeling offended that she barely notices the reflection behind her, a figure on the other side of the road watching her. She starts when she realises who it is. *The man from the churchyard!*

Her heart in her mouth, Cec does her best to pretend she hasn't seen him. She turns, walking swiftly away, further into Clifton Village, but he follows her, and she feels his eyes bore into her back. She walks faster, on the verge of a run, turning first one corner, then another. A quick glance back and, to her relief, there's no sign of him. The gate at Mall Gardens has been left open and Cec dashes in, taking refuge on a shaded bench to catch her breath. Confident she has escaped, she closes her eyes for a moment.

'Forgive me. I did not mean to startle you,' a voice says, and she sits bolt upright, staring at the very man she was trying to avoid, a brown scruffy dog tucked under his arm. The sunlight shines behind him, and it makes his white hair glow like a halo.

'What d'you want?' Cec asks, nervously.

'To help you.' His voice is smooth, a hint of an accent from elsewhere.

'How? Why?'

'You saw me for what I am. And I saw you in return.'

'I don't know what you mean, sir.'

He chuckles softly. 'We both know what we saw. The tile. The buttons in the air.' He holds his left palm out as Cec swallows. 'I'm nothing to be scared of. I promise you.'

Cec takes a good look at him. He's about the same age as Arter. Thin but not frail, despite his walking stick, which seems to her an affectation more than anything. He seems strong somehow, powerful. He bends to put his dog on the ground, smiling as he does so, and the sun shines straight into her eyes, making her sneeze. She reaches for her handkerchief, the black-bordered one Skarratt gave her at Arter's funeral, but it's nowhere to be found.

The stranger pulls out his own handkerchief and offers it to her at arm's length. Cec examines the markings embroidered around the edge – red hearts and black spades like her cards – before snatching it, blowing her nose loudly and revoltingly.

'How d'you find me?' she asks, as the man's small dog approaches, sniffing at her boots.

'The gravestone, at Arnos Vale. I followed the trail,' he replies. 'I wasn't sure how to approach without frightening you off again. But I was clumsy in my efforts, and you spotted me anyway.'

She offers him the snotty handkerchief and he raises an eyebrow. 'I think you'd better keep it.'

He pulls out a small card and hands it to her.

The Great Valentini
Illusionniste. Magicien. Prestidigitateur

'A magician?' Cec frowns, uncertain, handing the card back to him. Although she can read and write well enough – thanks to Arter – other languages are beyond her. For now, at least.

'My name is Valentin. Also known as The Great Valentini. You may find me at the far end of Royal York Crescent.'

Cec stares at him as he holds his left hand up again.

'We are alike, you and I,' he says, softly. 'A touch of the impossible. Although I hide in plain sight onstage, amongst the other performers.'

'D'you do séances and the like?' she asks, and he shakes his head.

'No. True magicians do not partake in such things. What makes you ask? Roderick Skarratt?'

Cec sucks her breath in. *This man, Valentin, he knows where I live.*

'He paid for the gravestone I saw you by. That's how I found you,' Valentin says with a faint smile. 'Roderick Skarratt is an interesting man, but one can be *either* a medium *or* a magician. Blurring the lines is a grey area indeed. Be careful whilst you're under his roof.' He tips his hat. 'That's all I wished to say. You know where to find me now, if you want to talk further or if you ever need help. Come on, Oz,' he says, and the little dog trails slowly after him.

Cec slumps back on the bench, her mind a jumble of questions, Valentin's embroidered handkerchief still in her hand.

Eadie beams with delight for her new assistant – and previous customer – the charming Mr Hodges, stands next to her behind the counter.

'I always wondered what the view was like from here!' he jokes, surveying the shop before him.

'Are you quite sure you'll be comfortable with the role? It isn't too much of a step down from the bank?'

'I'd rather be happy than rich, Miss Carleton. Photography has been a passion of mine for some time, as you know. And the chance to learn more about living pictures – well, how could anyone resist?'

She grins at him. 'And are you certain I can't show you around properly? There's the studio and workshop, the dark room upstairs and the projection room too.'

'I'm sure there'll be time for that in due course, but I'd better head to work before I'm too late. I'll ask for a day off – a trial run. Check we'll both be happy with the arrangement and, if all goes well, I'll see when I can start.'

'As soon as possible, please. Oh, I'm *so* glad you saw the notice in the window and didn't think it beneath you,' Eadie says, with relief.

'I think it could work rather well for both of us. Although, if it's not too much to ask, might we come up with a more grandiose title than "shop assistant"? I'm sorry to make such a request, only I'm not sure my father will be happy with my change of occupation. My mother wouldn't have minded, but my father is more conventional in his outlook.'

'I'm sure we can come up with something,' Eadie says. An image of the young, uncertain Miss Marsden flickers in her mind and she shakes it away. Mr Hodges is far more suitable. Knowledgeable *and* experienced at dealing with the public. But, nevertheless, Eadie wonders how the young woman is, wishing again she had noted the name of her employer so she could check all was well.

After Mr Hodges leaves, Eadie goes to find Louis to tell him the good news. Her brother had offered to help with the shop but it was clear to Eadie, after he slept for almost two days solid, that he needed more rest. Besides, how can she trust him with her customers when she no longer trusts him herself?

Louis isn't in the sitting room though, nor the kitchen or his bedroom. Eadie returns to the shop on the off-chance he's in the workshop but instead finds him in the studio, spatters of colour on his face and shirt, pots filled with paints by his feet. Pleased as punch, he stands in front of a newly painted backdrop, a scene of spring, beautifully rendered, with trees bursting into leaf and hills curving into the distance.

She recognises the view, even though he's disguised it, changing the horizon and adding a tower. Her chest tightens.

'I thought I'd make myself useful,' he says. 'You said you wanted a new backdrop for spring sittings. So I made you one overnight. Just finished it.'

But Eadie cannot reply. The view is of that from the Habingtons' house. Max's family home. The house they had visited so often, that she had thought one day might be her home too. *Max* . . . She has tried so hard to contain her grief at losing him, but now Louis is back, Max keeps resurfacing, catching her off-guard. The cherry tree he kissed her under is just out of view in Louis's backdrop, and she is grateful for that at least.

'You don't like it?' He frowns, and she shakes her head.

'It's not that,' she manages to say. 'All these pots, Louis! I'm supposed to have clients in here this afternoon and the mess—'

'It's all right,' he says. 'The Robinses came in earlier when you popped upstairs. The baby's poorly so they've had to postpone. And I can tidy up.' He smiles hopefully at her.

'I've found someone for the shop,' Eadie says. 'Mr Hodges. He's one of our customers and very knowledgeable—'

Louis's face falls. 'But I can help! I already offered! And surely it would be cheaper if I—'

'Louis,' she stops him, guiltily. 'Get some more rest. That's what you most need. And while we're discussing it, I'll be out tomorrow at lunch, with Mr Perris, so I'll close the shop for a while. Please, there's no need for you to stand in.'

'You don't trust me,' he says softly.

Eadie inhales. 'Oh, Louis! How can I when I don't know where you were? What you were up to all that time? How can I?' Her heart races as she says it, and he looks at her in silence for a moment.

'I was in Hungary,' he says quietly. 'For most of it. France at the start, then Hungary.'

Eadie lets the revelation sink in. 'Did you meet someone?' she ventures, and Louis shakes his head.

'No. Not like that. I was an English tutor to a boy, a nobleman's son. I pretended to be someone else for a while.'

'Why?'

He shakes his head and Eadie knows she'll get no more out of him. It's the most he's confessed since his return.

As she turns to leave, he clears his throat. 'I'll look around for something else,' he says. 'So I don't get under your feet. It means I can bring a bit of money in too. If you're going to pay for this Mr Hodges.'

Eadie can't bear to look at him, standing there all sorrowful. 'All right,' she says, not looking back. 'If that's what you want. Oh, and thank you for the backdrop. It's . . .' But she cannot bring herself to say what she really thinks. *It's beautiful. Vibrant. It's spring parties and picnics with Max.* It hurts her to look at it.

'I'd forgotten what a good painter you were,' Eadie says instead, flatly.

Cec's ears prick up the moment she hears Miss Carleton's name. She creeps closer to the dining-room door, open just a crack, to hear Skarratt talking with his sister, Marianne Carnesky.

'Technically, Miss Carleton is excellent. She fixed my device very well, as I told you before,' Marianne says, in her distinctive husky voice.

'There's no evidence Perris is working with her beyond that though,' Skarratt replies, thoughtfully. 'But if he is, then it's a great pity he got there before us. A good mechanician is worth their weight in gold, and he's already got the best in the Hogarth twins.'

'Why don't you try and make another appointment with The Professor?' Marianne suggests.

'After last time? We agreed never to mention that again . . .' Skarratt snaps.

'But his health is worsening, is it not? If the rumours are true, he might be a little more suggestible.'

'There's only room for me in this city, Marianne,' Skarratt growls. '*Me!* Not some new upstart, a damned incomer who's barely been here six months. Not George *bloody* Perris!'

'Calm yourself Roderick, you know how your temper can override your senses at times.'

'I'm perfectly calm, Marianne! *Perfectly* . . .'

Cec holds her breath as Skarratt paces up and down.

'Roderick, please. Perris cost me a handful of clients after his little outburst, but you don't see me lose my temper over it. You must remain calm.'

'Coming to Bristol, trying to take what's rightfully mine! I've been here for years! Bristol is *my* city, Marianne! *Mine!* *I'm* the rightful heir to The Professor's crown, not Perris. *I'm* the best magician of my generation! I can do everything he does, but *better*! Damn him to high hell!'

'So you keep saying. And that's all very well, but what are you going to *do* about it? This show, if it happens? What are you actually going to *do*?'

'Leave Perris to me,' Skarratt growls. '*Leave him to me!*'

Footsteps come towards her and Cec dashes to the hallway mirror, her head down as she dusts it. She bobs a curtsey as Skarratt's sister leaves, returning her gaze to the mirror.

For a moment, Cec imagines Valentin behind her, as he was outside Eadie's shop. She thinks of his sparkling eyes and the handkerchief he gave her that now lies in her pocket. He had said she was like him, but how can that be? It was she who killed Arter, she who made the tile hover in mid-air.

It *was* her, wasn't it?

Cec frowns, and her reflection frowns back at her.

To Eadie's surprise, a young woman is already seated next to George when she steps into the busy restaurant in the heart of the old city. The waiters buzz around her like clockwork toys as she's shown to the table, and she suddenly wishes she had looked in the mirror a little more closely before leaving home. Her late Great-Aunt Sylvia's words to her from when Eadie was in London, studying, echo in her head: 'You cannot afford to be seen looking shabby, Eadie. You ought to know that at your age. And, honestly, your table manners leave much to be desired. Always rushing!'

'Miss Carleton!' says the young woman, holding out her hand. She is little and curvy with dark wavy hair, arched eyebrows, and a small beauty spot above her lips. Eadie likes her immediately. 'Harry Perris, well, Harriet, but no one calls me that these days. I'm George's box jumper. Sorry! His assistant! I forget how full of theatre words I am. I'm also his sister. For my sins.'

The trio sit down, delicious smells wafting towards them from the plates and bowls that pass nearby, and George nervously plays with his napkin. He changes it into a dove, a hare, and an odd-looking hat, before giving up and fiddling with a coin instead, dropping it through the table and catching it underneath. He looks pale, Eadie thinks, as if he hasn't been sleeping.

'You've seen George's tricks before, Miss Carleton?' Harry asks.

'No, but my father was keen on legerdemain. He used to insist on performing for us when we were children. He was always trying out new ideas – he had a little notebook he used to scribble them down in.'

'I do the same,' George says. 'But then I misplace it and have to start a new one.'

'My father used to call his "the book of tricks".'

'Used to?'

'Yes, alas. He died. Over a year ago now, in India.' Eadie still finds it hard to say.

'I'm sorry to hear that,' George says, gently. 'Was that when you took over the business? That's quite an undertaking.'

'My brother Louis and I inherited it, together.'

'I thought Mr Waterfield was your business partner?'

'Oh, he is. Louis went away, travelling overseas, but he's newly returned. He's not involved in the business at present.'

'Well, you and your brother must come to supper!' Harry exclaims. 'I insist!'

'May I ask, do you still have your father's book of tricks?' George asks.

'Yes, thankfully. It arrived out of the blue, months after he died. Some of his other things too. He thought he'd discovered a new trick whilst he was in India, but I fear the fever had got to him. It's nothing but symbols and scribbles.'

'I'm glad it was returned,' George says. 'I wouldn't mind a look at it some time.'

'If you wish! I'm afraid you'll only find it disappointing. He was a brilliant inventor but his musings on magic are barely that of an amateur.'

'Well, an amateur is not necessarily inferior to a professional,' George says, warmly. 'Some of the best magic tricks were invented by amateurs! And surely there's a purity in creating work solely for one's own pleasure?'

'You wouldn't say that if you'd seen the amateur dramatic *Hamlet* at Clifton College recently,' says Eadie drily, and both Perrises laugh until George winces.

'Will you excuse me a moment?' he says, leaving the table.

'George has got a stitch again,' Harry explains. 'He's rather prone to them when he's under duress. He has to be fit for our shows, we both do of course, so it's not down to exercise. Personally, I think it's because he's inclined to not drink enough fluids. Except strong coffee and I'm not sure that helps! He's more anxious than I've seen him in a long while. Since the date of the show was confirmed – I know you're sworn to secrecy on it too – it's rather played on his mind. He's still struggling with his idea for the grand finale and Mr Greenhouse, his business partner, sometimes puts too much pressure on him.' She sighs, looking at Eadie. 'Please forgive George for doing tricks at the table. It's simply his way of steadying himself. He's always done it. Ever since he first started doing magic as a boy.'

Eadie smiles. 'So, have you always been George's . . . what was it? "Box jumper"?'

'Oh no, not at all. It was an accident. Chaplin, his old assistant, overindulged one day at lunch. He fell asleep on the job, ruined the matinee. He was supposed to disappear from a trunk but was instead revealed fast asleep inside, snoring away. George was furious and, despite Chaplin's pleas, sacked him on the spot. I suppose he didn't have much choice – trust, once lost, is not so easily regained.'

Eadie thinks guiltily of Louis as Harry continues: 'I was already familiar with George's act and found myself being talked into "just tonight's show." That was a year and a half ago.' She grins. 'To tell the truth, Miss Carleton, I rather like the applause. I'm sure you've noticed, George can be very passionate about his work, perhaps too much so at times. But he has a good heart, and he's truly the finest, most inventive of magicians. And collaborative too. He works closely with me, and with his mechanicians, the Hogarth brothers. You must meet them – identical twins as alike as peas in a pod! I'm sure you'd find their workshop fascinating. And now, of course, George is working with you too. And one thing *is* certain – he hasn't stopped talking about living pictures, or indeed you, Miss Carleton, since our trip to London.'

Eadie smiles, flattered. 'And are you interested in moving images, Miss Perris?' she asks.

'Harry, please. Of course! I loved the ones I saw in London. That glimpse of overseas. Who wouldn't like the idea of travelling the world from the comfort of one's own seat? But I must confess, I'd rather like to see it for myself – have my own adventures! I might even scribble them down, Miss Carleton.'

'Please, call me Eadie.'

'George!' Harry exclaims as her brother rejoins them. 'I was just about to suggest to Miss Carleton – *Eadie* – that she and her brother – Louis, wasn't it? – come for supper soon, before we get too deep in rehearsals. You see, Eadie, we've not been in Bristol that long, and it'd be nice to know others of a similar age. We've known the city for years through our grandparents, but we only moved here last winter. And, alas, we no longer have family here.'

'And I promise not to talk about work during supper, Miss Carleton,' says George. 'Although it is somewhat occupying my mind at the present.'

'I'm sure I can cope.' Eadie smiles as the menu arrives, then remembers her late great-aunt's reprimand about her poor table manners. She reddens as she examines the menu in detail before glancing up to find George looking at her intensely. He smiles at her and she cannot help but smile back.

'This is very lovely, I must say,' Harry says. 'I suggest a toast. To new friends.'

'And we should raise a glass to our animated pictures too,' George adds. 'Our forthcoming collaboration, Miss Carleton.'

'To the future then!' Eadie says, as the three of them raise their glasses.

It was normally Mabel's responsibility to look after Skarratt's dining room but, today, she had been called away for other duties and Cec was cleaning in there instead. She had already polished the silverware and swept up what little dust there was, but her attention kept being drawn to the tall mahogany cabinet in the corner. Mabel had told her to leave it well alone which, of course, had only piqued Cec's interest.

It was inevitable that curiosity would get the better of her. Cec carefully places her dustpan on top of the mantelpiece and listens in the hallway for a moment before tiptoeing over to the cabinet. It is so well polished that Cec could almost see her reflection in it.

She lightly flicks her duster over it and the left door creaks a little before swinging open on its hinges and Cec yelps, hand to her mouth, when she sees what lies inside.

A human skull. As polished and shiny as the cabinet itself. Blank eye sockets stare darkly at her. Teeth fixed in a permanent grin.

'I see you found my little cabinet.' Skarratt's voice comes from behind her and Cec turns to see him in the doorway. He smiles but his eyes are cold.

'Sorry sir, forgive me. Mabel told me not to touch it but I didn't want to leave anything in here undusted.'

'How dutiful of you,' he says, stepping past her towards the cabinet. 'I must have left it unlocked. Very careless of me.' He pulls out a small ring of keys from his waistcoat pocket before turning to her.

'Do you not want to see what else is inside?' Skarratt asks coolly, not waiting for Cec to respond. 'Not many are fortunate enough to see inside my cabinet of curios,' he says, lifting the skull out on a square velvet cushion. 'But as you were so intrigued by it, you shall join that lucky few. Alas poor Yorick.' He offers the skull to Cec and she shakes her head, repulsed by it.

'Death comes to all of us in the end, little urchin. This, though, is a very interesting specimen. From a criminal. A poisoner. You see, these small bumps on the head? One can read his predisposition to criminality right here in his skull. Fascinating, no? Cost me a small fortune at auction.'

Skarratt replaces it back in the cabinet, his eyes glinting, as he holds out another object, a slender wand with strange symbols engraved into what looks like ivory.

'Bone,' Skarratt says, running a finger up and down it. 'A special and rare object. An iron rod holds all these sections together.' He looks up at Cec and smiles. 'Human bone,' he says, as her stomach clenches.

'Are you sure you don't want to touch it?' Skarratt asks, amused, pushing it towards her as she backs away. 'I thought you would have more mettle in you!'

He laughs as he replaces it carefully in the cabinet, taking out a large ugly candle, a neatly written label wrapped around one side. Cec reads what it says. "Made from a hanged man of the name of John Morgan, 1762"

She recoils and Skarratt notices it.

'You can read?' he asks, surprised.

'Arter taught me,' Cec says quietly. 'He insisted I learn.'

'Well, well, little urchin. How full of surprises you are.'

Cec takes a further step back, revolted by Skarratt's collection, but as she does so, she knocks her dustpan from the mantelpiece. A tiny amount of dust puffs into the air and she sneezes, immediately reaching for her handkerchief with her left hand.

'Ah! A sinister!' Skarratt says, grabbing her left wrist. 'Intriguing! Left handed, are we?'

It's only then that Skarratt notices the handkerchief itself. He is upon her in an instant.

'What exactly is *this*?' He growls, snatching it out of her grasp, his face inches away. Cec has nowhere left to go, the mantelpiece already digging into her back as Skarratt waves the distinctive handkerchief at her. Red hearts and black aces edging the white silk cloth.

'It's just a handkerchief, sir!'

'Where did you get it? And where is the handkerchief *I* gave you?'

'I lost it. I'm sorry, sir. And this one, it was from a man. I don't know his name!' she lies, thinking on her feet.

'What man?' He glares at her. '*What man, Cecily?*'

'At Arter's grave. I went to visit and I sneezed, just like now, and a man at another grave, he lent it to me. That's all. He said he didn't want it back, that it was mine to keep. That's all, sir, I swear.'

'You'd better not be lying.'

'I'm not, sir! Honest, I'm not!' She trembles under his gaze, petrified.

'Are you spying on me?'

'Of course not! Who for, sir?'

Skarratt gives her a wry look. 'That is the handkerchief of a magician, Cecily. But you already knew that.'

'Please, sir! I didn't know the man. It's just chance, that's all. I'm not spying, I swear!'

He stares at her before pulling something from his pocket.

Cec's heart races when she sees what it is. A small, sharp penknife which he flicks open. She swallows as he leans toward her, pulling a lock of her hair loose. He fingers it for a moment not taking his eyes off her, before swiftly cutting the end off.

'You'd better *not* be lying,' Skarratt says sharply, as he throws the handkerchief back at her, before heading upstairs to his study.

Cec sighs with relief, realising she's been holding her breath. But the lock of hair, why on earth did Skarratt take that?

She racks her brains before remembering the stories Arter used to tell her, late at night, when she was younger. About eggshells and changelings, of witches using hair in their magic. She shivers, remembering the nightmares that followed afterwards. How Arter, if he was feeling cruel, used to pretend he'd hand her over to the witches if she didn't behave.

Nonsense, it's nonsense! That's all.

But then Cec remembers the dolls in Skarratt's box in his study.

Not dolls after all, but poppets. Representations of *real people*. The boy with the pin through his stomach. *That's* why Skarratt took a lock of her hair!

Cec touches her hair, feeling sick suddenly. She could run – she could. Go to that man, Valentin. Or even Miss Carleton. But what would Skarratt do to her if she did?

She looks at the cabinet of curios in the corner and understands better now what Arter meant. *Dabbling in the unknown*. It wasn't the séances he meant after all. It was *this*. The bone wand. The skull. And worst of all, the tallow candle. The wick trimmed, the drips around the sides. It had been used, she was sure of it, for there was a wax mark on the velvet cushion underneath. And she had seen something else on that cushion too. Embroidered onto the cover. A pentagram.

Black magic.

That night, when Cec finally goes to her room, relieved to have avoided Skarratt for the rest of the day, she pulls the chair up by the door and climbs up onto it, wobbling slightly. There is a pin in her hand attached to a short line of thread and a needle too.

Carefully and quietly, Cec pushes the pin into the plaster above the door and, using the needle and thread, scratches a faint circle around it. She moves the pin, creating another curved line within the circle, before repeating it again and again until the circle is filled with curved petals. A daisy wheel. To protect from evil spirits.

When Cec is done, she steps back down, ramming the chair firmly underneath the handle so that no one can open the door. She should feel safer now, but even so she sleeps fitfully, her dreams filled with poppets who walk, a skeleton who mouths emptily at her, and Arter, who transforms into a giant bird with wings that block out the sky.

It's a bright sunny morning and George and Eadie stand on the roof of her workshop, the city spread out below them. They have clambered out of the kitchen window, much to Jenny's amusement, passing out pieces of equipment, a folding table, props and more, and are nearly ready to film George's animated photographs.

There's a lightness in Eadie's step as she checks the camera whilst George sets up his backdrop over the kitchen window. It is not as large a space as they might have wished for, and the camera is situated nearer the edge of the roof than would be ideal, but the light is good and Eadie is hopeful of completing both films before the rain that is forecast later spoils their plans.

'Right. I'm ready,' George says, rubbing his hands. He stands behind a cloth-covered table, a huge sheet of stiff paper in front of him.

They have just thirty seconds of footage in each reel, and although George has practised whittling down his act to exactly that length, both he and Eadie agree he should rehearse at least once more in situ.

'It'll be loud when I crank it,' Eadie says, taking up her position behind the camera. 'I'll count you in. Backwards from three. Then forward – one to thirty, so you know you're on track. Ready?'

George takes a deep breath. 'Ready as I'll ever be.'

'Three, two, one . . . Go!'

George smiles at Eadie, bows gracefully, then his hands fly as he speedily folds the paper first lengthwise, then along the shorter side, creating a concertina effect. He holds it up and the paper unfolds itself as a Venetian blind. Swiftly, he folds the paper up again, pulling the ends together in a circle to create a large rosette which he pretends to adorn his suit with. Then he stretches it to create what looks like a tablemat before folding it into a large fan, which he comically cools his face with as if his efforts were strenuous.

Eadie almost forgets to count as she giggles.

'Fifteen . . .' she says. Halfway through and he's already created four effects, exactly on schedule.

It's the first time Eadie has seen George perform and, she must admit, he is rather enchanting.

George chuckles as he folds the paper again, creating a large urn which he balances on his shoulder as if it were filled with water. Then he twists it to create a sentry box before somehow pushing it together to form a giant paper bon-bon.

'My final trick!' he says, and with a few more twists, the bon-bon is transformed into a large paper dumb-bell. George slowly lifts it up and down with one arm, pretending it is heavy before collapsing underneath its 'weight', leaping to his feet for a final bow just as Eadie counts thirty.

'Bravo!' she says, applauding as she laughs. 'Although I'm going to have to ask you to do it all again, this time with the film in.'

'Will it look all right, do you think?' he asks nervously, as he resets, taking out a new sheet of paper and disposing of the already folded one.

'It'll look marvellous!'

This time, Eadie takes off the lens cap before she cranks the handle, a noisy rattle, as George's performance is preserved forever on a long roll of celluloid film, immortalised in black and white. A solo show, just for her, and yet thousands will see this little film. For now, though, in this magical moment, it is just the two of them, a filmmaker and a magician, on a sun-drenched roof in the heart of Clifton.

'Superb!' says Eadie, applauding as George takes his bow.

'I'm glad the wind was low.' He laughs. 'It would've been impossible otherwise.'

Eadie laughs too as she steps back, and her heel falls into empty space. For one terrifying moment she teeters on the edge of the roof, before George grabs her and pulls her back, his arm around her as she stumbles into him. His face is close and his panicked expression tells her how narrow her escape has been.

Eadie steadies herself, heart thumping as she gets her breath back.

'You have very fast reflexes, Mr Perris,' she gasps, noticing for the first time the colour of George's eyes: an unusual mix of blue and grey, flecked with gold.

'Used to do archery when I was little,' he says, and she laughs nervously until she thinks of Cupid and blushes, his arm still warm around her. She clears her throat and he steps back, shy suddenly.

'Miss Carleton, Eadie. The camera is too close to the edge and, for all your impressive skills, you are not invincible. Perhaps we should find somewhere else to film?'

But Eadie is already focusing her attention back on work. 'We can manage. If we push your table back a little further, that gives us more room. And the camera has to be this far back for you to be in focus. Besides, if we film your Magic Hat trick today, we'll have finished. You've brought the props, after all, and it's not as if either of us has much spare time.'

'Only if you're sure? I won't allow you to go near the edge again, though. Let us at least put a chair or something there. I couldn't bear it if—' He breaks off.

And there it is again, Eadie thinks. That intense look of his that confuses her, making the heat rise to her cheeks. She lifts up the backdrop and clambers back into the house to change the reel.

Less than half an hour later, George has rehearsed, reset, and Eadie is again ready to roll.

'Backwards from three?' she asks, and George nods, a top hat in his hand.

'Three, two, one. Go!'

George smiles as Eadie cranks her camera. He tilts the hat, showing that it is empty, before pulling out first one, then two, and finally a third white rabbit that he places on the table. He reaches in again and pulls out a card, then two, then four, before shaking the hat towards the camera, a flurry of cards flying out as he chuckles. Next out is a carafe of red wine, then an empty wine glass, into which he pours the wine. George grins before retrieving his final item from the hat, a bouquet of flowers, which he throws to the side of the lens before picking up the glass of wine and raising it.

'Cheers!' he says, as the film runs out and Eadie reaches her count of thirty.

She is surprised by how different George is when he's performing. That sporadic shyness, the awkwardness he sometimes has, all vanishes when there's an audience, even of only one.

'You have exceptional timing, Mr Perris,' she says, impressed.

'Leave nothing to chance! One of the rules of magic.' He smiles. 'Thank goodness that's over, though. It's always horribly intense performing in front of just one person, particularly when that person is—' He pauses, catching himself.

'Is—?'

'Well, is you,' he says, looking away. 'Right, all done? I'll pack away.'

He gently collects his rabbits, putting them back into their cage, folding down other items and placing them near the window, ready to be handed back into the kitchen.

Eadie watches him for a moment, more unsure than ever what to think of him. So rash, so impulsive – yet so creative too. An ability to turn on charisma as bright as limelight and switch it off again in an instant. And his performance! So entertaining, so *graceful*. She thinks of George's arm around her when she nearly fell, but then Max surfaces in her thoughts . . .

'Eadie,' George says, bashfully. 'I wondered . . . well, Harry and I are performing at a private party at Goldney Hall. I wondered perhaps if you might like to come along, as our guest? Your brother would be welcome too.'

It's tempting, Eadie thinks. But she has so much to do. Even with Mr Hodges having started, there are still projectors to be built and correspondence that desperately needs replying to – all things her new assistant cannot yet deal with. She feels woefully behind and the only way she might catch up is to work all the hours she can muster.

'I'm sorry,' she says. 'It's kind of you, George. Really. But I'm afraid I'm far too busy with work at the moment.'

George nods, trying to hide his disappointment.

When they finish hauling everything downstairs, George starts loading up a cab but a movement in E. D. Carleton Photographic catches his eye.

In exchange for free photographs of the bank's amateur football team, Mr Hodges had been released early from his old job and now stands behind the counter.

'Well, I'll be damned!' George says, startled. 'Your new assistant, Miss Carleton!'

'Mr Hodges?'

'Mr *Chaplin* Hodges. Your new assistant is my *old* assistant. He let me down onstage, and I was forced to let him go. He's why Harry performs with me now.'

Eadie glances back at the shop. *Good Lord!* Mr Chaplin Hodges! She remembers Harry telling her about the man who'd got drunk before appearing onstage. One mistake and sacked for it. Mr Hodges hadn't mentioned it, but why would he? He'd been at the bank for some time before he joined her employment.

'I hadn't known Chaplin was in Bristol,' George says. 'If you want my advice—'

She cuts him off. 'Come, George. Surely everyone deserves another chance? I don't blame you for sacking him given what happened. But it was some time ago and photography is his area of expertise now. His references were excellent, and I assure you I don't need him to wave a wand or hide in a trunk. I did, however, desperately need an assistant and he's invaluable. Really he is. In so many ways.' She holds out her hand. 'Thank you,' Eadie says, as George shakes it. 'For letting me film your performances. And, well, for saving me from falling. May I ask, what happens to your rabbits?'

'Oh, they live in the garden. A large hutch with a run – Harry insisted. I meant to say, I brought you these. Biscuits from Fortnum's. I got a tin for The Professor that I keep forgetting to give to him, but I thought you might like some too,' George says, handing her a pretty tin. 'And, Miss Carleton, Eadie, if I may be so bold, no one should be so busy with work if it means it stops them from enjoying life. From having fun. No work is *ever* worth sacrificing that for, surely?'

He gazes at her intensely before jumping into the cab, leaving Eadie in the doorway, bewildered.

Cec keeps her head down all day, doing her best to avoid Skarratt's gaze, but in the afternoon he catches up with her on the stairs. She's on her knees, brushing each step clean, and she shuffles to one side, to let him pass.

'I'm watching you,' he says, under his breath. Three words that stay with her for the rest of the day.

That evening's séance is only a small one. Skarratt and three sisters – the Thompsons – who come in the hope of contacting their recently deceased mother. The five of them sit around the table, hands clasped, forming a circle.

Mabel is feeling unwell so Cec is on duty tonight, waiting in the corner of the parlour as instructed. She is reluctant to be there and Skarratt is clearly displeased by her presence too.

'You will do only what I tell you and no more,' he had said to her sharply, as the doorbell rang, marking the arrival of the Thompsons. He had been all sweetness and light then, as soon as there were others to witness it.

The gas lights in the parlour have already been turned off and the room is lit only by a single large pillar candle.

'Let the spirits come!' Skarratt says, in a low voice, as the candle extinguishes itself, plunging the room into darkness. 'Come, my friends, come to me!'

It all happens so fast. The sound of someone struggling to breathe in the dark, gasping for breath. A sound of desperation. Cec doesn't even think to ask whether or not she *should* light a gas lamp but reaches for the nearest one automatically. An act of kindness.

The light reveals everything in stark brightness. Not just the youngest Thompson sister, hyperventilating, but so much more: the secret door in the wall half-open with Marianne, Skarratt's sister, crouching there; a pale papier-mâché face dangling from within the chimney on a piece of string.

A moment so still it is like a painting.

Skarratt turns to Cec and she knows by the look of fury on his face that he will hit her.

Chaos breaks out as realisation dawns. Howls of rage from the Thompson sisters. A ringing in Cec's ears as the three sisters storm out and Skarratt pushes roughly past her, trying to plead with them.

The front door slams – and then there is quietness. Cec holds her breath, frozen to the spot as Marianne glares daggers at her before disappearing back into the wall. Seconds, minutes, Cec isn't sure how much time passes.

It was the right thing to do though, wasn't it?

And then he is there, Skarratt. In front of her, his face cruel and twisted.

His punch knocks her to the floor. A bolt of pain across her face and then he is gone.

'We'll put a cold steak on it,' Mabel whispers, as she helps Cec take refuge in the kitchen. She had heard the commotion from her bed upstairs, and come down to see what the matter was, finding Cec, shocked and shivering, still lying on the floor of the parlour.

'He's not a bad man, Cec, honest,' she says, handing her a small cup of brandy. 'When the drink gets in him, he's maudlin more often than not. Never violent. Well, rarely. He's only ever raised a hand to me a few times – when I've deserved it.'

Cec looks at her in silence, horrified.

'You never deserve it, Mabel,' she says, taking her hand. 'No one ever does. Even if you love him, please know that.'

Mabel looks at her, surprised.

'A guess,' Cec says, thinking of the squeaks of the bedsprings she'd heard in the night. 'But you'd be better off elsewhere. We all would.'

Cec downs the small tot of brandy and leaves Mabel in the kitchen, heading upstairs to her room. She knows for certain now that she must leave, and she wonders if she has the courage to seek refuge with The Great Valentini.

Skarratt, mercifully, is nowhere to be seen on the ground floor or the first. Cec is careful to be silent as she tiptoes past the second floor landing where Skarratt's bedroom is and up the last set of stairs, but when she reaches the landing that leads to her room on the top floor, Skarratt blocks her way.

Cec pauses, watching him warily.

'I'm sorry . . .' he says, weaving gently from side to side, a whiff of whisky coming from him. 'If only you'd *warned* me you were putting a light on. If only!' He clenches his fists as Cec holds her breath. 'I'm not a bad man, Cecily. I do good. *I do*. I return happiness to the world, to those who've lost loved ones.'

He's suddenly too close to her. His breath hot. He puts a hand over her eye, covering the bruise that is already forming, his palm smooth and soft.

'They said I had healing hands as a child,' Skarratt slurs. 'I saved a bird once, restored it to life. I'll heal you too if you forgive me. You will, won't you?'

What choice does she have? She gives a tiny nod, as he mutters a string of words under his breath, before stepping back and releasing her, pleased with himself.

Cec slips past him to the door of her bedroom, opening it, only to find Skarratt right behind her.

He hovers in the doorway and Cec glances up at the daisy wheel she scratched above the door. Skarratt might not be tall but he is strong and determined. Cec's heart in her mouth, he sways there for a moment, before turning away.

'Good night, sweet Cecily,' he murmurs, and Cec realises she is holding her breath.

Her mind races as she shuts the door after him, once again putting the chair under the handle. She picks up her small case and packs her hairbrush, spare undergarments, and Eadie's red leather notebook. Her dresses must be left behind for they will not fold up small enough to fit.

He will be furious if I leave, she thinks, and hesitates, her courage faltering.

An idea strikes her and Cec reaches under the mattress and pulls out her playing cards. The first time in a while. She shuffles them, warming to the feel of them in her hands. She has missed them.

She chooses one and holds it out in front of her. *If you stay there without me touching you, even if only for a moment, I will leave this house and never come back.*

She stares at the card.

Slowly, she takes her hand away, watching as the nine of diamonds remains exactly where it is – a single heartbeat – before it flutters down onto her blanket. Decision made, Cec waits for first light.

'If we can get the main structure built by the end of next week, and the rivets done in a few days, might we be back on track then?' George asks, thinking out loud as he and Ollie Hogarth, one of his mechanician twins, walk at pace towards the docks. Despite The Professor's less-than-enthusiastic reaction to George's finale with the tank, in the absence of a better idea, George is still ploughing ahead, for now at least.

It's bright and early in the morning but the docks are already busy as they head to one of the cycling outlets nearby for Ollie to pick up a few small pieces of equipment.

'The timing's too tight,' Ollie says, shaking his head. He's taller than George, with pale brown hair, green eyes, and an earnest look about him. 'If I could somehow replicate both myself and Alex, we might achieve it, but there are only so many hours in a day. I'd ask Warnes and Hankinson to help, but they're flat-out on a show in Glasgow.' He stops outside a rather run-down-looking building.

'Will it even be open this early?' George asks.

'Special arrangement.' Ollie grins, using his shoulder to push open a stiff door that leads into a narrow alleyway. At the far end is a large outdoor space, partly covered by an assortment of materials to provide a patchwork roof.

A tall, thin young man with a mop of dark hair and a sleepy look bends over a rusting bicycle, spanner in hand. He looks up and smiles when he sees Ollie. 'Good to see you again,' he says warmly, standing up and shaking Ollie's hand before looking at George.

There's a smattering of freckles over his cheeks and George thinks for a moment there's something vaguely familiar about him.

'You must be the famous George Perris!' the young man says, with a grin.

'I wouldn't *quite* say that,' George says, embarrassed.

'Better famous than infamous.' The young man chuckles. 'I've heard a bit about you, and your animated pictures.'

'Oh?' George is surprised, for he has kept his collaboration a secret.

'My sister, Eadie. I'm Louis Carleton.' The young man grins again as he shakes George's hand.

The brother who has been travelling. Of course! 'But why aren't you working at Regent Street, with your sister?' George asks, puzzled, as he takes in the low-key premises.

Louis wrinkles his nose. 'Cameras aren't really my thing,' he says, softly. 'I prefer larger-scale work . . . you know – big canvases or, like this, welding and brakes, chains and cables and so on.'

'Welding?' George repeats. He glances at Ollie who nods eagerly, clearly thinking the same thing.

'Listen, Mr Carleton—'

'Louis, please!' the young man insists.

'Louis, then.' George leans forward with a grin. 'I don't suppose you'd be interested in a *really* large-scale project, would you? I promise there will be welding. Lots of it, in fact.'

'Cables too,' Ollie adds. 'And hydraulics.'

'And a chance to learn from this one,' George says, motioning towards Ollie, who looks bashful.

Louis's eyes light up and his smile widens. He glances down at the old bicycle before looking first at Ollie then George, and all three of them already know what his answer will be.

Valentin has been waiting patiently for this moment. At times, he has been certain the girl would come; at others, he doubted her very existence. Was she, perhaps, a figment of his imagination, like Olivia in Paris? But now here she is, the girl from the cemetery, on his doorstep. Her face stained with tears, a black bruise starting to blossom around her left eye.

'You'd better come in,' he says, holding the door open.

Cec stays silent as she trails him inside, into his sitting room, putting her small case down before sitting on the edge of an armchair, ready to flee at any moment. Oz sits by her feet, and she reaches down and pats him.

'Skarratt?' Valentin ventures, motioning to Cec's black eye, and she nods. 'What happened?' he asks. 'And please, there's no need to call me "sir". Valentin will do perfectly well.'

'I don't want to talk about it, sir – Valentin, I mean.'

He notes the traces of London in her vowels, the way she swallows the ends of her sentences. She glances around the room before turning her gaze back to him.

'Who are you?' she asks. 'Really?'

'I am a magician. And when I was about the age you are now, I found I could do "things that were a little different" – just like you – and it frightened me.'

'Is there something wrong with me?' she asks, her voice unsteady.

'No,' he says, thoughtfully, taking the seat opposite her and lacing his fingers together. 'No more than someone born with an extra digit on their hand is wrong. Or someone who can paint from the moment they hold a brush. You and I, we're different, certainly. A touch of the impossible. But there's nothing *wrong* with you, no.'

Cec sniffs and he smiles.

'I hope you've still got that handkerchief,' he says, drily. *She is so very young*, he thinks. And less like Olivia than he had thought too. Her nose is longer, her eyes darker and her hair not quite the same shade.

'That's what got me into trouble, sir,' she says. 'The first time. When he saw it. He said I was sinister. But I'm not, am I?'

Valentin shakes his head with a smile. 'No. You might be more inclined to use your left hand, just as I do. *Sinister* is Latin for left. And superstition over a period of time distorted it into something darker. That's all.'

She holds up her left hand and looks at it a moment.

'You became a magician because of it? Because of this?'

'Perhaps. Perhaps not. It doesn't make me a conjuror any more than someone being able to memorise a play of the Bard's would make them an actor. Or someone with perfect pitch picking up an instrument makes them a musician. They must still learn their craft. But it is an advantage to hide in plain sight onstage, I won't deny it.'

'The woman at the cemetery, the tile. Was that me then? Or was it you?'

'Honestly? I believe it was both of us, together. We *both* helped save that woman.' He sees a flicker of relief in her expression and leans forward. 'I've been looking for someone else like me my entire life. You are the only other one I've found. I heard tales once, of another, in the south of India. Many moons ago, I went in search of him, for it was said he had the power to render himself invisible right in front of you . . .'

'That really *is* impossible,' Cec says, quietly.

'Is it?' Valentin asks. 'When a train can power us from one city to another in mere hours? When light can be commanded at the flick of a switch? Electricity is invisible, is it not? And moving images, mere mortals immortalised, when the dead might live again? Ours is a world where things once thought impossible have become everyday reality.'

'I can't control it,' Cec says sadly, and he nods.

'Nor could I, at first. If you are like me, as I believe, then it's a small power you have been granted. A tiny piece of magic born within you. Something to marvel at, to harness, but with its limitations too. You cannot perhaps change the world with it, but you can light it up a little, nudge it in a particular direction. But be aware that others may seek to exploit you if they know the truth.' He sighs. 'Yet your biggest challenge will be simply to learn to live with it, with who you really are.'

'I don't want it! I didn't ask for it!' Cec protests.

'I know. I felt the same at first. But no matter how much, at times, I would have wished it away, it's part of me. Part of you too. I will help, however I can.'

'Why'd you want to help me?' She sniffs, wiping her nose on her sleeve before reaching for the handkerchief he gave her previously.

'Because we may be the only two in the whole of humanity. *Imagine that!* And I had no one to help me learn to live with it. It was a lonely place and I would not wish it upon another . . .'

Cec stares at him, confused. Since the moment the scaffolding fell, she felt as if she's been in a fever dream. Arter and his funeral. Skarratt and his séances. The boxes of strange dolls. The bone wand and skull. The daisy wheel for protection.

And now this man with his sparkling blue eyes and snow-white hair. All the nights of fitful sleep, of dark dreams – suddenly, it all catches up with her and the words tumble from her mouth as the tears come too.

'I killed a man,' she sobs. 'My friend. I killed him!'

It is her second confession for the same crime but this time she has an audience willing to listen. Valentin remains silent as Cec blurts it out, sobbing and sniffling. She tells him about Arter, the sort of scams they used to run together. She tells him too of how it ended, with the impossible card in the graveyard, the performance at St Andrew's. Her anger at Arter, and the scaffolding twisting and falling . . .

He waits, patiently, until her tale is told, and her sniffles subside.

'Child, let me assure you, with all my heart, you did not kill that man,' Valentin says, gently. 'After all my years, I could not even come close to hurting someone in such a way. To bring a tower of scaffolding down in the click of a finger? No. That was not you. That was the storm.'

Could he be right? Cec wonders, staring at him. *Was it really just the storm?*

'The simplest explanation is almost always the right one. One of the worst storms in years, a badly built structure. A stroke of bad luck. It wasn't you, child.'

'*I was so angry . . .*' Cec wails.

'You were tired and hungry. You think you haven't been that before or since? And yet you seem to have managed not to kill anyone else. What do *you* think the simplest explanation for that might be?'

He smiles kindly at her and Cec, for the first time since Arter's death, feels a glimmer of real hope.

'Because it really wasn't me . . .?'

He nods, satisfied.

'What happens now you know all of this?' Cec ventures, wiping her eyes. 'What happens now?'

'What happens is that we go to Mr Skarratt's house, and we collect the rest of your things. There's a spare room here you might stay in, for tonight, or for however long you need it. But before we do that, we'll go somewhere nice, eat something decent, and you'll tell me about yourself. After all, I don't even know your name.'

'Marsden. Cecily Marsden. But I prefer Cec or Cecil.'

'Cecil it is then. And my dog, by your feet, he's Oswald, but he prefers Oz.' Valentin smiles.

'But I'm scared of Mr Skarratt, sir. Valentin, sorry. I'm scared of him.'

'You'll be quite safe under this roof, I promise you.'

'Why are you *really* helping me?' Cec ventures. She doesn't want to be suspicious of this man but still, better to be wary after all that has happened.

'Because you're like me, dear girl,' Valentin says. 'And because you remind me a little of someone from long ago.'

'What happened to her?'

Valentin sighs and Cec sees his face fall.

'She died. And I could not save her, Cecil. But I can at least try and save you.'

The third of my headings is 'Transposition'.

Transposition can be a difficult effect to achieve for the amateur but is, in essence, the effect of one object travelling invisibly from one place to another.

Examples for the amateur conjuror might include a card leaving the pack and flying into the pocket of a member of the audience, or moving a ring from one's hand, or that of a volunteer's, to a padlocked box on the far side of the stage.

One of the most excellent transposition effects I have seen is that of the lamp that flies. A lamp, already lit, is put on a glass-topped table and a pistol fired at it. The lamp instantly disappears and reappears in an entirely different part of the stage. Crucially, the lamp remains alight! This trick, however, I am sorry to say, is quite beyond the reach of the amateur . . .

Extract from *The Secrets of Magic* by George Perris
(published by Saxon Press, 1895)

TRANSPOSITION

Eadie stands on the long golden sands of Weston-super-Mare, the sea stretching out in front of her and Chaplin Hodges standing beside her.

'Now!' she says, and Chaplin waves a red flag as she cranks her camera. In the distance, a small noisy vehicle comes rocketing towards them. Bristol's first motorised tricycle, it looks far faster than its top speed of twelve miles per hour as it whizzes past. The driver, Mr Johnson of the Bristol Motor Company, gives them a jaunty tip of his hat.

'Perfect!' Eadie cries, waving at Mr Johnson as he loops back to approach them, slowing to a stop in a spray of sand just metres away.

'Would you like a go?' Mr Johnson grins. 'It's tremendous fun, Miss Carleton!'

And so Eadie finds herself flying along the sands, holding tightly on to the spare seat bolted onto the back of the tricycle, laughing as she's bumped along, the wind in her hair. She hasn't been to Weston for an age and the light is so lovely, reflecting off the still-damp sand as the tide recedes.

A memory of her birthday here, five years ago, surfaces and her smile falls away. *Max*. His inscription in her card. *To my future wife*. She hadn't long left Great-Aunt Sylvia behind in London, returning home at last after two years studying at Finsbury Technical College. The start of the summer. Long lazy days with Max and Louis to look forward to until autumn, when the boys would return to Oxford. It had been a glorious day, filled with ice cream and laughter, and music too for Max had made up a song for her, a daft and forgettable ditty he'd sung on the beach, gathering a small crowd of passers-by as Eadie blushed crimson.

She had kept his card safely in a drawer – until news of his engagement arrived. It found its way into the hearth, along with all of Max's other notes and letters; Eadie's hopes turning to ashes too.

Later, when Eadie returns home and finishes unpacking, she processes the film of Mr Johnson in her dark room upstairs, leaving the strip to dry, curled over a drying rack. She focuses on work, trying to keep thoughts of Max at bay but George slips into her mind instead.

His signed contract for the projector lies on the kitchen table, where he dropped it off, accompanied by a generous bunch of flowers. *Ironic*, Eadie thinks. *I've not received flowers for such a long while, and now it seems everyone wishes to send them*. First Bill, now George. She wonders what Papa would have made of it, but when she goes to find his notebook, it's no longer in the sitting room. Not above the hearth nor in the kitchen. She goes to her bedroom too, but the note-book is gone. Vanished.

No one has been in the house except her and Jenny. And Louis, of course. She pounces on him when he returns from work. His recently acquired job at Vaughan's Bicycles seems to be good for him, she thinks, the light in his eyes begin-ning to return, along with the colour in his cheeks.

'Sorry, Eadie, I haven't seen it,' Louis says. 'Last time I saw Papa's notebook, it was in the sitting room. I did think of reading it the other night and meant to ask where it was but you'd already gone to bed. I'm sure it'll turn up. These things always do.' He looks at her. 'Even me,' he adds, drily, but she barely hears him, already checking the bookshelves again.

'Oh, and I met your Mr Perris earlier today,' Louis says, and Eadie turns to him, surprised.

'He's hardly *my* Mr Perris,' she replies, a little sharply.

'I like him,' Louis says. 'He's easy company and good fun. Full of ideas, and he wears his cleverness lightly too.'

'You're certain you haven't seen Papa's book?' she asks again.

'Yes, I'm certain! And listen, Eadie, I've got a new job. Something better than Vaughan's and I think it'll make me happy but—'

'Good,' she interrupts. 'I'm pleased for you, Louis. Really. Now where on earth is that notebook?' And with that, she's gone, leaving her brother to throw his hands up in the air.

The answer to the mystery of the missing notebook doesn't come to Eadie until she's in bed. The contract on the table. The flowers. *George Perris*. Jenny had let him in so he could deliver the contract. And he'd said over lunch that time, he'd like a look through Papa's notebook. But he surely wouldn't take it without asking. *Would he . . .?*

George leans against the side of the cab, desperately trying to think of ideas for his finale and failing. The cab passes along Regent Street and his thoughts turn to Eadie. Brilliant, inventive, sparkling Miss Carleton. It still seems odd to him that Louis isn't working with her. But he doesn't yet know him well enough to delve more deeply or to ask the question that burns through him – is Miss Carleton courting at the moment? It appears she wouldn't have time for such things but still, he'd like to know. He thinks of Chaplin Hodges behind the counter. The man always did have an eye for the ladies. Certainly, he always seemed keen on Harry. 'Invaluable,' that's what Eadie had called Chaplin. *Invaluable* . . .

George frowns as he instructs the driver to stop by Lansdown Place to deliver The Professor's much delayed biscuits from Fortnum's. In truth, he's been avoiding his mentor for some time, keen to avoid questions about his finale, but now he must face up to reality. Be honest with how far he still has to go. The metal tank is already being made, so he can fall back on that if need be, but he knows The Professor is right: it isn't his best or boldest idea.

George consoles himself that the date for the show still hasn't been made public – perhaps it might be pushed back a month or so? He'll never be ready otherwise . . .

He waits on the doorstep for some time, wondering if The Professor might be out. He's heard tale that an old friend of his has returned and George is eager to discover who it might be. But when the door finally opens, George's face falls.

Mrs Gray is dressed head to toe in black.

His heart plummets.

The Professor is dead.

His mentor. His champion. *My dearest friend.*

'He's gone, George,' says Mrs Gray quietly, unable to meet his eye. 'He's gone . . .'

George stands silently on the step, trying to absorb the shock. 'Might I see him?' he ventures, after a while, and Mrs Gray looks at him.

'Do you really wish to? Then I must warn you he no longer looks like himself. An empty shell, that's all.'

George nods. She's right of course. He mustn't see him like that, for it will haunt his dreams. He knows that from before. From the last time he saw someone he loved breathe their last. His mother, eleven years ago now, when he was just fifteen. He wouldn't wish it upon his worst enemy.

George sits outside The Professor's home, pale and shocked, on a bench in Victoria Square as a blackbird sings a hymn, the little tin of orange biscuits still tucked under his arm. His world as he knew it, his future, irreparably changed, his hopes shattered – but he cannot think about any of that. He can only think how much it hurts, and he begins to weep.

He weeps for the loss of his dear friend, for the sense of being robbed of more years with him, at the injustice of it all. And only when he is done does he allow himself to weep for the future too – for who is he now, without The Professor's guiding hand, without his support and affection? Who exactly is George Perris, when he is all alone?

'I'm here to see Mr Skarratt,' Valentin says, waiting at the bottom of the steps as Mabel comes to the front door, eyes widening when she sees Cec hiding nervously behind him.

Skarratt comes quickly, frowning when he sees Cec is accompanied by a stranger.

'Mr Skarratt. My name is Valentin.' Cec notices that he doesn't offer his hand for Skarratt to shake.

'Ah! The Great Valentini,' Skarratt says, raising an eyebrow. 'I heard one of The Professor's old rivals was in town, but I hadn't thought it to be you.'

Valentin continues, his voice steady and clear. 'I'm here to inform you that Miss Marsden will be leaving your employ with immediate effect. She is here to collect her things.'

Skarratt stares at Cec, his eyes icily cold, and she remembers the weight of his fist on her face. She is glad Valentin is with her for she doesn't feel she would have such courage on her own.

'Miss Marsden has a contract,' Skarratt says, crisply.

Valentin smiles politely. 'No. She does not. It was an informal arrangement and can be ended as such.'

'That handkerchief. The one with hearts and spades. It was *you* who had her spy on me?' Skarratt narrows his eyes.

'I assure you no one has spied on you, Mr Skarratt. Miss Marsden had need of a handkerchief and, like any gentleman should, I always carry a spare. She's told me nothing about her employ here and I've no wish to hear of it. Now, please. Let her collect her things.'

'I saw you perform once,' Skarratt says. 'In Paris. Last year. A surprise to even see your name. I had thought The Great Valentini to be long dead. A tired show by a tired performer. I was so disappointed, I left in the interval.'

Valentin sighs. 'And, unfortunately, Mr Skarratt, I saw *you* perform, too. Ambitious but lacking in talent. Unmemorable.'

'The reviewers disagreed. They were most favourable!' Skarratt snaps.

'I believe only *Le Matin* reviewed you favourably, is that not so?'

'What makes you think Miss Marsden will be any more loyal to you than she has been to me?'

'I'll simply have to have faith in her. Treat her as a person, not a dog,' Valentin says crisply.

'I never *once* treated her as a dog!' Skarratt exclaims, a note of outrage in his voice.

'You hit me,' Cec says, finding a wobbly version of her voice. 'You hit me!'

'An accident, Miss Marsden. A misunderstanding!'

Valentin goes up the steps, one by one, until he is level with Skarratt. He is riled now and Cec sees that his eyes are full of fire. 'You struck a young woman!' Valentin growls. 'Now, listen to me, Skarratt. You swear now that you will never speak to, approach, or have any contact whatsoever with Miss Marsden again.'

'Or what, *old man*?'

'Or you will have *me* to answer to.' Valentin squares up to him and Skarratt laughs.

'As you wish. If it's so important – I swear. And in return, I hope Miss Marsden keeps *her* promises too.'

Cec flinches as his gaze turns back to her.

'Now, if you don't mind,' Skarratt continues, 'that little urchin didn't leave any items of her own behind. However, she *is* currently wearing something that belongs to me. That dress is my property, and she must either return it or pay the price.'

'But my dress in my room! My Lady in White costume!' Cec protests.

'I'm unaware of any such dresses. Let that in itself be a lesson to you, Valentin. Miss Marsden is silver-tongued.'

Valentin takes his wallet out and hands Skarratt a note. 'That should more than cover it.'

'In that case, our business is at an end. Oh, and commiserations.' Skarratt smirks.

'What for?'

'Why, The Professor of course. How sad he's left us so soon!'

'What do you mean?' Valentin asks sharply.

'The Professor. He died this morning, hadn't you heard? Dear me! Then I appear to be the bearer of bad news. My condolences. I bid you good day and please, don't return here again. Either of you.'

He gives an insincere smile before the door slams in their faces.

Cec turns to Valentin, as a wave of emotion ripples over his face.

'Who's The Professor?' she asks, puzzled, but Valentin shakes his head, unable to speak. A single tear falls down his cheek and he closes his eyes as Cec watches him.

'He can't be dead!' Valentin whispers. 'He can't be!'

Mr George Perris

in his

Brilliant and Highly Refined Drawing-Room entertainment

Prestidigitation
A Varied and Extensive Repertoire, embracing Startling and
Original Novelties

Hand Shadows
A Unique and Amusing Display of Digital Dexterity

Mental Phenomena
Mr Perris's New and Interesting Feats of Memory. And an
Inexplicable Exhibition of Thought Transference, assisted by
Miss Harriet Perris.

Illusions
Mr Perris is the Inventor of the Successful Mystery, "Vice
Versa", performed at the Prince's Palace; and of the Illusionary
Sketch "The Artist's Muse" performed in London, Edinburgh,
Manchester, Birmingham and Leeds.

Mr Perris can accept Private Engagements at hours that
will not interfere with his touring commitments.

Tuition by Arrangement
Mr Perris's Séances exposing the methods that Mediums use
to mislead and prey on the vulnerable, are eminently suitable
for Drawing-Rooms etc., as he does not require any special
arrangement and uses no objectionable apparatus.

For Terms and Particulars,
c/o Messrs Greenhouse and Perris, St Michael's Hill, Bristol

George is in no mood to perform, but tonight's booking was made months ago, and he hates letting others down. He daren't even think about afterwards. The Professor's grand retirement show, so much excitement and hope – all gone. He sent a telegram to Greenhouse earlier and is dreading the response. So much money already spent and, with the show now cancelled, George could lose everything. He can't even think of The Professor without his heart cracking. To think he'll never see him again! Never joke and reminisce with him, learn from him! He never even got to show The Professor living pictures, let alone share his plan to include them in the show. *He would have loved them!* George sighs despondently, running his hands over his face.

'Are you sure about this?' Harry whispers, as they prepare their props in the side hall. 'It's not too late for us to pull out.'

George shakes his head. 'He wouldn't have wanted us to cancel. Would he?'

'You knew him better than I did. It's all right to be upset, George, really. Everyone will understand. It's a shock for all of us.'

George sits down on a bench in the hallway and Harry sits beside him.

'I'm so sorry,' she says, taking his hand.

'Me, too.' George closes his eyes, tries to focus his mind on the show he's about to perform – but instead his thoughts turn to his mother. To his last moments with her when he'd not long turned fifteen. She'd asked him to perform some of her favourite tricks at her bedside. Her last request. She had become so very frail. His fingers suddenly clumsy, George had fumbled, unable to comply, as she slipped away, still smiling, her thin hand on his arm. He had packed away all of his tricks that same night, giving magic up for good. Or so he had thought. Until months later, when his father took him to see The Professor's latest show . . .

George sighs. His mother always used to say that a man who made his living from his passion was the luckiest man of all. Yet today he feels anything but.

'Come on, Harry,' George says, opening his eyes and getting to his feet. 'We'll do it in honour of The Professor. We'll imagine him out there, watching us, making notes on where we went wrong to tell us later with great glee.'

'He'd be so proud of you.' Harry smiles, sadly. 'He always was. I think he'd have adopted you if he could. I felt like a spare part whenever the two of you were talking. But I did know him well enough to know how proud of you he was. I mean it, George.'

'I hope so . . .' George says, softly. 'I really do, Harry.'

'I had no idea this was here!' Cec whispers to Valentin as they stroll across the manicured lawn. She takes in the fancily dressed people circulating, champagne glasses in their hands. Despite her usual misgivings about the wealthy, she had to admit it was rather fun to be hidden right in their midst.

The grand gardens of Goldney Hall, in the heart of Clifton, welcomes them in. A huge private place with paths and orchards, greenhouses and grottos, it's filled with scent and colour, even this early in spring. There's a short canal in which a variety of fish swim, an impressive orangery, and a stone tower straight from a fairy tale.

Cec cannot help but smile as she looks up at Valentin, smart in his evening suit, she in a borrowed dress and shoes from a glamorous neighbour on the Crescent. Anything would have been better than living with Skarratt, but she hadn't expected this. She was surprised that, despite the death of his friend, Valentin had still insisted on attending tonight; surprised too that the performance was even going ahead if this Mr Perris was as close to The Professor as Valentin seemed to think.

After their encounter with Skarratt, Valentin had returned Cec to his apartment, leaving her with Oz, while he went to The Professor's home. Cec had been unable to resist a look around, rummaging in drawers and wardrobes, but it seemed Valentin has no secrets, not in his rooms anyway. A handful of personal belongings, suits, shirts and ties, socks and underwear. A few books. *The Great Valentini is an enigma.*

When he returned, he was red-eyed and tired, pleased to find Cec still there. It was true, he told her. His friend, The Professor, was dead. *He mourns for him as I still mourn for Arter*, Cec had thought. *But he bears his loss well, hiding his distress with a stiff upper lip.* Then she will endeavour to do the same . . .

'I'll talk to Perris afterwards,' Valentin says, as they head towards the orangery. 'I don't want to put him off before the show. The Professor wanted to introduce us but, alas, time was not on our side. I hope the young Perris will find solace in knowing another is grieving as he is.'

'Can we see the grotto too?' Cec asks, eagerly, for Valentin has already told her of the underground cavern filled with shells from around the world.

'We're not here to see the gardens, Cecil; we're here to see Perris,' Valentin says, gently rebuking her. 'Ah, here he is now.'

'Good evening, ladies and gentlemen!' says George, as he steps out at the far end of the orangery to a round of applause. 'What a fine evening to be here in the splendid gardens of Goldney Hall. My name is George Perris and tonight I will be assisted by Miss Harriet Perris, my sister.'

He motions with his arm and Harry steps out to join him, in a beautiful dove-grey dress. She smiles and curtseys as Cec's mouth hangs open with surprise. Skarratt said women had no place in stage magic – and yet here is one, at the very heart of the show!

'Before we begin,' George continues, 'I'm aware some of you will have already heard the devastating news. Our show tonight is in honour of our dearest friend, the wondrous wizard, The Professor, who tragically died early this morning. I hope you'll join me in raising a glass to him. He has been taken from us far too soon and will be sorely missed.'

The crowd murmur, whispering and nudging each other.

'To The Professor!' George says, holding up a glass as the crowd does the same.

'And now we must, as always, go on with the show.' George bows with a flourish. 'I'm pleased to say my sister has invented something rather novel which I hope might be of interest to you fine ladies and gentlemen.' He smiles charmingly. 'For, sometimes, when one is invited to an evening such as this, it's rather difficult to decide exactly what to wear.'

Harry nods sympathetically. 'I had been thinking of coming in evening dress tonight, in a ballgown perhaps, and now, ladies and gentlemen,' she says, 'I fear this simple dress is rather underwhelming for such a setting.'

A ripple of amusement runs through the audience and Cec grins. She feels a shiver of anticipation, just as she used to before a show with Arter. She's missed it. The excitement of live performance.

'Never fear!' says George. 'For my sister's magnificent invention will solve such worries in an instant. Behold . . . the Magic Cloak!' He reaches to a hatstand in the corner and holds up a large black cloak.

'Madame,' says Harry, extending her hand to a woman at the front. 'May I invite you to join me up here?'

The woman steps up, excited and embarrassed, as Harry asks her to check the dress she is wearing is secured properly. Satisfied, the woman returns to the audience.

Cec strains to see as the crowd jostles slightly in front of her.

'Behold, the Magic Cloak!' cries George as he throws the cloak around Harry, fastening it by her neck and covering her before spinning her around.

'Oh, dear! I feel rather dizzy!' says Harry. 'You'll have to spin me the other way too, George, otherwise I fear I shall never feel right again!'

George does so and Harry comes to a stop.

'Better?' he asks, amused, and she nods.

'Much better,' she says. 'Although I'm afraid this cloak is rather heavy for such a warm evening.'

George unpins it, removing it from her shoulders.

The audience gasps – for Harry no longer wears her dove-grey dress but a pink ballgown of satins and silks.

Cec's eyes are wide with disbelief. *But that's* . . .

'Impossible!' someone cries, as George grins and Harry curtseys.

'Ladies and gentlemen! The Magic Cloak!' cries George. 'Available now at all reputable tailors.' He chortles as the audience laughs and cheers.

Cec, too, applauds wildly, filled with joy. She's never seen anything like this. So different to the cheap music halls Arter took her to. So different to the scams they used to work. Her head feels close to bursting with ideas and inspiration.

Valentin smiles as he feels George's charm and warmth flow through the audience, performing a wide range of illusions to gasps of astonishment and enthusiastic applause. Cards first, clever tricks that combine thought-reading and sleight of hand. A fishing rod that George extends, casting it over the audience, to catch live goldfish from mid-air. There are scarfs that materialise from nowhere; juggling balls that change colour and vanish; floating pencils that hang in mid-air before George burns them in a top hat, transforming the ashes first into multi-coloured ribbons, and then into a Union Jack.

Finally, it's time for George's finale, his 'egg man' trick, an illusion Valentin has heard much about from The Professor.

'Ladies and gentlemen!' George bows. 'Now that we are acquainted, I feel able to make a confession. A strange thing has happened of late. Recently, my sister bought me a present: two white hens to add to our menagerie of rabbits and doves. They are pretty creatures, but, my word, they will not stop laying eggs.'

'They are most productive hens!' adds Harry, with a grin.

'Indeed,' says George. 'But the strange thing is, ever since they arrived – oh, Harry! It's happening again!'

With a look of shock, George produces a hen's egg from his mouth. He looks at it in surprise as the audience giggles.

'You see,' George says, suppressing a smile, 'this is what keeps happening! Ever since those hens arrived, I can't stop laying eggs myself!'

He produces another egg from his mouth, then a third one. The audience laughs, and ripples of applause fill the air as George rolls up his sleeves, showing his empty hands, before plucking eggs from the air, two in each palm.

He places them in a wicker basket Harry holds out for him, then reaches into his trouser pockets, pulling out first one egg, then more and more. Egg after impossible egg, dozens and dozens, until the basket is filled up, carried away by Harry as the audience falls into fits of laughter.

George chooses a young boy from the audience to help him retrieve eggs from his waistcoat, and still they do not stop. Dozens and dozens, *hundreds* of eggs, as if the stage itself were to be turned into a giant omelette. Finally, when the audience is sore with laughter, cheeks aching with glee, George shakes out one last egg from his trouser leg.

He holds it up, looking at the audience. 'Ladies and gentlemen, I do hope you've had a pleasant and entertaining evening,' George says, eyes twinkling. 'It's been a pleasure to perform in front of such a friendly audience, particularly tonight of all nights. I thank you from the bottom of my heart. One last thing – please don't forget that all the tricks and illusions you witnessed tonight are simply that. But as you've been so welcoming, I will entrust you with the secret of how they are achieved . . .'

He cracks the last remaining egg in his hand, revealing it to be hollow bar a small piece of paper inside. George unfurls it, smiling at the audience. 'All done by kindness,' he reads, before handing the paper to a member of the audience as a souvenir.

He and Harry bow, to rapturous applause.

Cec is speechless, her face full of wonder as she looks up at Valentin. He nods, impressed, as the crowd around them starts to move.

'Extraordinary. Less formal than my generation, but a warmth and charm all of his own. You know, Cecil, I think Mr Perris might do rather well for himself.'

He smiles at her expression. A look he recognises from his own, younger days: delight, astonishment, and a thoughtfulness too, wondering how exactly it was all done.

A crowd of well-wishers and excited fans swarms around George, removing him from view and, not wishing to further overwhelm the young magician, Valentin decides to postpone his introduction.

'Come, Cecil, we'll speak to him tomorrow. What a day. What a day for all of us . . .' He shakes his head, one last sad smile, before they take their leave.

When Valentin and Cec return to his lodgings on Royal York Crescent, Cec finds herself yearning for rest after such a long day. The bedroom he shows her to is a light and airy one with a door that, much to Cec's relief, locks on the inside. There's a wardrobe, a chest of drawers, a long mirror and a bed with snug blankets folded on top. Warm and cosy. A wooden chair sits in one corner, a small table and lamp next to it, and Valentin leaves her to settle in before knocking on the door with a cup of cocoa.

She sits on the bed as he takes the chair by the lamp, the glow confined to the corner for it is late now and the room is dark.

'Thank you,' Cec says. 'For rescuing me. For everything.'

'For everything?' he asks, smiling at her. They eye each other for a moment before Valentin lifts his hands to the beam of light from the lamp. The shadows of his hands make a swan come alive, above Cec's head, and she laughs with delight as it swims across the ceiling. Then a bear follows, full-bellied and wobbling, uncertain on his feet as he dances. Finally, the silhouette of an elephant, trunk swaying, moves slowly, ponderously, from the dark into the light before disappearing into the shadows.

Cec glances at Valentin, sensing he is not quite finished, and he nods towards the ceiling. She gasps as the trio of shadow creatures dances together on the ceiling. *All of them.* The swan, the bear *and* the elephant. And yet, each shadow animal takes *both* hands to create.

She looks at Valentin – who now sits with his hands on his lap, motionless.

'But that's . . .' she cannot find the words.

'It is,' he says, tired suddenly. 'One day you might do the same, Cecil. Better even.'

'D'you really think I could?'

'I do indeed.'

'Have you ever shown anyone else?'

'Once,' he replies. 'A long time ago.'

'Was it her?' Cec asks, tentatively. 'The person I reminded you of?'

He gives a small nod, before looking her in the eye. 'The Professor is dead, Cecil, and I must face up to it. He's left me with the onerous task of sifting through his paperwork and organising his funeral. I need an assistant. And so, I ask that you make a decision tonight. If you say no, I understand and you may leave in the morning, no questions, to wherever you wish to go. If you say yes, you'll stay here, with me.' He waits, allowing his words to sink in. 'I'll pay you a wage. A proper one. You'll be given bed and board and your own room. I know what happened with Mr Skarratt has no doubt tainted your view of magicians, but I promise you I am not him. I am not your Arter, either. I am my own self, for all my faults.'

'What sort of assistant?' she asks warily, and he smiles.

'A magician's assistant. Well, an apprentice. I'll teach you stage magic and I'll teach you how to harness your own element of the impossible too.'

'Really . . .? *Truly?!*'

He nods.

'Will I be your maid as well?' Cec asks, thinking of Skarratt, and Valentin chuckles, shaking his head.

'I am not offering a domestic position, Cecil, but an apprenticeship. The two are quite different. I will not be asking you to blacken the hearth or whiten the step for I have always believed such things are neither necessary nor important.' His face becomes serious and he leans forward. 'A true magician's assistant is crucial to the show. Without the assistant, there can be no magic. You saw that tonight with George and his sister, Harriet.'

She nods, lost in wonder, as he continues.

'Many years ago, when I was younger than you are now, someone gave me a second chance. I was at my lowest ebb and a conjuror called Lightfoot, a good man with a kind heart, saw something in me and took me on as his apprentice. It's only right I pass that good fortune on. What say you?'

She glances at her hands and wiggles her fingers. 'Do you *really* think I could do that? The shadows on the ceiling?'

'I think, with practice and training, and a belief in yourself, you could do more. You are quick and intelligent, a fast learner. Small enough to hide in a trunk. So I offer you this. A chance to learn, to hide in plain sight alongside me.' Valentin stands, takes out a small knife from his pocket and cuts a thin scarlet line across his left palm. 'A blood oath,' he says. 'An act of trust. Your choice, Cecily Marsden.'

She stands up too and he hands her the knife. The weight of it in her palm. The paths of different lives branch off in front of her like a tree. A choice, for once, that is truly hers. And just one moment in which to decide.

She slices the knife swiftly across her left hand.

BRISTOL MERCURY, Thursday 26 March, 1896

DEATH OF 'THE PROFESSOR'

We regret to announce the death of the distinguished conjuror known only as The Professor which took place in the early hours of yesterday at his residence in Lansdown Place, Clifton. His funeral will be held next Wednesday at two o'clock at St Peter's Church, Mary-le-Port. The church is expected to be filled with many from the world of entertainment. There had been speculation The Professor would announce his successor in what was to be his last public engagement but, although an insider at the Prince's Theatre confirmed a planning meeting had been discussed, no date had been announced.

Eadie steps out of the cab, opposite George's workshop underneath the railway arches at Gloucester Road, just as the man himself emerges in a well-cut brown suit. He looks pale and tired and his shoulders slump a little as he carries a large trunk. Eadie hides in a shop doorway for a moment, watching him. She had searched 5 Regent Street from top to bottom – even the workshop and studio – and there was still no sign of Papa's book. She cannot *really* believe George would steal from her – and yet, what other explanation might there be?

As George heads off, Eadie instinctively follows him, keeping her distance. He cheers up a little as he walks, his lips pursing in a whistle, but she cannot hear it, for the train above screeches on the rails, puffing clouds of steam as it heads towards Avonmouth.

George walks quickly and Eadie struggles to keep up as he heads past grand semi-detached villas and then down a narrow alleyway that emerges onto St Michael's Hill. A quick glance up at a grand building before he crosses the road and heads inside. The children's hospital.

George is already setting up in an empty ward when Eadie enters.

'Oh, Miss Carleton — Eadie! What a pleasant surprise!' George smiles, brightening up when he sees her. 'Did Harry say where I was? Don't suppose you could give me a hand?' He continues unpacking before realising she hasn't replied. 'Are you all right?' he asks, concerned.

'Harry didn't tell me where you were,' Eadie says, guiltily.

'Then how did you know I was here?' George frowns, puzzled.

'I, um . . . I followed you . . .' she says, carefully.

He looks at her, confused. 'You followed me? Why?'

She swallows. 'The notebook, of my father's.'

He pauses, thinking for a moment. 'The one you mentioned over lunch that time?'

'Yes. It — it's gone missing . . .'

'Oh, no! I'm sorry to hear that. But what on earth makes you think I can help?'

She has no need to answer, for George sees it on her face. 'You think *I* took it?' he says, realisation dawning.

'No, honestly, George, I didn't—'

'You are a *terrible* liar, Miss Carleton,' he says, his face crumpling.

Eadie sees what a mistake she's made, how much she's hurt him. 'George, please . . .' She steps towards him, but he turns away, busying himself with his tricks, laying them on a table at the far end of the room.

'Do you think so little of me? That I would steal from anyone, let alone *you* of all people?'

'I'm sorry, George. I'm sorry. I wasn't thinking straight!' Eadie tries to appease him. 'I've finished developing the animated pictures we filmed, perhaps I could show them to you this evening or—?'

'You don't trust me, do you?' he asks, full of disappointment.

His words cut at her heart, an echo of what Louis said when he showed her his painted backdrop. 'I *do* trust you, George—'

'Then you have a most peculiar way of showing it,' he says, firmly. 'Besides, I cannot come this evening.'

'Oh.'

'I need to prepare for a private show. For money. I sell a little bit of my soul, and gain an insight into how the other half lives. It subsidises me, allows me to do things like this. A free show to cheer up some poorly children.' He eyes her coolly. 'But perhaps you don't approve of that, either, Miss Carleton? Somehow, I seem to make a habit of irritating you.'

'George, that's not true! I know we had our differences to begin with, but I respect and admire you hugely and—' She breaks off, her words hanging between them.

'Well, pleasant though this is,' he says, 'I'm afraid we must resume this conversation some other time. I wish you luck in finding your notebook, but I have a show to put on.'

He looks up at her, furious and hurt, as she lingers. 'My word, Miss Carleton, I am *this* close to losing everything I hold dear! The Professor is dead, my dearest friend, and my entire career is on the rails. Investors pulling out left, right, and centre. I came here for a bit of respite – to avoid the endless depressing telegrams from my business partner. I came here to cheer some children and try and cheer myself up a little in the process. And now *this*. That you genuinely think I crept around your house and stole from you! Honestly, it beggars belief!'

A sense of shame creeps over Eadie's skin as if it wanted to tear itself away from her. 'I'm so sorry, George. I didn't know about The Professor. Please accept my condolences. I don't know what I was thinking. I'm sorry, truly—'

'Well, you'll excuse me, but I must finish my preparations, and I'm sure you wouldn't want me to keep the children waiting, would you?'

She shakes her head, lost for words.

'George . . .' she murmurs, his name catching in her throat. But it's too late. She turns and walks away, her head hanging in shame.

As the door shuts behind her, George whacks his fist down on the table, making his tricks jump in the air. *'Damn it!'* he mutters to himself, under his breath. *'Damn it!'*

Pages of handwritten notes lie scattered across the table in front of Valentin and Cec. All in The Professor's distinctive, scratchy script.

'Precise instructions.' Valentin sighs, running a hand over his short white hair as the sun shines into the sitting room. 'Everything from the order of his funeral to the wording on the memorial cards! I can't let him down . . .'

'It's all right,' says Cec. 'One task at a time. I'll organise the flowers and memorial cards for a start.'

'I can't believe he's gone . . .' he says, softly. 'All the years in which we never even spoke or exchanged a letter. After all of it, he's entrusted this to me.'

'I'm sorry,' Cec says quietly. 'Honest I am. But please, give me things to do, Valentin. I'm here to help, aren't I? Come on, I'll make some tea to keep us going.'

Valentin nods, gratefully, and starts to busy himself with a list of jobs that need doing as Cec puts the kettle on. She glances over at the piles of Valentin's cases stacked up in the corner of the room. A dozen or so trunks that arrived from France this morning, each one weighed down with secrets. Oz sniffs at them hopefully and Cec wishes she could open them all to see what lies inside.

When Cec brings over the tea, she notices a tatty green hardback with gold embossed writing on the table.

'You'll be needing this,' Valentin says as he slides it towards her.

'*Magic and More Magic*, by David Wighton,' Cec reads the title. 'It's been well used,' she says, flicking through the crumpled pages.

'I should hope so too. I learned an awful lot from it. Lightfoot gave it to me when he took me on as his apprentice. And now it is yours. Choose one trick and learn it well. Learn it until it is second nature, until you can do every move without thinking. Then learn another, and another. The patter, to you I think, will come easily. The more you practise, the better you will get. Even with your advantage, you'll find few short-cuts, Cecil.'

'Thank you,' she says, hugging the book to herself, genuinely touched.

Later, when they've made some progress on the list, Valentin opens the door to the balcony and steps out, looking at the spectacular view. He chuckles as first Cec and then Oz join him.

'What is it?' asks Cec, pleased to see him smiling.

'I was remembering an old trick we once did together. Long ago. In Morocco. Oh, Cecil, when Henry was on form, he could be extraordinary – The Professor, I mean. We had an illusion in which I was thrown into a fire and he would return me to life from the ashes.'

'Go on,' Cec says, intrigued.

'One evening, we performed it at a private event for a wealthy host. He was a man who did not like to be refused and had decided Henry would be a fine match for his youngest daughter. We were out of our depth, for Henry had no wish to marry a stranger, but no wish to offend our powerful host either. So Henry and I swapped places: he volunteered to burn himself and be revived. And I had to pretend the trick had gone wrong, that he'd been killed in a terrible act of misfortune. All as Henry was carried away, giggling, in a wicker hamper around the back of the stage, onto a train bound for the coast.' He smiles. 'Such mischief! Happy days!'

Valentin motions to the view in front of them, over the rooftops of countless houses to the curving hills in the distance. 'I told him where I was staying. Paying over the odds for rooms on the Crescent, for that view,' he says. 'You know what he said?'

Cec shakes her head.

'"You always were gullible."' Valentin imitates The Professor's rasping voice. 'But aren't we all, Cecil? Aren't we all, in one way or another?'

'To The Professor!' cries George, raising his glass for the umpteenth time as he drinks to the memory of his late friend.

He sits in the King William Ale House with Fintan Costello – the manager of the Prince's Theatre; the Hogarth twins; and new recruit, Louis Carleton.

The group has already drunk several toasts to The Professor, as well as toasts to forgotten friends and lost loves. They have drunk, it seems, to almost everything they can think of, and their heads are exactly as muddled as one might expect at this late stage of the evening.

'To new friends!' says Louis, replenishing their glasses.

'To new friends!' agrees George, hiccupping as he drains his glass, feeling both better and worse for drowning his sorrows.

He isn't someone who generally drinks to excess, but tonight is different. The Professor is gone, his own promising future disappearing into the ether. And to top it off, Eadie Carleton accused him of stealing!

He looks at Louis who is distinctly cross-eyed and in danger of falling asleep. George nudges him. 'You know your sister accused me of taking your father's notebook?'

Louis stares back at him, closing one eye in order to see better. 'She wouldn't mean it, Perris!' he snorts. 'Sometimes she's a bit rash, jumping ahead of herself.' He slurs his words. 'But she *likes* you. I don't see her much as she's always working but when I do, she's constantly talking about either you or that Chaplin Hodges fellow.'

George sighs. *Chaplin bloody Hodges.* 'Right, come on,' he says, as Louis slowly slumps forward. 'Homeward.'

Outside in the cold air, George, somewhat unsteady on his own feet, hails a cab and accompanies Louis back to Regent Street, helping him to the door. But Louis seems unable to unlock it, for his key either seems too big or too small or the keyhole isn't quite where he thinks. By the time he realises the front door isn't even locked, Eadie has opened it.

'What on *earth* is going on?' she huffs, as Louis tries to hold in a belch.

'It's my fault, Miss Carleton,' says George, trying not to slur his words. 'The tavern. My fault entirely . . .'

Eadie looks puzzled, as Louis gently pushes past her, clambering upstairs with a backward wave to George. 'I had no idea you two were friends!' Eadie says with a frown. 'Only that Louis had met you the once.'

'You didn't know he was working with us?' George asks. 'With the Hogarths, in our workshop?'

Her look of surprise is enough of an answer in itself and George, feeling as if he's swaying, reaches out to prop himself up against the wall.

'Are you all right?' she asks.

'*Fine!*' He snorts.

'Are you sure you're fine? You don't seem—'

'Fine! I'm *fine*, Miss Carleton. Perfectly fine.'

'George . . .'

'I would never steal, Miss Carleton,' he says quietly, looking her in the eye and feeling hurt afresh. 'You *must* know that.'

'I'm sorry, George. I *do* know that. Really, I do. You are, however, very drunk and you had best go home and sleep it off.'

'Very drunk? Come, I've simply had a few drinks – that's all!'

'A few too many I would say.'

He snorts again, emboldened by the number of toasts he has consumed. 'Look at you, Miss Carleton! So judgemental! Perhaps *you* should have some fun once in a while. For what is life if not for living? If the past few days have taught me anything it is that. Life is short! Live while you can! Enjoy it! Why everything so *buttoned up* all the time?'

'Buttoned up?!' she exclaims. 'It's easy for you, Mr Perris! For all you *men*! Imagine if I'd accompanied you to the tavern, drunk even half as much. My reputation would be in tatters by morning; my business would fold within a month. Whereas *you* . . .' She doesn't bother to finish the sentence.

'No, Miss Carleton! I beg to differ. It's not *quite* that easy!' George tries to defend himself, the alcohol muddying and magnifying his emotions. 'The Professor is dead. Do you understand? My mentor, my dearest friend. I could be bankrupt within the month, lose everything I've worked so hard for. And yet you accuse me, *you accuse me*, and now you judge me too! *You!* Always working so hard you never let your hair down! Prim and proper Miss Carleton who never dares take a risk!'

Eadie stares at him in silence for a moment.

'Are you quite finished?' she asks, quietly, a tremor in her voice.

George swallows. Despite his inebriation, he knows he's gone too far. 'Miss Carleton – Eadie – I'm *sorry*. Forgive me, it's the drink. I hadn't—'

But the door is slammed in his face.

Damn it, he thinks to himself. *Damn it!* He slides down the side of the doorway and sits on the cold stone step, letting the coolness sober him up before he walks home. A stitch slowly forms in his side as he picks over every harsh word he said.

When he returns, Harry is waiting up for him. She raises her eyebrows as he stumbles into the hallway.

'A visitor for you, George . . .'

'At this time of night?' he asks, puzzled.

'He arrived some time ago. Insisted on waiting.'

When George enters the parlour, an elegant white-haired man rises to his feet. 'George Perris?' he says, offering his right hand. The left, George notices, has a bandage across it. 'The Professor spoke very highly of you. He'd been hoping to introduce us, but circumstances conspired against it.'

'You're the old friend of his who has returned?' George says, shaking the man's hand warmly and trying not to hiccup. 'Then you have an advantage over me, for you know my name, but I'm afraid I don't know yours.'

'The Great Valentini. At your service,' says Valentin, as he bows.

George is struck dumb. He grabs the back of a chair to steady himself.

'Don't tell me,' says Valentin, wearily. 'You thought I was dead . . .'

'No!' says George, delight flooding through him.

'What then?' Valentin asks.

'It's *you*!' George blurts. 'My goodness! It's *you*! I saw you perform when I was a boy. It was you who inspired me to embark on this mad, foolish venture! I waited at the stage door, years ago. You signed my programme!'

Valentin smiles at George's enthusiasm although he has, of course, signed thousands of programmes for eager children over the years.

'Well, Mr Perris, I have come to offer solidarity at our time of shared loss. And I'm afraid I have come to ask for your assistance too.'

'Whatever help you need, I will offer it,' George says firmly, suppressing a belch rather less successfully than he might have wished.

'Then you must sober up very fast, Mr Perris. For, you see, I have instructions. From The Professor!' Valentin's eyes twinkle.

'What?' says George, mortified by Valentin noticing how drunk he is. 'Instructions for what?'

'Detailed instructions. On all things. And so, my new friend, we have a show to put on.'

'I'm sorry – *what?*' George thinks he's misheard. He must surely be more drunk than he'd realised.

'Oh, The Professor's instructions are crystal clear. I've just finished going through his papers this evening, hence this late call. You see, he very much wanted his grand show to take place with or, indeed, without him. According to his last wishes, I am to take his place and perform alongside you in his stead. As the saying goes, Mr Perris, "the show must go on!"'

The fourth of my headings is 'Transformation'.

This can be a more complicated effect than the tricks I have already described. Sometimes you might wish to produce an article, transform it, then cause another article to appear in its place. Transformation is often achieved through the aid of mechanical and visual devices but by no means always. When the amateur has got beyond the elementary stage, he will find many of the best transformation tricks can be performed by sleight-of-hand alone.

Examples for an amateur conjuror might include: pouring water into two glasses in which one changes colour; changing a candle into a bouquet of flowers; or a card trick in which a card is transformed into another suit or into a different object entirely.

One of my favourite transformation tricks is turning my assistant, my sister Harriet, into a boy and back again, but for that, I'm afraid you will have to come and see one of my shows!

Extract from *The Secrets of Magic* by George Perris
(published by Saxon Press, 1895)

TRANSFORMATION

Cec barely recognises herself. New dark green dress, new gloves, new shoes, *new Cecil Marsden*. Her hair trimmed and neatened too. She curtseys to the mirror in her room, and the young lady within curtseys back.

'Blimey,' she whispers, as her reflection smiles back at her.

Cec's newly purchased wardrobe, courtesy of J. F. Taylor of College Green and Cordeux and Sons in Clifton, is laid out on her bed. She had gawped through the windows of the department stores many times since she'd come to Bristol but today was the first time she'd dared step inside. Valentin even allowed her to choose her preferred colours and styles from off the peg. A luxury she never thought she would get to experience, for all her clothes until this point had been second or third-hand from the pawn shop.

She looks down at her feet and wriggles her toes inside her new pair of black lace-up boots from Derham Bros, their shiny metal eyelets reminding her of cats' eyes. There's a new hat, two new shawls, new gloves and even new under-clothing from C. Minifie, an outfitters Valentin had been reluctant to enter with her.

Best of all, there are two more dresses to come – ones made to fit, like a proper gentlewoman. One for daytime, one for evenings. Both specially made with pockets for her playing cards. Her old maid's dress from Skarratt's house has been sent for repair, to be dyed black for The Professor's funeral. She'll wear it one final time, a costume of her previous self, before casting it off. The empty cocoon of a butterfly that has spread its wings.

She looks at her grinning face in the mirror. *A conjuror's apprentice.*

'I look like *me*,' she says out loud to herself. 'Like how I was always supposed to.'

Oz – for Valentin has left him with her – gives a quiet woof of agreement from at her feet and the room rings out with her laughter as she scoops him up, burying her face in his wiry fur, giggling with delight.

Eadie was not expecting to see anyone at the breakfast table – not after Louis had come home in such a state – and she's startled to find Bill sitting there.

She slept fitfully, her mind racing from her clashes with George, both at the children's hospital and again, last night, on her doorstep. *Buttoned up, indeed!*

Eadie sits at the kitchen table and looks questioningly at Bill. *He seems calm*, she thinks. *Perhaps his time away has done him good?*

'I hope you don't mind me dropping by,' he says, after a while. 'I took the liberty of letting myself in.' He reaches into his pocket and pulls out a key which he pushes across the table. A spare front door key he sometimes used to access the dark room on the second floor. The gesture is clear.

'You're not coming back then?' she asks, and he shakes his head.

'I don't see how I can. But I'll ask one last time. The offer from Travers. Have you considered it? He's asked me again and that's partly why I'm here.'

'I won't sell. Please don't try and make me, Bill. This is my life. It always has been.'

'It's all right. That's what I thought you'd say. You appear to have coped admirably with my absence, Eadie. Better than I hoped you might, to be honest.' He smiles, and she feels a twinge of guilt.

'I've managed. But I won't pretend it's been easy. Far from it.'

'I see Mr Hodges is my replacement.'

Eadie laughs. 'No one will *replace* you, Bill. No one *can* replace you. And I'm sorry, I never meant to upset you. Really. I said some unforgivable things and I must apologise for it.'

Eadie thinks of George and her accusation over the notebook. She seems to be making a habit of saying unpardonable things of late.

'I'm sorry too,' Bill says. 'I think, perhaps, we both said things we regretted.'

'I'll always be grateful to you for stepping in when you did, after Papa died.'

'I've learned a lot, that's for sure. But while I was away, I thought about it. You see, Eadie, it's the *photography* that always interested me. Not living pictures. They're fine and all very well but they don't *excite* me. I'm not sure what they achieve. A brief bit of entertainment perhaps, but that's not enough for me.'

'So, what now?'

'I want to sell. And I know you don't, and I respect that, but I want to sell my half, use the funds to open up somewhere new. Photographs only. I've found a place in Exeter – a fellow who wants to retire. And it's far enough away that I won't be treading on your toes.'

Eadie nods. It's the outcome she'd most hoped for – E. D. Carleton Photographic to be her responsibility alone. Yet another investor will have to be found and quickly, for she knows the bank won't lend her enough to buy Bill out. She had wondered, before, if Mr Perris might wish to invest, but The Professor's death has clearly led to his own financial troubles. Besides, after their falling-out, she's unsure where they now stand with each other.

'Why didn't you say so before?' Eadie asks. 'About the photographs? I thought you liked living pictures!'

'Sometimes you're not that easy to talk to, Eadie.'

'Oh?'

'You can be rather . . . dismissive at times. I know you've accused me of that too – perhaps you're right. But Louis is back now, things have changed. And I hear you've been making some living pictures with one of those magicians.'

'George Perris,' she says, blushing despite herself.

Bill snorts quietly.

'What?' she asks.

'Eadie, sometimes I think you don't know yourself very well at all. Anyway, look, Exeter isn't too far for a visit. You'll always be welcome.'

'Thank you,' she says, suddenly remembering George's words to her last night. '"Prim and proper Miss Carleton who never dares take a risk."'

Well, Mr Perris, Eadie thinks, *here I am, about to take the biggest risk I've ever undertaken. So there.*

'A new era then,' Eadie says. 'For both of us.' She shakes Bill's hand.

'I'll make a start on the paperwork,' he says. 'And I'm sorry to ask, as the rental in Exeter doesn't start until June, but I'll need funds for the deposit as soon as you can. I don't want to lose the opportunity, you understand. It's a shame Mr Hodges no longer works at the bank, but I'm sure he'll get you a good rate through his contacts.'

It won't be enough, Eadie thinks, but somehow, she will do it.

'Thank you, Bill. For everything. And good luck in your new venture. I look forward to visiting. "Mr Waterfield Photographic" has a nice ring to it.'

Bill smiles. 'I'll write to Travers and turn him down. We've kept him waiting long enough, eh?'

They shake hands again and, as she lets go, nearly a year and a half of hard work, collaboration and partnership slip away too. A thrill of excitement too – the business now entirely hers. And Eadie hopes, fervently, she has not bitten off more than she can chew.

Cec is surprised to find Valentin waiting for her when she returns from walking Oz. The red notebook she stole from Eadie sits on the dining-room table, in front of Valentin, as a fire crackles in the hearth.

'You went through my things!' she says, affronted.

He raises an eyebrow. 'Please, Cecil, I hardly think you can take offence at the very same thing you did to me when you arrived. I am most particular with my sock drawer, and you left it in quite a state.' He smiles at her. 'I'm not angry. Only intrigued as to why you have this in your possession, and if you know what it is.'

'I took it. From a woman who lives on Regent Street. Miss Carleton,' Cec confesses. 'I don't know why really. I know I shouldn't have stolen it. Why? Is it important?'

Valentin leafs through it. 'Well, most things are important to someone. Has this been under Skarratt's roof the whole time you were there?'

'More or less.'

'Goodness. Well, in answer to your question, yes, I think it is important. Perhaps dangerous too.'

'Dangerous?' Cec gasps, surprised. 'How?'

'Have you ever heard of the Indian rope trick, Cecil?'

She shakes her head as she joins him at the table.

'It's a trick so audacious and impossible that it took on a life of its own. Magicians around the world tried to recreate it, even though they'd never seen it, only heard about it. Some became fanatical, obsessed, risking everything to try and be the first to recreate it in the west.'

Cec leans forward, eager to know more.

'There were those who came close to losing their minds over it,' Valentin continues. 'But it was impossible. For the trick did not exist.'

Cec draws her breath in and Valentin smiles.

'It had never existed. Cecil. The Indian rope trick was a fabrication – a lie, nothing but a story. But a powerful story, so powerful that men were driven mad by it. But it's an interesting question, is it not? For what if there really *was* a trick so wondrous, so incredible that someone might kill for it? And what if it fell into the wrong hands . . .?'

Cec's thoughts turn to Skarratt and she shivers. 'Better it be destroyed,' she says.

Valentin nods and opens the notebook. He rips a handful of pages out and throws them into the fire. They flare up in a ball of blue smoke before disappearing up the chimney.

Cec is struck dumb for a moment – until Valentin grins, flicking through the notebook to show her that it's still intact.

'You tricked me?' she says, relieved, and he chuckles.

'All tricks are a story in the end, are they not? But this stolen book is most fortuitous.'

'Why?'

'Because something in it has given me an idea. Here, you must return this to Miss Carleton sooner rather than later. I'm sure it means a great deal to her. Now, how are you getting on with the Wighton book?'

'I've read nearly half of it and chosen my first few tricks,' Cec says.

'Are you ready to show me where you've got to?'

Cec swallows, shy suddenly.

'You don't have to,' Valentin says kindly. 'If you don't feel ready yet.'

Cec takes a deep breath and puts a smile on.

'I'm ready,' she says. She takes out her pack of cards and shuffles them before fanning them out.

'Pick one,' she says and Valentin does so.

'The queen of clubs,' Cec says, holding it up in front of him. She rips it in two and lets it fall to the table. Then she reaches forward, covering the two halves first with one hand, then the other.

She slowly lifts her hands away but, to her dismay, the two halves remain separate, not made whole again as they should have been.

Her heart plummets.

'I can't do it . . .' she says, frustrated.

'What makes you think that?' Valentin asks. 'It was only your first attempt. One simply tries again.'

She reaches out her hands.

'Don't forget to breathe,' says Valentin.

Cec frowns with concentration but her mind slips to Skarratt. To the bone wand and the skull. *Black magic.* Her confidence falters and she takes her hands away. The two halves of the card remain on the table.

'Cecil,' Valentin says, softly. 'Magic only works if you believe in it too. I saw what you can do, I know what lies inside of you. You must believe in the trick but you must also believe in your ability to perform it.'

She takes a deep breath. And this time, when she lifts her hands, the queen of clubs is restored. She laughs with delight, holding it up in front of her.

'Keep your hand there for a moment,' Valentin says, softly. 'And when you're ready, when you feel the stillness inside of you, when there is only you and the card, release your hold.'

Cec breathes deeply and slowly. *Just me and the card.*

She takes away her hand and the queen of clubs stays there, suspended in mid-air. A heartbeat before it falls to the table. The first time Cec has deliberately controlled her powers in front of another.

'You see?' Valentin grins, proudly. 'You see what you can do when you put your mind to it, Cecil? Which reminds me, I have something else to ask of you.'

'Go on.'

'As you know, I am to perform in The Professor's stead at his grand show. I will need someone to accompany me onstage. Alas, The Professor's assistant has long since retired and my old assistant is in France with no wish to travel.' He pauses, looking at her. 'You are still in your very early days of apprenticeship. It is an awful lot to ask. I will be with you every step of the way, but time is short before the show and you are new to all of this. It will be long, hard hours. Repetitive. Demanding. You will be pushed to your limits and beyond.'

Cec looks at Valentin, wide-eyed, as her heart leaps.

'Everything that's happened since I returned to England – The Professor, Mr Perris, *you* – all of it has made me reflect more deeply than I have in some while. I think it's high time I retired too and so this will be my final show. A joint retirement with my late friend. One last performance. Your apprenticeship will continue, of course. But I ask, Cecil, will you join me? In the show of a lifetime? Onstage, as my performing partner, my *true* assistant?'

Cec stares at him, unable to take it in, before glancing down at the table, the queen of clubs looking back at her. Valentin is offering so much. An opportunity she could never have dreamed of . . .

'Do you *really* think I can do it?' she asks, unsure.

'I wouldn't offer if I didn't.'

Cec weighs it up. She had once thought Skarratt's offer to be his maid as an opportunity, but *this*, this was so very different. What was it Arter had said that last night? "If an opportunity comes your way, grab it with both hands, girl! Grab it!"

'Magic only works if you believe in it . . .' Cec says quietly and Valentin chuckles.

She gets up from the table and runs over to him, hugging him tightly.

'You really think I can do it?' Cec asks again, and he nods.

'I do, Cecil. Besides, there's only one way to find out . . .'

Eadie carefully assesses the sway of the small steamer from the back of the boat as it slowly chugs up the Bristol Gorge towards the suspension bridge.

'Is it steady enough, do you think?' she asks Chaplin.

'Hard to say. We'll only get one shot if we do go for it, though.'

Eadie sighs and Chaplin glances at her. 'Are you all right, Miss Carleton? Forgive me, you don't seem yourself today.'

'It's been a busy few days,' she says, trying to raise a smile. 'A busy few weeks, months even. And interrupted sleep too. Louis and Mr Perris turning up drunk on the doorstep. Yet he had the audacity to sack you for the same offence.'

Chaplin pulls a face. 'Well, I was working. I shouldn't have indulged myself. I imagine poor George probably needed to let off steam. I feel for him, Miss Carleton, really. He's never quite forgiven me for letting him down, but I'm sorry for his loss. The Professor meant a great deal to him, and he's lost this grand show as well as his friend. I'd been looking forward to seeing the two of them onstage. And George isn't someone who normally indulges in drink.' He pauses. 'In some ways he reminds me of you.'

Eadie is baffled. 'George Perris reminds you of *me*?'

'Of course! Clever and focused. Inventive and creative. Impulsive at times.'

'I'm *hardly* impulsive! George can be very rash.'

'Was it not impulsive to shut the shop early then? To see if we could procure a boat for filming?' Chaplin smiles, raising an eyebrow. 'George is *extraordinary*, Miss Carleton. I can see why he wanted to work with you. You must make for a formidable team.'

When Eadie returns home, she wonders if Louis is still in bed. She assumes he didn't bother going into work given George's show is now cancelled.

She's annoyed with him for last night but puzzled too. *Why didn't he tell me he was working with George?* Eadie goes to knock on Louis's bedroom door, but pauses. She finds it so hard to talk to him. They've been exchanging civilities of course, and she'd told him about Bill and the business – omitting to mention the proposal. She'd asked Louis, more than once, to tell her more about Hungary and France, why he really left, but every time, he evades her questions.

There's a sudden wail of distress from within his room and Eadie bursts in to find Louis sitting up in bed, startled.

'Are you all right?' she asks. 'I heard a noise.'

'A nightmare. Sorry,' Louis mumbles. He looks up at her, groggily. 'I'm sorry about last night too. Come in if you like?' He pats the bed and she shakes her head. *This room.* She can't bear to look at half of the things in there. The photo of Max. Papa's old clothes.

'Why *did* you leave, Louis?' she asks, her voice small. 'It was so hard. Not knowing where you were. If you were alive, even.'

'I'm sorry,' he says, awkwardly. 'I can't find the right words. They're here. In my heart. Sometimes in my head. But then they get stuck in my throat.'

They look at each other; still so much to say, and neither of them ready to do so.

'You'd better get some more rest,' Eadie says. And with that, she's gone, her question still unanswered.

The Prince's Theatre

'Our true intent is all for your delight'

DRAMA OPERA VARIETY

Refreshments available in the Lounge

Park Row, Bristol

Cec rolls the words around her mouth. *The theatre*. She stands outside the Prince's Theatre on Park Row where Valentin had said to meet him. A tall, impressive stone building, a grand canopy runs the length of the front, and four statues on the roof keep a look-out. Cec used to go to the cheaper places now and then, when Arter was flush, but she's never been anywhere as grand as this.

She pushes one of the glass doors open and steps into a deserted foyer, with thick carpet, electric lights, and colourful playbills.

'Cecil?'

Valentin stands at the top of some stairs in front of her. 'Welcome to the Prince's! Ever been backstage before?' he asks, and she shakes her head. 'You should see it from this side first. This is where our grand show will take place and I need you to know it like the back of your hand.'

He smiles as he opens the double doors leading to the stalls and Cec follows him into the biggest indoor space she has ever stepped foot in. It takes her breath away, this huge, cavernous room that Valentin tells her fits three thousand people. She follows him down the aisle and up onto the stage itself, and he puts his hands on her shoulders, gently turning her to face the auditorium.

Three levels of seating curve around the back, pillars holding up each floor, culminating in boxes nearest the stage for the wealthy to see and be seen in. Ornate carvings on every surface; even the ceiling – and who would think to look there?

'But this isn't the *exciting* side,' Valentin says, eyes twinkling. 'Come with me . . .' And he leads Cec into the wings and onward into a whole new world. A world of costumes, props, playbills, and lights. A world of trapdoors and ropes, backdrops and secret corridors, dressing-rooms and curtains. A labyrinth of brick hallways and doors and under the stage and minding your head. The dull soft smell of make-up and old scent. The whiff of oil and grease and wood. Bustling teams of people fluent in a strange language that Cec can only dream of one day translating: flys and get-ins and get-outs, techs and dresses. This underground, hidden world, a hive of secret activity that comes together to create something truly wonderful, so transient, so *magical*, each and every night.

'The theatre!' Cec murmurs, as she emerges from the labyrinth to find herself back onstage with Valentin. Together they look out at the empty auditorium, imagining all the hundreds of seats filled with people. Her heart thuds with desire, her mind brim-full of stardust and dreams.

Valentin sees in her lovestruck eyes the wonderful, unpredictable world of the theatre reflected back at him. *Little Cecil Marsden*, he thinks with a smile, *has just found her true calling.*

BRISTOL MERCURY, Monday 30 March, 1896

SKARRATT TO BE MAGICIAN'S SUCCESSOR

Mr Roderick Skarratt, the Bristol magician, has publicly claimed he is the rightful heir to the title of Britain's 'Greatest Living Magician.' Mr Skarratt maintains that the distinguished conjuror known as The Professor had confirmed he was to be named his successor, and that a grand show was being planned at the Empire Theatre. Mr Skarratt said his relationship with The Professor had long been close and that the conjuror had been as a father to him. The Professor's funeral, after his untimely death, will be held this Wednesday. It is not known what role, if any, Mr Skarratt might partake in it.

'He barely knew him! It's outrageous!' George is furious, throwing the newspaper down with a thump. He sits backstage in a small office in the Prince's Theatre with his business partner Hugh Greenhouse, theatre manager Fintan Costello, Valentin and Cec. The first planning meeting for the revival of The Professor's grand show.

'An opportunist, as I said,' says Greenhouse, picking up the paper before Oz has a chance to nibble it.

'A charlatan and a thief more like!' fumes George. 'A disgrace to our profession, mixing mediumship with magic. Now this! Valentin?'

'I think it's not worth replying to, or acknowledging, for he'll only claim the paper themselves concocted it. We know the *true* state of affairs and that is what matters.'

George glances over at Cec, who looks as anxious as he feels. He's still unsure what to think of her. She seems so young and inexperienced, is she really cut out for the limelight?

'That's all very well about not responding,' says Greenhouse. 'But George and I have a lot riding on this. As his business partner—'

Valentin cuts him off. 'The show continues as planned, except that I shall perform The Professor's elements now. My last show too. A joint retirement, if you like.'

'I'm sorry to hear that,' George says but Valentin shakes his head.

'The time is right, George. Really it is.'

'But how can any of us perform a show that is all about celebration when we are in mourning still?' George asks, quietly.

'Because The Professor *wanted* us to do this show. He planned *everything*,' says Valentin, putting a sheaf of hand-written notes on the table. 'Right down to the last detail. He knew what might happen, and he planned accordingly, far more than any of you could have known.'

George looks into Valentin's bright blue eyes and thinks back to the incredible show he saw aged just eight at the Théâtre Historique in Paris. He queued afterwards, waiting for The Great Valentini at the stage door. He had waited and waited as, one by one, everyone else gave up and headed home, until only George and his mother remained.

'Come on, George, time to go,' she had said, but he insisted they stay.

Valentin, when he finally emerged, had been astonished to see anyone still there. He had apologised profusely, explaining that something had gone wrong during the show and that it had to be fixed before the next performance. He thanked George for waiting, telling him patience and practice were the marks of a fine young magician. He signed George's programme with a flourish, handing him a handkerchief he had used in the show itself, embroidered around the edge with red hearts and black spades.

His generosity left a big impression. George still had the programme in a trunk of memorabilia under his bed; the handkerchief, alas, disintegrated long ago.

'I'll do it then,' George says. 'For The Professor. For you too, Valentin.'

'Then all is confirmed,' Valentin says, as Fintan Costello nods, noting it down.

'Just one thing,' George says. 'Is it possible to have more time? Another month or so? Only—'

'No,' Valentin replies firmly. 'I'm afraid not. The Professor was adamant the date be kept. And the Prince's is booked up until autumn.'

'Our busiest year so far.' Fintan grins.

George nods, another stitch beginning to form. *No more time then.*

'Now, George,' Valentin says. 'What exactly *is* the climax of your act? The Professor said you had yet to make a final decision. I've heard remarkable tales of your living portrait, the painting that turns into a real woman.'

'No, it can't be that,' says George. 'Skarratt stole the Artist's Muse from me and I want my half of the show to be entirely new. The climax must be bold and original. Different and more ambitious than anything I've attempted before.'

'Such as . . .?' Valentin asks, gently.

George thinks. *So many ideas and yet . . .*

Last night, he dreamed of Eadie. Lit up from within. A dress the colour of scarlet. He had walked towards her in darkness, a lantern in his hand. Her dark eyes, her long curls, that warm smile – so tantalisingly out of reach, however much he strove to close the gap between them. Until finally, she was in front of him, drawn towards his lamp. He'd reached out to embrace her, but his arms had clasped around nothing but air. For Eadie had vanished.

And George knows, as he recalls this, his heart quickening, that this, at last, is the right idea. His challenge now is to turn his impossible dream into reality and in only a handful of weeks.

He confides his idea in the group, omitting any mention of Eadie, the world around him sharpening into focus as he tries to describe the beauty inside his head.

'Ah,' Valentin says, tapping The Professor's sheaf of papers. 'It's full of promise, undoubtedly so. A technical challenge too, given the shortness of time. But that's by the by, for I believe we may have a slight problem.'

'Why?' asks Greenhouse. 'It sounds magnificent!'

'Because The Professor's finale is a vanishing act too,' Valentin says, wryly.

Eadie is in her workshop when Chaplin comes in to announce that she has a visitor. She's hoping it might be George Perris for she's very much looking forward to telling him how wrong he was about her not taking risks, but instead a tall, white-haired stranger waits for her by the shop counter.

'Miss Carleton.' Valentin smiles. 'I have a small piece of mechanical equipment that needs repair. A stagehand at the Prince's mentioned your name.'

'You're a performer?' she asks, and he nods, gracefully. 'I'd be honoured to help but I'm afraid I'm rather busy at the moment. New projectors, living pictures – this current fad for photographic miniatures. There may be a delay.'

'I know.' Valentin bows his head. 'Mr Perris may have mentioned you too. More than once.'

'Oh?' Eadie says. They eye each other, before the silence is broken by the rumble of Valentin's stomach and Eadie cannot help but laugh.

'Well, let me get you something to eat and we shall see what is possible. Did you bring this mysterious equipment with you?'

He nods and she notices the bag he carries. 'You did not ask the . . . the Hogarths? The mechanician twins that work with Mr Perris, to look at it?'

'I rather think they have their own work cut out.'

'How are you with untidiness?' she asks, and he shrugs, nonchalantly. 'Then come through to my workshop. Excuse the mess but I do at least have a stash of biscuits, and I fancy you might need them.'

They step through first into the studio, filled with props and painted backdrops, then through another door into the organised chaos of Eadie's workshop. The place she feels most comfortable, free to experiment and invent, fix and mend, to try out new ideas as her father always encouraged. To an outsider, she knows it looks a mess, but Eadie knows where everything lives, from the smallest bolts and paste pots to the screws and shutters, printing frames and even her father's burnishing machine.

She reaches up and retrieves a large, dented tin from the top of a cluttered shelf. 'It's clean,' she says, and Valentin raises an eyebrow at the smell of oils and polish, the tang of metal lingering in the air. 'The biscuit tin, I mean.' She laughs. 'So, what exactly do you need? For me to fix the mechanism?'

'Ah, Miss Carleton.' Valentin grins. 'I must confess I want a little more than that.' He sits down at her desk in the workshop and pulls out a bundle of papers, which he unfolds.

Eadie looks down at the inky diagrams and sketches. Scratched words and arrows and figures. Intrigued, she starts leafing through them, translating them in her head into metal and wood, into physical objects.

'You see, Miss Carleton . . .' Valentin pauses, theatrically, leaning towards her. 'I need you to help me disappear.'

Eadie and Valentin are still deep in conversation when Cec arrives, feeling sick at what she knows she must do. Eadie's notebook has felt heavy in her pocket all day.

'Oh! Good Lord! Miss Marsden!' Eadie says, surprised to see her, as Cec steps into the workshop, hastily followed by Chaplin.

'My assistant,' Valentin explains, as Chaplin nods, heading back into the shop.

Eadie frowns, for she has been so intrigued by Valentin's drawings she has forgotten to ask his name. 'Then you are, who exactly?' she asks, turning back to him.

'Valentin. Also known as The Great Valentini.'

'Not the same person as before,' Cec explains. 'I'm no longer under Mr Skarratt's employ. I was rescued.'

'Quite,' Valentin says, with a smile. 'And Cecil has something of yours, Miss Carleton. She wishes to return it.'

Cec places the notebook on the table and Eadie gasps, grabbing it and clutching it tight. 'Oh my goodness! My father's notebook! I don't understand—?'

'I'm *so sorry*, Miss Carleton!' Cec says, in a rush. 'But it was so beautiful, and I didn't know how to bring it back and Valentin told me I had to return it. I'm sorry, truly, I never should've taken it!'

She takes a deep breath. There. It is out. A relief in a way, just as Valentin had reassured her it would be.

'No, you shouldn't!' Eadie frowns. 'You've caused me a great deal of trouble. I accused someone else of taking it, even though he'd never do such a thing.'

'Not Mr Perris?' Valentin ventures, and Eadie nods, guiltily.

'A lucky guess.' Valentin smiles gently. 'But Mr Perris is a good man, Miss Carleton. One of the finest I've met. I suspect the only thing he might like to steal from you is your affection.' Eadie's cheeks redden as he continues. 'Now, before Cecil and I leave you in peace, may I ask, was it your father the notebook belonged to? Forgive me, but I leafed through it myself, not realising it was stolen property.'

'Yes, it was. He used it over a number of years.'

'And he went to India? Is that correct?'

She nods.

'I do not mean to pry, Miss Carleton, but may I ask what drew your father there?'

'Of course. There's no mystery. His best friend retired there. In the south. My father went to visit him, a reunion that's all.'

'And your father works here? For it is his name above the shop, it is not?'

Eadie looks away, a look of pain across her face.

'Miss Carleton,' Valentin says, gently. 'There's no need to answer if you do not wish to.'

'No, no. It's all right,' Eadie says, slowly, giving Cec the impression it is anything but. 'My father is dead. That's why the notebook means so much to me.'

Cec looks at her feet, guiltier than ever.

'It's my last link to him,' Eadie continues. 'He died when he was in India, you see.'

'I'm sorry to hear it,' Valentin says. 'My condolences.'

'Thank you,' Eadie replies. She looks up towards the top of a filing cabinet and Cec follows her glance towards a framed photo of a cheerful-looking man with a mop of dark hair, a curly beard and a wry smile.

'Felled by a fever. It feels as impossible now as it did then.' Eadie sighs. 'Such a strange thing, though. He was always so careful to wear something on his feet. An old habit from the workshop.'

Valentin frowns. 'Forgive me, Miss Carleton. I don't under-stand. Barefoot? What has that to do with a fever?'

'Oh, the fever muddled his mind. He was ill and must have wandered out, in the night. He was found dead, in the garden of the lodging house he was in. Bitten by a snake.' She hugs the notebook to her. 'Thank you for returning it, Miss Marsden. It means a great deal to me. Did you find anything of interest, Valentin, when you looked through it? I've never quite worked out what all his notes meant . . .'

Valentin shakes his head. 'I'm sorry, Miss Carleton.'

'What did you think might be in there, miss?' Cec ventures.

'Oh, I don't know. He was a clever man, and he seemed so excited in his last letters. He thought he'd discovered something remarkable. But I imagine that was the fever talking.'

She stands and goes to the small safe at the back of the workshop, turning the combination lock several times before opening it and placing the notebook inside. 'There,' Eadie says, locking it. 'Safe and sound. Now, anyone for some tea?'

George was not expecting thieves, let alone for them to be so brazen as to break into the Hogarths' workshop. It's early and he's not yet had coffee so it takes a moment for him to register that the two men trying to lever the padlocks off the doors are not in fact his mechanician twins, but rogues.

'No!' he shouts, as he runs towards them, noting as they look up that their faces are covered. He launches himself at the taller, thinner one, realising, too late, that he is one against two. The smaller man still wrestles with the padlock, a wrench in his hand, as George's fist collides with the tall man's chin.

There's a shout behind him and George turns to see Louis hurtling towards them, the Hogarth twins close behind. *Reinforcements!* George thinks, with relief, but then the tall man hits him on his jaw and he moans in pain. When the Hogarth twins enter the fray, keen boxers both, the burgling duo soon turn tail. They escape, running off down Gloucester Road as Louis and Ollie pursue them.

George leans on the door, wincing as he touches his lip, blood on his fingertips, as Alex, Ollie's twin, examines the bent padlock.

'You're early!' George says, as Valentin arrives, a look of shock on the older conjuror's face.

'What on earth—?' Valentin exclaims.

'Attempted break-in.'

'The vultures are circling,' Valentin says. 'I should have thought of it earlier. Jackdaws trying to thieve your shiny secrets.'

'Not the first time,' George says, wryly. 'Although normally ideas are stolen from onstage. I'm not sure I like this new, violent approach.'

'Envy is a powerful emotion,' Valentin says.

'It's one thing to see an effect onstage and wish to recreate it in your own fashion, but *this* . . .'

'You have been known to give your ideas away at times, George . . .'

'That was a small book with a limited print run for Christmas,' George says, defensively. 'The tricks within it were for the home. Besides, knowing how a trick is done doesn't mean you can do it yourself, as you know. What about the story? The patter? The presentation?'

'Speaking of books, I saw Miss Carleton yesterday,' Valentin says, smoothly.

George stiffens. 'You know she accused me of stealing her father's notebook?'

Valentin nods. 'You'll be glad to know it's been safely returned. Her professional demeanour belies a warm heart. I think she rather likes you.'

'Then she has a strange way of showing it.'

'Come now, George. She clearly admires you and you admire her too, no? And she's had much to deal with of late. At the forefront of living pictures, expanding her business, and her brother unexpectedly returning, after he disappeared.'

George is startled. '*Louis?*'

'I believe so. Certainly a young man who vanished a year or so ago returned recently, out of the blue. His name had been kept out of the papers, but I'm fairly sure it's Miss Carleton's brother. The Professor mentioned it in passing – you know how he always was tapped in to the latest Clifton gossip.'

It's at that moment Louis himself rejoins them, out of breath from pursuing their attackers, Ollie beside him.

George stares at him, dumbfounded.

'Sorry, George, we lost them,' Louis apologises. 'I don't think I'd recognise them again either, given their faces were covered.' He nods at Valentin who smiles at him.

'Come on,' Ollie says, as his twin finally wrestles the battered padlock off the door. 'I'll make some tea. I think we all need it.'

Louis follows the twins inside, and Valentin pats George on the arm before heading in too.

George watches them go, his mind reeling. Both Eadie and Louis had said he'd been travelling, but if he had disappeared, George can't imagine how hard it must have been for Eadie. He wonders what the cause of it was. *Some sort of falling-out. perhaps? Or something to do with their father dying?*

George hasn't seen Eadie since that night on her doorstep. He's sent flowers and a letter of apology but he knows he must brave her face to face. He feels so guilty for his harsh words, yet he still feels hurt by her accusation of thievery too. The revelation about Louis makes him soften though. If Eadie hadn't known where Louis was, perhaps she didn't even know if he was alive or not. The worry must have been overpowering – and hadn't she said that her father had died a year or so ago too?

After his own mother died, George had learned all about how grief changes the world around you. He had tried to put on a cheerful face, writing letters to Harry at her boarding school, concealing his own deep grief, as a gulf opened up between him and his father. And then his father had fallen apart, right in front of him, and he hadn't seen it – not until it was almost too late . . .

Cec is on her way to George's workshop to meet Valentin, a spring in her step as she hums happily to herself. She's getting to know this part of the city better now and has already worked out a shortcut using a narrow, somewhat overgrown alleyway. The brightness of the sunshine disappears as she steps inside and, for a moment, she wonders if this was the right way to come after all. As she walks on, approaching the light at the far end, a figure steps in front of her. A flicker of fear for she recognises him right away. *Roderick Skarratt.*

'Ah!' Skarratt says, smoothly. 'Good morning to you, urchin!'

Cec tries to ignore him, but there's not enough room for her to get past.

'Please, sweet Cecily! No need to run away! It *is* a surprise to bump into you again but Bristol is a small city, is it not?'

'What d'you want?' she asks, nervously.

'I wondered what you might have told Valentin about me.' He smiles, but Cec sees the coldness in his eyes.

'I've told him nothing, except that you hit me,' she says, defiantly. 'I promised when you took me on, I wouldn't talk about you or your house and I keep my promises, Mr Skarratt.'

'If you're lying, I'll find out.'

She tuts, offended. 'I'm not lying. Besides, *you* swore to leave me alone. And yet here you are. Which makes me wonder if *you* keep to your promises.'

She goes to squeeze past him but he mirrors her movement like a dancer, blocking her path as her heart races.

'Come now! What do you think "The Great Valentini" can do to protect you? He's an old man! You think he can beat me, in the prime of my life?' He looks at her pityingly. 'I hadn't taken you to be quite so naïve!'

'What do you *want*, Mr Skarratt? Out with it so I can get on with my day.' She takes a step forward but so does he and his face is suddenly inches away. Cec realises how vulnerable she is: a dark alley, no witnesses, and she is suddenly, overwhelmingly, frightened of him.

'This grand show of theirs. Is it cancelled or not?'

'What does it matter?' Cec asks nervously, slowly stepping backward. 'Why d'you even care?'

He eyes her coolly before leaning forward, his voice low. 'You and I, Cecily, we are cut from the same cloth. We must toil for every opportunity. Edging our way forward, inch by inch, through grit and determination. What if someone, another young woman like yourself, took what you thought – what you *assumed* – was yours? What if, when you returned to Valentin this evening, there was no room for you as his assistant? Another young woman standing there instead.'

He steps back as Cec puzzles over his words. And then she understands. *He thinks George Perris has stolen his place.* But The Professor had freely chosen George, hadn't he? Why blame George for what was someone else's decision?

'You understand now?' Skarratt says. '*That* is why I care, Cecily. One last thing. I wouldn't tell Valentin about today if I were you. After all, it's merely happenstance we are in the same place, at the same time.'

She nods warily, quietly defiant, swearing to herself she'll tell Valentin everything as soon as she sees him.

'I'm glad we understand each other.' Skarratt smiles, tipping his hat. 'I'll see you at The Professor's funeral, no doubt. How fortunate to come across you like this. Good day to you, sweet Cecily!'

He smiles again, all white teeth, before leaving her there, furious and frightened. She'd been so happy, in her new world, a bright new future opening up. She frowns to herself, determined not to let Skarratt spoil it.

When Cec arrives at the Hogarths' workshop underneath the arches at Gloucester Road, she is taken aback by how big it is. A long, large space with an arched brick ceiling, it's full of raised platforms, cluttered workbenches, and a variety of apparatus. She is surprised to find no sign of Valentin but it's her first encounter with the Hogarth brothers, and she marvels at the miracle of identical twins. If it weren't for them wearing different outfits, she would never tell them apart.

The twins move a large piece of scenery to one side, revealing George in a brown suit and blue neck-tie sitting at the back of the workshop, with Valentin opposite him. *Valentin!* A sigh of relief. She can tell him all about Skarratt!

As Cec steps towards them, George stands, wincing as he does so, almost doubling over as he holds a hand to his stomach.

Valentin leaps to his feet, concerned.

Cec's eyes widen as she remembers the box she found in Skarratt's study. The poppet with the distinctive brown suit and blue neck-tie. The poppet with the sharp pin right through its midriff.

Skarratt's poppet, the one she had held in her own hands, was of none other than George Perris!

Eadie glances up at the observatory tower, long before it is due to open, remembering the first time Papa brought her here. She had been entranced by the camera obscura's moving images projected onto the white concave bowl in front of her. She had reached out, wanting to touch them all: the people and carriages crossing the suspension bridge, the ships sailing up towards Avonmouth. Papa had held her up so she could clasp the wooden handle, rotating it to change the view. She had loved it. Spying on a secret world that had no idea it was being watched.

She hadn't understood why those beautiful images couldn't be taken out of that room.

So, Papa had shown her how to make her own version: a blind over her window, a single pinprick in it, the image, upside down, on the far side of her wall. Magic but temporary. Unfixed and, many had thought, unfixable.

Yet Eadie and others like her have found a way to achieve the impossible. To fix movement. The results far better than a magic lantern – no longer a contraption of slides, but *real* images that flicker and dance. All those years of experiment-ation, that thirst for understanding – for Eadie, it began here. At the top of a tower, a day that changed the way she saw the world.

Last night, Eadie had projected the two films she had made with George in her screening room. It was the first time she'd watched them, and she was delighted, both by the quality and, she must admit, by George's performance too. She knows she must eventually show him the fruits of their collaboration, but she's still upset about his drunken rant, still guilt-ridden too for her own accusation of thievery. He had sent flowers and a card by way of an apology, and surely it is now her turn to extend the hand of peace.

It surprises Eadie to acknowledge it, but she misses him. Although Chaplin is interested in living pictures, he doesn't have the same passion and enthusiasm as George. She thinks again of the look of wonder on George's face when he had first seen her moving pictures, the flecks of gold in his eyes . . . She stops herself. She mustn't become side-tracked, for look what happened before, with Max. All those years and nothing to show for it but a broken heart.

Preoccupied, Eadie circles the edge of the Downs, passing groups of fashionable Bristolians taking the air, before looping back along the tree-lined avenue of Clifton Down. She glimpses a couple ahead – a man with black hair who, from the back, reminds her faintly of George, and a distinctive young woman with a lightness in her step. Eadie's heart leaps. *Harry!* Perhaps *she* might be able to advise how best to deal with George, given how close they are?

She picks up her pace, trying to catch up with the woman she thinks might be Harry, along tree-lined paths before emerging into a leafy clearing. And there she sees Harry – for it really is her – sitting on a bench facing a man with his back towards Eadie.

The man leans forward and brushes Harry's cheek gently before pulling her towards him in a passionate embrace.

Eadie gasps and Harry looks up, springing to her feet as Eadie hurries away.

'Eadie, wait! Please!'

'I'm so sorry!' Eadie says, deeply embarrassed, as Harry catches up with her. 'I hadn't meant to interrupt—'

'It's all right,' Harry says. 'I expect you'd have found out sooner or later. Come on. There's someone I'd like you to meet.' She takes Eadie's hand and leads her back to the bench.

Eadie's mouth falls open as the man sitting on it turns towards her.

'Eadie – Mr Chaplin Hodges,' Harry says, bashfully. 'But, of course, you already know each other.'

'Miss Carleton,' says Chaplin, standing and shaking her hand. He smiles, self-consciously, as he puts an arm around Harry's shoulders.

'This *is* rather a surprise . . .' Eadie says, piecing it together in her mind. The couple must have met when Chaplin worked with George. She frowns. *Hang on – hadn't George been surprised to see Chaplin here in Bristol?*

'Oh, my goodness!' Eadie says, the truth dawning upon her. 'George doesn't know, does he?'

A vase of fresh tulips and a plate of Bath buns sit on The Professor's dining table as Mrs Gray pours Valentin a cup of tea.

'I'm so glad you came back,' she says. 'It feels so empty here without him.'

'I wish I'd returned earlier,' says Valentin. 'Been able to spend more time with you both, before all of this.'

'Oh, you were such good friends for so long. Almost like brothers. But better late than never, isn't that what they say?' Mrs Gray fixes him with a certain look, her lips slightly pursed.

Valentin remembers that look well – the same one she gave him after he had taken her out a few times, many years ago. After Olivia died. And Nellie Buchanan, as she was then, had looked him in the eye and told him she wouldn't be doing it again. That he was still in mourning and she wouldn't be second best. The truth of her words had stung. Not long afterwards, she had met Daniel Gray. It was the night before their wedding that Valentin had left England for good.

'Mrs Gray . . .' Valentin begins.

'There was a burglar here last night,' she says calmly, picking up her cup of tea.

'What?!'

'He had a scarf pulled up over his face but I caught a glimpse as he headed out through the window.'

'Did you recognise him?'

'He reminded me of someone, certainly.' Mrs Gray looks thoughtful. 'Roderick Skarratt,' she says. 'Do you know him?'

Valentin growls at the mention of Skarratt's name and Oz, lazing on the rug, grumbles faintly back at his master.

'He's called here before, several times, but not for a while,' Mrs Gray says. 'The Professor didn't think much of him. A second-rater, Henry called him.'

'You're certain it was him?'

'Not entirely I'm afraid, no. But Skarratt is rather distinctive. Handsome but clumsy. As he slid down the drainpipe, there was a certain inelegance that brought him to mind.'

'Did he steal anything?'

'No, but it's why I asked you to come over. I wanted to warn you, in person. Someone is after your secrets.'

'Someone's always after my secrets, Mrs Gray. But burglary? That's very low indeed.'

He tells her about the attempted break-in at the Hogarth's and she nods, thoughtfully.

'Will you be safe here, on your own?' he asks, concerned.

'Oh, quite safe. Don't worry about me, Valentin. I'm perfectly suited to looking after both myself and this place on my own. For now, at least. Besides, look.' She goes to the sideboard and takes out a small black revolver.

'I hope you won't ever need to use that,' Valentin says, carefully.

'I hope so too, but you never quite know who you can trust these days.' She smiles at him. 'I've been meaning to ask, Valentin. That girl of yours, Miss Marsden, she seems bright, eager to learn, but she's so new to all of this.'

'She's quite something,' Valentin says, softly.

'Do you trust her though? Really?'

'With all my heart.'

'Be careful, Valentin. I mean it. I know she bears a slight resemblance to Olivia, but she is not her. Trust must be earned, not given. We can't afford to take risks. We can't let Henry down.'

Valentin nods. 'I do trust Cecil. I trust her absolutely, Mrs Gray.'

'Then I hope you are right to do so, Valentin. For all our sakes.'

Damn Roderick Skarratt! Cec sits at Valentin's sitting-room table, practising a new trick from the book he had given her, but Skarratt slips into her mind. His cabinet of curios. The box of poppets. *George.* But black magic wasn't real. *Was it . . .?*

Cec sighs, tired suddenly, her whole mind and body aching. She has spent ages poring over schedules, running through preparations for The Professor's funeral, and on top of it, practising tricks from the book too. Every day, every night. Every spare moment. Valentin had shown her some physical exercises she should do on a daily basis too, to keep her supple, and she had bent and stretched herself until she felt like rubber.

Cec yawns before getting up from the table and stretching her shoulders, looking out of the window to the view beyond. She hadn't mentioned her encounter with Skarratt to Valentin in the end for she knew how ridiculous it would sound. But then Cec thinks of the daisy wheel she carved above her bedroom door, how it seemed to keep Skarratt out on her last night in his house. She remembers too the sharp prick of the pin in Skarratt's poppet when she picked it up and her shock at seeing George wearing the exact same outfit, doubled over in pain.

'Stomach cramps,' George had called it, but Cec wasn't so sure. Besides, if both she and Valentin could do 'things that were a little different', who was to say Skarratt couldn't? Perhaps she *should* say something to Valentin but he had so much on his mind, particularly with The Professor's funeral imminent. And Cec had promised Skarratt she wouldn't reveal what was in his house and she couldn't abide it when people went back on a promise. She would wait until after the funeral and mention it then. Yes! That's what she'd do.

Pleased with her decision, Cec picks up a playing card from the table and holds it up at arm's length. She breathes slowly and deeply before taking her hand away and the card flutters straight to the floor.

Cec looks down disappointed. Try again. That's what Valentin would say. Try and try again. But the box of Skarratt's poppets flickers through her mind again and she finds she no longer has the heart to do so.

'Oh! Miss Carleton! Eadie!' George turns scarlet as Eadie nearly walks into him on the landing. She is startled to see him emerge from her sitting room and he seems equally surprised to see her.

'Mr Perris? What on earth—?'

'I invited him, Eadie!' Louis calls, from the sitting room. 'He was dropping by with some flowers for you so I invited him in. You're home earlier than expected.'

'Mr Perris. George. I'm sorry, I — I hadn't expected to see you!' Eadie is wrongfooted both by his sudden appearance and by the large bunch of flowers she can see on the sitting-room table.

'I owe you an apology, Miss Carleton. I'm *deeply* sorry,' George says, face still flushed. 'I spoke completely out of turn the other night and I apologise profusely. It's rare that I am "in drink" and I was unbearably rude and insensitive. A double fault. I hope you can find it within yourself to forgive me.'

He looks at her hopefully and she can no more be cross with him than she could with a puppy. All the angry words she had imagined she would fire at him like arrows long forgotten as her anger had abated.

She gives in and sighs. 'You were grieving for your friend, Mr Perris. I'm sorry for shutting the door on you when I should have offered tea and consolation. And I'm sorry too for the misunderstanding about my father's notebook. I think, perhaps, we are even. If you'll accept my apology too, of course.'

George smiles and Eadie notices his lip is swollen, as if he's hurt himself. She goes to reach for it but stops herself just in time as George blinks, and she steps back, startled.

'I wished to see you anyway,' George says, shyly, 'before The Professor's funeral tomorrow. And before this dinner party Harry's been planning. Not just to apologise, but I wondered, the living pictures we made together . . .'

'They're quite something. Would you like to see them?'

George smiles. 'I'd like nothing more.'

As he follows her up the stairs, she turns to him, affecting an air of nonchalance. 'Oh, by the way,' she says. 'Mr Waterfield's leaving the company. I'm buying him out. So, you see, I *am* someone who dares take risks, after all.'

Eadie relishes the look of surprise on George's face.

'Then, congratulations! Most sincerely!' George says, impressed.

'Now then,' Eadie says, as she stands outside her projection room. 'Are you ready to see yourself on screen, Mr Perris?'

The shadow George looks both like him and not. Fatter somehow. Different. Yet there he is. Immortalised on film. It is an odd sensation to see one's own self projected on the wall, like coming face to face with one's ghost. The first time George has seen a living picture of himself. His shadow double. He finds it hard to look at. An echo of himself trapped, frame by frame, onto a long strip of celluloid.

'Is that *really* what I look like?' he says out loud, and Eadie smiles.

The shadow George giggles silently as he folds his sheet of paper into myriad different tricks, before bowing. Then Eadie changes the reel and a whole new shadow George leaps onto the screen, pulling item after item from his inexhaustible hat.

George thinks of The Professor's funeral tomorrow and wishes his old mentor had been recorded for future generations. If only he could have seen this!

'Perhaps I *did* look better with a moustache . . .' George mutters, as the reel ends and his shadow-self vanishes.

'I assure you that you didn't,' Eadie says, wryly, recalling his disguise at the séance. 'Are you pleased? I think they've turned out rather well.'

But George is too overwhelmed to answer.

In Affectionate Memory of

THE PROFESSOR

Conjuror Extraordinaire, Wizard Supreme

Who died at Clifton, March 26th 1896
AGED 60 YEARS

REMEMBERED AT ST PETER'S 1st APRIL

(Interred at Arnos Vale)

How short is life, how sure is death,
Our days alas are few,
Our mortal life is but a breath,
'Til God grants us life anew.

The church is packed, all the space in every pew taken. George looks around at the gathered crowd: performers of all kinds, stagehands, friends, newspaper men and more. The Professor was not only popular but famous, and gossip-mongers, driven by nosiness and the hope of a free meal at the wake, have also flocked here en masse. There are others, too, George knows, only too glad to see the back of the mischievous magician.

George's eyes automatically go to the faces he knows, others he only half recognises. He thinks he glimpses Eadie at the back of the church but then spies Roderick Skarratt. *The audacity of that man!* George cannot prove it was Skarratt behind the break-in at his workshop, but he has his suspicions.

He turns his glance back towards the chancel, to the raised wooden coffin containing the body of his beloved mentor. A white plaster death mask on one end, a small bouquet of hand-tied marjolettii tulips in the centre. George's eyes well up as Harry, to his left, takes his hand and squeezes it. On his right, Valentin, sitting next to Cec, gives him an encouraging nod. *Time to say goodbye.*

Reverend Richardson steps out and the congregation settles. *An audience no one ever wishes to perform in front of*, thinks George. He struggles to concentrate on the reverend's introduction, focusing instead on containing his emotions enough to be able to muster the words for the eulogy he is to give.

The organ starts and the hymn begins, a long droning thing. And yet, George thinks, as his eyes blur, it is strangely stirring. Valentin pats him on the back, and George realises the Reverend Richardson is looking expectantly at him.

He stands, legs like jelly, walks to the front, and looks out at the sea of faces. 'I first met The Professor just over a year ago,' George says, hands clutching the notes he has rehearsed a dozen times or more. 'That's what he would have told you, anyway. But, like many of The Professor's stories, it's not entirely true.

'I first met him when I was fifteen. My mother had died six months previously, and my father took me to see The Professor's show in London, on Shaftesbury Avenue. As a child, I was a keen student of all things legerdemain, but I gave them up upon my mother's death. I put away my cards, my boxes of tricks, and my books. My childish things, as I saw them. They were relegated to the attic, to gather dust in the darkness. I lost my love of magic, for it vanished along with my mother.' He looks at Harry, who nods encouragingly. 'But I accompanied my father to the show anyway, to humour him.

'When the curtains lifted and the lights dimmed, The Professor stepped out onstage, bare-headed. He bowed and went to remove his hat before realising he wasn't wearing one. In that famously raspy voice, he asked for a volunteer to lend him one for the duration of the show – and a barrage of headwear was flung onto the stage. A hailstorm of hats. The Professor chose one, put it on, and immediately took it off again. For underneath it, standing on his head, was a white dove which fluttered off into the wings.

'Baffled, The Professor reached into the hat and pulled out a handkerchief which he threw to the floor in a fit of pique. He reached in again. A wig this time, then tin cups and tumblers, a lit lantern. All the while, The Professor became more and more furious with the hat. He pulled out bird cages with birds singing inside, cannon balls, bottles of wine, a line of flags, even a violin. He reached his arm in and drew out, in quick succession, such a gloriously mad succession of goods as anyone could ever hope to see. A live chicken, a spaniel, an entire leg of ham and, finally, a disgruntled baby . . .'

The crowd in the church quietly titters.

'It was the most remarkable, wonderful thing. And I laughed and laughed at this ridiculous sight. It was the first time I'd truly laughed in weeks, months perhaps. And he made me remember what a privilege it is to perform for others, what a gift it is to share the joy of magic. I still have my signed programme from that night. I'll never forget it. When I finally got to the front of the queue, The Professor smiled. "You look like a young man who is secretly a conjuror!" he said, with a glint in his eye. It meant the world to me.'

George glances towards Valentin and smiles. 'The Professor was not the first to inspire me, but he was the one who made me fall in love with magic all over again. That same night, when I returned home, I clambered up to the attic. I brought down my cases, my books, my boxes of tricks. And I began practising again . . .'

George clears his throat. 'But, of course, The Professor would contradict all of this. He would say we only met for the first time early last year. At the Theatre Royal in Bath. And this time it was him waiting for me after the show. To my great surprise, he came to my dressing room, this man who changed my life – he paid me what I thought was the greatest honour of all, attending my show and telling me he'd enjoyed it. But the greatest compliment was still to come. For this man, who I admired so much, became my friend.' George looks down for a moment, choked. 'And that was the greatest honour of all. To be friends with this irrepressible, magnificent man.'

George looks back up with a quick smile, acknowledging the appreciative murmurs. 'But The Professor would still say that was not the first time we met. He would say the first time we *really* met was when he invited me to his home. He'd been looking forward to it all week, he told me later. And no wonder. For, unbeknownst to me, he'd rigged up a network of pulleys and strings. As soon as I walked into his sitting room, a balloon full of water landed on my head and exploded, drenching me.'

The audience chuckles.

'Oh, that wasn't all,' says George, warmly. 'When I went to the bathroom to sponge myself down, there was another water balloon in there. The Professor, struggling to contain his glee, suggested I warm myself by the kitchen hearth. I opened the door to the kitchen and, well, you can guess what happened . . .'

The congregation laughs and the sound echoes around the church.

'I only hope that when I too am in my sixties, I have as much energy, as many ideas and as much vigour for life as The Professor. His brilliance will shine on for decades to come in the memories of all those lucky enough to have watched his incredible shows, and in the world of magic where he inspired and encouraged so many. From professionals and amateurs to all of his audiences, we owe him a great deal. What an honour to have lived in the world at the same time as this marvellous, mischievous wizard.'

George pauses for a moment. 'But there is another here who knew him far better and for longer than I ever did. I pass you now to him.' He bows, returning to his pew, and Harry takes his hand, squeezing it tightly.

'Nicely done, George,' whispers Valentin, as he steps out in front of the congregation.

Valentin looks out at the gathered crowd, recognising some from many moons ago, their hair, like his, now white or grey. He sees too that they are struggling to place him. Whoever they were expecting, it was not him.

'I am The Great Valentini,' he says loudly, and his voice echoes around the church, gasps of astonishment dashing after it around the stone walls.

'I thought he was dead!' someone mutters and Valentin exhales through his nostrils in a sound some might consider to be a tut.

'The Greatest Living Magician is no more,' says Valentin, glancing at the casket behind him. 'We must mourn the loss of our dear friend, but we must celebrate his legacy too, for he has left us with much. He immeasurably enriched the world of magic; he spread joy and wonder throughout many lands, and he inspired the next generation – as Mr Perris has demonstrated. He invented, pioneered, and teased with his impish humour. He was an incredible conjuror, a brilliant man, and I am honoured to have called him my friend.'

Valentin reaches into his pocket, takes out a sealed envelope and opens it. 'The Professor instructed me to read this to you today.'

Everyone in the church holds their breath as Valentin unfolds the letter.

'"Do not mourn for me, for I am still with you. In your memories and hearts,"' he reads, voice quivering. '"I do not want sadness, friends, but laughter, wonder and joy. Do not mourn for me. For I am gone to a better place. Do not mourn. For the show must go on."'

'He has this to say too. "My instructions are clear. In three weeks' time, the show I was planning to perform will still go ahead."'

For the second time in the service, there are audible gasps and a murmur of disbelief.

'"This show is my final wish. It will be the exact same show I planned, but"' – Valentin swallows – '"as you can see, I am alas no longer in a fit state to appear. Instead, my old friend, The Great Valentini, will perform my part."'

Valentin glances up at the awestruck faces, hanging on to every word The Professor wrote.

"'This show will see George Perris, the greatest young magician of his generation, inaugurated as my worthy successor. I promise you that the impossible will become, for one night only, possible. This is my final, dearest wish."

'That is all,' Valentin says, folding up the note. He reaches into another pocket and pulls out a wand. 'George,' he says, handing the wand to the younger magician as he joins him by the casket.

Their eyes meet and George snaps the wand in two. A crack echoes around the church, before he gently places both halves upon the coffin.

'Farewell, old friend . . .' says Valentin quietly and they stand silently for a moment before the organ strikes up and the choir starts to sing. Their fine voices dance around the stone walls of the church, soaring through the stained-glass windows and out to the surrounding streets.

BRISTOL MERCURY, Thursday 2nd April, 1896

THE PROFESSOR'S LAST REQUEST

The funeral of Bristol's world-famous conjuror, known only as The Professor, took place yesterday at St Peter's Church, Mary-le-Port. Fellow wizard Mr George Perris led the eulogy, followed by The Great Valentini, a formerly popular magician who has not performed in this country for many years. To the congregation's surprise, The Great Valentini announced The Professor's retirement show will still take place under detailed instructions from the late conjuror. The show, honouring The Professor's successor, Mr Perris, will be at the Prince's Theatre on Park Row on Friday 24th April. Demand for tickets is expected to be high.

'Well, what are the odds! We *must* stop meeting like this, sweet Cecily!'

Roderick Skarratt loiters outside a restaurant on Berkeley Square, cigarette in hand, as Cec walks by, Oz reluctantly trailing her. She is startled to see her old master again and her heart quickens as she crosses the road to avoid him. She suddenly regrets not telling Valentin about their previous encounter, but she had been so busy, and it was too late now. She hears Skarratt chuckle behind her, and she turns to face him.

'What d'you want, Mr Skarratt?' Cec asks, forcing herself to look him in the eye.

'Come, come! No need to be unfriendly. If you insist on dragging that mongrel around the streets, it's inevitable we'll occasionally bump into each other.' He smiles insincerely.

'What d'you want?' she repeats.

'This show of theirs — it's really happening, then?'

'You know it is. I glimpsed you at the back of the church at The Professor's funeral.'

'And what tricks and treats might they have up their sleeve this time, I wonder?' Skarratt muses.

'Who could say?' Cec says, trying to be bold.

'Well, *you* could,' Skarratt says, continuing to smile. 'Couldn't you?'

She looks at him suspiciously. 'No. I couldn't.'

'I think you could . . .'

'Are you asking me to *spy* for you, Mr Skarratt?'

'Come now, Cecily, really!'

She scoffs, turning away, her heart beating fast, but he dances into her path.

'No,' she says, firmly.

'Come! It would be nothing as serious as that. Merely sharing the odd morsel, a nugget of information. Hardly informing, is it?'

'I can't and I won't. I'll tell Valentin *everything*!'

'What, exactly? That your path crossed with mine in the city in which we both live? Hardly much to tell, is there? You said before you would stick to your promise not to say a word about your time under my roof. Will you break that promise now then? I had thought you to be someone whose word could be trusted. Come, little urchin, I'll reward you for any information you get me . . .'

'I'm not interested in your reward. Why does it matter anyway?'

'It matters because it should have been *me*, Cecily! Because The Professor was *my* friend until Perris stole him away. It matters because I don't like to be wronged. I'm a victim of Perris's ambition. The Great Valentini and Perris – you don't know them! But *I do!*' He spits the words out. 'I know Perris and I know Valentin's type too. They'll wring you out, use you, then cast you off and leave you behind. Why do you think Valentin fled England all those years ago? What exactly was he running from?'

Cec frowns.

'You see? You don't even know! Listen,' Skarratt continues. 'You know what you are. A con artist. A trickster like Arter. But you're also like me. Someone who wishes to use their power to help others.'

Cec stares at him, wondering exactly what power he might be talking about. *Black magic.* The two little words float around her head again.

'You don't belong to the likes of these new friends of yours,' Skarratt says. 'False friends. People who will use you. You belong with someone who wants to do good. Work with me. *Please.* And I'm sorry, truly, for my behaviour that night. I didn't mean to strike you. And come, I've been kind, haven't I? Despite the fact you left with no notice. Join with me again, Cecily. I'm offering you another chance . . .'

'*No.*' Cec says, firmly, and Skarratt sighs.

'I hear The Great Valentini will retire after this grand show. So where does that leave you, little urchin? But I will help you — if you help me, now.'

Cec thinks to herself. It *is* true that Valentin is retiring. He had said he would see her right and that her apprentice-ship would continue, but what did that *really* mean?

Oz growls softly and Cec looks closely at Skarratt. She thinks of his fist on her face that night. The cold iron smell of the raw steak Mabel put on it. How her face still twinges occasionally.

'*No*,' she says. 'That's my final answer.'

He blocks her way.

'Wait,' Skarratt says, taking a lock of hair from his pocket. A glimpse is enough for her to recognise it as her own.

'I know you found my little poppets . . .' he says softly.

She stares at him, wordlessly, and he smiles slowly. *That sharp pin. The pain George was in.* Cec swallows, knowing only too well that impossible things can, in fact, be possible.

'Poppets aren't real,' she says, boldly, hoping he doesn't hear the tremor in her voice.

'Aren't they now?' Skarratt gazes at her. 'Are you sure about that?'

And suddenly she isn't. She isn't sure at all.

'George . . .' she whispers as her own hand reaches protect-ively to her stomach. Skarratt tilts his head and lowers his voice.

'So you won't mind me making a poppet of you then, will you?' he asks.

'*No!* Please don't!' Cec begs and he smiles at her.

'You must know by now what I'm capable of. Or why else would you have scratched that mark of protection above your bedroom door?'

Cec's insides clench and her breath is sucked out of her. She gazes at him, full of fear.

'I see *everything*, Cecily,' Skarratt says, his eyes glinting. 'You're clever, but you're not cleverer than me. Now listen. You don't have to say anything; you don't even have to

acknowledge it. But you *will* help me. You have no choice.'
He puts the lock of hair into his waistcoat pocket and
taps it.

'No . . .' Cec says, uncertainly. She can't betray her new
friends, *she can't*. 'Please!' she cries, shivering where she stands.

He smiles, looking at her expectantly. 'You would make
such a pretty little poppet too. What will it be then, little
urchin?'

Cec swallows. She's doesn't want what's happened to
George to happen to her. And who knows what else Skarratt
might be capable of? She thinks of his bone wand, the
pentagram, and tallow candle . . .

'It's not spying,' Cec murmurs, her voice barely a whisper.
'You said it wasn't. Not really.'

'Of course it isn't!' Skarratt reassures her. 'Merely sharing
the odd piece of information. For mutual benefit. Come,
come! That's hardly spying now, is it?'

Cec feels sick as she nods, hating herself, as Skarratt smiles.

'There now. That wasn't so hard, my sweet Cecily.
Was it?'

'Here we are,' Eadie says, smoothing her emerald-green dress
down as she and Louis arrive at the Perrises' home on
St Michael's Hill.

It's the night of Harry's long-promised dinner party and
Eadie glances up at the large Georgian townhouse before
lifting the unusual door knocker, shaped like a key.

Harry answers, a grin of delight, as she welcomes them in.

It's a wildly appealing place inside, full of nonsense and clutter. Wherever Eadie looks, there are more delights to take in: the head of a velvet 'unicorn' mounted in the hallway as if it were a stag; a 'phoenix' feather framed in a box; carpets from the Far East; and throws from Persia. Blankets and scarves, throws and rugs, a clash of colours and patterns, all old and faded, lived with and loved. And there are books everywhere: shelves crammed to over-flowing, stacks on little tables next to comfy armchairs. It is chaotic and delightful in equal measure, and Eadie loves it.

Louis follows Harry through to the dining room as Eadie trails behind George, peering in at the sitting room on her left and glancing up at the stairs on her right. To her aston-ishment, a black cat appears in the hallway, having apparently walked through a solid wall.

'I see you've met Ambrose.' George smiles as the cat winds itself around her legs, purring.

Eadie drops to her knee and examines the wall. A small hole, just big enough for a cat, carefully concealed by trompe l'oeil. She puts her hand through, smiling as she realises the trick.

'My grandfather's little jest.' George grins. 'Good, isn't it? I was fascinated by it as a boy. He used to create things like that all the time to entertain us when we came in the summers. We always loved it here, so when we inherited it, it seemed obvious we should move here. Bristol's such an exciting city, after all.'

George smiles at her and Eadie feels, for the first time, as if she's beginning to truly understand him.

She'd attended The Professor's funeral partly on impulse and partly out of curiosity, but George's eulogy had given her a new insight into him. That vulnerable boy she sometimes catches a glimpse of in his eyes. The loss of his mother that he still feels so deeply, just as Eadie feels the loss of her own Papa. Perhaps, Eadie thinks, remembering what Chaplin had said, she and George really are more alike than she might care to admit.

They go into the dining room, a large light space full of an eclectic assortment of furniture: a mishmash of styles with chairs that don't match, a dresser painted Moroccan blue, and a kilim that looks worse for wear.

'Sorry about the mess,' Harry apologises as they all find a seat around the table. 'I'm afraid neither of us are particularly tidy, and we're still working out where everything lives.'

'It's lovely,' says Eadie, truthfully.

'Our grandparents travelled a lot,' George explains. 'Brought back all sorts of souvenirs. Old necklaces, mirrors, rugs. They once brought back some shrivelled dates, asked if we wanted to try them . . .' He raises an eyebrow. 'Apparently they'd been found in an ancient tomb. Hundreds of years old, maybe more.'

Louis chuckles. 'Our father travelled a bit too,' he says. 'Always in search of a new idea that might lead to some new invention. He was rather eccentric too. Named both of us so that we'd have the same initials as the shop. I'm Edward

David Louis and Eadie is Edith Dorothy – E. D. for both of us. And, of course, he liked the fact his initials sounded the same as Eadie's nickname . . .'

'I think the truth of it is that he wanted me to be a boy,' says Eadie. 'But he had to wait until Louis came along.'

She glances at George, who is gazing at her so intently that she looks away.

'Did you say you came here as children?' Louis asks, and George nods.

'We used to spend summers here,' he says, wistfully. 'Having grown up in the flat outskirts of London, the hills were such a novelty. Bristol always felt like our true home. And after Mother died and Father remarried and moved north, we became even closer to our grandparents. Mother grew up here, you see, so we couldn't contemplate selling it.

'It's a rambling beast of a place. And it's hard to heat in winter,' Harry says. 'Father warned us of that but I think he was happy we kept it, regardless. We hope he'll come and visit soon, but the Highlands are so far away and Jane, our stepmother, keeps him busy too.'

'May I ask, how are the plans going for the Prince's show?' Eadie asks.

'Hard work!' Harry says, and George nods in agreement.

'I'm negotiating my new finale with Valentin at the moment,' he says. 'And the Hogarths are heads down on the technical aspects, ably supported by Louis, of course.'

Louis smiles as George continues. 'Costumes are all in hand with the aptly named Miss Pegg. The pressure is on! But it's good to be kept busy, the distraction is welcome.

Stops me from wallowing. And I take solace in the fact we're carrying out The Professor's wishes to the letter.'

'Oh, Louis, I meant to show you this book!' Harry says, reaching for the nearest bookcase as George leans towards Eadie and lowers his voice.

'I'm afraid to say I've foolishly agreed to another perform-ance,' George says. 'One in which I rather hoped you might help. A couple I met at Goldney Hall are hosting an event at Ashton Court, the place over the gorge – a spring party, some sort of charity event. I hope you don't mind but I mentioned your films and they'd very much like to show some of them. I'll be there anyway, performing of course, but perhaps I might introduce your pictures, as they do in the capital? And you could project them yourself, exactly as you wish them to be shown? It would be a good show-case and a sort of trial run before the Prince's. What do you say?'

'That's very kind of you!' Eadie says, surprised at him being so generous after their recent falling-out. Who knew what other connections this Ashton Court event might lead to? Other investors she sorely needs, so she can buy Bill out. 'How can I say no?' She smiles. 'Although I really am taking on too much. Oh, I should say too, I've been working on an improved projector for you. I'm hoping it'll be quieter and smoother.'

'Excellent!' George looks delighted. 'And The Theatre Royal in Bath might be interested in a projector,' he continues. 'I'm performing at a children's party next Saturday and I believe the father is on their board. I could mention it then?'

'Please!' Harry says, turning towards them. 'Enough of work! Can you not arrange a meeting to discuss such things? We're here for dinner, not business!'

'Exactly!' cries Louis. 'Honestly, Eadie, this is a rare evening out! Especially for you.'

George holds his hands up. 'My fault. I apologise. Although just one more thing. You must come and visit our workshop, Eadie. I think you'll find plenty of interest, and the Hogarths are keen to meet you.'

'*Enough!*' Harry says as George chuckles, guiltily, and he and Eadie smile at each other.

Cec is a thief. A liar. A traitor. She is all of these things and worse. The lowest of the low. Here she is, betraying Valentin who has offered nothing but kindness. She came so close to confessing everything last night – but he went to bed early, saying he felt unwell, and the last thing she wanted was to add to his worries.

And Skarratt was right, wasn't he? This *is* who she is. A con artist. A trickster. Someone who lies for a living.

Valentin has offered her so much. Safety and security, a roof over her head. A job with prospects. He has given her nothing but support and encouragement. Every day she learns more from him, as if he was pouring all his knowledge into her as fast as he could. And now here she is, the plans for a grand illusion rolled up tightly under her arm, on her way to see Skarratt, loathing herself more than she ever thought possible.

When she turns up at their planned meeting place by the corner of Holy Trinity Church in Hotwells, Cec is surprised to find Skarratt's sister, Marianne Carnesky, waiting instead.

'Do you have what he asked for?' She asks as Cec glances around them, scared of being seen.

'We are quite all right here,' Marianne says. 'No one will suspect two women talking by a place of worship.'

Cec looks up at the church, remembering the day of Arter's funeral and how empty it was inside. She takes a deep breath before holding out the plans.

'It's all I could get,' Cec says. 'And I need them back. He can have them for two days but no more. Else they'll get suspicious.'

Marianne takes the papers in her gloved hands.

'I'll let him know,' she says.

'Why are you doing this?' Cec asks. For she has herself heard Marianne Carnesky trying to calm her brother's rages. Why then is she helping him, encouraging his ruthless ambition through thievery and blackmail?

'Because he's my brother. Why else? Family comes first.'

Cec stares at her. 'But Arter was your family too. And you didn't even attend his funeral.'

Marianne eyes her sharply. 'Mr Evans was a relative so distant he was almost on another planet. If my brother decided to indulge him both before and after death, then that was his decision. Not mine.'

'And this?' Cec says, pointing to the plans. 'You know it's wrong.'

Marianne smiles. 'As do *you*. But sometimes wrongs must be done in order to restore a right. And my brother is the one who has been wronged, after all.'

'Wronged? But it was The Professor's free choice, surely?' Cec asks, puzzled.

'Goodness! All these questions! What a chatterbox. Look at you! Pretending to take the moral high ground, and yet here you are, offering me stolen goods. How tiresome you are. I'll tell you this for nothing, little Miss Marsden, you don't want to make an enemy of my brother. And for the love of God, neither do I.'

She smiles at Cec pityingly, and with that she's gone, taking the papers with her and leaving Cec to wonder what hold Roderick Skarratt has over his own sibling.

It's a few days since George saw Eadie at supper and he's excited by her visit to the workshop. He can see she loves it from the moment she steps inside, and it warms his heart to see her so impressed by something so integral to his own life.

'This is quite some set-up!' she says, spotting Louis at the back of the workshop, engrossed in some sort of spinning mechanism. She waves but he's too engaged in his work to notice her.

'I'm very fortunate,' George says. 'And the twins understand me better than I sometimes understand myself. Come, I'll introduce you.'

Alex and Ollie look to Eadie so identical she is unsure how anyone other than their own parents can tell them apart.

George laughs when she tells him this, out of the twins' hearing. 'You wouldn't need to spend more than a day with them to notice the difference, I assure you. Alex is more methodical and outgoing, Ollie is shyer but more creative. A dab hand at painting too. I think that's partly why he and Louis have hit it off so well.'

Then, somewhat apprehensive of what she might think, George tells Eadie of his copper tank, and she laughs with delight. He confides in her too: details of his latest idea, of a woman drawn to the light before vanishing, right at the front of the stage – although he omits to mention it was inspired by a dream of her.

'Horribly complicated and I fear impossible,' he says, bashfully.

'If you can find a way of doing it, it'll look spectacular!'

'I'm not sure I can, not given how short of time we are. But The Professor wasn't keen on the tank, so if I *can* work out how to make the woman instantly vanish, I'd feel much happier. And I'll still need your living pictures, of course. Was it, er, two pounds each?' He looks at her, cheekily, and she chuckles.

'No, George! Three pounds, as you well know!'

'You drive a hard bargain! I've been wondering too, how we might do something unique – maybe use film and magic *together*? Not just project your animated photographs but *interact* with them somehow? It's probably far too ambitious but if you could think about it, perhaps we can come up with something between the two of us.'

Eadie screws her face up in concentration and George laughs. 'You don't have to think on it *right this minute*, Eadie.'

'No, but the thing is, if you could somehow *synchronise* what's onstage with what's onscreen . . . I see what you mean, George! That would be *extraordinary*. But so many things might go wrong: split-second timing, and you'd need a reliable projectionist, someone you absolutely trusted—'

'Would you do it?' he asks and Eadie hesitates.

'I don't seek the limelight . . .'

'But if we back-projected, which we'd surely have to, you wouldn't be visible to the audience anyway.'

'I'll think about it,' she says, shyly, as George's heart skips.

'There's something else I wished to tell you about too,' George says. 'It's rather a secret, I'm afraid.'

'How intriguing! I promise not to tell a soul.'

'All right. Well, here it is. I'm looking to set up a new home of magic. Here, in Bristol.'

Eadie is surprised. 'A rival to London? To the Egyptian Hall?'

George smiles at her, pleased that she's heard of it. The famed Egyptian Hall, a distinctive building on Piccadilly with a grand façade of statues and hieroglyphs that houses within it the most marvellous magic shows. George had performed there on more than one occasion and had even been offered one of their prestigious residencies. It was clear he would have to stay in the capital in order to accept though, and he had made no secret of the fact he was moving to Bristol.

'Not a rival to the Egyptian Hall as much as a sibling, I suppose,' George replies, thoughtfully. 'Another home of magic, here in the west of England and I was thinking, perhaps, a home of living pictures too. After all, why should the capital have all the best things?'

'Why indeed? Goodness, that is a bold ambition, George. I cannot help but admire you for it. Your secret is safe with me, I promise.'

Eadie smiles warmly at him, and George thinks then how much he would like to lean forward and kiss her, to unpin her hair and run his fingers through her curls. He finds himself staring at her until she blinks and turns away, and he feels the heat rise to his own cheeks.

'I wonder where Valentin has got to?' George says, glancing at his pocket watch. 'He's never late . . .'

The world flickers at the edge of Valentin's vision like a reel of film stuck in a projector, black and white shards obscuring his view. *A migraine is a strange sort of magic*, he thinks. *To be able to look directly at something, to know it is there and yet be unable to see it.* He groans as a wave of nausea rolls through him.

'Valentin, let me call a doctor, *please*,' George says, placing a damp flannel on the older conjuror's forehead.

'No, no. I'll be all right . . . I suffer with migraines from time to time. Usually when under duress. Thank you for coming to check on me, you're very thoughtful.'

'Where's Cec?' George asks.

'Out with the dog . . .'

George pulls the blankets up and fetches a glass of water. He sits beside Valentin and takes his hand.

'Thank you, George,' Valentin murmurs, closing his eyes. 'You are kind.'

George sits in silence, looking at The Great Valentini's hand within his, a hand that can weave marvels from thin air.

'Why *did* you and The Professor fall out?' George wonders out loud.

Valentin shifts in his bed, opens his right eye a crack. 'It was a long time ago . . .' he says, quietly.

'Of course. Forgive me. I shouldn't have mentioned it.'

Valentin exhales, memories forming in the cloud of his breath. So many years ago now. He had never met anyone like Olivia before. So vibrant, so full of ideas and conversation. He had fallen in love so gradually that the realisation came as a shock. He closes his eyes and remembers those last months with her. The way her kisses goodnight lingered. Even before she snuck into his room in the dead of night that first time, complaining of the cold. She had crept in under the covers next to him and he had held her, warm in his arms, safe in the knowledge neither of them would tell anyone.

And then today, it had all come flooding back. The walk into town, past the scruffy antiques shop on Narrow Wine Street. The name above it. Ernest Harding & Son. Dealers in Antiquities of Every Description. Valentin had looked through the windows and seen him. A ghost from his past. The once handsome rogue with a silver tongue. The man who got by on wits and charm. His hair thin now and his face lined. A sea of memories flooded through him: anger and bitterness, regret and sorrow. And then he saw the small framed photograph, in the corner of the window. *Olivia.* The fresh flowers on her grave then, they were from Harding. Valentin had walked away, his mind in turmoil. All the times he had thought he could kill Harding with his bare hands. All those years of demonising him, of hating him. The migraine arrived soon afterwards.

Valentin sighs, opening his eyes and looking at George.

'The Professor's sister. Olivia,' he says, slowly. 'She was . . . very dear to me and vulnerable at the time. Unmarried. A brief affair with a man who left her with child. The Professor's rooms at that time were rather small, so she shared with me instead. As a friend of the family. We'd known each other some years by then. Holidayed together. And then the baby arrived . . .'

Valentin could still see him so clearly, still feel little Robert's tiny fingers curling around his index finger, clinging on as if his life depended on it. His rich, burbling chuckle when he was swung into the air. His gurgles of delight when Valentin played with him, reaching out with his chubby arms to be picked up and held. The smell of his warm downy head, the snuffles he made as he slept. The warm wriggling weight in his arms. Valentin had loved him so very much.

'A little boy. Baby Robert,' he says, softly. 'A joyful little thing. Hungry for all the world. Dimples in his knees and elbows. And a bawl that would wake the dead. I adored him. We all did.'

George waits, silently, for Valentin to continue.

'We were at the theatre,' Valentin says, slowly. The memory is so agonising to recall that his head tightens, as if the migraine might crack it open and the painful past come spilling out. 'The three of us. Me and Olivia and Baby Robert, five months old by then. I'd been rehearsing, trying out a new idea for the show. Olivia wanted to see it, to be my eyes for a trial run. She was always so good at working out how an illusion could be improved. I had a range of props, each of which glowed in the dark. An umbrella. A hat. And a bottle of milk – luminous paint that in the dark shone so very brightly but in daylight, looked utterly ordinary. And for the trick I was planning, I'd decanted it into a feeding bottle. A visual gag to play out onstage.' Valentin sighs, slowly. 'It seems so obvious now. And I'd seen it, George, I'd seen that damned bottle earlier that day and thought, "*I should put that to one side. Somewhere safe.*" But I didn't. Instead, I walked by, preoccupied by the show that night. By my own ego. My god, I would give anything to go back, to throw that blasted bottle away. Smash it against the wall, pour it down a drain. Anything. It was not the nursemaid's fault. No one's fault but my own. It looked like a normal feeding bottle, after all. She'd already fed Robert half of it before he started coughing and gasping. She sniffed the bottle, realising her mistake. Not milk after all, but paint. Poison.'

Valentin remembers it all. He casts his mind back to that awful day. To the theatre. To those velvet curtains he can still see hanging on the stage. To the nursemaid who blamed herself for what was, surely, his own mistake – that little glass bottle filled with paint.

Then the realisation gradually dawning, the angry hot sobs of hopelessness, the hollowing out of Valentin's heart. The cry for the doctor, the too-long wait as the baby choked and spluttered, vomited and wailed.

A bawl to wake the dead.

The panic spreading through the handful of staff in the empty theatre, Olivia had run onstage to him, distressed and holding Robert out, willing him to help, to do something, *anything*. He remembers every moment. The convulsions, the little boy's temperature rocketing as Valentin tried to soothe him. And how, suddenly, Robert had gone limp in his arms as if he were made of nothing but rags.

Valentin had stood motionless, numb with disbelief; Olivia wailing as she snatched the baby back, a raw, unearthly sound that still pierced Valentin's heart and he had known that nothing would be the same again.

'We could not save him,' he says, as tears run down his cheeks. 'No matter how hard we tried.'

'Oh, Valentin,' George says gently, sorrowfully. 'You must not, *cannot*, blame yourself. It was an accident. An awful accident.'

Valentin turns to him. 'But I went onstage that evening, George! The contract I signed bound me to it, so I made myself. I walked out, plastered on a smile as if it were a mask. Because that's what we do, isn't it? The show must always go on . . .'

'We are but flesh and blood,' George says, softly.

'You are wiser than I,' Valentin says. 'And when I came off stage, I was already too late.'

'Too late?'

'Olivia. She'd taken that damned bottle, hidden it upon herself. The only time I had not been by her side was when I was onstage. And, that night, she drank the remainder.'

Valentin hears it still, the sound of her in distress, the sobs and retching, the yowl of despair. The memory still so clear. How he had felt the life go out of her even as he clasped her in his arms. Her face contorted, eyes empty. No more breath in her. And the black hole that opened up underneath his feet like a trapdoor, swallowing him in his entirety.

When The Professor had arrived, moments after the doctor had pronounced she was gone, he had looked at Valentin with such rage. The trust between them – *such old friends!* – broken forever.

'This is *your* fault, Valentin! All of it!' The Professor was furious and wild, restrained by the doctor as Valentin stood there, hollow, looking down at her in his arms. All his hopes, his love, crushed to dust.

'The Professor blamed you?' George asks, softly.

'How could he not, George, when I blamed myself?' Valentin wipes away his tears. 'I'd have done anything for Olivia. *Anything*. And for Robert too. I loved them with all my heart. And I lost them both. It *was* my fault. I knew it then and I know it now.' He shifts in his bed. 'I ran away, tried to drown myself in drink. I returned to Bristol, for a while, hoping to make peace, but The Professor could not forgive me – and I could not forgive myself.'

'Valentin. It wasn't your fault; it was an accident. You *must* see that?'

'Perhaps. Perhaps not. But it doesn't matter in the end whose fault it was. Because the end result is still the same. I lost the person who meant the most to me in all the world. And I lost my best friend and that beautiful baby boy too.'

Valentin hadn't been Robert's father, he knew that, but he was *becoming* his father. He had fed and nursed him, bathed him and played with him. He had *loved* him.

'Can we stay with you forever?' Olivia had asked, the night before that awful day, nestling into his shoulder, Robert fast asleep in his crib.

'Always,' he replied. 'Of course.' And she had turned her face to him and kissed him, a long lingering kiss as his heart leapt. He had wrapped his arms around her, his smile as wide and full as hers. And they had fallen asleep like that, happily entwined, until Robert woke them with a hungry cry in the early hours.

A glimpse of another life, full of love and children, of happiness. It breaks him to think of it, even now.

'I cannot bring them back,' Valentin says, sadly. 'I cannot change the past. But perhaps it is time I accepted that now.' He reaches for his water, drinking it, before lying back. 'Thank you George,' he says, closing his eyes. A weight lifts from his shoulders even as his chest feels close to bursting. 'Thank you for listening.'

The sound of footsteps alerts Cec to his presence. Even in the dark of night, there's something distinctive about the way Roderick Skarratt walks. She stops underneath a streetlamp and turns to see him lounging by a set of railings on the far side of the road, his face in shadow.

'Thought you were clever, little urchin?' he says. 'Those plans you brought Marianne were old ones. Don't try and mislead me again, else you'll pay for it.'

His tone is light but Cec hears the sharpness behind it. Then her small element of resistance had failed. She had asked the Hogarth twins for old plans, unperformed illusions with a fault inherent in them. This was what she had handed to Skarratt's sister, hoping it might buy her a little more time – but he had seen right through it.

Cec steps away but Skarratt comes closer, stepping into the patch of light she had just been standing in. His golden hair glistens under his hat.

'You can't avoid me, urchin. You still owe me! You agreed to help and I *need* something from this show of theirs. Something *new*.'

'I can't. Please!' She tries to look him in the eye but can't.

'We've been through this. Of *course* you can.'

'I can't take things, and no one notice. *I can't*!'

Two strides and he's right by her, his hands suddenly tight around her neck.

'*This isn't a game!*' he snaps. 'Perhaps it's just a jest to you, but it isn't to me. There's too much at stake!'

She tries to shake her head but his hold on her is tight and she struggles to breathe. Oz growls at her feet and Skarratt aims a kick at him.

'Please . . .' she manages to utter. '*Please!*'

He squeezes her neck tightly, just for a moment, before releasing her. Cec falls to her knees, gasping for breath, Oz by her side, licking her hand and whimpering.

Skarratt looms above her as she reaches for her neck, red and sore. 'No more games. Get me the plans for Perris's finale. *Detailed plans*. I don't care how. Understand?'

Oz growls again and Skarratt smiles, all shiny teeth. 'That little mongrel has quite the attitude. Rather like you.'

He offers Cec his hand but she ignores it, on the verge of tears as she clambers to her feet.

'I'll meet you at lunch time tomorrow,' she whispers, her throat burning. 'I'll have to be quick. At the bottom of Christmas Steps, round the corner from the theatre. Five minutes, that's all.'

'That's more like it,' Skarratt says, charmingly. 'Five minutes is all l need. And see this as your final warning. Don't *ever* try and mislead me again. Else I'll be getting your poppet out of its box and you *really* won't like that . . .'

He tips his hat and disappears back into the shadows, leaving Cec standing there, breathless and distraught.

'I feel woefully underprepared, Mr Perris,' Eadie says, the next morning, as their cab approaches the suspension bridge and the ground falls away beneath them. She resists the temptation to grab George's arm as he looks out along the gorge towards Avonmouth.

He looks particularly handsome today, she thinks, in his pinstriped suit and green necktie.

'They simply want to meet the both of us beforehand, to discuss a few practicalities,' George says, fiddling nervously with his cufflinks.

Eadie laughs. She feels so much more at ease in his company since Harry's supper and her visit to his workshop. 'You're as nervous as I am, George!'

'What makes you think that?'

'The fact you are dressed even better than usual—'

'*Even* better?' he says, with a wry grin.

'And you're playing with your cufflinks! Fidgeting away!'

'I suffer very badly from nerves, if you must know. I suppose I always will. But the moment I step onstage, it's like I'm meant to be there.'

'But you're not performing today, surely?'

George shrugs as the cab approaches the gatehouse at Clifton Lodge, stopping for a moment before being waved through and into the grounds of Ashton Court.

'I've never been here before,' says Eadie. 'It feels like a forbidden land.'

'Sir Philip and Lady Packer are only human, like us.'

'Only with considerably more wealth,' Eadie says, drily, as they head down a long tree-lined drive. She leans out of the cab window as the grounds open up, swathes of soft grass sloping away into copses and woodlands.

'Good Lord!' she says. 'I've never seen the like!'

'Landed gentry not amongst your friendship circle? You surprise me, Eadie!' George chuckles as she pulls a face at him.

The cab bears left, downhill, skirting a large wood and onwards, past a wide grass area where a herd of red deer look up at the sound of the cab.

'Lady Packer's recently set up a convalescent home for women at Long Ashton,' George explains. 'The spring party is to raise funds for it.'

'They could just donate their house,' Eadie says, as the cab pulls up at the front of an enormous mansion, all turrets and windows and wealth.

'Excellent idea!' says George. 'I'll let *you* suggest that.'

She takes a deep breath, suddenly anxious.

'Don't worry, Miss Carleton.' George leans towards her. 'I've already vouched for you. You don't need to be on your *very* best behaviour but do *try* not to swear.'

Her mouth falls open in mock surprise as he steps out of the cab and offers his hand to help her down.

'We are so excited to have you here,' Lady Packer says, as she and her husband take them on a brief tour of the gardens.

They enter a fairy tale of meadows and roses, lawns and glasshouses. There are regimented teams of staff – gardeners, cooks, maids and servants – and in every direction, spectacular views.

Eadie and George are shown into the impressive Great Hall, where drinks will be served, before stepping out through the south doorway to the huge lawn that spans the length of the house. This is where the guests will proceed, when all is dark, for the highlight of the evening: George's magic show and Eadie's films. After the entertainment, there is to be music and dancing on the lawn, with the city spread out below and the hills in the distance.

'Here, I think,' George says, looking back at the house. They stand in a naturally sloped area, the lawn gently sweeping down towards them.

Eadie nods her approval, trying to imagine the space full of people in their finery. It will be just her and George on the night, for Harry will be away in London. A little thrill runs through her when she thinks of it.

'I hate to ask as I know you're both preparing for this grand show at the Prince's,' Lady Packer says, 'but might it be possible to show some *exclusive* animated photographs at our event?'

'New living pictures,' her husband Sir Philip says, with a nod. 'Ones that haven't been seen anywhere else. Something a bit different, you know?'

George glances at Eadie. 'Well, Miss Carleton and I have made two films together already. Perhaps one or both of them might be shown here first?'

'I'd have to think very seriously about committing to any other new pictures at the moment,' Eadie says. 'My time is very short, as is Mr Perris's. But I'm sure we might come to some arrangement. For a price.'

'Of course!' says Lady Packer. 'We only want the very best.'

George manages to hold his laughter in until they are safely back in the cab for their return journey.

'Eadie Carleton, your gall is quite something,' he says, admiringly, as the cab moves off.

'Well, my time *is* very short. As is yours! Besides, they can afford it,' she retorts.

'That they can,' he says.

She looks out to see the vast mansion disappear behind the trees. 'Imagine living somewhere like that!' she says.

George splutters. 'I'd hate it! Wouldn't you?'

'Of course! Think of the housework! And the heating!'

'Ha! That's why they have whole armies of people working for them. But it's why I rather like private parties. Insights into other worlds. It's endlessly fascinating.'

'I can imagine,' she says, glancing out of the window again, her mind whirling with excitement – where to put the projector, how big the screen should be . . . what it might feel like to be onstage beside George.

'Eadie,' George says, after a while. 'I hope you don't mind me asking, but why exactly *were* you at Mrs Carnesky's séance that night? Was it only to return that piece of equipment?'

'Partly. But I wanted to see her tricks for myself too, see how convincing she might be,' Eadie says. 'I wouldn't have exposed her as you did, George. I planned on taking her device out and returning it to her at the end, after everyone had gone. To preserve the feelings of those attending.'

He looks at her thoughtfully. 'Perhaps that's what I should have done too.'

'Perhaps.' Eadie smiles.

'The thing is,' George says, quietly, 'the reason I get so irate about people like Mrs Carnesky . . .'

'Go on,' Eadie says.

'When I was fifteen, my mother died,' George confesses. 'She became ill very suddenly, and it was a great shock to all of us. Harry was away at school, so was sheltered from it a bit at least. I was back home after my boarding school didn't work out.' He sighs. 'It wasn't easy, not for any of us. But, about seven or eight months after my mother died, my father developed a keen interest in séances. Almost obsessive in fact. One particular medium made him come to believe my mother was waiting for him to join her. On the other side.'

'Oh, George . . .'

'The lies she told poisoned his mind, Eadie. I came *so close* to losing him. But I found him, just in time. He was over halfway through a bottle of whisky, a hot bath already run, a razor in the bathroom, and it all came tumbling out. We sat up together all night, talking, listening, until dawn broke. Something we should have done long before. And it worked out in the end. The governess I had at the time helped enormously – dear old Jane. They got married some years later. But it might so easily have ended very differently. That's why I feel compelled to expose them, to stop them from hurting others. Do you see now? Why I did it?'

'I do,' she replies, putting her hand on his for a moment before the movement of the cab jerks it away. 'Really, I do, George.'

When Eadie returns home, her head and heart are entirely full of George. Kind, thoughtful, passionate George, with his handsome face and neat figure. There's an elegance about him, but an awkwardness, a vulnerability too. The combination draws Eadie to him like a moth to a flame.

At first she had put it down to his enthusiasm for living pictures: a shared understanding, a meeting of minds – despite their unfortunate first encounter at the séance, and their misunderstandings since. But there is something else too, a spark of something big and bright, something more powerful than either of them alone.

Eadie barely dares admit it to herself. The flicker of excitement she has tried so hard to ignore, the energy in his gold-flecked eyes.

But she had been so mistaken in Max. To discover that money spoke louder than love had broken her heart. What then if she is mistaken with George too? And the situation with Bill had surely proved why it is best that business and pleasure do not mix. *Emotions only ever get in the way*, she tells herself as she hammers a piece of sheet brass flat in her workshop. All those years of study, the looks she used to get at the technical college as one of only a handful of women in the electrical engineering classes. All that hard work.

She cannot risk it, for anything, for anyone.

Not even for George.

Cec skurries out of the Prince's theatre like a mouse, looking around nervously as she heads down Christmas Steps, papers for George's most precious illusion rolled up under her arm.

And there he is. Roderick Skarratt. Waiting for her at midday, just as he had promised. Cruel and cold, gimlet-eyed and greedy. As she hands over the plans, Cec thinks of his fingers around her neck, a piece of her dying inside.

Skarratt leafs through, swiftly assessing them, as Cec continues to monitor the flow of people passing, hoping no one from the theatre sees her.

'Ah, now that *is* clever . . .' Skarratt mutters. 'Complicated and yet so very simple. Obvious now I think of it. Classic Perris.'

He starts to roll the plans back up and Cec reaches for it, desperate to get away from him, to return to the safe confines of the theatre.

'Please, I can't do this again!' she pleads and he laughs, moving the roll of paper away and out of her reach.

'Come, little urchin. It's an investment in our future, that's all.'

'What'll you do? Now you've seen the plans?'

'Never you mind. Here, take them back. I have everything I need.'

She snatches at them and he grabs her wrist, holding it tightly. 'Careful! Don't want to damage them now, do we?'

He smiles suddenly, loosening his grip as she pulls her arm away.

'I'm sorry for last night,' he says, motioning to her throat. 'But I do so *hate* to be disappointed in those I work with. You understand?'

He reaches out, brushing a hand against her cheek as she flinches.

'You know, when all this is done and Valentin is retired, you'll have to return to me properly. Permanently. I'm rather looking forward to having you back under my roof. Such an accomplished thief. No wonder Arter was fond of you . . .'

He chuckles as she turns away, repulsed.

'Who else would take you in after all that you've done? We make a good team, sweet Cecily. Don't forget it!'

Cec walks towards the theatre as fast as she can, on the verge of tears. If only Arter were still here, she would never be in this mess! But then she would never have met Valentin either . . .

Guilt churns in Cec's heart as she glances down at George's beloved plans. If only she'd told Valentin at the start of all this! Too late now. She is well and truly trapped. She has betrayed her friends but she has betrayed herself too. When she left Skarratt's house she had promised she would never return. The cabinet of curios, the bedroom door without a lock – she cannot go back, she *cannot*!

Yet although Valentin said he had plans for her after his retirement, he has evaded her questions since, only saying that she must trust him. Cec cannot bring herself to believe that Valentin would abandon her, yet she cannot tell him the truth either. *It will destroy him.*

If only she could use her own powers on Skarratt somehow! Valentin had said Cec could not change the world, only nudge it in a certain direction. She wishes she could nudge Skarratt away then! But last night, she wasn't even able to suspend a single playing card in the air. What use are her own small powers if she cannot even control them?

Traitor. Liar. Thief.

How can she stop Skarratt when he holds all the power?

THE GREAT VALENTINI
AND MR GEORGE PERRIS

ONE NIGHT ONLY
Performed according to
THE PROFESSOR'S last wishes

The Prince's Theatre, Park Row

Farewell Bristol, take a magician's adieu!
Never more will he astonish your people and you ...
Never more on your walls will be posted his name,
Nevermore will he ask you to add to his fame
Far away o'er the sea to the fair land of gold
He goes to seek new friends, as true as the old.

Then casting aside all his magical might
In retirement he will see rest and delight
Nor ever more come where he's now to be found
Where for one night only he'll be in wonders abound.
If you fail to behold him, no words sure will tell
The regret that you missed the magician's farewell

**The Great Valentini's final show
as instructed by the legendary late conjuror, The Professor.**

**Introducing Mr George Perris as the next
Greatest Living British Magician.**

One night only. Friday 24th April.
Never to be repeated. Do not miss out!
Reserved and numbered seats 5s and 4s, area 3s.
The best 1s balcony in Bristol. View equal to the dress
circle of other theatres. Children under 12 half-price.

The huge poster, illuminated by a nearby streetlight, stops George in his tracks as he leaves the workshop.

"'The next Greatest Living British Magician.'" George frowns in the dark, certain he would not have approved the use of the grandiose title for himself. The Professor always hated it as a label and George doesn't much like it either.

'Bloody Greenhouse . . .' he mutters.

The clock is ticking. Only two weeks left to perfect the show.

To his disappointment, George has had to shelve his idea of the vanishing woman for he and the Hogarths have been unable to work out how to achieve it to their satisfaction, and time is running out. The metal tank illusion, the one The Professor was unimpressed by, is still set to be the climax of his act, but George will have Eadie's films at least and, despite Greenhouse's initial misgivings about living pictures, George is confident they'll bring the house down, he's sure of it.

He checks his pocket watch, dismayed at how late it is, before waving farewell to the security guards behind him, overnight men he's worked with before, grateful they are there, but worried again about haemorrhaging money. Like any other business, illusions need capital, and the larger the scale of George's ambitions, the more capital is required. Although George has been honest with Eadie about enjoying private parties, they're also a necessity to cover his bills. More private engagements – with and without Harry – are confirmed, and Greenhouse has encouraged him to book a tour later in the year, an offer he's had to accept.

His dream of setting up a new home of magic in Bristol recedes into the distance. Success, George is realising, comes with a new and different set of pressures and expectations – and he isn't sure he can meet them all.

As he picks his way home along darkened streets, his thoughts return to Ashton Court, and to Eadie. Their visit had been such a delight – Eadie such easy company, so much fun. The prickliness he first felt from her and the misunderstanding over the notebook has long since faded. He runs his hands through his hair as he walks home, breathing in the night air. He has fallen for women before, of course he has, but not like *this*. Not someone who intrigues him so much, who challenges and questions him, makes him push himself. Not someone who sparks such a strong sense of excitement every time he sees her. Not someone whose presence burns through him as if he were made of nothing but paper . . .

So, this is what love really feels like, George thinks – his entire insides bubbling over, singing with joy at the thought of sparkling, clever Eadie Carleton with her sharp wit and soft curls. The young woman who has stolen his heart. Sometimes she smiles at him so knowingly, yet at others, he feels her to be so far away. George barely dares hope Eadie might return his affection, for he cannot risk offending or upsetting her when so much depends upon their collaboration. He frowns suddenly, remembering how enthusiastic she was about her recruitment of Chaplin Hodges. Yet, despite all of it, he has to admit he's never wanted anyone more.

When he finally turns in for the night, George once again thinks of Eadie. An image of her lingers in his mind, merging with his grand illusion that he has now been forced to put a hold on. As his eyelids grow heavier, he dreams of her stepping towards him before stopping, frozen, as if in a photograph. She reverses suddenly, like a film cranked in reverse, moving away from him, no matter how much he strives to reach her. She disappears into the darkness as he cries out, waking himself with a start before the first blackbird has sung even a single note.

9, Royal Crescent,
Bath
Thursday 9th April

Miss Carleton,

Please forgive this brief note but I am advised I need to give you advance notice, in writing, of the fact I will need you to vacate the premises of 5, Regent Street and its associated shop and workshop post-haste. Please reply at your earliest convenience.

Yours sincerely,

Mrs Michael Fearnley

Eadie sits, pretending to sip tea, at her landlady's house in Bath. She has been full of worry ever since receiving Mrs Fearnley's letter yesterday. The projectors, the films, the work for Valentin on his mechanism, the running of the shop, the confirmation of the loan from the bank to pay Bill's deposit – she's barely had time to think about new investors – and now this!

Mrs Fearnley sits opposite her in silence. Her husband, Michael, a flamboyant character, partial to waving his handkerchief around to emphasise a point, had been a friend of Eadie's father and Eadie had been fond of him too.

She is well aware she must play it carefully today or risk making an already bad situation worse. The letter was wholly unexpected. Eadie's father had rented long term from the Fearnleys, and there was no reason to expect anything would change.

'Why now?' Eadie asks suddenly. 'If I may ask such a question, Mrs Fearnley. Our arrangement has previously been long term and, I had believed, perfectly satisfactory to both sides.'

Mrs Fearnley shifts in her armchair, barely meeting Eadie's eye. 'Two nights ago I spoke to my husband, Miss Carleton. He told me that the work you are doing, these moving images of yours – they are the work of the devil.'

Eadie is so surprised that all of her words fall out of her head. For Michael Fearnley has been dead and buried for well over nine months.

'You spoke to your *husband*, Mrs Fearnley?' she asks, slowly. 'How?'

'Through a medium. She was marvellous, Miss Carleton. Really she was. It was all real – certain things only my husband knew, little details. There is no doubt.'

A medium! Eadie stares at her, dumbfounded, before piecing it together. 'Her name wasn't Mrs Carnesky, was it?' she asks, tentatively, and Mrs Fearnley nods.

'She said you might know of her.'

'I'm sure she did,' Eadie says, trying to contain her frustration. 'Mrs Fearnley, I'm sorry to break this to you, believe me, but Mrs Carnesky is a fraud.'

Mrs Fearnley coughs and looks away. 'She said you might say that too.'

Eadie is bemused. She cannot fathom why Mrs Carnesky would go to such efforts to take revenge on her.

'Mrs Fearnley, please. Living pictures are nothing to be afraid of. It's like a magic lantern, that's all, simply updated for a modern audience and—'

'No, Miss Carleton. I will not be convinced! Please do not try and persuade me. You have one month to find somewhere else. That is all.'

One month! Eadie's mouth falls open. *It's nowhere near long enough!* She gathers her thoughts. 'Mrs Fearnley. *Please.* Your husband and my father were great friends and our families have been connected for many years. Please, I beg of you, give me *two* months at least. I'm working with The Great Valentini and Mr Perris in memory of The Professor, who I know your husband was very fond of seeing onstage. Give me two months so I can complete my work with them and find alternative accommodation elsewhere. *Please.*'

She waits on tenterhooks, silence filling the room, as Mrs Fearnley ponders the request.

'Agreed. Two months, Miss Carleton. But not a day more.'

'Thank you,' Eadie says, relieved. Two months is not enough but it buys her a little more time. She must persuade Mrs Fearnley to change her mind, although she cannot fathom how.

'One last thing,' Eadie says, as she stands to leave. 'Why, when Mr Fearnley has been gone over a year, would he choose such a specific request? Why would he not speak to you about something more important? More personal? It's worth thinking on, is it not?'

Eadie remains furious the whole way back to Bristol, her train journey passing in a flash. Why try and exact revenge on her now? She wasn't the one who had exposed Mrs Carnesky. Perhaps it's because she's working with George – but her films are only a part of his show, so why would it matter? She puts her head in her hands. The thought of losing Regent Street was too much to bear.

Later, after Eadie closes up for the day, and Chaplin has left; on impulse, she takes her new, improved living pictures camera to the bottom of Park Street, near the Tramways Centre.

Preoccupied with the worry of losing her home, Eadie is halfway through filming when the roll gets stuck, the cranking handle resisting the pressure of her hand.

It's because I'm anxious, she tells herself.

Cursing quietly and breathing slowly to steady herself, she manages to gently dislodge whatever was causing the problem, fervently hoping she has not torn the film and ruined her efforts.

When Eadie returns home, hoping her brother might offer some consolation over the situation with Mrs Fearnley, she's disappointed to find that Louis is absent. *He must be working late again*, she thinks, finding some small solace in the fact that he's found new friends in the Hogarths. With no one to distract her, for Jenny has already left for the day, Eadie heads to the dark room and develops the roll of film, relieved to discover it has not been torn after all.

It's only in the morning, when she looks more closely at the images, that she discovers a most unexpected thing has occurred.

Cec is trying to practise a new juggling trick in front of the large mirror on the roof of the Prince's Theatre. She likes it up here, a semi-secret place, accessible only through a small wooden door and up a rusted spiral staircase. A brief respite from the hustle and bustle below. She loves feeling as high up as a bird, like one of the gulls circling overhead. Other people must come up here too, for it wasn't her that brought the large, gilded mirror or the faded throne in the corner, weather-worn and sun-blasted. But today, the roof feels like her very own secret.

She tuts to herself as one of the small rubber balls she has been practising with falls from her hand, bouncing away. She knows it is best to keep herself busy for it helps keep her guilt at bay. But she's exhausted. Since Skarratt came back into her life, she has been sleeping badly, and preparations for the show are pushing her to her limits – physically and mentally. Every muscle aches and her brain is crammed full of dates and times and sequences of events. Every time Cec thinks about the size of the auditorium and how vast it appears when looking out from the stage, she shivers. Valentin has put so much faith in her. If only she could find a way to tell him about Skarratt!

Her betrayal gnaws away at her and her head tightens. The scar across her left palm twinges, reminding her of her broken blood oath. *I am a traitor.*

Cec looks at her reflection in the mirror, the lies looking back at her from within. Ashamed, she turns away and walks to the edge of the roof, the city spread out beneath her. Spires and towers, tall ships in the harbour, and the hills beyond. The theatre lies just underneath her feet. Cec is surrounded by people yet never has she felt so alone.

Arter's death wasn't her fault, she knows that now. But this is. She has betrayed those who have been kindest to her and Skarratt has bound her to him in such a way that it is too hard for her to tell the truth. Where would she even begin? And who would believe a word she says when she has lied so very much?

She takes out her pack of cards and looks at them. Of late, Cec has been struggling to suspend even a single card but she tries again now. The king of hearts in her left palm as she slowly takes her hand away. The card flutters off as she gasps, reaching for it, but too late. It disappears over the edge of the roof, the faint breeze taking it in the direction of the harbour. Lost forever. Cec's favourite pack of playing cards now incomplete.

She tries — and fails — again. Frustrated and upset, she tries again and again until the air around the back of the theatre becomes full of fluttering cards. Reds and blacks. Diamonds and hearts, clubs and spades. The entire pack scattered into the air. Not a single card suspended for even a heartbeat.

It is only when the view over the city becomes blurred that she realises she is crying.

George cannot believe it. A magic trick within Eadie's film. The impossible projected right in front of him.

'I know!' Eadie exclaims, seeing his expression. 'I couldn't believe it either! Let me play it again for you.'

She rewinds the reel before cranking the handle forwards and George sees it all for a second time. In the blink of an eye, an omnibus transforms into a hearse, and a group of men walking, with hats and sticks, becomes a group of women in dresses and bonnets.

George laughs afresh. 'How on earth did you do it?' he asks.

'Honestly? The reel of film got stuck. It usually gets torn when that happens, but I managed to unstick it and clearly the traffic changed in that same moment.'

'A transformation within the camera itself. But then . . .' George thinks. 'That means you could, with a little planning, do it deliberately. Am I right? You could pause the filming, change something in front of the camera, and continue. An illusion printed directly onto the celluloid . . .'

'Exactly! This was an accident but—'

'A happy one, Miss Carleton! A very special effect indeed. I'm so pleased you asked me here to see it.'

'Marvellous, isn't it?' She smiles. 'Imagine what else might be done with it . . .'

And that's when it comes to him. A combination of ideas surging into George's head. He sees it in his mind's eye as if the film had been projected directly into his imagination.

'Do you have any more blank reels at your disposal? I've got an idea.'

'George, really. I'm very short of time. There is *so* much going on.' She lifts the blind and the room floods with light.

'I know. I remember you saying Mr Waterfield was leaving. I understand how busy you are, and I am *so* grateful to you for every moment you spend working with me, but, *please*, Eadie. It'll be worth it, I promise. I need to make a few props, and I'll need a stand-in. Someone roughly the same height and build . . .'

'Chaplin?'

George grimaces. 'I suppose if Hodges is the only option . . .' He recalls Eadie calling Chaplin 'invaluable', and wonders again what exactly she meant by it.

'Tell me,' she says, stepping towards him. 'Go on, George. Tell me what's got you so excited.'

He grins delightedly as he describes it, fresh from his imagination, acting it out and waving his arms around so animatedly he nearly knocks her projector over.

'All right. We'll do it,' she says, her eyes alight, his enthusiasm infectious. 'If we film in the next few days, I should be able to develop it in time for Ashton Court. Come, let's talk to Chaplin. Oh, George, I have *so* much to do, but how can I resist?'

'Let's film it at the Prince's, on the roof,' George suggests. 'It's south-facing, flat and, crucially, big enough that no one will fall off.' He smiles for a moment, remembering how he'd saved her, his arm around her waist. 'Give me a day to make the props,' he continues. 'Work out the details, and rehearse to check whether or not it's even possible . . .'

'Tuesday, then?'

'Tuesday.' He exhales. 'Oh, Lord. It's too much. A man has to sleep . . .'

'Tuesday,' she says. 'Come on, George! We *have* to do it! I won't sleep until I know if it can be done. And neither will *you*, Mr Perris,' she says teasingly. Her eyes sparkle – and there's a moment where he could do it, really he could – gently pull her towards him, his lips on hers, his arms folding around her.

Encouraged by her smile, by her enthusiasm, his hand impulsively unfurls by itself, about to risk everything . . .

'Come, let's talk to Chaplin!' she says, heading towards the stairs, and the moment is lost.

BRISTOL MERCURY, Saturday 11th April, 1896

FINALE FOR GRAND MAGIC SHOW REVEALED

The Mercury has been informed that Mr George Perris, the Bristol-based conjuror, is to present a spectacular illusion involving a large, purpose-built copper tank, at the Prince's Theatre on Park Row. The show, to honour the memory of Bristol's well-loved conjuror, The Professor, will feature Mr Perris's never-before-seen trick in which he will transform himself within the tank into a woman, a large ape, and finally into a bowl of goldfish. The tank is being constructed by mechanician brothers, Mr Alexander and Mr Oliver Hogarth, and will be used solely for the sold-out show at the Prince's.

'It's not quite the disaster you seem to think, George,' Valentin says, sagely.

They are sitting around the Perrises' dining table in the evening: George and Harry, the Hogarth brothers, Eadie, Louis, Cec and Valentin, as George reads the article out again.

Cec feels sick. This is Skarratt's doing. *Her* doing too.

'But who would have leaked it?' George asks, despondently. '*Why?*'

'I'd lay money that Skarratt's behind it,' Valentin says as Cec tries to maintain a neutral expression. 'His uncle's a newspaper man, is he not? And Skarratt himself is always hungry for publicity. But, George, this will only help drive excitement for the show, that's all!'

'It ruins the surprise!'

'Only one element of it. And as you've said yourself, it's the storytelling that matters – and that hasn't leaked. Merely the concept.'

'Someone at the theatre must've said something!' George says, frustrated.

'You think it was one of us?' Eadie asks gently. 'Why would we do such a thing? We're all working towards the same goal – to make this show a success.'

George runs his fingers through his hair. 'You're right. I just wish sometimes we could still ask The Professor for his advice.'

'We could always hold a séance,' Eadie jokes and George raises a smile, the first time he has done so all evening.

'Speaking of séances,' she adds, 'there's something I should tell you.'

They sit in silence as Eadie tells them about the clash with her landlady and the ultimatum she's been given for 5 Regent Street.

'I wonder,' Eadie says, 'if Mrs Carnesky is working with Mr Skarratt?'

Cec is desperate to tell her the truth, that Marianne is Skarratt's sister, but she doesn't have the courage, for what if the rest of the truth tumbles out? Dry-mouthed, she reaches for her glass of wine and takes a sip.

'Almost certainly,' Ollie Hogarth says. 'Skarratt and she are brother and sister. Did you not know?'

'No, I did not!' Eadie says, surprised, as Cec stares at the tablecloth. Her head is pounding and she wonders if, perhaps, Skarratt is experimenting with his poppet of her. She rubs a hand over her forehead, nauseous suddenly, a vision of a sharp pin running right through her head.

'I'm sure your landlady will come to her senses,' George says. 'And, if she doesn't, then we'll all help, however we can. There'll always be room for you and Louis here. We have several spare rooms.'

'And in our workshop too,' Ollie adds, shyly, with a smile. 'All Carletons welcome.'

'Thank you,' Louis says, as Eadie nods.

'I hope it won't come to that,' she says.

'Do you know who we mean by Mrs Carnesky, Cecil?' Valentin asks and Cec nods, guiltily.

'I think so. His sister, Marianne,' she replies. 'She's a regular at his house and at the meetings he hosts. I've heard her referred to as Mrs Carr too.'

'Then it's not just Skarratt we should be worried about!' exclaims George. 'But a whole team! The attempted burglary at the workshop, now this with Eadie!'

'And Mrs Gray witnessed an intruder too,' Valentin says.

'But what can we do?' George protests. 'We have no proof! I reported the break-in to the police but to no avail.'

'We must stay focused,' Valentin says. 'Keep our attention on the show. After all, there's barely any time left for Skarratt to thwart our plans and, unpleasant though it is, you're right. George. There's not a great deal we *can* do.'

As the talk turns back to technical matters and costumes, Cec feels sick to her stomach. *They have no idea what Skarratt is capable of! Or that there is a traitor in their midst* . . .

The group enjoys a convivial dinner of roast fowl and a fruit pudding, but Cec barely eats a morsel. She rubs her forehead, feeling as if her very skull is tightening.

When Cec goes to retrieve her shawl, for the Perrises' house is rather draughty of an evening, Eadie joins her in the hallway.

'Are you all right?' she asks.

'Yes. Of course,' Cec lies, avoiding her eye.

'I notice you didn't eat much at supper.' She looks at Cec sympathetically. 'Valentin's relying very heavily on you, there's a lot of pressure on your young shoulders.'

'I'm fine,' Cec insists. 'A little under the weather maybe.' She cannot bear Eadie being kind to her when, if she knew the truth, she would surely never speak to her again.

'You know you can always talk to me,' Eadie says, gently. 'I know it might be hard sometimes to talk to an older gentleman about worries and such.'

'I'm so sorry about your notebook,' Cec blurts out. 'Truly.' But really what she wants to do is apologise for the mess she's got them into, one she cannot seem to untangle, no matter how much she would wish it.

Eadie smiles. 'It's long forgiven. And you were right, that time. How are we to change the world if we don't try to do it ourselves? We womenfolk must stick together. If you ever do need to talk, you know where to find me.'

'Thank you,' Cec says, lowering her eyes, Eadie's sympathy only serving to make her headache even worse.

'Well, in some ways, it might be for the best,' Louis says as Eadie stares at him, horrified, a breakfast cup of tea halfway to her mouth.

'How could it *possibly* be for the best?'

'It's just a building, Eadie! I know we grew up here and it's full of memories, but perhaps we're living in the past.

And, listen, I've been meaning to tell you: Alex and his fiancée Helena are looking to set up somewhere, after their wedding, and Ollie will have a spare room.'

'You're moving out?' Eadie's so startled she can barely speak.

'No. Not necessarily. I wanted to speak to you about it first and . . . Look, Eadie, what I mean to say is that *you're* what makes 5 Regent Street special. *You*. Your cameras, your brilliant brain. I hope Mrs Fearnley does see sense but, all I'm saying is, if she doesn't, it's not the end of the world. You'll find somewhere else. Buildings are important, but they're only bricks and mortar and wood.'

She stares at him wordlessly.

A question rises unbidden to her lips. One she's wanted to ask for so long. 'What really happened with you and Max?' she asks, and Louis's face crumples.

'Not now, Eadie,' he says, simply. 'Not now.'

'Why *did* you row with him, though?' she asks, softly. 'I still don't know why. And then he left, abandoned us for *her*.'

Louis's eyes burn right through her. 'Oh, Eadie. He didn't abandon us!'

'What happened then? Please. You never argued, then suddenly you were both refusing to talk to the other.'

'*No*, Eadie.'

'Tell me,' she says, her voice trembling. '*Please*, Louis. You owe me that. You know I loved Max. I loved him so much, and then he left me.'

'No!' Louis says firmly, pushing his chair back and going to the door as Eadie stands too.

'Louis. *Please!*' she says.

Louis stops, and turns to her: 'You really want the truth, Eadie? Then know that I loved him. I loved him too—' He breaks off, puts his hand to his chest, the words so hard to say. 'Do you understand? I loved him, Eadie. *I loved him like you did!*'

Eadie cannot think straight for Louis's words make no sense. She stares at him as it slowly begins to sink in. Her brother had never shown much interest in the fairer sex, but she'd always thought it was because he could be shy sometimes. It had never occurred to her that his heart already lay with someone, let alone a man! And now this! *Max!* His best friend and the very man she had been set to marry . . .

'Oh, Louis . . .' she says, full of pity. How hard it must have been for him! All this time he had loved Max too, unrequitedly! She steps towards him but Louis holds his hand up to stop her.

'*No.* That's only the half of it.'

'What do you mean?'

'He didn't abandon us, Eadie.' He swallows. 'I made him go.'

'What? *Why?* Because he was in debt? The gambling? That's why he married her, wasn't it? The money?'

'It wasn't that, Eadie. It was *all of it.*'

'All of what?'

He looks her in the eye. 'Eadie. I'm sorry. Max. He wasn't . . . I don't know how to tell you this. But Max. He loved me too. And we hid it. For years. From everyone. Even from you.'

Eadie's world slides around her, the walls of the house looming in, as the breath goes out of her and Louis's eyes fill with tears.

'No!' she murmurs, as her mind fills with the three of them. The lakes, the picnics, the dances. The theatre trips, the visits to London when she was studying. The picnics and parties. The terrible trio – thick as thieves. But Max had loved her, he *had*! Her heart shrinks. And the pact! To marry each other when she turned twenty-five – except Eadie had turned twenty-five last summer, alone.

'No!' she says. '*No*, Louis!'

He must be mistaken, she thinks, but she sees the truth in his face. And there is suddenly not enough air in the room.

'Get out!' she cries, sobs coming thick and fast as she reaches for the wall to hold herself up. '*Get out!* Leave me alone!'

Louis stands, distraught, as tears fall silently down his face.

'This is why I couldn't tell you,' he says, quietly. 'Do you understand now? Because it would've been a lie if he'd married you. He would've made you live a lie and I couldn't allow it. Not for you, Eadie. Not of all people.'

She turns her back on him, gasping for breath, weeping, as she runs upstairs to the safety of her bedroom. She throws herself on her bed, oblivious to the slam of the front door, as she wails into her pillow.

Her heart fractures, slicing at her memories, hacking them to pieces. Her chest contracts, withering, as she weeps and moans, sobs and wails. The pillow becomes damp with her tears until there is no more water and no more rage left in her.

Her cheeks slowly dry, salt-crust streaks over them as her sniffles gradually subside. She sits up slowly on the edge of her bed, closes her eyes, and she remembers . . .

Max and Louis. The little glances they shared. The secret language they once made up until she fought with Louis to tell her the code. The way they would finish each other's sentences, their words as entwined as their lives. That time she burst into Louis's room without knocking and Max's shirt was off and all she could think was how beautiful he was, not why he might be half naked in her brother's room. She thinks of the swimming in the lakes, the splashing, the laughter. The two looking at each other with light in their eyes. The way Max looked over his shoulder from the front of the church on his sister's wedding day. That knowing smile. And Eadie understands now that he wasn't looking at her. He was looking at Louis, seated right next to her.

Eadie allows the memories to flood back: the dancing in the garden, looping round and round in Max's arms. The delight of his company. The kiss under the cherry tree by the edge of the cornfield, soft pink petals cascading around them. That tender, *perfect* kiss where Max had pulled her towards him and her heart flew out of her like a dove released from her ribcage. He had laughed, catching her hands and dancing around the tree, until Louis found them, furious they had disappeared.

'That's what you wanted, wasn't it?' Max had said, mischievously, laughing as he ran back to the house, racing to catch up with Louis who'd stamped off. She'd seen them, in the distance, as Max had thrown his arm around Louis, tousling his hair, as her heart had tumbled and skipped. Too blinded by her own desire to see the truth in front of her.

'That's what you wanted, wasn't it?' he'd said, and it *was* what she had wanted, what she'd *always* wanted. But he'd been toying with her all along. Perhaps Max had loved her, in a way, just not in the way she had believed him to.

When Eadie finally opens her eyes, she sees it all clearly. The real reason Louis lost himself. First Papa's death and then Max, not just his friend but his . . . She struggles to find the word in her head. *Lover.* The word she'd thought of as her own for Max, but he'd been Louis's love instead. A secret love. And Louis had lost him. Pushing him away to save *her* from the lie of a loveless marriage. And the pact between her and Max. How much of it had been assumption, fuelled by her hopes and dreams, egged on by comments from others? All this time she had thought Max abandoned her, that Louis had abandoned her too, when the truth was far more complex . . .

'Oh, Louis . . .' She sighs. How *could* he have told her? When he knew how much she loved Max, how could he have said anything?

She puts her hand to her forehead, hot suddenly. Louis's disappearance. *Of course!* A love that could see him thrown in gaol . . . How could she have been so *blind*?

But when Eadie goes downstairs, her brother is long gone.

'Louis?' she calls, frantically checking all the rooms, panic rising. '*Louis?*' She suddenly recalls what he said, when he first came back – 'I thought, perhaps, this world would be better without me in it' – and, for a moment, Eadie has to again hold herself up against the wall.

She must find him, she must! She cannot bear to lose him again!

As Eadie steps outside onto Regent Street, the world around her feels strangely slow, as if it were a film cranked at half-speed. Cabs and carriages, carts and cycles, everything moves as if caught in treacle as the wind captures one of her stray curls and blows it slowly across her face.

Louis is nowhere within view and so Eadie runs, right through the slow world around her, breath and heart tight and fast, not thinking where she is going. She runs down a handful of streets before she forces herself to stop, to think, and the city unfolds itself in front of her, a giant pop-up book with so many hiding places for a person in distress. Docks and gardens. Bridges and gorges. Caves and houses. And only her to find him. . . .

George is the first person she thinks of who might help. Not Harry, not the Hogarth twins, not even Chaplin who is, at that very moment, standing outside E. D. Carleton Photographic, checking his pocket watch, and wondering when Eadie might open up the shop.

Instead, Eadie runs straight to the Hogarths' workshop, her boots thumping on the pavement, not caring how she looks. *Please let him be there! Please!*

But there's no sign of Louis. Ollie is concerned to see Eadie in such distress but he cannot persuade her to tell him the cause of her upset, for Louis's secret is not hers to share.

She runs for the Prince's Theatre as soon as she knows George is there. A gasp of relief as she sees him in the foyer, playing with a pack of cards, and she bursts in through the glass doors.

'Eadie?' he says. 'Why, whatever's the matter?'

'Louis!' she sobs. 'I've done something terrible! I've lost him . . .'

George's arm is around her, gently guiding her towards the auditorium.

'It's all right. He's inside. He turned up half an hour ago, as upset as you. He didn't want to talk to me, only Harry.' He holds a hand to her cheek, his thumb wiping a tear away. 'Eadie, it's all right. Whatever's happened, it'll be all right.'

He guides her in, to the darkness of the stalls, bright lights onstage as her eyes adjust and there he is, next to Harry in the back row. *Louis*. His eyes full of hurt as he looks up at her.

'Louis,' Eadie sobs. 'Oh, Louis . . .'

He stands slowly as Eadie dashes forward, throwing her arms around her younger brother, holding him *so very tightly* as he embraces her in return. The two siblings wrap around each other like a spiral as Harry takes George's hand, slipping silently out of the auditorium behind them.

'I'm sorry!' Eadie whispers. 'I'm *so* sorry . . .'

Louis's arms tighten around her.

'I'm sorry too, Eadie . . . I never meant to hurt you.'

Louis now safe in her arms, Eadie realises, guiltily, this is the first time she's embraced him since his return.

Later, when their tears have dried, Louis and Eadie sit on the roof of the theatre, watching the pigeons flutter overhead.

'All those years . . .' Eadie sighs, drained by it all.

'Do you blame me?'

'No! How can I blame you for loving him too? I wish you'd told me, but I can see why you didn't. Is that why you went overseas? Because of what happened with Max?'

Louis nods. 'I lost myself, Eadie. Papa's death was so unexpected. And Max. I knew if he proposed you'd say yes. I always knew that. He told me, on the day of the row, that it would be a way for us to stay together, secretly. I couldn't let him do that to you. And I knew time was running out because on your next birthday, you'd be twenty-five. The expectation of it! And his debts, so much worse than I realised. I gave him an ultimatum: tell you the truth or leave. And I knew it would be the end. Because if I couldn't bring myself to tell you, how could I expect him to?'

'You know last summer, when I did turn twenty-five, he sent me a huge bunch of flowers,' Eadie says, sadly. 'A note, not signed. Just one word. "Sorry."'

'That wasn't Max, Eadie,' Louis says, softly. 'That was from me.'

She looks at him for a moment, silently.

'I wish I'd known,' she says, breathing out slowly. 'I don't think I knew Max anywhere near as well as I thought. I allowed my imagination to run free instead of looking at who was in front of me.' She sighs. 'Perhaps our pact was only a joke to him in the end, but to me it was so much more. I grieved for him after that announcement in the paper, knowing I'd lost him to someone else. But not as much as I grieved for you, Louis.'

'I'm sorry. I couldn't keep on as I was. Pretending everything was all right. To the rest of the world, to you, Max was simply my best friend. But to me he was *everything*, he had been for such a long time. Do you understand now why it took me so long to come home? To tell you the truth?'

She nods.

'I knew I'd have to tell you,' he says, quietly. 'One day. Do you forgive me?'

Eadie gently nudges him in the ribs. 'Only if you forgive me too,' she says, looking up at the bright blue sky above. 'Did anyone else know?' she asks. 'About you and Max.'

'Papa never said anything, but I think he suspected.'

'When did you know – that you loved him?'

Louis looks away bashfully. 'That first day. At Clifton College. A rush of blood to the head. The golden boy like something from a fairy tale. You know how he was. Do you believe in love at first sight?'

And Eadie remembers Max too. But George flickers through her mind. The first time she saw him. That strange evening at the séance. His lively eyes and boyish energy, his wide smile and passion for justice.

'I don't know,' she says, heat rising to her cheeks. 'It's not that simple.'

'Isn't it?'

'People are complicated.' She hesitates. 'Do you know if Max felt it too, that same day?'

'Yes, but he took a bit of time to win around. He thought I was a show-off.'

'Because you used to walk into parties on your hands?'
she teases.

'Probably,' he says. 'I loved those street jugglers. It's why
I love the theatre too. Misfits of all sorts.'

Eadie looks at the Louis sitting before her, the old one
still somewhere inside, the joyful one that somersaulted and
swam and walked into parties on his hands. Past and present
together. A double exposure. And yet, in the past few weeks,
he had been so much more like his old self. Ever since he'd
been working with the Hogarth brothers . . .

Oh!

'Ollie . . .' she says, softly, and Louis glances away, shy
suddenly.

'I can't keep on living in the past, Eadie,' he says. 'I know
I'll always have to hide who I am in some ways, but I don't
want to hide it from you. Not anymore. And I'm sorry.
Really I am. I know you loved Max and I don't believe
he meant to mislead or hurt you. He thought – we both
thought – you'd grow out of it, meet someone else who
meant more to you. I know you must miss him. I know
I do. Probably always will in some ways.'

'It's true,' she says. 'I do miss him, but not as much as I
missed you, Louis.' The truth of it stings her eyes. Such a
long time since she has been so open with anyone.

Louis puts an arm around her in silence, and a little piece
of them both is finally restored.

The three of spades flutters down onto Valentin's dining-room table and Cec puts her head in her hands.

'I can't do it!' she cries. 'I can't!'

'Oh, Cecil! I'm sorry!' Valentin apologises. 'Please, put your cards away. It's my fault. I talked you into this and I shouldn't have done. We're both tired after a long day.'

Cec nods, despairingly, her confidence knocked, and Valentin reaches out a hand.

'I'm sorry,' he says, softly. 'I believe in you, Cecil, really I do. I only wished you believed in yourself half as much. Now come, let us take Oz for a quick turn outside. A breath of fresh air will do all three of us good.'

They stroll along the crescent together and circle through the village, Clifton so handsome at night with the streetlights reflecting off the innumerable windows of its terraces and shops. Valentin links arms with Cec as they walk and, for a moment, she feels a sense of happiness. A reminder of how things were before Skarratt came back into her life. All too soon though, they loop back to the far end of the crescent and up the steps onto the raised pavement that runs the length of it.

Cec's heart stops when she sees him in the shadows beneath. *Skarratt.* She knows it's him from the way he walks, trailing them in the road below. Oz growls gently and Cec picks him up, finding comfort in his warm wiry fur.

'He doesn't like the cold much,' Valentin says and Cec nods, unable to speak. *What does Skarratt want with her now?*

When they reach Valentin's front door, Cec loiters outside for a moment as Valentin unlocks the door. She leans over the railings on the pavement, looking down to the road below and there he is.

'Tomorrow,' Skarratt mouths, tipping his hat to her – a flash of golden hair, the gleam of his white teeth – before he silently slips back into the shadows.

'Are you coming in?' Valentin calls to her, and Cec nods, her feet feeling like lead as she goes inside. *What on earth does Skarratt want now?* she wonders, worrying to herself, and knowing that, again, she will not sleep well tonight.

This is the last Will & Testament of The Professor, also known as William Henry Bagshaw, of Clifton in the City of Bristol, Conjuror and Wizard. I bequeath all moneys which I may have at the time of my decease in the bank of Prescott, Dimsdale, Cave, Tugwell and Co in Cornhill, Bristol and in any other bank, to my dear friend Valentin Perche, also known as The Great Valentini, Conjuror and Wizard, subject to the payment of my debts and funeral and testamentary expenses.

As to the residue of my estate (and effects including my entire collection of items relating to the performance of, and history of, magic) – excepting my apartment on Lansdown Place – I give and bequeath the same unto my friend George Perris of St Michael's Hill in the City of Bristol, Conjuror and Wizard.

I give and bequeath my residuary personal estate of 8, Lansdown Place to my dear friend and loyal housekeeper, the widow Mrs Penelope Gray.

I appoint Mr Perche as Executor of my Will hereby revoking all other Wills in witness whereof I have hereunto set my hand this twenty-fifth day of March one thousand eight hundred and ninety six.

Signed The Professor, William Henry Bagshaw
....

Signed and acknowledged by the said Valentin Perche, the testator as and for his last Will and Testament at his request.

Signed Valentin Perche ....

On this twenty-fifth day of March 1896, Probate of this Will was granted at Bristol to Valentin Perche, the Executor.

George and Eadie have had a busy morning, preparing for tomorrow's charity gala at Ashton Court, and now they are setting up for George's experimental film on the roof of the Prince's Theatre. Chaplin carries the camera as Eadie lays out a black backdrop and a tablecloth with a hole cut into it.

As George heads downstairs to bring up the last of his props, Eadie takes the opportunity to speak with Chaplin.

'Does George *still* not know about you and Harry?' she asks.

'No.' Chaplin sighs. 'I know we should tell him. But it's so hard to find the right moment. You know he still holds a grudge against me. I have to prove myself to him. Only then might he forgive me.'

Eadie puts her hand on his forearm and gently presses it. 'You *must* tell him! *No more lies!*' she says, just as George returns, a look of puzzlement as he sees Eadie's hand on Chaplin's arm and she hastily removes it.

'Ah, George!' Eadie says, taking a step back. 'I'm afraid you'll have to talk me through it again. I'm not sure where this belongs . . .'

Another hour and everything's in place. Eadie's notes are next to her on a small table, held down by a rusting gilt crown commandeered as a paperweight. Chaplin stands beside her, dressed in an identical shirt and bowtie to George. The rehearsals have been intense and Eadie can see how impressive the idea is, but still, can they *really* pull this off?

'Ready?' George says, sitting on a chair behind the cloth-covered desk. 'Let's go!'

A countdown from three and then he's off, as Eadie steadily turns the handle of her camera. Inspired partly by George's 'egg man' trick and partly by the popular trend of stage magicians 'decapitating' themselves, George's performance is divided into three sections. Between each, Eadie must stop her camera whilst the next section is prepared: a strange combination of George performing real magic, as he does now, producing two eggs in each hand from nowhere, and tricks that will only become apparent after the film is developed. It's exciting, bizarre, and with much that could go wrong, yet Eadie cannot help but grin as she pauses her camera for the first time.

'Change!' George cries and Chaplin switches places with him, pulling on the conjuror's jacket along with a black mask that covers his face, rendering his head invisible against the dark backdrop. George dips beneath the table, smiling at Eadie as he disappears.

'Ready?' George's muffled voice shouts as Eadie cranks her camera once again. Chaplin, now sitting where George was, places a giant fake egg to one side of the table. A crack appears on it and it opens into two halves as George pushes himself up from underneath the table, his head appearing within the egg as Eadie laughs out loud.

Another pause as Eadie rests for a moment, watching Chaplin throw the jacket back to George as they swap places, Chaplin now underneath the table and George back in his chair. *They work so well together*, she thinks, a little glimpse of how they would have performed onstage.

Finally, it's time for the third and last section. Eadie counts out loud as she cranks the camera and George and Chaplin time their performances to the second.

'Perfect!' Eadie cries, as George bows to the camera and her reel comes to an end.

George mops his brow as Chaplin crawls out from under the table, chuckling as he pulls off his mask. He leaps up and shakes George's hand as they approach Eadie.

'I'll process it overnight,' she says, excitedly. 'See what the morning will bring. Keep your fingers crossed . . .'

'Does that affect the development?' George asks, wryly.

'No, but it'll make me feel less nervous.'

'Gracious,' says Chaplin, looking at his pocket watch. 'I'm terribly sorry. May I—?'

'Go!' says Eadie, knowing perfectly well he has a rendez-vous with Harry. 'George and I can pack this up. If that's all right with you, George?'

'Of course, but I must be gone by four. Valentin wants me for the reading of The Professor's will. Then straight back to rehearsals and another late night. There's still so much to do.'

Chaplin shakes George's hand again. 'You'll be fine. It's been good to work with you again, Perris,' he says, giving a quick nod to Eadie as he leaves.

'Chaplin's a good man, George,' Eadie says, thinking of Harry as she starts to pack things away. 'I only wish you could see it too.'

'He was always rather too fond of the ladies.'

'I think he'd make for a very loyal companion,' Eadie says, with feeling.

George frowns as he watches her, recalling her hand on Chaplin's arm earlier. *Damn Chaplin and his easy way with women.* He always seemed to know what to say and do, how to be charming and courageous. *If only*, George thinks, *I could find it within myself to be as bold . . .*

The bells of Holy Trinity Church peal as Cec reluctantly hands over a full copy of the rehearsal schedules to Skarratt. Eleven o'clock – she should be in bed by now.

'Is that everything?' he asks and she nods as Oz growls at him. 'Excellent! Then I thank you, sweet Cecily. You really are turning out to be most valuable.'

He tucks the papers into his coat and smiles. 'See? That wasn't so bad now, was it? One final thing, is Perris's copper tank finished yet?'

'I don't know,' Cec says quietly, her voice barely a whisper. She cannot bear to look him in the eye. 'Why?'

'A little idea I had, for one of the wheels the tank sits on. How easy might it be for you to access it?'

Cec shakes her head. 'Not very. Valentin and I are barely at the workshop.'

Skarratt looks thoughtful. 'No matter,' he says. 'Leave it with me.' One last grin and he's off, leaving Cec behind full of worry.

What exactly is he planning now?

Cec is so preoccupied as she slowly begins the walk uphill, back to Clifton, she doesn't even see Mabel loitering in the shadows. She almost walks into her as she turns the corner, gasping as she sees the maid's black eye.

'What happened?' Cec cries and Mabel shakes her head.

'What was that you handed to him?' Mabel asks.

Cec swallows, guiltily. 'Papers, ' she replies. 'You don't want to know.' She shakes her head. 'He's a bad man, Mabel. Dangerous too.'

'You don't trust him?' Mabel asks.

'Not as far as I could throw him,' Cec replies, firmly. 'Look at what he's done to you.'

'You know, he said he'd marry me. He promised,' Mabel says, her eyes brimming with tears. 'When the time was right.'

Cec looks at her in silence, her heart breaking for the maid. 'And do you honestly think he will?' she asks quietly.

'I don't know. Not anymore. That's why I followed him this evening. Saw him with you and. . . .'

Cec takes her hands. 'Mabel. Please. If you get a chance to escape that man, *please* take it. Otherwise he'll hold you in his clutches forever. *Please*. Swear it. I beg of you.'

Mabel looks at her silently. 'And you?' she asks, slipping her hands away.

'I thought I'd escaped him,' Cec says quietly. 'But then he trapped me, good and proper. He's a bully and a violent one at that.'

Mabel suddenly embraces her and Cec nearly weeps at the warmth of it.

'Good luck,' Mabel whispers in Cec's ear. And then she is gone.

Cec is quiet when she heads back into Valentin's apartment, quieter still when she hears George's voice coming from the sitting room. She lingers in the hallway a moment, eavesdropping.

'She's the only one in our group who knows Skarratt. And you've said yourself, Valentin, you've not known Cec long. What if Skarratt put her in your way? What if this is some kind of set-up?'

Cec puts her hand to her mouth to stop herself from crying. She holds her breath as George continues. 'It's not that I don't like her, Valentin, far from it. She's enormously talented and from what I've seen, she's immensely warm and likeable onstage. But please, this is important. Are you *sure* she's not the source of our leak?'

'Quite sure,' Valentin replies. 'I trust Cecil with my life. And I assure you, George, our paths crossed because of her remarkable talent. It was nothing to do with Skarratt.'

The tears run down Cec's cheeks as Oz nudges her leg softly. She cannot bear to hear Valentin defending her in such a way. *If only he knew!*

'Come on, Oz,' Cec whispers, wanting the respite of the chill air outside. She quietly heads back out, Oz pattering behind.

The penultimate of my headings is the 'Defiance of Natural Science'.

This is an effect that can easily mystify an audience and includes any tricks in which there is a seeming defiance of natural laws. This might include the suspension of a person in mid-air, the plunging of a sword into someone's body to no apparent harm, or even the shooting of a person without injuring them.

A simpler trick for the amateur might be that of the 'floating cards', in which the only apparatus needed is a pack of cards and some ordinary cotton thread.

If pushed to say which effect goes down best with an audience, I have always found that the 'decapitation' trick — removing one's head and taking a bow with it under one's own arm — is always a winner but, of course, never to be undertaken lightly, let alone by an amateur!

Extract from *The Secrets of Magic* by George Perris
(published by Saxon Press, 1895)

DEFIANCE OF
NATURAL SCIENCE

'You've really not watched it yet? You have admirable powers of self-restraint!' George says, stepping into Eadie's projection room.

'I had to wait! It seemed only fair!' she replies, excitedly.

'Go on then. Let's see whether it's a delight or a disaster.'

'We should really wait for Chaplin . . .' Eadie says, biting her lip as she looks at George. 'Oh, he won't mind, I'm sure! And it was your idea, after all!'

She grins as she turns the cranking handle and George watches himself back as the projector gently rattles away. The black-and-white George smiles charmingly from the screen, and produces an egg from each of his empty hands, then from his mouth too. He claps twice, draws an oval shape around his face using his hands and, in the blink of an eye, his head transforms, impossibly, into a giant egg.

'Ha!' George says, pleased.

The onscreen George removes his giant egg-head, placing it on a stand to the left, leaving a headless George behind. Cracks appear on the giant egg and it opens, hatching to reveal George's head inside wearing a look of bemusement.

'It's worked!' George chuckles. '*Eadie!* It's damn well worked!'

The headless George grasps around, reaching for his disembodied head, catching in one of his hands a final egg George produces from his mouth. He then picks up his head and reattaches it, stretching his neck as a whole George is once again restored. Satisfied, he pulls out a fan, flicks it open, and wafts it at the giant egg to close it back up. A bow to camera, and the magic is over.

George laughs, a breathless, raucous laugh of relief and delight, as tears stream down his face. It is a hundred, a *thousand* times better than he imagined. His first trick film! An impossible illusion, defying all laws of science, that he could never have achieved onstage! So much more than he could have dreamed of when he sat in that dingy theatre in the capital and watched living pictures for the first time.

He rights himself, still chuckling. He's feeling pressured still, very much so, but now there is *this* . . . this remarkable trick film! *And then there had been yesterday too . . .*

He was rendered speechless by The Professor's will. He'd never imagined his old mentor would leave him anything, for the wizard's affection and friendship had been more than enough. Yet he is now the proud owner of an enormous collection of magic paraphernalia, a collection that could easily form the heart of his planned home of magic here in Bristol, after all.

George feels, despite all the setbacks, that things are truly looking up.

He looks at Eadie, radiant with delight, and despite his suspicions about Chaplin – her hand on his arm, calling him 'invaluable' and saying he would be 'a loyal companion' – George has never been more wildly in love.

'Are you all right, George?' Eadie's eyes shine with excitement.

'I can't believe it!' He grins. 'It's brilliant, Eadie! *Brilliant!*'

'It is *marvellous!*' she says. 'Far better than I imagined. You can't show it at Ashton Court though.'

'Why ever not?'

'*George!* This has to be part of your show with Valentin! We've other films we can show at Ashton Court. But not this. You *must* save it! I won't allow you to show it tonight. In fact, as your projectionist, I forbid it!'

'All right.' He laughs. 'If it's so important to you.'

'*Of course it is!*'

They gaze at each other, holding their breath, and the room feels as if it might spin around them like a carousel, the world and all things pausing for a moment.

'Eadie? George? Are you there? I got your note to come up!' Chaplin's shout comes up the stairs and the world resumes.

'Chaplin?' says Eadie, unable to take her eyes off George. 'We're in the projection room! It's the most marvellous thing!' and she loses herself in George's smile as Chaplin's feet thud up the stairs towards them.

It's a bright morning, with all the promise of blue skies, as Cec walks beside Valentin and Oz along Park Row, on their way to the theatre. It's their usual route, for Valentin is a creature of habit, so much so that he even likes to cross the road at the exact same point. He glances both ways before stepping out, Cec next to him.

The cab careens towards them out of nowhere. Cec is frozen to the spot, transfixed, as the horse bears down upon her. Thunderous hooves. Rolling eyes. Foam bubbling from its open mouth.

Valentin grabs her, pulling her back, and the wheels miss her by less than an inch. The push of air as the cab flies past. The sweat on the horse's haunches. A whiff of warm hay.

She topples backwards onto the pavement as Oz barks furiously and the cab disappears down the road. Valentin helps her to her feet before reaching into the road to retrieve his walking stick, mercifully unbroken.

'Someone was in a hurry,' he says, wryly, dusting his coat.

Cec is so startled she can't even speak as they carefully cross the road and Valentin gently guides her towards the theatre doors.

'Honestly, Cecil, the drivers are worse here than in Paris and I never thought I'd say that!'

Later, when Valentin is checking the trapdoors onstage, Cec is suddenly called into the wings by one of the stagehands.

'A Mr Greenhouse for you in the dressing room,' he says. 'Just you, not Valentin, he said so specifically.'

'Mr *Greenhouse*? Are you sure?' Cec asks, puzzled, and the stagehand nods. *What might George's business partner want with her?*

But when Cec goes into her dressing room, she's surprised to find it empty. She glances at her own puzzled reflection in the mirror – only to jump when she sees a figure behind her. Skarratt himself, wearing a black bowler hat and gold glasses.

'Do you like my little joke?' He grins, pleased with himself.

'How did you get in?' Cec cries, turning to him, distressed. 'You can't be here!'

'I have my ways. Now look, there's something I need you to do.' He takes out what looks like a bolt and gives it to her. 'You need to replace the main bolt on one of the wheels of Perris's copper tank with this,' he instructs her. 'Doesn't matter which one, any of them will do. The night before the show, no earlier. You understand?'

Cec stares at him. He's asking her to sabotage the show! Leaking information is one thing but *this*!

'*You* do it,' she says, defiantly. He stares at her before grabbing her arm tightly, speaking between gritted teeth.

'I would happily do it myself but, as you know, Perris's precious tank is still in his workshop and won't be here until the get-in. And *that's* when they step up security . . .'

He releases her, calm again, a smile playing across his lips. 'I don't like it when you make me cross, little urchin. Don't do it again.'

He goes to the door, turning as he reaches it. 'One last thing. You haven't seen Mabel recently, have you?'

Cec shakes her head.

'Not since I left your house,' she lies, repressing a smile. *Then she has left him! Well done, Mabel, you brave soul!*

'Well if you do happen to see her,' Skarratt says sharply. 'Be sure to let me know.'

Cec is lost in her thoughts the rest of the day, the bolt Skarratt gave her already in the dressing-room bin. She won't put her friends in danger, *she won't*! Mabel's defiance has inspired her. Cec feels proud of the maid, wishing she too could find it in herself to escape Skarratt's clutches. Only then does she remember the close call with the cab that morning, how she herself had given Skarratt a copy of the rehearsal schedule. She grows cold. He would know *exactly* what time she and Valentin would arrive at the theatre. Cec had believed Skarratt to be focused only on George, but what greater way to get revenge on his rival than in scuppering the *entire* show? Could it have been Skarratt himself in the cab? Or was it merely a coincidence? She frowns to herself, mulling it over.

'What would *you* do, Cecil? If you unexpectedly inherited a lot of money?'

Valentin interrupts her thoughts and she looks up at him, standing above her in an open trapdoor at the Prince's; only his head visible from where she stands beneath the stage.

'Spend it?' she suggests, trying to concentrate.

'On what exactly?'

'Fine wine and food, clothes, and travel. Fun.'

Valentin smiles fondly at her. 'The voice of youth,' he says, drily.

'Well, I would!' she says. 'But I'd want it to last too. The good times never lasted long enough with Arter.' She swallows, wishing the good times with Valentin could have lasted longer too, before Skarratt ruined it.

'If you can do anything, do good,' Valentin says, as Cec reaches up and he pulls her through the trapdoor and up onto the stage.

'It's not always possible though, is it?' Cec says, quietly. 'Because sometimes, things don't work out how you want. And one bad person can cause so much ill.'

She looks up and out at the vast auditorium, imagining all the people sat there, watching the show, watching *her*. *All those faces*. Her nerves come like a bolt of lightning and she puts a hand to her head.

'A headache again?' Valentin asks, concerned, and she nods. 'Water and a sit-down,' he says. 'I'm working you too hard.'

She gives a tiny nod as a feeling of nausea comes over her.

'Oh, and Cecil,' Valentin says softly, 'you're right. One wicked person *can* do so much wrong. But one good person can do so much right too. That's true too, is it not?'

He holds his left palm up, the faint scar visible, and Cec looks guiltily down at her own matching scar as her headache starts to throb.

Eadie stands in her distinctive emerald-green dress feeling strangely out of her depth as crowds of fashionably dressed people mingle around her within the Great Hall at Ashton Court.

A light touch on her arm and George is by her side. She's relieved to see him, his warm smile reassuring as always.

'There are a *lot* more people here than I was led to believe,' he says, and she nods. So many people, so many faces, a fug of champagne issuing from their loud chatter.

'Come on,' he says, gently taking her hand. 'Fresh air. Being in here isn't helping either of us.'

They sneak outside into the cool evening, Eadie's boots softly crunching on the sand path as they walk away from the house towards the area in which they will soon perform.

George inhales nervously as he looks at the stage and Eadie laughs.

'Nerves again, Mr Perris?'

'Always, Miss Carleton,' he says, fidgeting with his jacket. '*Always.*'

'Me too,' she murmurs, thinking how handsome he looks, his black jacket with its satin trim, his watch-chain a flash of silver across his chest. His tie though, is wonky. Without thinking, she reaches forward to straighten it, and as she does so, that intense look of his appears in his blue-grey eyes, flecked with gold.

'That's better,' she says, awkwardly, patting the knot of the tie.

'You look rather lovely,' he says, and she blushes a little.

'I feel woefully under-dressed, truth be told. Besides, you saw this dress at supper the other night. And all those women in there, dressed in the latest fashions . . .'

'Their sleeves are ridiculous,' he says, and she laughs.

'Come on, Eadie, they are! I know it's called "a leg of mutton" sleeve, but it must be based on a giant sheep the likes of which the world has never seen! And as for the hats! Why anyone would wish to recreate Kew Gardens on top of one's head is quite beyond me . . . You look far nicer than anyone in there,' he adds, shyly, and she turns to look at the horizon so he won't see the heat in her cheeks.

'The light's beginning to go now,' she says, as George pulls out his pocket watch and examines it.

'Half an hour.'

And although they don't know it, their hearts skip a beat at the exact same moment.

They wait nervously, soaking up the atmosphere as a succession of flambards are lit, ready to show the way for the hundred or more guests currently being entertained inside. A troupe of musicians passes by, to set up at the far end of the lawn for dancing later, and George nods at them.

'We'd better ready ourselves,' he says, and Eadie gazes at him, her heart fluttering. All this hard work and now here they are. Just the two of them.

'Best of luck, George,' she says.

'You too.' He grins suddenly. 'Oh, come on, Eadie, let's not be *too* nervous! Tonight, we are in the business of entertainment! This will be joyous! This will be—' He reaches for Eadie's hands, whirls her in a circle. 'This will be *enchanting*!'

She laughs excitedly, butterflies in her stomach, as she looks again at the remnants of sunset painted across the sky, the glow on the horizon. The air cools around her and a scent of spring lingers in the breeze. She breathes it in.

'I'm ready,' she says, turning to him, and his smile lifts her heart.

The well-dressed, fashionable crowd has gathered: aristocrats, businessmen, members of parliament and more. Bristol's wealthy and influential, together in the same place. All eyes on George where he stands on his small stage, the twelve-foot-wide screen behind him hiding both Eadie and her projector from view. He is lit from the front – bright arc lamps that cast his shadow straight through the screen, and backstage to Eadie. She smiles as George's shadow bows elegantly and he introduces himself, not a trace of doubt in his now confident voice.

'Ladies and gentlemen!' cries George. 'Good evening and welcome! What a glorious setting this is, high above the city and with the beautiful grounds of Ashton Court surrounding us. My name is George Perris, and I am a conjuror.'

Eadie grins as she sees George's shadow-self through the screen, silhouette black against bright white, as he performs trick after trick. She deciphers them through the shadows, aided both by the audience's reaction and George's charming patter.

She gasps, along with the gathered crowd, as she hears him read the mind of three audience members, one after another. Then his shadow-self places a top hat on his head, lifting it to reveal a dove underneath that flutters off, disappearing into the darkness above as Eadie's heart flutters along with it.

She checks her equipment for the dozenth time as George continues to perform just feet away.

He balances an empty wine glass on his nose and another on top of it, then a third filled to the brim, and somehow the wine transfers itself from the top to the bottom glass. He sprinkles a handful of seeds into three oversized pots, covering them for a moment, before revealing instantaneous shrubs in full bloom. He introduces his tank of 'educated goldfish', who proceed to spell out words suggested by the audience, plucking lettered tiles from their bowl. Finally, George takes out his inexhaustible hat and pulls out a range of impossible items.

It's the last of his illusions before Eadie's living pictures. She holds her hands out, tries to steady the tremor of her fingers. *To be a part of this . . .*

And then George is introducing the films. *Her* films. *Their* films.

'Ladies and gentlemen. The final act of my show this evening is something very special indeed. An incomparable display of the latest, most original, entertaining, and exciting living pictures – the most wonderful scientific marvel of our age. The living pictures you are to see tonight include the very latest, most entertaining subjects and, I assure you, hand on heart, having seen the animated photographs of other makers in our capital city, the work of Miss Carleton of Bristol can no more be classed alongside them than flickering rushlights could be compared with a thousand-candle-power arc lamp.' He pauses for effect. 'There will be a short inter-lude between each living picture as the reel is changed but, fear not, I will demonstrate the ancient art of hand shadows to entertain and amuse during these pauses. Ladies and gentlemen, please enjoy our finale.'

He steps around to Eadie's side of the screen, bright-eyed and breathless, as the lights at the front are extinguished, plunging the crowd into semi-darkness. Eadie switches the arc lamp of her projector on, a steady hiss as her screen floods with light.

One deep breath before she turns the handle, transporting her audience to Clifton suspension bridge and a girl running through a flock of pigeons. Eadie cannot, dare not, hear the audience, partly for the rattle of the projector and partly because she's concentrating so hard on keeping her hands steady, on not letting George down.

As the first film ends, Eadie slides a special plate over the projector, focusing the beam of light through a small circular opening. As she swiftly changes the reels – two minutes at her fastest – George entertains the audience. He stands by the side of the beam and lifts his hands into the light, wiggling his fingers so the audience can see they are really his, before effortlessly shaping them into shadows. Suddenly there is a bulldog on the screen, a fearsome shadow-beast that rolls his eyes as Eadie finds herself laughing along with the audience.

Five more films follow: Zebi the elephant at Bristol Zoo reaching out to steal a passer-by's hat, a tall ship that makes its way into Bristol docks, a fire engine extinguishing a small inferno, George's paper-folding tricks, and Mr Johnson's motorised tricycle whizzing along Weston's sands. And in between, more shadow shows created from nothing more than George's hands. A floating swan that pecks and preens, a bull that silently bellows, a billy goat with a tufted chin and, finally, an egg that hatches into a tiny chick.

And much too soon, it's the final film of the night and Eadie is sad suddenly, not wanting it to stop, not wanting to take her eyes away from George. A feeling of sheer joy flows through her as George turns to her and smiles.

'Last one,' he mouths, and she nods, turning the handle of the projector a final time to show the happy accident. The omnibus transforming into a hearse, the men into women. It brings the house down as George steps around the front of the screen to take his bow.

He runs back to fetch Eadie, eyes alight, reaching for her hand and pulling her forward, out from behind the safe confines of the screen and onto the stage. The audience is revealed to her, faces flushed with delight, cheers so loud she can barely think, George's hand wrapped tightly around hers, the faint scent of his cologne in the night sky.

He turns to her as the applause deafens them, his smile so bright it is like an arc lamp in itself, and she cannot help but beam back, relieved it has all worked so perfectly.

They bow together, in perfect unison, once, twice and a third, final time before disappearing behind the screen together, giggling like children, as the roars of the appreciative crowd echo around them.

'Should we not—?' Eadie suggests, but George shakes his head as he releases her.

'Always leave them wanting more . . .' He holds her glance.
'Well, I think we've earned that glass of champagne now.
What do you say, Miss Carleton?'

When Eadie walks out into the party, she steps into a whole
other world. A world full of colour and vibrancy, so vivid,
so bright. A glass of champagne is pressed into her hand,
and she sips it, soft bubbles tickling the back of her throat.
George takes her other hand, holding it tightly, and they
walk together – the toast of the evening – towards the
gathered throng as the music rises around them. Lady Packer
approaches, congratulating them both before kissing Eadie
on the cheek and peeling her away from George to introduce
her to various ladies of high standing. Eadie, half-dazed, still
moving as if in a dream, glances back over her shoulder to
see George being swamped by a group of admirers. He looks
over at her and mouths, 'I'll find you!' with such earnestness
that her heart sings.

And suddenly there are people. So many of them. Women
with high hair and puffed sleeves. Men with waxed mous-
taches and neat beards. There seems to be a never-ending
stream of them. Face after face, Lord and Lady this or that,
Sir thingummy – they all merge into one, eyes and noses,
eyebrows, mouths and hair. Clipped voices with no discern-
ible accent. And perhaps it is the champagne, but Eadie
suddenly feels a little light-headed . . .

A hand on her arm and George's familiar face beams at her.

'Care to dance, Miss Carleton?' He grins, and there is
nothing more she wants in the world.

Her hand once again clasped in his, they move through the throng as it slowly parts to let them through. And then she is whirling with him, the world around flashing into flickers of colour as he looks into her eyes, and she feels herself falling. But her legs are steady still, and she laughs, giddy with joy as they waltz, holding each other close as they spin and glide across the large lawn surrounded by other couples.

Alas the last dance comes all too soon, and they must pack up before they leave. Eadie dismantles her screen as George counts out his props, placing them back into their trunks, humming to himself as he does so. They work quietly, enough at ease in each other's company now to be comfortable with silence.

'It's been a beautiful night,' George says, as they pack up the last few things.

Eadie murmurs her assent, wishing they could have danced for longer. She remembers how much she used to love it, before realising with a jolt that tonight was the first time she has danced since Max left.

When they are safely back in Clifton and George has unloaded the last of Eadie's equipment from the cab, he looks up at the clear sky above them.

'Look at the stars!' George marvels, and Eadie looks up from where she stands close beside him, a glimmer of his warmth seeping into her. He points up at the scattered pinpricks lighting up the velvet sky, and a shooting star slips out, from the tip of his finger, sparking from east to west, an impossible trail of silver.

'*George!*' she breathes.

'Now *that* was magic!' He laughs. 'Although a trick I fear may never be repeated!'

He puts her last case down on the doorstep of 5 Regent Street. 'Right. That's everything,' he says, but, as he stands back up, he is somehow too close to her, their faces mere inches away. Eadie smiles, and George reaches out a hand, gently brushing the side of her freckled cheek as her eyes widen, and then his lips are suddenly on hers.

He tastes of champagne and promises. Shared breath and heartbeat. The warmth of him floods through her and Eadie cannot help herself as she pulls him closer, her hands running through his hair. She breathes him in as a wild burning rises within her. As if she could merge with him somehow, become a single person . . .

But then Max is in her mind, Max with his blond hair and the cherry tree blossom falling around her. 'That was what you wanted, wasn't it?' echoes through her mind, and her hand is suddenly on George's chest, pushing him away as she gasps for breath.

She sees the hurt in his eyes, the confusion.

'George, I . . .' She swallows.

'I'm sorry,' he mumbles. 'I'm so sorry, Eadie. I don't know what came over me . . .'

'No, George, I—' but she doesn't know what to say, how to explain. Only that she wishes she could rewind time, just those few moments, to go back to his lips on hers, to his arms around her, to that impossible shooting star.

'It's been a long day,' he says, not meeting her eye. 'The champagne must have gone to my head. Please. Forgive me.'

He briefly glances at her, looking away again as if even the sight of her causes him injury, and she wants, more than anything, to make it right, to reach out and pull him back to her. But how can she explain pushing him away when she doesn't quite understand it herself? That fear of falling. Of opening her heart to him. Because look what happened with Max . . . *A dream, that was all. An illusion.*

'My sincere apologies, Miss Carleton,' he says, and then his hat is on and he steps into the cab and the horses' hooves rattle off down the road.

Eadie stands motionless and alone on the cold stone step of her front door, wondering what on earth just happened. Her heart on fire, her mind still waltzing with him somehow. She reaches up, runs a finger over her lips, the taste of him still there. And then there is salt water, silently dripping down her cheeks, and she realises she is crying.

BRISTOL MERCURY, Friday 17th April, 1896

ASHTON COURT CHARITY GALA

The spring novelty at what is planned to be an annual 'Ashton Court charity gala for women in need' was an exhibition of E. D. Carleton's latest developments in the area of continuous photography, whereby animated pictures from scenes of everyday life are thrown upon a screen. Renowned conjuror Mr George Perris acted as introduction, in addition to performing his own magical wonders. Miss Carleton's apparatus showed a series of pictures of photography come to life and taken 'in the action'. The lady inventor's animated pictures are likely to prove as popular in Bristol as in the capital, for the attraction may be revived again and again by new pictures.

Mr Perris, meanwhile, can be seen at the Prince's Theatre, in just one week's time, with the magician known as The Great Valentini. An insider informed us there would be disappearances, brand-new animated photographs, and never-before-seen illusions in the much-anticipated show held in memory of Bristol's beloved wizard, the late conjuror known only as The Professor.

George is crushed. How could he have been so *foolish*? Yet he had been certain Eadie wanted him to kiss her. The way they danced together so closely, both of them unable to look away. That warmth in her eyes, that openness. He would never have dreamed of kissing her otherwise! His heart crumples. She had warned him, hadn't she? Too busy for everything; too busy for romance then, as well.

He'd asked Louis a few days ago whether or not his sister was courting and Louis had hinted at something in Eadie's past that had hurt her deeply. George curses himself. He should have been more cautious. And yet *that look*, he had seen it deep in her eyes. *Desire*. And *she* had pulled *him* closer, hadn't she? He thinks of her soft hands running through his hair, the faint scent of roses, the taste of champagne on her lips . . .

'Penny for your thoughts, George?' Valentin asks.

George sighs. 'Not sure you'd want to hear them.' He glances at Cec leafing through the latest rehearsal schedules where they sit, in the Hogarths' workshop. He frowns, wondering again who was responsible for the leak to the papers.

'Nerves about the show?' Valentin suggests, and George shakes his head.

'Miss Carleton . . .?' Valentin ventures.

George looks at him with surprise.

'Ah.' Valentin nods, knowingly. 'Cec, you couldn't fetch us some coffee, could you?' and Cec disappears, leaving them alone.

'It's not important, Valentin. The show is all that matters.'

'Life is for living, George. You know that better than I. May I ask, what exactly has happened?'

And so, as Valentin had confided in him previously, George feels at ease to do the same in return. He recounts the evening's events at Ashton Court, the dancing afterwards, how the cab took them to Regent Street and then . . .

'Rebuffed?'

George nods, deflated.

'Perhaps it's simply that she's a little apprehensive,' Valentin guesses.

'Of me?'

'Not you, per se. More of what you represent. Change. Commitment. She has taken on a lot with her business ventures, begun to really make a name for herself. Perhaps her independent spirit thinks a romance might complicate things. Particularly with an existing client.'

'Perhaps,' murmurs George. 'Oh, I don't know, Valentin. I don't want to ruin things. Now I am nothing but doubts.' He sighs, thinking again of Chaplin. 'It was reckless of me.

And, my word, I don't want it to affect our working relationship, not so close to the show.'

'Neither will she.' Valentin smiles at him. 'Bide your time,
George, but clear the air for your own peace of mind. And
please, promise me: if you have happiness within your reach,
hold on to it with all your might.'

George nods, remembering Valentin's own confession, the
great loss the conjuror clearly still felt.

'Now come, we've got a lot to be getting on with!' Valentin
says, patting him on the arm.

George and Valentin are deep in conversation when Cec
returns with two steaming hot coffees with a dash of milk,
just as she knows they like it. George smiles as Cec puts his
coffee down but she can't quite bring herself to return it. If
only he knew how much she'd betrayed him!

'Those stitches you were suffering from – they've disappeared then?' Valentin asks, and Cec's ears prick up.

'Completely!' George grins. 'Those chalk pills helped,
thank you for that, and an acrobat I bumped into at the
Prince's gave me some stretches to do. He gave me quite a
talking to, told me to drink a lot more liquid. But yes, thank
goodness, the damn stitches have been gone for days. I feel
so much better!'

Cec stares at him, stunned. George's pains have gone! *Vanished!*

But if the cure was simply to drink more liquid and stretch,
then . . .

She inhales deeply. A wave of understanding.

Then George's pains were never caused by Skarratt in the first place!

'Are you all right, Cecil? You've gone rather pale,' Valentin says and George leaps to his feet, helping Cec to a chair.

Her mind reels as she sits, silently.

Could it be true? That it was nothing but a trick of her own imagination?

"Magic only works if you believe in it," that's what Valentin had said. But so too do lies . . . and Cec had fallen for Skarratt's.

Oh, he had been clever! Playing on her existing worries and beliefs. The daisy wheel Cec had drawn served not to keep him out of her room, but to give him an insight into her own mind, knowledge that he played on to his advantage. And her frightened reaction, when he threatened to make a poppet of her. . . .

Cec groans quietly to herself, piecing it together, seeing how Skarratt had deliberately fed her powerful imagination, tailoring his lies, and luring her in until she was well and truly trapped.

The bone wand, the skull and tallow candle. Perhaps Skarratt himself believed in his poppets, but Cec sees now that they were no more than cloth and stuffing. His attempts to dabble in black magic nothing but wishful thinking and lies.

'I feel *such* a fool,' Cec says out loud, and Valentin goes to her.

'Why? What's the matter, Cecil?'

She shakes her head. All of it, her betrayal, her lies, her thievery, Skarratt had convinced her to become scared of her own shadow. He was *nothing* like her and Valentin – Roderick Skarratt was simply a violent bully and a fraud!

George offers her a glass of water and she gratefully gulps it down.

'Thank you,' she says.

'Not a headache again?' Valentin asks, concerned, and she shakes her head, lost in thought.

The scales have fallen from Cec's eyes. Fuelled by jealousy and self-importance, Skarratt has played her for a fool. Ensnared her tightly in his web of deceit. Then she will play *him* for a fool too. She has no idea how or when, but Cecily Marsden vows right there and then that she'll get him back, and this time *he* will be the fool.

Eadie has just finished oiling Valentin's trapdoor mechanism when she decides to take a break. Even though she has been trying so very hard to push it from her mind, memories of last night edge back into her mind. Ashton Court. That impossible star. *George* . . .

She tries to shake him from her head as she picks up the photo of her father in the corner of the workshop, wishing he were still here so she might ask his advice. The bank loan is secure, so Bill can pay his deposit, but Eadie is still low on new investors to help her buy him out. Two wealthy men with an interest in philanthropy, both of whom she thought had a good chance of investing, have already turned her down. One of them even told her that, in his view, a woman should not be running a business at all and certainly not one centred around new technology. Then there's 5 Regent Street itself. She cannot believe it will no longer be hers in just a matter of weeks, and she can't bear to think about losing it, yet she cannot risk losing the business either.

As a result, Eadie is throwing herself into work and scaling up production of her films. The profit margin is good and the more successful she is, the better investment prospect someone with deep pockets will surely find her.

George slips back into her mind again. His lips on hers, her pulling him towards her, wanting him so very much. Then the moment of panic, of fear, the sense of falling. She swallows. *Focus, Eadie. Focus!*

She heads into the shop as a customer is leaving, and Chaplin turns to her with a smile. How different everything is in here, Chaplin so much more at ease with people than Bill. And they've had more new customers of late too. Eadie's appearance at Ashton Court and the resultant press coverage has reopened doors to her father's old clients, some of whom are returning for the first time since she took over.

'You've worked wonders, Chaplin,' Eadie says, approvingly, and he nods, pleased.

'Who's that?' he asks, and Eadie realises the photograph of her father is still in her hand.

'My papa.' She smiles fondly as she puts the photograph down on the counter. 'I've been meaning to ask,' she says, awkwardly. 'About George. You said, that time, he reminded you of me. Did you like working with him?'

Chaplin looks surprised. 'Did I *like* it? Of course! How could you not? He's brilliant! Clever, determined, he cares passionately about everything he does. His attention to detail, well, you've seen it. Of course he reminds me of you.'

Eadie raises a faint smile as Chaplin continues. 'And, like you, he's always thinking about the next idea. His imagination's never off. I admire the two of you enormously. I wish my brain worked like yours both do.'

He laughs suddenly. 'We went to see a show once, George and I, by Howard Manners, you know, the famed American magician. He did some excellent tricks, a levitating woman, but the incantation, oh Lord, it was one of the funniest things I've ever heard. You perhaps wouldn't know to look at me, Eadie, but my mother was Hindu you see, and although I can't write or read Hindi, I can speak and understand it well enough. Manners had clearly asked for some 'magic words' when he was off touring in India and, as a joke, they'd taught him a succession of insults. He clearly had no idea what he was saying, he must have learned it phonetically. I started giggling, I couldn't help myself. Imagine! This magician, standing on stage, waving his arms around a floating woman, and saying, in all seriousness, things like "You cursed idiots! Your chins look like a baby's head! You smell of milk and stupidity!" George asked me what the matter was, so I translated it, whispering in his ear. I'm ashamed to say both of us were so helpless with laughter, we had to leave in the interval.'

Chaplin chuckles. 'I *loved* working with him, Eadie. I've kicked myself a thousand times and more for over-indulging that lunchtime. I knew I'd blown it. I broke his trust and, to him, that's everything. I'm sorry it ended badly; but then if I'd never worked with him, I'd never have met Harry.'

'Well, I'm glad you've ended up here instead,' Eadie says. 'I appreciate you taking the risk to do so, giving up your position at the bank.'

'Well, my heart will never lie in finance. And I'm glad I came too, even if it means I have to spend an eternity photographing amateur footballers as penance. Oh, I forgot to say, I bumped into my old manager. I hope you don't mind, but I mentioned about the premises here and he knows someone with a shop on St Nicolas Street, in the heart of town. There'd be no rooms above it, but it's an option at least. For the business.'

'Thank you,' Eadie says, quietly, hoping it won't come to that. 'You know Chaplin, the films are really beginning to sell now – throughout the south-west and beyond – we need to make sure we can offer a ready supply of new ones. I've been contemplating making a smaller camera with a light-weight case.'

'A travelling camera?'

'Exactly. And you know I've long admired your eye for composition. Why don't you come up with some ideas, for films that might require a trip away? I know Harry is keen to travel too, so . . .'

He grins. 'If you insist!'

The bell rings, interrupting them, and Valentin steps in, brass-tipped stick tapping against the floor as he takes off his hat.

'I'm in a bit of a hurry, I'm afraid, Miss Carleton,' he says, after greeting them. 'Is it ready?'

Eadie nods, going into the workshop, and retrieving his mechanism.

'Excellent, thank you.' He smiles. 'I'll test it and report back.' He leans in, looks at her closely. 'Oh, and Mr Perris sends his regards,' he says, smoothly.

'Oh . . .' she murmurs, heat rising to her cheeks.

Valentin's hand is on her arm, a slight pressure as he whispers in her ear. 'Love is a rare and beautiful thing,' he says softly. '*By God, don't waste it, Eadie.*'

He releases her and puts his hat back on, the bell ringing as the front door slams behind him, and Eadie stands, speechless, her heart full.

It is strange, muses Cec, as the queen of hearts floats, suspended in mid-air, in front of her, as she sits on her bed, left hand outstretched. *How powerful bullying and lies can be.* Skarratt's hold over her had been so strong and only now does she see the truth of it.

She tilts her head and, to her surprise, the card tilts too. A gasp of surprise as the card falls to the bed. Pleased, she scoops it back into the pack, tucking it into her pocket.

She cannot change all that has happened, cannot confess her sins either for she is too deeply ensnared, but Cec is almost looking forward to seeing him today. To see his reaction when she finally tells him no, once and for all. A last glance in the mirror, a nod to her reflection, and she is ready.

Cec is deliberately a little late when she turns up at the meeting place she suggested, by the docks near Bristol Bridge. Oz accompanies her, and she feels further emboldened by the small dog's presence. She looks Skarratt directly in the eye, seeing him clearly now. A bully who uses his talent for ill.

'Mr Skarratt,' she says, with a knowing smile, as he nods a greeting. The hubbub of the docks surrounds them, no one taking any notice of two more figures in their midst.

'You seem rather pleased with yourself . . .' he frowns.

'I see you, Mr Skarratt,' Cec says, defiantly. 'I see you for who and what you really are. Your poppets! They are *nothing*. They are simply cloth and stuffing and I will never be afraid of such things again.'

To her surprise, he laughs.

'George Perris has never been in better health!' Cec says, sharply. 'And neither have I. You know, Mr Skarratt, someone once told me that a few lucky people have a touch of *real* magic about them. I thought perhaps one of them might be you. But there's nothing special about you, only jealousy that turns your veins green with envy. So no more skulking, no more lies. I'm done. Understood?'

He smiles, impressed. 'Well now, little urchin, you are quite something! So that's why you called me here today.

But, you forget, I always hold the upper hand. You must surely know by now that I'm far cleverer than you.'

She glares at him. 'Maybe you are cleverer – you have the advantage of years, certainly. But I have an advantage too.'

'Oh? And what might that be?' He looks at her, amused.

'I have *friends*, Mr Skarratt. You only have your sister. And I'm not sure she even likes you. Perhaps she's afraid of you too.'

Cec sees a flash in his eyes and takes a step back.

'Urchin, please. You might have friends *now*, but you won't when they discover you've been spying on them. And then you'll have to come running back to me.' He smiles, wolfishly. 'For all your bravado, let us not forget who holds the cards. Because it isn't you, is it?'

Cec stares at him. 'But your attempts at sabotage, they'll fail without me.'

He chuckles and adjusts his cravat.

'Little urchin, you're very sweet. But I'm not the fool you think me to be. Who's to say I haven't recently recruited someone else? Someone closer to Perris who looks set to be *most* informative. You are not as important as you like to think you are. Know that I will scupper this show with or without you. Now, off you run. Thank you for your service. I know where to come when I need you next.'

The threat is unmistakeable, yet Cec feels a surge of triumph too for Skarratt has let slip he has another collaborator. If she can only find out who it is, she can tell the others, perhaps confess her own sins at the same time. A glimmer of hope. *But who on earth might it be? Closer to Perris . . .?*

Skarratt steps away, narrowly missing a dock worker who curses him. 'Until next time, sweet Cecily!' he says, tipping his hat before striding off.

Oh, Mr Skarratt, Cec thinks with a wry grin, *for all your bravado, it's not you who holds* all *the cards after all.*

Eadie stops, startled. Papa stands with his back to her in the open doorway of Louis's bedroom. *Impossible!* Then the figure turns and it's none other than Louis himself, dressed in Papa's old jacket and hat.

'I thought I'd clear it out in here,' he says. 'Want to give me a hand?'

And suddenly it's all too much. Papa. Louis. The thought of losing Regent Street. Knowing her brother will soon be moving out. And *George*. Kind, brilliant George who she has rejected and hurt when that was the last thing she wanted.

She bursts into sobs.

'Eadie! What's the matter?' Louis puts his arm around her and hands her a handkerchief as she sits down on the edge of his bed. 'What is it?' he asks, concerned, squatting down beside her.

'Everything really.' She sighs. 'It's all too much. The business, the films, not knowing if I can stay here. Not wanting to let anyone down. Valentin. *George* . . .'

Her heart cracks when she says his name.

'Louis,' she ventures, wiping her eyes. 'When you and Max . . . the first time you . . . kissed, were you scared?'

'Petrified,' Louis says, softly. 'It was New Year's Eve, years ago, and he said he'd always wondered what it might be like to kiss a boy. I thought he was teasing me, that he'd guessed how I felt. He told me later that I was his New Year present. But of course I was petrified. So much to lose. But so much to gain too. Why do you ask?'

She shakes her head and he knows better than to push her.

'And Ollie?' she asks.

'It's different,' Louis says, blushing as he smiles. 'Very different. But he's wonderful, Eadie, really he is.' He takes her hands. 'Look, I've had longer to get used to everything about Max but he's gone, Eadie. And even if circumstances had been different, he never would've deserved you anyway.'

'He never deserved you either,' she retorts, and he smiles as he stands.

'It's partly why I wanted to tidy up this room, clear things out. A fresh start. And, besides, you clearly haven't been in here in an age — it's full of dust.'

Eadie looks around at the jumbled items in the room. Failed inventions of her father's, some of his old clothes, the photo of her with Louis and Max. For so long she has shut everything away but perhaps Louis is right. Maybe it is time to face up to it all.

She thinks of George again. The way his face lights up and his eyes glitter when he comes up with a new idea, his laughter as catching as his enthusiasm.

But business and pleasure don't mix, everyone knows that. It was surely for the best that she had already turned down George's supper invitation for tonight . . .

Yet while she can lie to the rest of the world as much as she likes, Eadie Carleton cannot convincingly lie to herself.

It's the night before the get-in – the evening when the team's equipment, costumes, and more, are finally taken inside the theatre. The last few days before their wildly ambitious show.

To mark the occasion, George and Harry have again invited everyone for dinner, to raise a glass to the much-missed Professor, and to celebrate how far they have come.

Cec has promised Valentin she will join them straight after her costume fitting but, once again, she is lying. Miss Pegg, their costume mistress, is long finished by the time Cec sneaks down to Dowry Square. She wears the same maid's dress she wore when she worked for Skarratt, dyed black for The Professor's funeral, grateful that she hadn't got rid of it as she'd first intended.

Ironic, she thinks, *to be wearing his uniform when I'm here to spy on him.*

It's nearly seven o'clock as Cec walks down North Green Street, parallel to the square, heading for a section of wall that leads straight into Skarratt's garden. He might meet this new informant of his anywhere, but surely, when the show is this close, he would go somewhere private. What better place than Skarratt's own house then? And seven is usually the time Skarratt holds his gatherings . . .

Cec is swiftly up and over the wall, grateful to Valentin for his stretching exercises that have made her so supple. She drops to the other side, silently as a cat, darkness around her as she spies the long ladder lying in the grass. The same one she had stood on for Skarratt's séance, after Arter's funeral.

She glances indoors, where the lights are on. Cook busy in the kitchen, steam coming from the range, a clatter of pans. There is no sign of Mabel.

Cec stretches, cracking her knuckles, before lifting the ladder up. It's heavy and she struggles for a moment before finding her balance. As silently as possible, she places it up against the back wall of the house and then steadily climbs it until she finds herself directly underneath the drawing-room window.

It's a cool evening, and the window is only open a crack. Cec can make out Skarratt's voice, though, and Marianne's, too. She waits, biding her time, trying to fend off a faint feeling of cramp in her left foot as she huddles on the ladder, her doubts beginning to grow. What if this is a wasted venture? What if she is seen when she looks through the window? *Come now*, she tells herself. *Have courage! You are finally doing the right thing . . .*

The sound of glasses clinking alerts her and she slowly peeps up to see Skarratt and Marianne talking at the far end of the drawing room. And there, in front of her, a glass of red wine by his lips, is someone whose face she knows well.

The man she has seen many times in Eadie's shop.

'Mr Hodges!' she whispers to herself, covering her mouth with her hand in surprise.

Chaplin, seeing the movement out of the corner of his eye, glances up to see her peeping in at the window. A look of horror as he drops his wine glass and both Skarratt and Marianne turn towards him, puzzled.

Cec's heart is in her throat as she ducks, sliding down the ladder as fast as she can. '*Mr Chaplin Hodges!*' she gasps to herself.

This time, she knows *exactly* where to go.

Eadie is surprised to find a flustered Cec on her doorstep, dressed, for some reason, in a maid's outfit.

'You said I could talk to you! About anything, you said!' Cec pleads.

'Of course!' Eadie says, puzzled. 'Come in. What's the matter?'

'Chaplin Hodges!' Cec says, as she follows Eadie upstairs. 'Mr Hodges who works with you. He's been spying on you, on George and Valentin! He's been spying for Roderick Skarratt!'

Eadie turns to her, astonished.

'*Cec!* I cannot—'

'I *knew* you wouldn't believe me!' Cec cries. 'I barely believe it myself. But I saw him! At Skarratt's! I saw him!'

'Perhaps there's some other explanation?'

'It *is* him, miss! I know it is.' Cec looks down at the floor. 'I know it because Mr Skarratt had been making *me* spy on you all, for weeks. Then he let slip he'd found someone else. And I couldn't tell you before, because—' Cec bursts into tears.

Eadie stands speechless, shocked by the young woman's outburst. She puts an arm around her. 'Oh, goodness! Cec! It'll be all right. But first you have to tell me *everything*. The whole truth. Look me in the eye and tell me you'll do so.'

Cec looks up at her, teary-eyed. 'I swear, I never wanted any of this to happen. Skarratt lied to me; he tricked me!'

'You'd better start at the beginning,' Eadie says, firmly.

Cec does so. All of it tumbling out. The strange events at Skarratt's house, the poppet of George. She tells Eadie everything.

'Oh, Cec,' Eadie says to her softly, when she has finished. 'You've been taken advantage of – blackmailed and bullied. Perhaps you should've come to one of us sooner and told the truth, but I can see why you didn't. I must say, though, I still can't believe Chaplin would betray us.' She pauses, to think. 'George and Harry are hosting this supper tonight and everyone will be there. If we hurry, we can catch them. Tell them everything you've already told me.'

'All right,' says Cec, swallowing. 'Do you think they'll believe me?'

'Oh, Cec . . . You just need to tell the truth, that's all.' Eadie smiles at her, sympathetically, before smoothing her day dress down. She isn't dressed for supper having planned not to attend.

'I'll have to go like this I'm afraid,' Eadie says. 'I've been working late.' The thought of seeing George again makes her heart ache and now she must go to this supper of his after all *and* bring this most unexpected of news. 'Come,' she says, reaching for her coat. 'We must make haste. And, Cec, you must tell *everyone* the truth, no matter how hard it is.'

'I didn't think you'd believe me,' Cec says, quietly. 'He said – Skarratt – when you all knew the truth, you'd shun me forever.'

'Oh, Cec! That's not how friendship works!' Eadie says. 'Now, come on, let's do this together.'

She offers her hand and Cec takes it, holding it tightly as they leave.

George takes out his pocket watch and checks the time, impatient for Harry to arrive so they can get supper over with as swiftly as possible. He leans on the bookcase in the parlour, wishing he were working. At least then he could distract himself, but all he can think about now is Eadie. 'Too busy with work – unlikely to be able to attend but thank you for the invitation,' her note had said, but he knows she's avoiding him.

He sighs. Tomorrow, then, will be the first time he's seen her since Ashton Court, and he has no idea what he might say.

'You hate poor time-keeping as much as Eadie!' Louis laughs, taking a sip of wine as George looks away.

'George, please. Sit down,' Valentin says. 'This is supposed to be a happy occasion! Besides, Cec isn't here yet either. It's not just Harry we're waiting on.'

Valentin motions to a chair and George relents, sitting for a moment, before the doorbell rings and Oz barks.

'I say, Valentin, that's the noisiest I've ever heard that dog,' George says. 'I don't suppose you've replaced him? Those terriers all look the same to me.'

Valentin laughs, heartily, as Cec bursts in with Eadie by her side. George is startled to see Eadie so unexpectedly, and he blushes, noting that her cheeks flush at the sight of him too.

'Chaplin Hodges!' Cec says, out of breath.

'What about him?' George asks, bemused.

'Roderick Skarratt. Marianne Carnesky,' Cec says in a rush. 'And Chaplin Hodges.'

'What on earth do you mean?' George leaps to his feet.

'Cec believes Chaplin has been spying for Skarratt,' Eadie explains, apologetically. 'And I'm afraid Cec herself was being blackmailed by Skarratt too. For some time.'

A wave of horror flows over George. *So it was Cec who leaked the plans after all!*

'Good Lord!' says Louis, his glass of wine frozen in mid-air.

'My God! *Cec!*' George says, furious and hurt. 'Why didn't you tell us? Do you know what we've put into this venture? And all this time . . .'

Cec's chin wobbles as she stands there, ashamed and on the verge of tears.

'It wasn't her fault, George,' Eadie says, firmly. 'Skarratt is clever and far more manipulative than we'd given him credit for. Please.' She steps towards him, and the touch of her consoling hand deflates his anger for a moment.

George glances at Valentin, who looks as if he's aged a decade or more.

'I'm so sorry . . .' Cec whispers, as Eadie takes up her story for her: the poppets; the blackmail; the cabinet of curios; and the séances. She asks Cec to clarify the details, all as George's mind is a-whirl.

'He has a *poppet* of me?' George runs his hands through his hair, bemused.

And then Eadie mentions his stitches. That all this time Cec had thought they, and her own headaches, were caused by Skarratt.

George sighs. *Such a simple deceit, brilliant in a way.* He remembers then an after-show party, in London, last year, when a stitch had come upon him at the drinks reception. Skarratt had been there, uninvited of course, and George had noticed his eyes upon him, a watchful smirk upon his face.

'I promised Mr Skarratt I'd never tell what went on,' Cec says, sorrowfully.

'You made a promise to me too, Cecil.' Finally, Valentin speaks, holding up his left palm.

'I'm *so sorry*, Valentin! I'm so sorry, all of you,' Cec says, trying not to cry. 'I never wanted to hurt anyone. I never wanted to lie. I've never felt so happy in my life than working with you all. And, Valentin, you've been kinder and more generous than I ever knew existed in the world. He made me betray you! I'll understand if you never want to see me again, I will.'

'Chaplin *bloody* Hodges!' George says, between gritted teeth.

'It might not be all that it appears . . .' Eadie says, softly, her hand still on George's arm. 'I believe he's a good man, George. There *must* be some mistake.'

'I'm sorry!' Cec says, tearfully. 'Believe me, I'm so sorry.'

'You're sure, Cec?' George asks. 'About Chaplin?'

She nods. 'I saw him through the drawing-room window. Just the three of them. Him, Skarratt and Marianne.'

George nods. 'Then what other possible explanation could there be?'

But the answer comes sooner than any of them expects as Harry bursts into the parlour, closely followed by Chaplin Hodges himself.

'You've got a damn cheek being here! Selling our secrets to Roderick bloody Skarratt!' growls George as Louis gets to his feet and helps Eadie gently restrain him.

'But *she's* the one leaking information!' Harry cries, glaring at Cec. 'She's been the leak all along!'

George is too furious to listen. Blinded by his own fury, he wrestles himself out of Louis and Eadie's grip, and swings at Chaplin, hitting him on the nose and knocking him to the floor.

'*George!*' Harry cries, flinging herself to her knees at Chaplin's side, as Louis grabs George by his elbows and pulls him backwards. '*I asked him to do it!*' she says furiously, glaring at her brother, as Chaplin sits up, startled, trying to stem the blood trickling from his nose.

'What?!'

'I asked him to do it! You bloody *idiot*, George! You really think I'd let all our work go to waste? I've been so worried! The attempted burglaries, the leak in the paper! A determined effort to target us. I was certain Skarratt had an insider, someone within the team who he had direct access to.

Chaplin's been waiting for a way in. And tonight Skarratt finally let slip that one of his old maids had been "very useful." Who else might that be but *her*?' Harry helps Chaplin to his feet, glaring at Cec as she does so.

A smile unexpectedly starts to creep up Valentin's face and he titters, a titter that evolves first into a chuckle, and then a guffaw, as tears roll down his cheeks.

'Valentin?' ventures Eadie, as everyone turns and stares at him in surprised silence.

'I'm afraid,' he says, wiping his tears, 'there have been *two* double agents at work for our little team today.' He looks at Harry and Chaplin. 'Cecil has rather beaten you to it. Skarratt has played a lot more dirtily than any of us realised. I wish Cecil had told us the truth before tonight . . .' Cec hangs her head in shame. 'But, as her guardian, I must take responsibility too.' He turns to Cec. 'I should have taken better care of you, Cecil. And I certainly should have known better than to trust a rogue like Skarratt to keep to his word. Mr Hodges, we owe you an apology. Perhaps George most of all.'

'Well,' says Louis, releasing his hold on George, 'I don't know about anyone else, but I'm going to need more wine.'

George exhales loudly. *This is what you get*, he thinks, *when people aren't honest*. 'I think we're *all* going to need more wine,' he says, quietly. 'I'm terribly sorry, Hodges. It seems I'm the one who must apologise this time.'

'Think nothing of it, old chap,' Chaplin says, good-humouredly, his voice muffled by the handkerchief clutched to his nose.

'Just one thing, Harry,' George says slowly, thinking things through. 'Why did you ask *Chaplin* to help?'

Harry and Chaplin glance at each other guiltily.

'We thought it would be a good cover,' Harry says, quietly. 'You having sacked him before. That perhaps he might be out for revenge. And' – she hesitates – 'now's probably not the right time to tell you but, well, Chaplin and I are engaged, George. We have been for some time.'

George lets her words sink in. *Chaplin. Engaged to Harry.* He glances at Eadie and she shrugs, a faint smile too. *Then there is nothing between Eadie and Chaplin!* He had hoped as much but here was the proof! *It may not change the fact she pushed me away but it is*, George thinks, *a much-needed glimmer of light*.

He turns towards Chaplin and pulls him into an embrace, reaching for Harry too. 'Then congratulations!' he says. 'That's the best news I've heard in an age! Welcome to the family, Hodges!'

Harry and Chaplin exchange a look of surprise over George's shoulder. Whatever reaction the couple had been expecting from George, this was certainly not it.

When Cec and Valentin return to Royal York Crescent, Cec is still petrified he'll throw her out; that this glorious new world he introduced her to will be lost forever.

The whole way back, in the cab, he doesn't say a single word, and now he simply gestures for her to seat herself at the dining table, wordlessly making her cocoa, before he joins her.

'Cecil. I'm not angry, I promise,' he says. 'But I do need you to tell me everything again. Slowly, and in as much detail as you can muster.'

And so she does. From Skarratt's exact words, to the strangeness of his study. She tells him of Skarratt's rage after her mistake with the lights, the papier-mâché face hanging in the chimney for all to see. She describes the ladder at the back of the house, the boxes of notebooks and cabinet of keys, of her suspicions about the cab that nearly ran them over. All of it.

The truth pours out of her, unstoppered. She confesses all of her sins — and her worries too: her nerves about the show, how queasy she feels standing onstage, looking out at the vast auditorium. How terrible she feels for letting them all down.

Valentin listens silently, nodding encouragement.

When Cec has finished, she waits for him to speak, but it is some time before he finally replies.

'I had thought you were a little like Olivia,' he says, softly. 'I suppose I hoped that by taking you under my wing, by saving you from Skarratt, somehow, I was saving her too. I let the past blind me to the present and I put too much on your young shoulders, neglecting my duties as your protector. Much as I might wish to make up for the past, you are your own self, Miss Marsden. And so, it is I who must apologise too.'

'You won't throw me out then?' Cec asks, hopefully.

'Oh, Cecil, really! All these years of searching for someone else like me! You don't get rid of me that easily. Not yet.'

'I wish I'd told you the truth sooner,' Cec says, quietly. 'After that first time with Skarratt – but seeing George doubled over in pain and having found that box of poppets . . . Knowing what you and I can do, it seemed so real. I feel such a fool.'

'Skarratt is a nasty man, Cecil. I think we all know that now. But alas the law does not work very effectively when it comes to such things. One must have evidence, something we are sorely lacking.'

'But he's dangerous, Valentin! He'll stop at nothing. Please don't underestimate him. He got into the dressing rooms, pretending to be Mr Greenhouse didn't he? And he wanted to sabotage George's copper tank!'

She looks at him pleadingly and he smiles reassuringly at her.

'But, Cecil, the get-in is tomorrow. Skarratt has failed. We have security on the doors of the theatre every hour of the day. No one without permission can get anywhere close to getting inside. What could he possibly do?'

'But he can be so unpredictable, so violent! And he said he'd scupper the show, come what may.'

'Cecil. Please. Put your mind at rest. Everything is in place, I promise you. He has failed.'

Cec nods reluctantly, hoping with all her heart that he is right. She looks at Valentin as the light from the hearth flickers over his face.

'Valentin . . . This Olivia,' Cec says quietly. 'You've never really told me who she was. And I think I'd like to know.'

Valentin looks away as his face falls and he takes a deep breath before turning back to her. 'Very well,' he says. And he tells her everything, much more than he had George. The holidays, the friendship, the laughter. The years of happiness. And that dreadful day that robbed him of both Olivia and baby Robert.

Cec reaches out and tightly holds his hand, the faint parallel line of their scars touching, as Valentin wipes away his tears.

So that is why he left England, all those years ago. This kind, generous man who has given her so much. Cec only wishes she could give him something in return.

Early the next morning, Cec is at the theatre with her small notepad, crossing off every item as it arrives. She's taking her duties very seriously, more grateful than ever for this second chance. It was all out in the open now – and Skarratt had been wrong; Valentin and Eadie, George and Harry, they remain her friends despite it all.

This time she will not let any of them down.

There has been no sign of Skarratt and security on the front doors of the theatre – the only way in or out – is now extremely tight and will be until the show is over.

Cec smiles as she ticks off props from The Professor's collection that Valentin and she are to use in the show. Boxes and trunks, a greenhouse flat-packed into glass and steel, boards and ropes, silks and chains. A medley of intrigue and mystery.

Valentin watches from the stalls until Cec waves him over.

'All in,' she says, showing him the checklist.

'Good,' he says, with a sigh of relief.

'I've been practising too!' Cec says. 'Look!' She holds her notepad out before making it disappear, leaning forward and retrieving it from within Valentin's waistcoat as he laughs merrily.

Cec grins, flicking through the notepad to pull out a single card which she places in his jacket pocket. She taps it three times and pulls out an unopened pack of cards, handing it back to him.

Valentin's eyes twinkle proudly. 'We'll make a fine conjuror out of you yet, young Cecil!'

Outside the theatre, George and Harry are helping Louis and the Hogarths unload their engineering marvels from a huge cart. To hide their secrets from prying eyes – and to better drum up excitement – George has covered everything in brightly coloured cloths, and a crowd gathers to watch the mysterious items be taken inside. There's a loud cheer as the last object finally heads in and, as a thank you, George performs a couple of tricks for the impromptu audience. One last bow and then George disappears inside too, doors locked behind him.

'You couldn't resist!' Harry teases, and George grins as they walk arm in arm into the auditorium, the huge space filled with a flurry of activity. *Not long now* . . . Despite Skarratt's efforts, they have surely succeeded.

George smiles as he spots Cec next to Valentin in the wings, frowning with concentration. All of them, from

Valentin to his own self, had asked an awful lot of someone so young and inexperienced, despite her obvious flair for performance. Valentin was right – as her guardian, he should have kept a closer eye on her.

Eadie walks out onstage, to supervise where her projector will sit, and George's heart skips. After the revelations last night, she had made her excuses and slipped back to Regent Street whilst he was still talking to Chaplin. He had so hoped to talk to her, to say *something*. He shouldn't have kissed her, but yet she *did* pull him towards her – didn't she? He's gone over it so many times in his head that he can't truly remember.

Harry nudges him. 'Go on,' she says. 'Talk to her!'

'It's awkward, Harry . . .'

'Listen, I don't know what's going on between the two of you, but please, go and un-awkward it!' she says, pushing him forward. But a stagehand accosts George and by the time they've finished speaking, Eadie has vanished.

Later, after almost everyone has left for the night – the technicians; the stage manager; even Miss Pegg, the costume mistress – a small group remains in the backstage office: George and Harry, Valentin, Cec and Eadie.

'Everything's on schedule,' Cec says, checking her list again.

'All to plan.' Valentin smiles. 'Although, just one more thing . . . A little entertainment before we leave for the night.'

Cec stands, looking nervous. 'Mr Perris, there's something behind your ear,' she says.

George frowns, reaching behind his ear to find a folded playing card. He laughs, unfolding it to reveal it as a joker. 'How ever did you do that?' he asks, incredulously.

'Oh, and Eadie, you might wish to look up your sleeve,' Cec says, growing more confident as Eadie reaches for her sleeve, only to find a handful of red paper hearts inside. She shakes them out onto the table with a smile, catching George's eye and looking away with a blush.

'And, Harry,' Cec continues. 'There's something in your hat!'

Harry goes to the hat stand and jumps with surprise. 'Oh, my goodness! I thought it was real, but it's carved from a carrot!' She laughs, holding up an orange goldfish. 'Oh, Cec! That's marvellous!'

She applauds and the others follow suit as Cec bows and Oz barks his approval.

'And, Valentin, you might wish to check your waistcoat pocket,' Cec says. He reaches into it and takes out a playing card. On the back is written, 'All done by kindness', and he shows it to the little gathering.

'I hope you don't mind me borrowing it, George,' Cec says. 'It just seems right, after last night. You've all been so kind, so forgiving, more than I could've hoped for.'

'And your last trick?' Valentin reminds her, and Cec reaches into her pocket, only to realise she's left her playing cards in the wings.

'Oh! I'll go and get them,' she says. 'Sorry! I forgot I left them there . . .' She slips out of the room and upstairs, heart filled with light and happiness at performing for her friends, at having been accepted back into the fold. *Friends* – the word still feels a little odd to her.

When she reaches the stage, all is in darkness, just as they had left it. Her pack of cards on a small side table in the wings, where the stage manager will sit for the show. She grins. *Not long now, Cec*, she tells herself. She goes to reach for the main lights but something makes her pause before she does so. Her senses suddenly alert. A tingling in her palms.

Someone else is here.

Puzzled, she stands still for a moment, straining to listen. She is sure none of the others followed her up here – then who might it be?

There's a faint shuffle, a footstep that isn't hers, and silently Cec pads forward. She edges her way around the curtain to see a lit match. A glow of orange that suddenly goes out. She waits, holding her breath, until another match is struck. *Skarratt*. Lighting a cigarette. She freezes, panicked suddenly, unsure what to do.

Another match flares and she sees him more clearly this time, holding the light up as he examines George's giant copper tank onstage. *Almost as if he were admiring his own reflection!* Cec thinks, angrily. But how did he get in? The doors are locked, Fintan the theatre manager made sure of it, and the security men are keeping watch outside. Only Valentin has a spare key, to lock up after they leave tonight.

'I see you, Mr Skarratt!' Cec says boldly, her voice echoing around the empty auditorium. 'I don't know how you managed to get in, but I suggest you leave immediately.'

Another match strikes, a sly grin, as he looks towards her. 'Sweet Cecily. I'd have thought you'd be in bed by now.'

'So you snuck in? Thinking the theatre to be empty?' she replies, sharply.

The match goes out and darkness encompasses her. *The roof!* Cec thinks suddenly. *The door to the roof! That's how he must have got in!*

She listens for his footsteps but there is nothing. Then his voice, directly by her ear, through gritted teeth.

'Oh, little urchin, what *trouble* you cause me . . .' She feels his hands grabbing at her, holding her fast. 'Even more than my wife and she was a difficult wretch!'

Cec exclaims and he puts a hand over her mouth to silence her.

'You think it's funny?' he snaps, his voice cold as ice. 'I know it was you who made Mabel leave. Now Mrs Jamieson has gone too. The house empty! And me left to fend for myself like a pauper! *I won't have it!* I won't be defeated by Perris or by any of you!'

Cec bites him on his hand and tries to wriggle free, but he knocks her to the floor, where she lies for a moment, winded.

A match flares again and Cec sees him, centre stage, his eyes wild, as he throws the lit match onto the boards.

A spark, a flicker.

'*No!*' she moans, reaching for it with her left hand from where she lies, hoping to extinguish it, to crush it to nothing with her touch of the impossible. The golden flame dies and Cec's heart races with relief as she struggles to stand. She dashes to the wall and blindly searches in the darkness for the switch for the main lights.

'Help!' she tries to cry but she is still breathless from being pushed to the ground. Suddenly someone is next to her and she gasps, thinking it to be Skarratt again, but Valentin's voice is in her ear instead.

'It's me. I know he's here. I heard him. Are you all right?'

She gives a sob as a flicker of light bursts into life onstage. A glimpse of Skarratt's silhouette by the rich velvet curtains over the far side of the stage, as they catch fire behind him. And then he disappears, a running shadow, along the back of the stalls and out into darkness.

A loud click and the house lights come on. Valentin stands beside Cec, his hand on the switch, face stone-like with fury.

'Fire!' Valentin shouts. '*Fire!*'

Everything becomes a blur. The sound of running feet as the others rush to join Cec and Valentin, leaping into action. George's look of horror as he fetches buckets of sand and water, passing them to a shocked Eadie. No time to talk, to explain, they all focus on extinguishing the fire as quickly as they can. Cec takes the bucket from Eadie and passes it to Valentin who throws the contents at the flames before passing it back along the line. Harry is despatched to fetch the fire brigade and, for a moment, Cec thinks it might be all right, containable. That the whole event will be a nasty incident, no more.

She is wrong.

The inflammable curtains are proving to be anything but as the fire spreads up into the fly. Backdrops splutter, spitting sparks as the flames lick around them. Doggedly, the four of them – George and Valentin, Cec and Eadie – continue their efforts, but the supplies of sand soon start to run low . . .

By the time Harry returns, the fire has escalated, greedily turning everything it touches into ash and smoke. The air now thick with a dense smoke that catches at the back of Cec's throat even as she doggedly passes along the buckets, hand to hand. Too little, too late.

None of it will be enough.

An intense heat starts to build, and George's metal tank begins to lean to one side, softening in the heat. Cec sees the anguish on his face as the truth of it dawns on him.

They have lost control. Their faces now covered in black soot, the smoke builds, sweat running in rivulets down their backs.

'Everyone out!' George orders. '*Now!*'

He catches sight of a figure in the wings and runs towards it on impulse, but as George gets closer, he realises it's simply a hatstand bearing a cloak and a hat, a prop from a past show. Not a person at all. Yet it had seemed so real!

He turns back just in time to see Valentin collapse in the aisle and Cec trying to break his fall. George runs to them, bending down and picking Valentin up, lifting him over his shoulder, Oz barking at his feet.

'Get out!' George cries, his voice desperate. '*Everyone out! Now!*'

Cec scoops Oz up under her arm and counts everyone in her head. *Valentin with George, Eadie and Harry behind, Oz under my arm.*

She sobs as she follows George along the aisle but there's a noise behind her, a strange creaking groan, as if the theatre itself were alive. Cec turns as a piece of the ceiling, a huge ornate chunk of plaster, plummets to the ground, the smoke making it impossible for her to see where it lands. A scream of agony pierces her to the marrow and she knows she must turn back.

'Go!' Cec cries to Oz as she steps into the foyer and pushes him out of the front door. 'Out!' and with that she turns, heading back into the auditorium and the direction of the scream.

Eadie crouches by Harry, trying her best to lift the heavy plaster from her friend's leg – but it's too much for her to shift alone.

'I won't leave you!' she shouts as Harry pushes her away, face pale, insistent that Eadie save herself.

When Cec appears, face streaked with tears, Eadie is relieved to see her. The two of them work together to try and lift Harry out, even as the fire works its way towards them, up the rich woollen carpets, along the velvet-covered chairs.

'*Hurry!*' Eadie says, but although, between them, they can just about lift the plaster, they cannot also pull Harry out from underneath.

Cec suddenly frowns, her face full of concentration. She closes her eyes and breathes slowly through her nose, lifting her head up to the ceiling. And it's the most extraordinary thing — and later, Eadie will think she imagined it — but it's as if an extra pair of hands is helping them. The plaster lifts, more easily this time, falling to one side, and Eadie and Cec pull Harry out, by now unconscious.

And then George is there, covering his mouth with his sleeve, coughing with the smoke. Eadie had been so focused on Harry that seeing George almost overpowers her. He gently lifts his sister up, carrying her in his arms, Eadie and Cec following, as the firemen finally arrive, urgently ushering them out onto the street.

The little group stands, soot-stained and shocked, on the far side of Park Row as flames shoot out of the theatre's roof and windows, the whole of the interior now alight.

Valentin slowly revives, Cec by his side and Oz licking his hand, but Harry remains unconscious, her leg at a peculiar angle, as a distressed George tries to wake her. Eadie watches, numbed, as the police arrive, carrying stretchers for the injured. They gently lift Harry onto one and Valentin, protesting, onto another.

A hand on Eadie's shoulder. She looks around to find George there, his face streaked with tears. 'There's nothing you can do,' he says, softly. 'Nothing any of us can do now. Go home, Eadie.'

And with that he's gone, accompanying Harry to the Royal Infirmary as Eadie stands, motionless and broken-hearted, unable to look away from the inferno as everything they worked so hard for disappears into smoke and ashes.

BRISTOL MERCURY, Thursday 23rd April, 1896

BLAZE AT PRINCE'S THEATRE

The Prince's Theatre on Park Row was destroyed by fire last night. Flames were discovered at eleven o'clock in the evening and, four hours later, only the stone walls were left standing. The rooms and office in the basement were also destroyed, although the Bristol Fire Brigade prevented the fire from affecting neighbouring buildings. The magicians Mr George Perris and The Great Valentini, who were employed in the theatre at the time, have lost all their effects, and the scenery was also consumed. Mr Perris's assistant, his sister Miss Harriet Perris, was seriously injured but no lives were lost. The building had been described as one of the finest in the South West.

He looks so thin, Cec thinks, as she sits beside Valentin's bed in the ward, wrinkling her nose at the strange whiff of chemicals and starch.

'I feel much better, really I do.' He smiles faintly. 'Enough to return home, anyway.' He coughs into a handkerchief. 'The smoke must have overcome me.'

'It's all my fault,' Cec says, miserably. 'If only I'd told you earlier about Skarratt!'

'But even if you had, Cecil, who could have predicted he would stoop to such a thing?'

'We must tell the police! We must tell them everything!'

'Come now, you seriously think he will not have an alibi? His sister ready to swear on oath he was home all evening? Our word against his. I know it was him, I heard his voice, caught a glimpse of him as he ran. But would it stand up in a court of law? No, it would not.'

'Then he'll get away with it!' Cec drops her voice to a whisper. 'I tried, Valentin – the first spark, onstage. I put it out, I know I did! And then with Harry, I helped lift the plaster off her, I did. But what difference did it make in the end? We've lost everything!'

'Not everything, Cecil. We are alive, are we not? And a little magic is always better than none.'

'But what use is it if you cannot *save* things?'

'You saved Harry! You went back for your friend and helped rescue her. You think you cannot change things, Cecil? Harry would not be here if it weren't for you!'

'I couldn't save the theatre, though!'

He sighs. 'No one could . . .'

'But how do we get Skarratt back? He's ruined *everything*!'

Valentin pushes back his blankets and swings his legs out of bed. 'At times like this, it's easy to think that all is over, Cecil, but it isn't. Not yet. We are alive, that's the main thing.' He looks at her. 'When one is angry, it's always best to let it cool before deciding on a plan of action.'

He smiles, slowly getting to his feet. 'Now, come, you need to get me home. Oz will be pining, and we can't have that, can we?'

George stands in what's left of the auditorium, surveying the wreckage: strange shards of metal twisted and curled into abstract shapes; the remnants of the stage still smouldering as rags and tatters of curtains and backdrops flutter in the breeze.

There's nothing left of George's beautiful copper tank bar a lump of blackened metal. It had cost so much to build, hammered into curves, riveted into shape, polished until it shone.

George coughs, the smoke still irritating his lungs. He has lost much, yet he knows it could have been worse. He thinks of Harry and is grateful she is safe. The break in her leg is clean and expected to heal well, and he takes some solace from that at least.

A crunch of feet behind him makes him turn to see Eadie, tired and pale.

'I thought you might be here,' she says.

George nods, glancing up to where the roof once was, to the open sky now filled with gulls circling overhead, oblivious to the disaster that has unfolded beneath them.

Eadie looks towards where the stage was, at the melted mass that was once her beloved projector. At least she has others, in the workshop, along with copies of the films she was going to show. She counts herself relatively lucky. Unlike George, who has lost his props, his show, and nearly his own sister too . . .

'George . . .' she ventures, and he turns to her with a look of such sadness that it takes all her willpower not to just throw her arms around him and weep.

'We should talk to everyone. See if anything might be salvaged. Valentin suggested meeting at your house tomorrow. It'll give us time to gather ourselves.'

He nods slowly and Eadie's heart breaks for him. She had so wanted to be onstage with him again, hoping that the joy of performing together as they had at Ashton Court might restore things between them. That perhaps he might lean into her one more time, his lips on hers . . .

She reaches out to him; she can't help herself, her hand on his shoulder, but he steps away, too distraught to even register her touch.

Rebuffed, Eadie takes one last look at the charred wreckage, before turning and picking her way out of the ruins, leaving George behind, staring on in disbelief.

At least he is dressed properly today, Cec thinks, glad to see him back in his suit and no longer in his pyjamas, as Valentin slowly walks into the sitting room to join her. He had slept for hours after returning home from hospital but it's been two days now and both he and Cec have barely left the house.

'More post has arrived!' she says, brightly, gesturing to the large pile on the table as she hands him a cup of tea. Harry has still not been discharged from hospital and George has postponed any planned gathering until her return. In truth though, all of them are still trying to process the shock. An electrical fault. That's what the police believe to have started the fire. But Cec knows differently. Her fists clench without her even realising. Roderick Skarratt. *He could have killed us all!*

'We need time,' Valentin says, sipping at his tea. 'Time and fresh air.' He glances at her fists. 'You're thinking of Skarratt again, Cecil. But our focus must be on justice, not revenge.'

'Why? What's wrong with revenge?' Cec frowns.

'Revenge is fuelled by anger. An eye for an eye, a tooth for a tooth. We could set fire to Skarratt's house if we were so inclined. End up in jail ourselves. Revenge would have been served but not justice. For that we need a clear head. And we will have justice, I promise you.'

'How?'

'We'll work it out. Between us.' He smiles, finishing his tea. 'I'll take Oz for a walk.'

As they both step outside, Valentin turns to her.

'Actually, would you mind, Cecil? A little time on my own.'

'All right,' she says. 'But what am I to do? Please, give me something, Valentin. I feel useless otherwise.'

'You can make a start on opening those letters if you like.'

She embraces Valentin suddenly and he laughs.

'Go on,' he says fondly, releasing her. 'Off with you.'

She watches him go, Oz trailing behind, but when she turns back, there's a figure at the far end of the crescent. She recognises him at once. The hat at a jaunty angle, his distinctive walk as he comes towards her.

Skarratt.

The sight of him fills her with rage but she takes a deep breath to calm herself. *Justice not revenge*, she tells herself as he approaches, a smile on his face. But there's something different, in his eyes, and she can't quite place it.

'My sweet Cecily,' he says, smoothly. 'My little urchin.'

She waits for him to speak.

'You know, the police came,' he says. 'Asked if I knew anything about the fire.'

She waits for a moment, her anger rising as she stares at him.

'I'm sorry for Miss Perris,' Skarratt says, quietly. 'That was most unfortunate, but it was all right in the end. Wasn't it? After all, no one died.'

Cec frowns at him. With a jolt, she realises what the look in his eyes is. *Fear.*

'Why've you come?' she asks. 'If the police *were* sniffing around, it's nothing to do with me. I've not whispered a word of it to them. What good will it do? It won't bring the theatre back.'

'And Valentin and the others?'

Cec thinks on her feet. Better to keep Skarratt on side. For now at least.

'None of them know the truth,' she lies, seeing the fear vanish from his eyes, the relief on his face.

'Good,' he says. 'Best they don't, eh?'

'You shouldn't have done it,' she says. 'Any of it. But you got what you wanted. George is a wreck. The theatre destroyed. You've won.'

He smiles slowly, all white teeth, and Cec loathes him more than ever. *Calm*, she tells herself, her heart racing at the mere presence of this cruel and nasty man. *Justice. Not revenge . . .*

She looks him in the eye. 'Oh and it's sweet *cicely*, by the way,' she adds, before heading back indoors. 'The flower. It's not Cecily at all, Mr Skarratt. I thought you should know.'

When Cec is safely back in the warmth of Valentin's sitting room and has calmed herself down a little, she looks at the pile of unopened letters and telegrams on the table. So many of them! Valentin hadn't yet felt up to opening any of them let alone reading their contents and now she must do so on his behalf. Cec takes a deep breath, reaches for the letter opener, and begins.

Eadie's hair still smells of smoke no matter how many times she tries to wash it out. Whenever she shuts her eyes, she sees it again. The flames. The panic. Harry's anguished face as she lay, trapped underneath the plaster. And George. *Oh, George* . . . The last time she saw him, he had stepped away from her in the rubble of the theatre, out of her reach. Chaplin has barely left Harry's bedside at the hospital and Eadie hasn't been able to face opening the shop on her own. For the first time in years, E. D. Carleton Photographic has been closed for an entire week.

'Eadie, what on earth are you doing?'

She glances up from where she stands, in the workshop, beating a thin sheet of metal on a workbench as Louis stands in the door.

'Making a start on a new projector,' she says quietly, before resuming her hammer work.

'Eadie . . .'

'It's fine, Louis, really.'

'It's not fine. Look at you! You have to rest.'

'I *am* resting!'

'Work isn't resting!'

'Well what else can I do?' she snaps at him. 'What else can I do, Louis? George is barely replying to my notes. Harry's only today being discharged from hospital. All this time I've been waiting for us to meet up. To see what might be salvaged, but no one else seems ready. Not even Valentin and Cec.'

She reaches for the tea that Jenny made her earlier only to find it stone cold.

Eadie hits the metal sheet again with a hammer, harder and harder, until she drops the hammer on the floor, narrowly missing her own feet. She howls. And Louis is suddenly by her side, his arms around her, holding her tight as she bursts into sobs.

'Eadie, you can't *keep* bottling things up,' he says, softly, as she leans into him. 'It's not good for you. And it will be all right, I promise.'

How will it? She wants to ask. *How?* But she cannot bring herself to say it.

George stands, bereft, by The Professor's mausoleum in Arnos Vale cemetery. 'I wish you were here . . .' he says quietly, under his breath, looking up at the large marble structure. 'By God, I wish you were still here.'

He's barely allowed himself to think of the consequences of the fire for he's surely bankrupt, all that investment and equipment turned to ash. And yet, it could have been far worse. *Harry.* He'd spent days going back and forth to the hospital, sitting by her side, until she gently pointed out that she wanted some time alone with her fiancé. He had left Chaplin and her to it. Instead, he had distracted himself by clearing out the loft, re-laying some of the timbers and using it for storage. He'd kept himself busy in the empty house, avoiding the flood of letters and telegrams that had come, avoiding too Hugh Greenhouse's requests for a meeting.

He glances at his pocket watch, knowing that Harry is due home shortly, before taking one last look at the mausoleum. He wasn't entirely sure why he'd come, perhaps hoping for some miracle, a glimmer of hope or inspiration. Instead, he'd found only birdsong and sorrow. His mind turns to the offer made to him all those months ago, the residency at the Egyptian Hall, and for the first time, he regrets turning it down.

George runs his hands through his hair. Everything feels so topsy turvy. He knows he should have made an effort to see them since – Valentin and Cec, and Eadie too. *Oh, Eadie!* But like the ever-growing pile of telegrams and letters he'd been ignoring, even the thought of it was too overwhelming.

The toll of a nearby church reminds George that he needs to be on his way home, to be in time for Harry. A final nod to The Professor's resting place and then he is gone.

The subsequent gathering, a few days later at the Perrises' home, is a rather subdued one as the group sit, crammed together in the dining room. A despairing George sits at the top of the table with Harry on his left, and Cec and Valentin beyond. On his right sits Eadie, then Louis and Chaplin, with the Hogarth twins squeezed in at the far end.

'I spoke to Greenhouse earlier,' George says, quietly. 'He's talking to the investors to see what might be recovered but Skarratt's won. If he wanted to ruin me, he has well and truly succeeded.'

'No,' Valentin says, firmly. 'He's *stopped* us, George. For now. But he cannot stop us forever. Jealousy must never be allowed to win.'

'But we cannot bring him to justice!' George protests. 'An electrical fault indeed. And he has an alibi just as you predicted! Then how can we possibly defeat him?'

'I wish we could disappear him somehow!' Ollie Hogarth says, sharply. 'I still don't understand how he got past security.'

'The roof,' Cec says. 'It's the only explanation. The buildings either side are almost the same height. And none of us thought to put a look-out up there.'

George groans to himself.

'Perhaps we might try Ashton Court, George? We could build a stage and seating area there?' Eadie suggests, trying to cheer him. 'I'm sure Lord and Lady Packer would help.'

George shakes his head. 'It's no good, Eadie. More than half our tricks require fly towers and curtains. Trapdoors. All the other theatres in Bristol and Bath are booked up months in advance. We're done. Finished. I'm ruined.'

Cec and Harry exchange a glance but George is too upset to notice.

There's a knock at the dining-room door and the Perrises' maid comes in, struggling with an armful of letters. 'More letters, sir!' She beams. 'For you and Miss Harry. Hand-delivered, some of them.' She tips them onto the table, dozens of them spilling out across the tablecloth.

'Ugh. I can't bear to look,' George says, his head in his hands, as Cec looks at Harry and smiles.

'George,' Harry says slowly, putting a hand on his arm, 'the reason I insisted on us all gathering here tonight . . .' She nods at Cec who takes over.

'Harry and I have got something to share with you. And it involves all these letters that keep arriving.' Cec gestures at the missives on the table.

'Why? What are they?' George looks up. 'People demanding their money back?'

Harry smiles. 'No, George! Far from it. I know you've not felt up to going through all the post that arrived after the fire. So I took the liberty of doing so. They're offering condolences—'

'That's very kind. But how does that —'

'You didn't let Harry finish!' Cec berates him. 'Valentin's had the same too. Dozens and dozens of telegrams and letters. It's not just sympathy they're offering, George, but help.'

'Help?' George asks, puzzled.

'Yes! Help! From all sorts of people!' Cec pulls out a handful of letters from her jacket, placing them one by one on the table.

'That's from a stagehand who came to The Professor's funeral. This one's from a theatre mechanician. And this from an elderly engineer who read about the fire in the paper.' Cec looks at George. 'There are dozens more, hundreds even. And more are still arriving, every day!'

'But how can they help?' George says, puzzled. 'We've lost everything, our props, our entire venue! I'm quite possibly bankrupt. You're injured, Harry, out of action for months. How on *earth* can they help?'

'In any way they can,' Cec says.

George glances at Valentin and he nods.

'It's true, George. Cec and I have gone through all of ours. Every single note, telegram, and letter. It's quite something. There are offers of help from everyone and anyone you can think of, from members of the public to the very best magicians and technicians, even those who retired years ago. They all want to help us start again, to still perform the show in The Professor's memory.' He leans towards George and smiles. 'The public still want the show to happen, George!'

'Well, come on, help me with these ones!' Harry says, spreading the recently delivered bundle out across the table. Eadie smiles, reaching forward, and Louis does the same.

'But how many are offering to help?' George asks, a glimmer of hope rising.

'If it's anything like those we've already opened, well then, all of them, George! *All of them!*' says Cec, looking at the mountain of paper on the dining table. She catches Harry's eye and bursts into laughter.

Two days later, and still more letters and telegrams are flooding in. A groundswell of support. This time, the group gathers at the Hogarths' workshop.

Ever efficient, Harry and Cec have recruited Louis and Ollie to divide the offers of help into different categories: costumes, props, engineering and so on, each in separate boxes.

Valentin takes charge of the meeting. "'Whatever it takes,'" he says, reading out a recent telegram. 'From Renata Karas, one of our finest opera singers, and a substantial donation too.' He looks at George. 'If we don't try again, Skarratt will have taken away your chance in the limelight *and* destroyed the final wishes of Professor. We cannot let that happen.'

'All right, all right.' George sighs, giving way a little. 'I'll humour you. Let's go through this sensibly. We'd need a venue of course, but before we even think about that or possible dates, we need to know how long it will take to rebuild everything. Is it even possible?'

He looks at the Hogarth twins and Ollie pulls a face. 'The metal tank will be hardest, because of its size,' Ollie says. 'The rest, four to five weeks minimum, and that'd be working flat out. Possibly longer. The tank would be two months at least. We're only a small team after all.' He glances at Louis, who smiles encouragingly at him.

'Then forget about the tank, George,' Valentin says. 'I know The Professor never liked it. Could you replace it with something else, perhaps? What about your idea of the woman vanishing onstage?'

'And we have our living pictures still,' Eadie says, softly.

'But what about Harry?' George gestures towards his sister. 'She can't possibly perform on crutches!'

'We have someone else who already knows most of our show . . .' Harry says, looking at Cec.

'No!' Eadie protests. 'Cec has already been pushed to her limits! It's unfair to ask more of her!'

'I can do it,' Cec says, confidently. 'I can, Eadie. *Please*. I owe it to you, George, after everything. I'd be honoured.'

'Then you have props and an assistant,' Valentin says. 'I'll need The Professor's equipment rebuilding too, but we have more than enough offers here, two of which are from mechanicians I worked with myself, some decades ago.'

'And how are we to afford all of this?' George asks. 'I spoke to Greenhouse yesterday and even if the insurers pay out, it'll take months to recoup the damages.'

'A decent sum has already been offered in donations,' Valentin says. 'And The Professor left me a great deal in his will. Money is no problem, George.'

George is so touched by this that it takes him a moment to gather his thoughts. 'That's very generous of you, Valentin, truly.'

Valentin chuckles. 'It's my retirement show too, perhaps not as selfless as you may think.'

'All this,' George says, thoughtfully. 'Money and props and so on. Even if we could do it, how will we find a venue? Everywhere is booked up so far in advance. Unless we postpone it a year?'

'I might be able to find us a venue.' Harry grins. 'Elena Spaven has offered to help.'

'The music hall star?' Louis asks, and Harry nods.

'An old friend of mine. I saw her in London a while back. She's due to perform at the People's Palace, on Baldwin Street, in just over three weeks' time. A short residency. I've spoken to the venue and both they and Elena are happy for us to use the dates instead.' Harry smiles. 'What do you say?'

Ollie whistles. 'Three weeks is incredibly tight! We have the prototypes and technical drawings so it's not entirely impossible. But it'd be a *huge* challenge.'

'What if you and Alex managed a larger team? Of other, experienced mechanicians who could assist? Would that speed things up?' Valentin asks.

Ollie looks at his brother and they nod.

'We'd have to throw everything at it. Absolutely everything!' George says, excitement beginning to rise.

'We have a venue then,' Valentin says. 'We have performers. We have props and sets, and animated pictures. We have enough money to try again. But do we have the *will*?' He looks at everyone, one by one. 'We must put this to the vote. George?'

'I've nothing left to lose,' he says. 'I think it's madness but, well, why not?'

'Eadie?'

She sees the hope in George's eyes. How can she possibly say no? 'Of course.'

'Ollie? Alex?' George asks, and the Hogarth twins simultaneously nod.

'I'm in too,' Louis says. 'Whatever you need me for.'

'Me, too,' Cec says, determinedly and Harry nods.

'And me.'

'Then, my dear George' – Valentin grins – 'my troupe of friends. We are in agreement. Perhaps it is impossible but all we can do is try.'

'What about Skarratt though?' Eadie asks, and the temperature in the room drops.

'Funny you mention that.' Valentin raises an eyebrow. 'I have a telegram here from the man himself, offering his condolences.'

'How *dare* he?' George fumes.

'No, no, George. We must be clever. We know our opponent much better now.' Valentin glances at Cec and she beams back at him. 'Cec and I have a little plan, to keep him close and to deal with him, once and for all.'

BRISTOL MERCURY, Monday 4th May, 1896

MAGIC SHOW STAGED DESPITE INFERNO

The wizards Mr George Perris and The Great Valentini are to stage their tribute to Bristol's beloved late magician, The Professor, at the People's Palace on Baldwin Street after the inferno that destroyed The Prince's Theatre. Performers, mechanicians and stagehands of all varieties are to assist in this new version. The auditorium is to be reconfigured in order to accommodate the expected crowd. All tickets for the cancelled show will be valid at the People's Palace on Saturday 23rd May. The Great Valentini has confirmed there will be additional illusions, along with animated photographs courtesy of Mr Perris's collaboration with Clifton's E. D. Carleton Photographic.

Skarratt looks different, Cec thinks, as she joins him in the small room upstairs at the King William Ale House, having snuck in through a side entrance.

He looks wild-eyed, golden stubble emerging from his chin and cheeks when he is normally clean-shaven.

'They can't *seriously* go ahead!' he says, picking at his fingernails. 'Can they?'

Cec waits, silently, for him to continue.

'It's not enough time! They can't turn it around so fast. Can they . . .?'

He scratches at his stubble.

'Mr Skarratt,' she says eventually. 'What you did only destroyed the theatre, not the show. You underestimated George Perris.'

Skarratt growls and thumps his fists on the table. 'What *will* it take to stop him then? *Damn him!*' he shouts.

He looks at Cec, the very picture of innocence, her face concealing how much he disgusts her.

'I didn't mean for the theatre to go up in flames like that!' Skarratt whispers, leaning forward. 'I only wanted to give

Perris a taste of what happens when things go wrong. It's always so easy for him and—'

He breaks off. Even if Cec hadn't seen him drop the lit matches herself, she can see the lie deep in his eyes. This bitter man, eaten up with envy, prepared to put others' lives at risk to serve his own ambition.

'You were right about one thing, though,' Cec says, carefully. 'Valentin's made it clear he'll have no further use for me after his retirement. That's why I asked to meet up with you today, Mr Skarratt. I've thought long and hard about it all and you were right. About me. I'm nothing but a con artist and a thief. And when all this is done, if you still want me, I'll come back to you.'

He looks at her suspiciously.

'I knew you wouldn't believe me,' she says. 'At first. Even though I've told no one about your involvement in the fire. I keep to my word, like I always said. But I thought I'd offer something else too, prove that I'm serious.'

'What?'

'I found something . . . Something I think might be of great interest to you,' she says softly, seeing his eyes light up. 'A notebook. It belonged to Miss Carleton's father but Valentin has it now.'

'What of it?'

Cec leans forward, lowering her voice. 'Valentin looked through it and told me there was nothing in it, but he was lying. There was a story once about a man in India, in the far south, who claimed he'd discovered a secret. An impossible trick. How to disappear right in front of you.'

'I've heard tales of such a thing . . .' Skarratt says, intrigued.

'But the notebook, Mr Skarratt!' breathes Cec, shaking her head, awestruck. 'It's like nothing I've ever seen!'

'How so?'

She leans further forward, not taking her eyes off him. 'It's said that if you write your deepest, darkest secrets in it, *the key to disappearing will be revealed.*'

'Ridiculous!' Skarratt scoffs, sitting back in his chair.

'I thought that too. At first. But there *is* something peculiar about that notebook . . .' She looks at him with utmost sincerity, a silent thanks to Arter for having trained her so well in the art of the con.

'Peculiar how?' Skarratt leans forward again, his interest piqued.

'It's like nothing I've ever seen before. Like the pages are *alive*. It's impossible. You'd have to see it for yourself, to understand. Who cares about George Perris when you could have *this*?'

'Do you have it with you?' There's a greedy gleam in Skarratt's eye and Cec resists the temptation to smile.

'No, but I can get it if you want.' She waits for her offer to sink in.

'He hasn't tried it for himself? Not confessed his own sins?'

She shakes her head. 'Someone he loved died in a terrible accident, years ago now, but he blamed himself. I don't think he could ever relive it, and he'd have to write it all down in order for the secret to reveal itself.'

'Bring it to me then!' Skarratt demands. 'Ha! My word, that *would* beat Perris at his own game! A *genuinely* impossible illusion! It cannot be real, but I'd like a look, nevertheless. To see for myself.'

'You'll understand when you see it, I promise.' Cec nods, sitting back in her chair. 'But you'll have to wait. I need to get a replacement made, else Valentin will notice it missing from the shelf. He has eagle-eyes, that man. And I'll need the cost of it too. To cover expenses.'

Skarratt frowns and Cec stares at him until he gives in and blinks.

'If you put me to expense for your benefit and gain, sir,' Cec says, firmly. 'It's only right that I am recompensed accordingly. Besides, Valentin only pays me on a monthly basis and the next time is a way off. You understand?'

Skarratt gives in, reaching into his pocket and pulling out a handful of coins. She takes them, repressing a smile as she does so.

'You'd best hurry,' he says, crisply. 'I'd like to see this book of yours as soon as I can.'

'I'll do my best, Mr Skarratt,' Cec says, modestly. 'I always do. Oh and one last thing. The fire was officially an electrical spark. Nothing to do with you. But given they *are* going ahead with this new version of the show, what better way to prove your innocence then by volunteering to help?'

Skarratt thinks for a moment before chuckling.

'An excellent idea! Bravo! Ah, little urchin! I'm so glad we can continue this mutually beneficial arrangement. It works rather well, don't you think?'

Cec nods, keeping her face straight. *Oh, just you wait, Roderick Skarratt! Just you wait . . .*

The Hogarths' workshop is once again buzzing with energy. Two neighbouring spaces along the arches have been commandeered, and are now filled with mechanicians, old conjurors, and all sorts. There are friends and past colleagues of The Professor's, and many George knows only by repute. Stagehands, engineers, and costume makers, all divided into different teams, led by a trusted, hand-picked supervisor.

George stands and watches, not quite believing it to be real. Such a huge effort by so many people working together to attempt the impossible. It's so daunting, so ridiculous, to think they can recreate such an ambitious show in a short space of time. He smiles to himself, wishing The Professor could have seen this, to know how loved and respected he was that so many have turned out to help realise his last wishes.

Much to his relief, George has also finally worked out how to make his vanishing woman disappear onstage. The fire that raged at the theatre had led to one good thing, when he'd seen the figure in the wings that was nothing but a hatstand and a cloak. Then that was the solution. The costume was all. A winged costume that could lock together, retaining the shape of a person even if the wearer were no longer inside. At last, George has a fitting finale and one he knows, instinctively, The Professor would have loved. Valentin had jumped to his feet when George had told him of it that morning, applauding wildly and delighting in how, even in his darkest hour, George could still find inspiration.

George's mind turns to Eadie, remembering how it was she who inspired the idea in the first place. He wishes, with all his heart, he could make things right between them. But it seems impossible to get any time with her alone, not now the show is full steam ahead. Both of them are so busy, he's barely seen her.

A tap on his shoulder and George turns to find Valentin there.

'All good, George?' he asks. 'Just to let you know, I've taken up Skarratt's little offer of help – with all due gratitude, of course.' He winks. 'I've got him at work on something rather special. A mirror that appears to be entirely devoid of tricks. I've got him gilding the frame, trying to puzzle out what it will be used for. I believe it'll keep him occupied for some time and my spies are, of course, keeping a close eye on him at all times.'

'I still feel deeply uncomfortable with him working on anything to do with the show.'

'Ah, but it will keep us safer in the end. You know the saying, George, "Keep your friends close, your enemies closer."' Valentin leans in, a twinkle in his eyes. 'One other thing,' he says. 'Have you spoken with Miss Carleton of late?'

Two boys are juggling as a duo as Eadie walks past Clifton College, running through the animated pictures she is to show at the People's Palace in her mind. The pigeon film, the omnibus transforming into a hearse, the 'egg man' film . . .

And that's when it comes to her. A spark of an idea. A flicker of inspiration. A solution to the puzzle of how George might interact with film onstage. She can almost see it! Her mind floods with images of how it might be achieved and all she can think about is how excited he will be.

On impulse, she heads straight towards the Hogarths' workshop as the clouds gather overhead.

Rain starts to fall, lightly at first, then heavily. Eadie has left her purse at home and forgotten her coat, and she rebukes herself for doing so as a cab passes, splashing her with mud. But her excitement drives her on and then she is there, in the doorway of the workshop, mud-spattered and drenched.

She pushes the door open and George looks up, surprised to see her. She realises how awful she must look as he approaches. A drowned rat.

'I had an idea,' Eadie says, wiping the rain from her face. 'For the show, I worked out how you might interact with the screen, a living picture and you performing together, simultaneously. And I wanted—'

She swallows. '*I wanted to apologise,*' she wants to say, '*for pushing you away when that wasn't what I meant at all. I wanted you to kiss me. I wanted that for so much longer than I realised. Perhaps even since I first saw you at that dratted séance.*'

But she doesn't say any of this. For how can she?

'I wanted to run it past you,' she says, instead. 'To see if you thought it might work. If I can beg for some more of your time, one last film, possibly even for your finale . . .'

She explains her idea and his face widens into a grin. 'It's brilliant!' he exclaims. 'My word, Eadie, you're *ingenious*! I'll need Cec, though, and we'll need to be quick about it. I can't afford for us to miss any more rehearsal time.'

'The weather looks better on Wednesday,' Eadie says, conscious of looking half-drowned, even as the rain stops and the sun breaks out behind her.

'My goodness! Eadie, forgive me!' George says, ashamed. 'Please, come in and dry off. I shouldn't have stood here talking to you in the doorway!'

'Actually, I should get back,' Eadie says, looking down at her muddy, sodden self and avoiding George's eye. She turns away but George follows her outside, the streets glistening and steaming as the sun tries its best to burn off the puddles.

'Eadie. I've been meaning to talk to you,' George says, awkwardly. 'Properly, I mean.'

Eadie looks into his gold-flecked eyes and feels herself falling.

'I wanted to talk to you too,' she says, bolstering her courage, her voice full of nerves. 'About Ashton Court—'

She pauses. *Come on, Eadie, say it!* And there's a brief moment when she nearly does, but then Louis calls from the workshop and George turns, waving a hand to ward him off.

'It's all right,' George says, shy suddenly, second-guessing what she's going to say and getting it wildly wrong. 'It's all right, Eadie. Let's never speak of it again, I promise. I'll see you for the making of the film. We could do it on the roof of the People's Palace, perhaps?'

She nods, silently, as he gives a bow, and heads back inside. Eadie watches him go, taking her heart with him.

It's dark and late and Cec is nervous, unsure whether or not she can pull off what she is about to attempt. And here she is, waiting in the very room in which Skarratt holds his séances, the perfect venue for her very own illusion.

She stands awkwardly in the dimly lit parlour until Skarratt joins her, shutting the door behind him.

'Well?' he says, motioning to an armchair, and Cec sits down opposite him.

She holds out a red leather notebook and he takes it, unwrapping the fastener before opening it and leafing through.

'It's . . . blank?' he says, frowning at her.

'That's what I thought, at first. But it's not. Look closely, sir. *Really* closely . . .'

Cec has been practising with Valentin for this for days. Her own original idea that he has helped her finesse. So much more challenging than suspending a card. She breathes slowly in.

Magic only works if you believe in it.

As Skarratt peers into the book, Cec concentrates, channelling her thoughts. She thinks of Arter and his small stingy gravestone, of Skarratt's hands tight around her neck, of his threats and violence. She thinks too of Valentin's kindness and his lost love Olivia, of his hand shadows dancing across the ceiling, and her own floating cards. She thinks of extinguishing the flame of Skarratt's match in the theatre, of lifting up the heavy plaster that was crushing Harry . . .

And then Cec concentrates on simply *feeling* instead: allowing her touch of the impossible to flow through her. A strange sense of calm.

The faint scar on her hand feels warm as she slowly raises her left palm.

Magic . . .

And there it is. A flicker on the page, inky symbols and figures dancing like candle flame, as if the ink were alive. They flow first across one page, then another as Skarratt stares on, astounded. He turns the page and the figures flow over, skipping and twirling, evading his finger as he goes to touch them.

It lasts, perhaps, only seconds but time stretches somehow.

Cec exhales and the inky shapes vanish into nothingness, the pages once again blank as she sits, drained by her efforts.

'*Impossible* . . .' Skarratt breathes. '*Beautiful!*'

Cec reaches for the notebook, but he snatches it away. 'No!'

'Please sir! I know I said you could have it, but Valentin will want it back!' she objects.

Skarratt looks at her askance. 'You want it for yourself?' he asks, and she shakes her head.

'What on earth would *I* do with such a thing? I'm no magician, sir. Not like you. But please, what if he finds out?'

He smiles at her greedily. 'That wasn't the deal. You had a replacement made, there's no reason to think he'll even notice it missing. No, little urchin, this is mine now. Agreed?'

Cec nods, as she represses a smile, amazed by having tricked him, marvelling too at her very own illusion, the best she has ever done.

'You're dismissed,' Skarratt says, not looking up at Cec, as she stands to leave. She pauses at the door, glancing back to see him lost in wonder, examining the book by the light of the fire. And, only then does Cecily Marsden allow herself a triumphant smile.

Eadie is struggling, for there is not just one but a hundred and more George Perrises emerging in front of her.

She's developing the juggling film she made with him and Cec earlier, and now she must look at him over and over again: his bright eyes, high cheekbones, his wonky necktie that she didn't dare straighten this time, *that smile of his* . . .

So many tiny George Perrises not much bigger than her thumbnail, catching juggling balls from off screen, his face laughing as they change colour in his hands from white to dark grey and back again.

Frame after frame. So many Georges they make her heart ache.

Eadie takes the wooden drum out of the developing fluid, hundreds of Georges coiled around it, and ties it up to drip-dry over the tank below, sighing to herself.

George had been so focused today that Eadie felt he barely looked at her. Only when the rehearsals were done and the performance began did he look up – and even then, he just looked straight into the lens, performing for an audience who weren't physically there. The sense of him performing *just for her* utterly absent this time. And she missed him, so very much, even as he laughed and threw the final ball to Cec, professional to the last.

Let us never speak of it again. That's what he had said. But surely they will have to at some point? She cannot bear this gulf between them. *Oh, George . . .*

She runs a hand over her forehead. Perhaps some tea might help steady her? But all she can think of is that shooting star across the night sky, the feel of George's lips on hers, and the taste of champagne.

Valentin is delighted. So many elements finally coming together, and so many surprises – not just for the audience, but his colleagues too.

'You won't tell anyone, you promise?' he asks, as Chaplin lifts the camera up, ready to return it to the shop.

'Of course not. I may not approve of secrets, Valentin, but I know only too well one must sometimes keep them, for all manner of reasons.'

'Excellent,' Valentin says. 'I knew I could count on you, Mr Hodges.'

'And that's really all you wanted me to film?' Chaplin asks and Valentin nods.

'So be it then!' Chaplin grins. 'You're quite an enigma, you know that?'

'One last thing,' Valentin says. 'I know Miss Carleton has agreed to be George's projectionist but, at the very end of the show, might *you* be able to operate the projector? Just for this film – and no telling Eadie. A little surprise, that's all.'

Chaplin considers it for a moment. 'Well, she has been showing me how to run the projector, but she'd be far better than me I'm sure,' he says.

'No, no. I'd rather it was you. I'll give you instructions on the day, but it'll be quite easy. I promise,' Valentin says, gleefully.

'All right.' Chaplin smiles, intrigued. 'If you're sure?' Valentin grins and Chaplin smiles back at him before disappearing into the theatre, leaving the conjuror alone on the flat roof of the People's Palace.

It's all coming together now, Valentin thinks. *It's coming together very nicely indeed!* And The Great Valentini laughs out loud, the sound echoing around the whitewashed walls before floating off to join the gulls wheeling overhead.

'Friends, Romans, conjurors! Lend me your ears!' George grins as he leaps up onto a large wooden trunk onstage. The get-in is done, the People's Palace has survived the night unscathed, and technical rehearsals are about to begin.

George is buzzing with energy, surrounded by the large team that is to run the show. He looks around at them all, lighting, costume, the stage managers, technical crew, a whole village of helpers who have already gone above and beyond.

Skarratt is noticeably absent and George smiles to himself, safe in the knowledge that wherever the rogue goes, he is shadowed by two watchers from their security team. *Not long now*, he thinks to himself.

'I'm afraid that today is going to be long and difficult,' George says. 'It'll almost certainly be frustrating, but with patience and hard work, we'll get there. You'll have noticed the *extremely* tight security we have in place. That's because, I'm afraid to say, of what happened at the Prince's. Not just the fire but certain nefarious individuals trying to scupper our efforts. But we will prevail, my friends! This show will be spectacular because it is down to you. A team effort from every one of us. And I know, as all of you do, it will not *look* spectacular today. It will look messy and chaotic, and at times, it might even be dangerous, but we will prevail. As a team. As a family.'

He sees Eadie at the back of the crowd and cannot help but smile, the sight of her warming his heart.

'Let's go!' he says, leaping off the trunk.

A few hours later, Eadie sits in the stalls, half-watching George onstage, practising with Cec. She doodles on a small notepad, sketching out an idea for a new sprocket wheel, when a rushing sound makes her look up.

She is just in time to see her projection screen plummet like a stone, out of control, crashing onto the boards of the stage. A glimpse of George glancing up before the screen comes down, seemingly on top of him.

A deathly silence, a hush of disbelief.

Cec stands, confused and alone onstage as the screen masks whatever disaster has occurred.

Eadie is on her feet in a breath. She runs, faster than she's ever run in her life, boots thudding on the carpet, up the stairs to the stage. *George.* He lies on his back behind the screen, eyes closed and deathly pale.

Blood rushes in her ears as Eadie stands, immobile suddenly. Harry appears from the wings, dashing out on her crutches and throwing herself down beside her brother. Silently, the stagehands emerge from the wings to see how bad the accident is.

A collective holding of breath . . .

With a roar, George shoots up to sitting, rubbing his head gently. 'That was close!' He laughs with relief as Harry kisses him on the cheek and heads back to the wings to console the distraught stagehand responsible. An easy mistake to make: he'd forgotten to lock one of the ropes in the fly system – the structure of counterweights and ropes that enable scenery to be brought on and off stage quickly and quietly.

Eadie kneels down beside George. 'Are you all right?'

'A bit shaken that's all. Could've been worse.' He looks at the screen. 'Damn near killed by living pictures. Perhaps they are dangerous after all. Come on, help me up. Worse things happen at sea.'

She pulls him up to standing, a little too close, still holding his hands.

'George—' Eadie says, looking into his eyes. *It's too late,* she thinks. *I had my chance and I missed it. If only I hadn't pushed him away!*

'Right,' she says, brushing down his lapels. 'Best get back to work.'

The colour returns to his cheeks as she walks away, glancing back at him for a moment, wishing she could rewind time as easily as one of her reels of film.

Cec loves being onstage more than anything. Every element of it brings her joy. The smell of hot lights and warm varnish. The silent trapdoors and hidden pulleys. The lightning-fast costume changes. The illusion of it all; the audience only ever seeing a fraction of what makes a show come alive.

She thinks of Skarratt and allows herself a smile, hoping her plan has worked. There are so many things that could still go wrong but she won't let him defeat them: not now, not ever. She had been so frightened of him before, but now she feels her own power growing along with her confidence. She stands onstage at the People's Palace, no longer petrified by nerves but excited. For, if she can fool Roderick Skarratt, then performing to a packed theatre surely holds no fear.

Cec sparkles in rehearsals, remembering every cue, adrenaline seeing her through even the longest day. George had once told her that he preferred being a magician to a man and she understands what he means now. She belongs here, onstage. She always has done.

Finally, it is time to run through the section of the show that has required the most complex planning: a select group of stagehands and crew members taking a vow of silence around it. Some aspects cannot even be rehearsed as it relies on certain audience members who, unbeknownst to them, will play a crucial part. In less than 24 hours, all will be done. The show will be over.

So much that could still go wrong.

'Ready to go again?' Valentin asks, stepping towards Cec in his top hat.

She grins. 'Always.'

'From the top!' he cries, as their half of the show is re-set once again.

'Cec is fantastic, isn't she?' Harry whispers to George, her plaster-cast resting in the aisle as they watch Valentin and Cec perform.

George smiles, for Cec is indeed superb. Tiny and nimble, she's hugely charismatic, outshining even Valentin himself who, he claims, is saving his energy for the real show. George glances at Harry. He'd missed performing with his sister, but then, he'd missed performing with Chaplin at first too. A new era for all of them. And Harry is so excited about the prospect of travelling with Chaplin, filming new living pictures for E. D. Carleton Photographic. Brand new adventures with her soon-to-be husband.

George fidgets. His rehearsal had mostly gone to plan, although the timing of Cec's disappearance, the winged woman who vanishes, was slightly off. He has only one more rehearsal and that's it. Nothing until the show tomorrow, and so much riding on it!

Eadie sits ahead of him in the stalls and George feels the pull on his heart. He thinks of how she turned up, drenched and full of ideas at the workshop, and he'd wanted to kiss her more than ever. But there were so many people, and he couldn't bear to embarrass her again. Then earlier, when she helped him up after the screen nearly felled him, that same look in her eyes. Every time he gets close, something seems to stop him . . .

And then it's time for George's final rehearsal, his live section culminating in Cec vanishing right in front of the audience. Then onto Eadie's films, ending with the brand new one of him interacting with his screen self. A real George and a screen George working together. The most impossible thing he has yet created. *This* then is his finale. A new climax to his show combining both live performance and recorded, merging old and new, unmatched in ambition, a unique collaboration between magician and film-maker . . .

Eadie joins him onstage as the projection screen is lowered and the films are shown. One after another, and then the very last: of George juggling with his on-screen double. The timings must be exact otherwise the illusion will fail, and although Eadie, as projectionist, keeps time perfectly, it is George who fumbles, dissatisfied as the rehearsal comes to an end.

Even after another attempt, he still isn't content.

'It's a good thing to be a perfectionist, George, but there is such a thing as over-rehearsing,' Valentin says. 'It worked perfectly well from where I was sitting.'

'I'm happy to go through it again,' Eadie says. 'But I'm tempted to agree with Valentin. Besides, it's late. We need to at least try and sleep.'

'A big day tomorrow.' Valentin smiles, and George feels he has no choice but to give in.

When they finally leave, the doors are locked securely behind them, security men on guard everywhere – even on the roof this time. The lights are extinguished and the theatre turns as dark as the night sky outside.

Tomorrow, thinks George, his heart thumping, trying not to think of all that could go wrong. *Make or break. Tomorrow.*

And now for my final effect – 'Disappearance'.

In many respects, disappearance is simply the reverse of production: instead of producing an article, one must vanish it. There are, of course, many ways of effecting the disappearance of an article, and it would be impossible to list them all here. Some objects can be made to disappear with sleight-of-hand or by means of trap tables or doors, others by more ingenious methods.

As a rule, the larger the object you wish to vanish, the harder you must work to achieve it. Any budding conjurors must surely understand that it is far harder to vanish a man than a handkerchief . . .

Extract from *The Secrets of Magic* by George Perris
(published by Saxon Press, 1895)

DISAPPEARANCE

Valentin watches his reflection as he carefully shaves off his beard. When he is done, he tilts his chin, and the face of a younger man emerges in the mirror, as if he had been hiding behind his beard all this time.

Shiny-faced and new, he smiles at his double in the mirror.

Today is the day The Great Valentini will disappear.

A knock at the door interrupts his thoughts. Cec has already left for the theatre so Valentin must answer it instead.

'Ah, Nellie!' he says with a grin, his eyes twinkling. 'Bang on time. Won't you come in?'

George has checked and double checked everything under the stage, the Hogarths helping him, for they know his ways well enough to understand his need for reassurance. When he emerges onstage, he finds Eadie at her projector doing the same, checking the bolts are tightened, and that everything is well oiled.

'Everything in order?' He smiles, and she nods.

'Nervous?' he asks, and Eadie pulls a face. 'Me too,' he says, quietly.

'You'll be brilliant, George, you always are,' she says, smiling at him before looking out into the auditorium. 'I've invited Mrs Fearnley tonight – my landlady. I hope she comes. It's my last chance to change her mind.'

'It'll be all right, Eadie,' George says, softly. 'I'm sure of it.'

'I don't want to let anyone down,' Eadie says, and George takes her hands without thinking.

'Oh, Eadie, you won't! Think of Ashton Court and—' He breaks off as she looks at him, her eyes wide. He'd promised never to mention it again, hadn't he? 'Tonight will be even better, I promise,' he says, awkwardly, only then realising he's still holding her hands.

Eadie smiles at him and George feels himself falling.

'Tonight will be magical!' he says, grinning at her. 'For we are in the business of entertainment, are we not?'

He whirls her around and she laughs as he does so, his heart skipping a beat as they come back to standing.

'On with the show then,' Eadie says, a little breathlessly, and George nods, unable to take his eyes from her.

'On with the show . . .'

Cec feels like royalty as she looks at herself in her dressing-room mirror, bright lights shining. A buzz of excitement runs right through her.

A rap on the door and George and Harry enter, George handsome in his satin-edged suit, Harry elegant in a dark pink dress that she has painted her crutches to match.

'A quick interruption, Cec, if you don't mind,' says George, as he and Harry catch each other's eye and grin. He pulls out a hefty envelope from his jacket and hands it to Cec. 'Here,' he says.

'What is it?' Cec asks, puzzled.

'A good-luck card,' Harry says. 'Tradition on opening night.'

'And something else too . . .' George beams as Cec opens the envelope to pull out both a card and a lengthy document. She exclaims upon seeing the word 'Contract' at the top of it.

'Well,' says George, 'Harry's off to marry that Chaplin fellow and they're going travelling, making new films for Eadie. So really, Cec, I need a new assistant. A permanent one. Someone with a passion for performance and eager to learn. Someone who might be in need of a new job, perhaps.'

Cec is speechless.

'Don't feel pressured into saying yes,' George says. 'Have a good think. I'll pay you properly of course – it's all in the contract – and you'll be involved in creating new illusions, just as Harry has been. If you want to develop your own tricks, I'll support and help however I can. We're a team. But it's hard work, erratic hours – all the things you know so well now.'

Cec thinks of all that has happened since Arter died. The horrors of Roderick Skarratt, the joy of Valentin. The betrayal and blackmail. The forgiveness and acceptance. Her new theatre family who have welcomed her into their world . . .

'Oh, goodness!' says Harry, as Cec flaps her hands in front of her eyes.

'Please don't make me cry! I've only just finished my make-up! I don't need to think about it – *Yes! Yes please! Thank you, George! Thank you!*' She stands up, bursting towards him and hugging first him then Harry, as Valentin puts his head around the door.

'You asked her, then?' He chuckles.

'*You knew?*' Cec beams at him. 'The answer's yes! A thousand times yes! Thank you, thank you, all of you!'

'And what will *you* do, now you've lost your assistant as well as your facial hair?' Harry asks, wryly.

'Oh, I've got a few things lined up.' Valentin's eyes sparkle. 'You might be surprised!'

The house is open and the audience trickles into the auditorium. Magicians from all over Britain make their way to their seats along with the public, a gathering not just of The Professor's fans, but the crème de la crème of those who perform magic too. A crackle in the air as the excitement feels its way through the warren of backstage tunnels towards the dressing rooms beneath.

'Good luck, Perris,' says Chaplin, popping into George's dressing room to wish him well. George pulls him in for a quick hug, their friendship now restored as Valentin enters in his old-fashioned coat tails, wand in hand.

'George. How are you feeling?' Valentin asks as Chaplin leaves.

'I'm fine,' George replies, trying to hide his nerves. 'Really.'

'I have *every* confidence in you,' Valentin says. 'Just as The Professor did. It's been an honour, George, an honour and a pleasure. You've done The Professor proud, and you've done me proud too. You are an *exceptional* conjuror and a truly kind-hearted young man.'

George smiles. He wants to say how much he's learned, how much Valentin means to him, as his friend and champion, just as The Professor had. But he cannot find the words. 'I'll miss working with you,' he says instead, shaking Valentin's hand. 'Really I will.'

Valentin chuckles. 'In no time at all, you'll be standing where I am, handing over to the brightest star of the generation after you. Enjoy every minute: you've earned it. And thank *you* for all you've taught me too.'

'Taught *you*?' George asks, puzzled, as Valentin goes to leave.

'Maybe I don't need a wand after all.' He shrugs, shutting the door behind him.

George's palms are damp, and he fidgets with his cufflinks as he walks out of his dressing room, Cec beside him, along the maze of corridors towards the stage. Stagehands smile and nod with encouragement, as Miss Pegg, the wardrobe mistress, stops Cec for a final adjustment to the bodice on her green dress.

George waits, leaning against the brick wall, trying to calm his nerves, and his heart melts as Eadie appears down the far end of the hallway, dressed in a bright cornflower-blue.

'You look beautiful, Eadie!' Cec beams, and Eadie blushes as she makes her way past her, towards George.

'Well, it's what's inside that counts,' she says, quietly.

'You do look lovely, though,' George says, bashfully, as Eadie reaches up and straightens his tie, just as she did at Ashton Court.

'Nervous still, Mr Perris?' She smiles.

'Always, Miss Carleton.'

'You'll be *brilliant*, George. I told you before. You always are.'

George smiles back at her. 'Not *always*.'

'Ever the perfectionist . . . I wanted to say good luck, that's all.'

'Good luck to you too, Eadie,' he says, shaking her hand.

'Good luck, George,' she says – and she leans forward and kisses him on the cheek. Her lips linger just a moment too long, her hand gently pressing his.

She steps back and they gaze at each other, wide-eyed, as their hearts skip a beat at the exact same moment.

'Right,' says Cec, suppressing a smile at George and Eadie, as Miss Pegg finally approves of the tweaks to her dress.

Louis pokes his head around the corner of the hallway and grins as he sees them all, Valentin strolling up behind Cec to join the group.

'Everyone's in position,' Louis confirms. 'And both Skarratt and Mrs Carnesky are in the audience.'

'I knew they wouldn't be able to resist those free tickets!' Cec giggles.

'Let's hope they stay for the second half,' Valentin says, drily. 'Then all that remains is to wish everyone the best of luck. Good luck, all!'

George and Cec stand together in the wings with Valentin opposite, on the far side of the stage. The curtain is still down, and the hubbub of the excited audience fills the air. George's stomach somersaults as nerves fizz through him. All these months of work, all the worry and stress. The loss of The Professor. Skarratt's spying. The fire at the Prince's. And despite it all, here they are.

It is time.

The house lights go out as the curtain rises and two bright follow spots come up, white circles at opposite edges of the stage.

'Here we go,' mutters George, stepping into the light as Valentin does the same. The audience leap to their feet, filling the auditorium with the sound of applause. The two conjurors walk towards each other, meeting in the centre of the stage and turning to the audience with a bow.

'Good evening,' Valentin says, holding his hand up for quiet as George's heart thumps in his chest. 'Welcome, all!' Valentin smiles charmingly. 'I am The Great Valentini. And this, of course, is Mr George Perris.'

George bows again, trying not to feel sick, as the audience cheers.

'Tonight is a show of two halves,' Valentin continues, as the crowd quietens. 'I am, as you might guess, representing the older, more formal style, and young Mr Perris, the energetic and new. But we must remember it should never have been me performing here tonight but the late, great Professor. The most marvellous magician, the most cunning of conjurors – but he, alas, left life's great stage too early.'

Valentin bows his head for a moment, before continuing.

'As you may be aware, we should have performed some weeks past at the Prince's Theatre. We owe a debt of gratitude to many of you here for your help and goodwill, without which tonight would not have been possible.

'And now, we must on with the show! Mr Perris will perform his half first. And, my word, you have a treat in store. The finest magician of his generation, he truly is the perfect successor to The Professor. His is a show to astound, to fascinate and above all, to entertain. There will then be a short interval before I perform, followed by a joint final performance that unites both old and new. Without further ado, ladies and gentlemen, I give you – Mr George Perris!'

Valentin walks into the wings, leaving George alone onstage.

'Ladies and gentlemen.' George smiles at the packed auditorium, the biggest audience he has ever performed in front of. 'Boys and girls. The Professor would be delighted to see you all here. As for myself, I'm afraid I'm rather embarrassed – and after such a lovely introduction too. For you see, I've misplaced something crucial to my show, and it's out there, with you in the auditorium. And unfortunately

I must retrieve it before the show can begin . . .' He holds his hand up. 'House lights, please!' he says, his confidence growing as he begins to relax into his performance.

He steps out into the auditorium, past the first few rows, where Eadie's eyes burn right through him, and down the main aisle.

'Ah,' he says, pulling out a small wooden trunk from underneath an audience member's seat. 'Is this yours, sir? No? Never seen it before. You don't know what it's doing there? Can you hold it up? Oh, very light, is it? And with a padlock too. Well, I'm bound to have the key somewhere.'

George heads towards the stage, trunk in hand. 'It *is* very light,' he says. Then: 'Oh!' as he trips up the stairs, and the box tumbles onto the stage, doubling in size. The audience gasps and then cheers.

'How very strange!' George exclaims, leaping to his feet as the house lights dim. He lifts the box and throws it into the air where, impossibly, it doubles in size again, big enough to fit a child. A final throw and it's large enough for a small adult.

'It's never done that before!' George says, a mischievous grin as he fumbles in his pockets. 'Now, this *is* embarrassing!' he says as the audience titters. 'Lost the case, now the key – I don't suppose someone from the audience might be kind enough to lend me their hat?'

A dozen or so hats are flung onstage and George smiles as he picks one, showing that it's empty before reaching in and pulling out a white rabbit, then a goldfish in a bowl. His little homage to the very first show of The Professor's that he saw all those years ago.

'It's in here somewhere . . .' George says, as the audience laughs, and he pulls out a toy soldier from the hat, handing it to a girl in the front row.

'Can you keep that safe for me please, young lady? Thank you. I may need it back in a while.'

Finally, out from the hat comes a shining gold key that George holds up, victoriously, as the audience applauds. He mops his brow with mock relief before unlocking the padlock and opening the chest.

Cec emerges from inside, curtseying in her pale-green dress to a deafening wave of applause.

'My assistant – Miss Cecil Marsden!' George cries, holding his hand out to introduce her.

Eadie claps and cheers from where she sits in the front row, feeling the warmth of the audience wrap around her as George and Cec bow together onstage. She looks at Harry to her right, beaming with pride, Chaplin next to her, before glancing towards the wings. Louis is part of George's backstage crew, and Eadie smiles, glad to be sharing this with her beloved brother.

'Now, some of you may not know,' George says, 'but before Miss Marsden and my sister, Harry, I used to have another assistant – an excellent fellow. And much as I love my sister, and wonderful though Miss Marsden is, sometimes all these dresses and ruffles rather get in the way of magic. A gentlemen's outfit is so much better supplied with pockets.

And so behold my new invention, the Changing Cabinet, where I can transform my assistant in an instant!'

A long rectangular frame of a cabinet is wheeled out by Louis and Ollie. It has no sides, no front or back, just thin struts to hold it together and silk curtains rolled up on each side.

'If you wouldn't mind?' George says, and Cec steps inside.

'I'd best tie her in.' He grins at the audience as he takes out a long length of rope, tying the middle around Cec's waist. 'After all, I wouldn't want you to think I was cheating.'

George keeps hold of both ends of the rope as he walks off stage and into the stalls, handing the ends over to the audience. 'Would you mind passing that along? Thank you. Not too tight, sir, you don't want to topple her over. Yes, like that. Excellent.'

He leaps back onstage and drops the silk curtains down, tapping his foot impatiently. 'I usually count to thirty,' he says, checking his pocket watch. 'But I think that's long enough, don't you?'

The audience roars in agreement as George pulls up the silk curtains to reveal a moustachioed man in Cec's place, the rope securely tied around his waist.

'Behold the powers of the Changing Cabinet!' George giggles, cutting the man free.

Eadie laughs, knowing how Cec disliked wearing the suit under her dress. 'It's so hot underneath!' she'd said to Eadie in rehearsals.

George continues as Eadie watches him light up the stage. His presence, his ease, is utterly enchanting and she has never felt more desperately in love with him.

His tricks fly by in a whirl of delight as Cec rejoins him onstage, now back in her pale-green dress. A pack of cards changes into white doves that flutter out into the audience. A long thin glass tube that links two mangles that George somehow travels along in a compressed, elongated form as the audience cries with laughter. Then a mind-reading trick in which Cec, hypnotised, follows instructions from the audience, followed by an illusion in which George transforms the toy soldier from the girl in the front row into a real-life soldier, also played by Cec.

Eadie glances at the row behind her. A pair of children held utterly spellbound, a group of brightly dressed women who roar and cheer as loudly as the men, and a large bearded fellow with a particularly loud laugh. All of them are having the time of their life, and Eadie's heart swells with pride.

'And now, ladies and gentlemen, a conjuring trick using only myself!' George proclaims as a large glass box is lowered onto the stage, a smaller wooden one suspended above it.

'Solid wood and solid glass,' George says. 'One shall fit into the other and, dear audience – fingers crossed as this never worked in rehearsals – I shall conjure myself out of this double box in front of your very eyes!'

He climbs a short stepladder, clambering into the wooden box with a cheery wave, before the wooden box is lowered into the larger glass one, Cec securing the lid.

'A little bit of peace whilst he's gone!' Cec grins, and the audience laughs. 'Now come, who would like to step onstage and see Mr Perris disappear? For I know I'd like nothing more!' She encourages a dozen or so audience members from the stalls onto the stage, directing them into a semi-circle as the double box is hoisted up eight foot or so, still in full view.

The sound of thunder cracks through the air and the wooden box suddenly disappears, leaving just the empty glass box swinging, as the audience exclaims. One man in the small audience onstage – a young man with a straggly moustache and a mustard coat – seems particularly impressed. The audience quietens as the man says, 'Brilliant, quite brilliant! Never seen the like!' before whipping off the moustache and coat to reveal he is none other than George Perris himself.

The crowd is on its feet, laughing and cheering for more, as George and Cec bow. Then George holds his hand up for quiet as Cec leaves the stage.

'Before I unleash the wonders of living pictures upon you – the most cutting edge of technologies that bring the real world to life like never before,' George says, 'it's time for my final act. An act inspired by a collaboration with Miss Eadie Carleton of Clifton. An idea of being drawn to a new technology, an impossible marvel . . .' The lights onstage slowly fade, the follow spot on George lingering just enough to make him visible. 'For you see,' he says, striking a match and using it to light a small lantern that he holds, 'sometimes in life, one finds oneself drawn to the light . . .'

The audience gasps, for behind him, appearing out of the shadows, and in the beams of George's lantern, is young Cec, now wearing a rainbow-coloured silk dress with huge beautiful wings like those of a giant butterfly.

George moves a little way off – and Cec follows, drawn to the light, unable to take her eyes from it. She follows him up and down the stage before he heads to the very front, close to the audience. He puts the lamp down for a moment and, as she draws near, George reaches to embrace her.

Cec turns away, as if shy, lifting her arms up for a second. In a heartbeat, she vanishes. Disappears in mid-air. Dissolving into nothingness, as if she had never really been there at all.

A collective intake of breath. Three thousand people silent with wonder, before they break into wild applause and shouts of 'Bravo! Bravo!'

Eadie's eyes well up. This brilliant illusion, over in but a moment, took so much effort to create, so many days of trial and error, ingenuity and imagination.

Eadie knows all about the wings that conceal thin steel cables inside them, how Cec hooks them together to hold the shape of herself, even as the trapdoor glides her downwards. She knows too about the hydraulics that pull the empty dress through a black tube rising up through a small hole in the stage, 'vanishing' Cec in mid-air.

She knows all of this, and still it takes her breath away.

Eadie is tearful and proud as the lights come up, and George welcomes Cec, now clad in a scarlet dress, back onto the stage. They bow together, grinning at the audience, and Eadie glances around to see the bearded man wiping away tears of joy, the group of women on their feet yelling their approval and, best of all, the awestruck faces of the children, their mouths round with delight.

But, suddenly, George is introducing her, *'Miss Eadie Carleton and her living pictures'*, and Eadie finds herself on her feet, applause ringing in her ears as she steps onstage to join him, heart fluttering as he takes her hand, gently squeezing it to reassure her. They bow in unison, and three thousand people cheer them on.

Eadie's projection screen flies gently down behind them and Eadie takes her place behind it, hidden from the audience, as the lights dim and she flicks her arc lamp on . . .

She laughs as the time flies and the local crowd recognise their home city: the monochrome girl by the suspension bridge, the omnibus transforming into a hearse on Park Street. Their cheers echo in her ears as they watch a cheeky elephant steal a hat at the zoo, murmuring in awe at the tall ship coming into harbour, gasping as a falcon flies towards them on the Downs. When Eadie plays the 'egg man' film, her heart soars as the sound of cheering almost deafens her.

Finally, it's time for the last film – and their finale. George stands to one side of the screen, juggling for a moment before throwing the balls, one by one, to an onscreen George, who catches them before juggling with them himself. He changes the size of the balls and the colour too – from white to grey and back again – before throwing them back to the real George, who catches them – one by one – in his hands.

It is impossible. It is *wondrous*. It brings the house down.

Cec and Eadie join George, bowing beside him, faces flushed with relief and excitement, applause thundering in their chests.

The curtain falls, cutting them off from the audience, 'All Done by Kindness' in large letters emblazoned across it as the house lights go up for a short interval.

George is too overwhelmed to speak as Cec hugs him and
Harry comes over on her crutches, teary and proud. Eadie
catches George's eye and they hold each other's gaze for a
moment, beaming with delight, before being ushered off
stage in readiness for Valentin's half.

'I'm so proud of you, Cecil,' Valentin says, watching Cec
adjust her make-up as Oz circles their dressing room, unusu-
ally active for an evening.

She beams at him from the mirror, her eyes sparkling.
'I never want it to end!' she says. 'All of it, Valentin. The
moment when I stepped onstage, all those faces! All these
people, here to be entertained . . . It's like all my dreams at
once! And the applause! It's so deafening!'

'It's not over yet!' Valentin smiles. 'And the second half
will be harder for it's less predictable. But all this, Cecil, for
you it's just beginning. Harness it. Harness that piece of the
impossible within you. The spotlight will be shining on you
for a long time yet. You are so very special, dear girl. I hope
you know that now.'

'I have so much to learn!' she says. 'It's so exciting!'

'And you must never stop learning. That's the mistake I
made. It's only since returning, seeing The Professor again,
meeting you and George, that I dared push myself. And I
feel more like me than I've felt in years. Decades, even. For
that alone, I am indebted to you.'

Cec grins and Valentin thinks how very fond of her he is. This fierce, determined girl who has snuck so deep into his heart. He never did get to be a father in the end, but he feels he has become one, for a while at least.

He will miss her.

'I have one last thing for you.' He smiles. 'Many years ago, my Olivia gave me this, but I think you should have it now.' He hands her a small book: a guide to the butterflies of Britain. As she opens it, Valentin raises his left hand, and the butterflies on the page lift up, fluttering their colourful wings. They rise, out of the book, and circle around the room.

'*Oh, Valentin!*' Cec gasps, delightedly.

A knock on the door and a voice shouts, 'Five minute call!' as the butterflies fall back into the book, nothing more than ink and paper.

'That's one for you to practise.' Valentin grins, putting his hands on her shoulders. He looks at her reflection in the mirror. 'Now, little one, before we go out there, I want you to remember something. You have a new family now, and they adore you as much as you do them. Let that then be my true gift to you, Cecil. May magic and the theatre bring you the same happiness it brought me for so long. George will teach you well. I've given you all I can and, like the butterflies, it's time for you to spread your own wings.'

She nods as Valentin smiles mischievously at his reflection.

'The grand finale then. Just as The Professor requested.' And when Valentin winks, Cec isn't sure if he's winking at her or himself.

The audience is noisy, chattering like a flock of birds, but when the house lights go out, plunging them into darkness, the hubbub falls into a hushed silence.

George sits between Eadie and Harry in the front row, his heart racing. The Great Valentini's final show – and The Professor's too: the culmination of two lifetimes of work.

A collective intake of breath, then silence, as a small golden light is seen at the back of the stalls – a candle, held by Valentin, cupped by his hand as he walks slowly down the aisle. He gently touches audience members on the backs of their heads as he passes, as if blessing them, before walking up onto the stage.

'I am The Great Valentini,' he announces. 'Master of darkness and of light.' He pulls out his wand and aims it at the ceiling. 'Let there be *light*!' he says, and the crack of a gun whistles through the air as the curtain rises and the whole stage is lit with candles. Thousands of them. Flickering and shifting with the faint breeze of the audience's breath.

Applause rings around the auditorium and Valentin holds up a hand. 'And now, I command there be *darkness*!' he says, turning to the candles and blowing at them, left to right. One by one they extinguish themselves, like stars in the night sky covered by clouds.

Valentin points his wand towards the ceiling, the sound of another pistol crack before the lights go up to reveal a bare stage, the candles having vanished.

'An old trick but a good one,' Valentin says, charmingly, with a bow, as a glasshouse is assembled behind him, all steel frames and glass panes. There are blinds on the side facing the audience and Valentin pulls them down, one after the other.

'It feels as if this last winter was the longest in an age.' He smiles. 'But one thing I'm certain of, ladies and gentlemen, is that we are always glad to welcome in spring!'

As he says 'spring', every blind flies up to reveal the glass-house transformed, full of blooms, flowers of every colour and kind. Cec, dressed as a beautiful nymph, steps out and dances elegantly across the stage, before joining Valentin.

'Miss Cecil Marsden!' he cries, as the audience cheers.

Cec curtseys, delighting in the applause, before dancing into the wings.

George grins. Valentin is the most compelling he's ever seen him, lighting the stage up as brilliantly as his candles. He glances at Eadie next to him in her cornflower-blue dress and his heart swells, for she has never looked more radiant. Louis, on her far side, catches George's eye and smiles back at him.

From the left of the stage, Cec wheels out a barber's chair as a stagehand brings out a table with a basin and cut-throat razor. From the right, a sideboard appears. Valentin sits as Cec throws a cloak over him, leaving just his head visible.

'I would ask for a volunteer, but no one is ever brave enough.' Valentin smiles, as the audience titters.

Cec pretends to clumsily shave him, before, with a swish, cutting his head off. The audience gasps, some even leaping to their feet with a shout of alarm, as Cec lifts up Valentin's disembodied head, placing it on the sideboard.

'This is most uncomfortable, Miss Marsden,' Valentin's head says, as the audience laughs with relief. 'That'll teach me not to hire a professional barber!'

He tells Cec he's hungry and she feeds him a piece of apple before giving his disembodied head a sip of water. She then picks his head up, reattaching it to his body, and Valentin laughs, throwing off the cloak and bowing alongside her.

The audience cheers and the bearded man behind Eadie guffaws so loudly that he sets off an entirely new wave of laughter all by himself.

More illusions follow in quick succession. A slim portfolio, such as that used for holding drawings and sketches, from which Valentin produces a birdcage filled with singing birds, glasses of champagne, Oz the dog, and finally, Cec herself. A doll's house on a tall stand from which tiny automaton figures emerge and circle around the garden before Cec bursts out of the roof of the house. Then a large trunk, that contains within it three distinctive items of clothing in separate drawers: a lavish hat, a silk dress and a pair of heeled boots. Valentin closes the trunk, re-opening it to reveal Cec dressed from head to toe in the same items. The audience stamps their feet, roaring their approval.

'And now,' Valentin announces, 'I wish to invite Mr Perris back up here.'

Eadie gives George a smile of encouragement as he leaves his seat and heads onstage to applause. He bows as he joins Valentin.

The lights dim and Cec wheels out a large blackboard, as a follow spot illuminates Valentin.

'I need a volunteer from the audience,' Valentin says. He waves his wand at the blackboard and writing appears, written in what looks like chalk. *Roderick Skarratt.*

A murmur of surprise rumbles around the theatre, many of them recognising the conjuror's name, as the house lights go up.

'Ah! Mr Skarratt!' says Valentin, with a wry grin. 'A fellow conjuror! Please, sir, step right up!'

The audience cheers, excited by this unexpected guest appearance. Cec suppresses a smile, seeing Skarratt's puzzled face, a hissed conversation as he turns to his sister next to him. He's reluctant to leave his seat but the audience grows impatient.

'Come on!' someone bellows out and Skarratt is left with no choice but to join them onstage.

Cec's heart thumps loudly in her chest for this is by far the riskiest part of the whole show. After all, Skarratt has no idea what is about to happen.

Justice, Cec thinks to herself firmly. *Justice not revenge.*

As Skarratt walks onto the stage, stagehands bring out a round table, four chairs, and a large pillar candle.

'Please, be seated,' Valentin says, pointing to a chair, and Skarratt bows elegantly, trying to get the audience onside, before he sits.

'One more volunteer!' George cries, motioning towards the blackboard as the name of Skarratt disappears, replaced by another in the same chalky writing. *Marianne Carnesky.*

'Ah, Mrs Carnesky! Your sister! I believe she was seated next to you, Mr Skarratt!' Valentin proclaims.

Mrs Carnesky, however, appears even more reluctant to leave her seat, looking anxiously around.

Cec steps forward. 'A round of applause for Mrs Carnesky!' she says, as the audience cheers, urging her on. And, like her brother, Marianne has no option but to join them onstage.

Valentin directs her to the table and he and George take a seat either side of the siblings. 'I am the master of dark and light,' Valentin says, lighting the large pillar candle on the table. 'Remember, dear audience, everything you see tonight is a trick, nothing more than an illusion. Now, come, let us take each other's hands. The circle must be complete after all.'

Skarratt and Mrs Carnesky reluctantly take Valentin and George's hands as Cec steps into the wings. She sees Mabel in the shadows, her face pale, and Cec gives her a reassuring smile, a gentle touch of her arm, before waiting for her next cue.

'Mr Perris and I, we are the enemy of imposters,' Valentin says. 'The scourge of those who prey on the innocent and vulnerable. The bringers of truth. So let us see what truths we might unearth tonight. Come, spirits! *Come!*'

A pale disembodied face suddenly rises, impossibly, from the centre of the table, a worried look upon it, as audience members draw in their breath. Skarratt tries to pull his hands away but George and Valentin hold him tight.

'Speak, oh spirit!' Valentin says. 'What say you?'

'I say whatever you wish!' Cec says in a deep voice, throwing her voice from the wings. 'For I am the trick of a ventriloquist. Nothing but paper and glue. A mask, a rod, and a rope. Just as Mrs Carnesky uses in her séances.'

The lights go up onstage and the audience gasp as they see the spirit for what it really is: papier mâché and paint.

Mrs Carnesky stands in angry protest, exactly as Cec predicted.

'Why, Mrs Carnesky, what's the matter?' George asks, innocently. 'Do you deny you use these tricks?'

'What's the meaning of this?' Skarratt snaps, standing up to join his sister.

'We have witnesses, Mrs Carnesky,' George says, sharply. 'Dozens of testaments from those you duped. Bereaved men and women, those who have lost children. Even your own maid testified against you!'

The audience is silent, spellbound by this strange drama playing out in front of them.

Valentin claps his hands and a sheaf of papers appears from nowhere. Skarratt catches sight of Cec in the wings and glares daggers at her as she allows herself a faint smile.

'Mrs Carnesky, you have fooled the people of Bristol long enough!' George says firmly, as the audience starts to boo.

She turns to them. 'No! The spirits, they do come!' But her voice is uncertain.

'Like your brother's dead wife?' George asks drily, as Skarratt frowns. 'Or should I say estranged? For despite Mr Skarratt's many tales of being a widower, his wife did not drown in a river, but is alive and well, living in Northumbria, far away from his clutches. You lied, Mr Skarratt, telling a story to engender pity.'

'For shame!' someone shouts from the crowd, to mutterings of approval.

'That's only the beginning of Mr Skarratt's crimes,' Cec says, walking onstage, Mabel beside her, both carrying boxes. Skarratt is shaken to see his ex-maid and a look of panic comes over him. 'No!' he mouths silently, and Cec knows they've truly got to him.

'Contained within these boxes are books of notes, details on every person Mr Skarratt and his sister, Mrs Carnesky, preyed upon,' Cec says loudly as she and Mabel put the boxes in a stack beside the table. 'A file for each of their clients. Coded notes, but easy enough to decipher. And that's not all. Attempted burglary, first at The Professor's home, then at Mr Perris's workshop. He blackmailed a young woman, threatened those who worked with him, and resorted to violence on many occasions. All motivated by envy,' she says, her voice cracking a little as Mabel gives her a nod before returning to the wings.

'For shame! *For shame!*' The cry comes from the stalls and galleries, echoing around the theatre as the booing grows louder.

'Nonsense! All nonsense!' cries Skarratt, taking his sister's hand. 'You cannot prove a thing!' He goes to walk off stage but the wings are blocked by the Hogarth brothers and numerous stagehands. A flicker of fear as Skarratt turns back to Valentin.

'*You will sit back down*!' Valentin commands.

Skarratt reluctantly takes a seat as his sister does the same and Valentin holds his hand up for silence.

'Blackmail and violence,' Valentin says. 'Attempted burglary. Deliberate deception. And Mr Skarratt dabbles in black magic too, making poppets of his enemies. Yet perhaps the worst of his crimes was to light the fire that destroyed the Prince's Theatre!'

The revelation strikes the audience dumb for a moment, before shouts of disapproval and booing start anew, louder this time, angrier.

'Lies!' Skarratt jumps to his feet. 'Scurrilous lies! You have no proof!'

'Wrong again, Mr Skarratt!' Valentin says, and with a clap of his hands, a large mirror is wheeled on – much to Cec's surprise. She glances at George who gives a tiny shake of his head. He wasn't expecting this either.

This isn't what we rehearsed!

Valentin catches Cec's eye and winks. 'Trust me,' he mouths, and she nods. *Always*, she thinks.

'Watch!' Valentin says, as the lights dim. 'Justice will be served! For we have one final spirit to produce . . .' Valentin gently pushes Skarratt back into his chair before spinning him around to face the mirror, his back to the audience.

'Why, Mr Skarratt! This is the very mirror you helped work on over the past few weeks, is it not?' Valentin says. 'A mirror you know well. A mirror you know contains no tricks for you looked over it yourself, did you not?'

A look of dread comes over Skarratt's face as Cec watches him. Valentin smiles faintly before gesturing towards the large mirror. A chill rises in the air as the audience fall deathly quiet.

'Is anyone there?' Valentin asks. 'Anyone who wishes to give this man, Roderick Skarratt, a message?'

Valentin flicks his wand at the mirror, once, twice and a third, final time. For a moment, nothing happens – Valentin and Skarratt's own reflections look back at them – but then, far away, in the depths of the mirror, a faint red glow appears.

The audience members suck in their breath. A figure in the distance, coming closer. Skarratt is terrified.

'No . . .' he moans, shivering with fear. '*No!*'

The figure within the mirror comes closer still. A tall, unusual-looking man with high cheekbones, grey hair, and a large nose. A man who, Cec thinks, her mouth falling open, looks *exactly* like the photos she has seen of—

'*The Professor!*' someone cries, and a murmur of surprise ripples around the audience. *Impossible! How could it be?*

The figure remains silent, his eyes full of fire. He stares at Skarratt and lifts his arm, pointing at him with a single finger as if he could destroy him in an instant.

Skarratt recoils in shock, his face filled with horror.

'Oh, ghostly figure!' cries Valentin. 'Tell us what we should do!'

The figure turns towards Valentin. The corner of his mouth curves and he throws an object out, from within the mirror, that Valentin catches. Then the figure clicks his fingers and, in a flash, disappears. The mirror empty once again.

Cec cannot believe her eyes. *It must be a double, a man who looks like The Professor, a dim light playing into their imagination! Mustn't it . . .?* She glances at George, as dumbfounded as she is, staring at the empty mirror with wonder.

'Why, what do I have here?' Valentin says, holding up a red leather notebook and leafing through it. 'A confession. In Mr Skarratt's own hand. *Everything*. The fire, the séances. His collaboration with his sister and his bullying of her too. The seduction of vulnerable young girls and women.'

Skarratt glances towards Cec, and she smiles triumphantly, as Valentin continues.

'This man has let jealousy and greed overcome him. He has become drunk on the power of his own lies, addicted to falsehoods.'

'You're a disgrace, Skarratt!' yells someone from the audience as the sound of booing grows and Skarratt shrinks into his chair. 'You'll never work again! *Shame on you!*'

'Enough!' Valentin says. He motions to Cec and she runs over, a large white cloth now in her hand, embroidered around the edge with red hearts and black spades.

'If we cannot punish the fraudsters and vagabonds, the creators of chaos and misrule, in our art, when can we? For far too often they escape judgement in our real lives,' Valentin says. 'Mrs Carnesky, Mr Skarratt.'

Valentin takes the cloth from Cec and stands behind Skarratt and Mrs Carnesky, both stunned into silence, still in their chairs. He throws the silk up in the air, over the three of them, and it lingers for a moment, the shape of them briefly silhouetted underneath, before collapsing into nothing.

Vanished.

The audience cheers and whistles, drumming its feet with approval.

Cec curtseys, picks up the silk and throws it over herself – but this time, when it slips off, Valentin stands up next to her, restored.

There is no sign of Roderick Skarratt or Marianne Carnesky.

Cec and Valentin bow, the audience cheering as Valentin holds his hand out for George to join him. 'Mr Skarratt and Mrs Carnesky will shortly be found in a police cell in the local gaol,' says Valentin. 'Along with a package for the constabulary that contains sworn affidavits from those he and his sister duped, and Mr Skarratt's confession in his own hand. Justice is served, my friends.'

He pauses for a moment, a slight bow of his head, before continuing.

'We are, I'm sorry to say, coming to the end of our show tonight. But I do have one last, final illusion. Mr Perris, if you please.'

George stands next to Valentin and the older conjuror puts an arm around his shoulders.

'Mr George Perris, ladies and gentlemen – an extraordinarily talented young man. I dislike farewells and so too did The Professor. He couldn't bear them, in fact. So, I'll keep this short.

'Mr Perris represents not just the best of his generation, but the best of humanity. He brings a kinder magic, brighter and lighter than the arts of myself and The Professor. It has been an honour to work alongside him and Miss Marsden these past months. What then, might I give The Professor's successor, the inheritor to the conjuror's crown? I would give Mr Perris my wand, but he does not use one. I could offer him my cloak, but he has his own. And so, in the end, I can offer George nothing, bar my enduring love and respect – and one last, final illusion. For The Professor left me with strict instructions – to go out with a bang.'

Valentin nods to Cec, who throws him his walking stick, brass-tipped with the head of a beast that is part dog, part dragon.

'Incidentally' – Valentin smiles charmingly as the house lights go up and he walks off the stage and down into the auditorium – 'this is a trick Mr Perris himself came up with – I merely put an old man's spin on it.'

George watches onstage as Valentin heads along the main aisle in the stalls, growing more sprightly, younger even, with each step.

Ten rows down the aisle, Valentin is meant to turn left, where the trapdoor Eadie made for him is, and vanish. But instead The Great Valentini pauses. He glances back at George and Cec, one last mischievous grin, before turning right.

George's heart skips a beat.

The wrong side of the aisle! The trapdoor is to the *left*! Valentin must have *forgotten*! George panics, wondering how he can rectify his friend's mistake – but he has no need to.

'Ah, Mrs Gray!' Valentin says, smoothly, to The Professor's housekeeper, sitting spellbound in the audience. 'How lovely to see you! I cannot, of course, oust a lady from her seat, but perhaps the row behind you—? Ah, this gentleman. Might you oblige, sir?'

A tall man with gold glasses and a neat grey beard struggles to stand, and Valentin helps him before taking his place. The man shuffles off, disappearing into darkness at the back of the stalls.

'Mr Perris!' Valentin cries, towards the stage. 'Thank you for all you have taught me! May they cheer your name for generations to come. You are the future, George! I and The Professor are the past. Three cheers for Mr George Perris! *Three cheers!*'

Valentin throws his walking stick up into the air, brass handle catching the light as it flies high. 'Hip hip hurrah!' he cries, catching it as it falls. 'Hip hip hurrah!' he repeats, as he flings the walking stick up again, the audience now joining in.

'Hip hip hurrah!' cries the whole theatre one last time, all three thousand of them, waiting for The Great Valentini to catch his walking stick.

But it bounces into an empty space.

For there is no one to catch it.

No Valentin.

Nothing but an empty seat.

He has vanished whilst all eyes were upon him. Vanished in front of a whole theatre. Into a space where there is no trapdoor.

'*Impossible!*' breathes George, eyes round with disbelief. He looks at Cec, her mouth a circle of wonder as she turns to him.

The entire theatre roars with delight, leaping to their feet, clapping, cheering, whistling. A moment of wonder and amazement, of *pure magic.*

Darkness falls as the house lights suddenly go off and Eadie's screen comes slowly down, Cec and George instinctively moving to one side.

Another surprise, George thinks, as Chaplin cranks the projector and a bearded Valentin appears onscreen in his suit and top hat.

He peers into the camera before breaking into a grin. Then Valentin turns, walks a handful of paces and stops, looking back over his shoulder. A doff of his cap as he winks at the camera. One last charming smile before he walks away, and the film rolls into nothingness. A single slide with two words in white.

The End.

As the lights come back up and the cheers raise the roof, Harry joins George and Cec onstage, beckoning Eadie up, as they wait for Valentin to join them.

But The Great Valentini is nowhere to be seen.

'Perris! *Perris! Valentini!* Perris!' The crowd continues to whistle and applaud, everyone on their feet as those onstage – George and Harry, Eadie and Cec – bow again and again as the cheers fill their ears.

'Where is he?' Harry mouths, and George shakes his head. For it is impossible. *It is all impossible.*

They bow one final time – still without Valentin – and the curtain falls.

'Where on *earth* is he?' Harry asks. 'How did he *do* that?'

But he does not come. He does not come as they wait onstage for him to join them. He does not come even as Cec tries to find him, worried something may have happened, squeezing through hallways packed with excited stagehands, fumbling her way underneath the auditorium still rumbling with the audience's cheers. The trapdoor untouched, locked shut. Still no Valentin. He does not come as they head to the dressing rooms, minds reeling, clasping each other's hands.

And they know, each and every one of them, that they have witnessed something extraordinary.

Deep in their hearts and souls, they already know the truth.

He does not come because he cannot. The Great Valentini is no more. He has vanished, and the man called Valentin has vanished with him.

As a brief appendix to my little pamphlet, I feel I should add a few words about magic in general. Conjuring, I should say, is a capital hobby for ladies and I have never been able to understand why it should not be as popular with them as it is with boys of all ages. It is a most graceful accomplishment; and I sincerely hope this book encourages at least some ladies to give it a try. I would also strongly advise any budding conjurors, male or female, to write their ideas down in a notebook. They might be surprised what an inspiration they will prove to be in later years.

And, finally, anyone who wishes to become a conjuror should bear in mind that the best secrets will be those that he — or she — discovers for themselves. When the magician has discovered a wholly original way of doing and presenting an old trick, or when he has invented an entirely new one, he may consider he has a better secret than any that a book, such as this, can impart, because it is their own. And, of course, having achieved such a success, the conjuror has, at last, found the true and best answer to the question — what is magic?

Extract from *The Secrets of Magic* by George Perris
(published by Saxon Press, 1895)

THE MEANING
OF MAGIC

Cec sits in her dressing room looking at herself in the mirror, tears streaking the make-up on her face. She knew he would leave, of course she did. *But not like this . . .*

Oz barks at her feet and she lifts him up, burying her face in his wiry fur, cuddling his solid belly.

'Oh, Oz . . .' she murmurs as he yelps, and she puts him back down. She is so glad Valentin left him for her to look after, although puzzled too, for the conjuror had always been so fond of his little dog.

'Is he really gone?' Cec whispers, and Oz yips at her.

Valentin's walking stick, retrieved from the auditorium, leans against Cec's dressing table and, on a whim, she picks it up. The strange brass head feels loose and Cec twists it only for it to unexpectedly fall off, revealing a hollow inside.

Intrigued, she tips it up, and a wand slides out. A single card is wrapped around it: a joker, and on the back, in Valentin's neat writing: 'For Cecil. My other loyal terrier'– and she can't help but laugh, tears of joy and sorrow bursting from her.

A knock on the door and Harry and Eadie tentatively enter.

'Are you all right?' Eadie asks.

'I think so.' Cec sniffs.

Harry puts her hands on Cec's shoulders, just as Valentin had in the interval. 'We'll look after you, Cec,' she says, to their reflections. 'Me and George.'

'Me too,' says Eadie.

Cec smiles and wipes her eyes. Her new family. The one she has chosen, the one that chose her.

'Where is George?' she asks, and Harry and Eadie glance at each other.

'He's taking a moment,' Harry replies.

George has locked his dressing-room door so as not to be disturbed. He sits staring at the folded note in front of him, trying to unravel a puzzle that his brain cannot yet comprehend. *The man in the mirror. Valentin's disappearance.*

Whispers of understanding float just out of reach, in the far corners of his vision, as if, by turning his head fast enough, he might just see them and finally understand.

He and Valentin are the toast of the town. A huge success. A show as never seen before. And justice has been served too: Skarratt and Mrs Carnesky both dealt with at long last.

A rap at the door interrupts him.

'George . . . it's me. Eadie.'

He goes to the door and unlocks it, letting her in and shutting it behind her.

'The whole world wishes to congratulate you.' She smiles.

George tries and fails to smile in return. He unfolds the farewell note Valentin left for him in his dressing room and that he's already read a dozen times or more. He hands it to Eadie.

'Farewell Bristol, take a magician's adieu!
Never more will he astonish your people and you . . .'

My dear George,
   I did warn you tonight would be full of surprises . . .
   It has been a true honour, Perris. You have done us proud, both me and The Professor. I meant it when I said I could not bear a long farewell. It is, we have always thought, better to go out with a bang . . . Please then, forgive an old man's indulgence of leaving without a farewell.
   Great things await you, Mr Perris. You know that as well as I. You have always known. Follow your heart, for it will lead you true. And please, look after your new assistant. I know you will, of course, but Cecil is a rare treasure.
   'All done by kindness.'
   With the greatest of affection,
   V

'But it's impossible!' George says. 'Utterly impossible.'

'Maybe that was the point. His final gift to you,' says Eadie. 'For what else could he give you, George? No wand, no cloak, but a memory instead. A touch of *real* magic . . .'

'Which doesn't exist. *Cannot* exist!'

'He duped me too, don't forget! That film he made with Chaplin. The trapdoor he didn't end up using after all my work!'

George thinks for a moment, before shaking his head. 'It's still impossible.'

'Perhaps. Perhaps not. Now, are you coming to dinner, or are you going to sit here all night?'

George rubs his hands over his face before loosening his necktie. 'I wish I could rewind time, Eadie, like one of your reels. Find out what he'd *really* been up to all this time. Don't you wish that too?'

'To rewind time?'

George nods.

'In a way,' Eadie says, quietly. 'But we can't, can we? We must live forwards, not backwards.' She goes towards the door. 'I'll leave you to get ready. We'll meet you outside. Your father and Jane are coming. And your Mr Greenhouse wants you to meet some investors for a toast beforehand too.'

'All right.' George sighs.

'One last thing, George.' Eadie builds up her courage. 'You must know, if I could rewind time, I would. Please know that.'

He looks at her, puzzled, as she smiles at him. She holds her left hand out, extends a finger, and draws, with her other hand, a shooting star that flies out from it, just as it did that night after Ashton Court.

And then she's gone, the door shutting behind her, as George is left to wonder.

Later, much later, after the photographs and journalists, after the flowers and congratulations, champagne and supper, a sizable troupe heads back to Eadie's sitting room. But as the evening wears on, the numbers drop as first George's father and stepmother leave for their hotel, then Alex Hogarth and his fiancée go too. Soon there are only seven left: Louis and Ollie, Eadie, George and Harry, Chaplin and Cec – not including Oz, who seems particularly vocal.

'Perhaps he's missing Valentin,' Cec says, picking up the dog, who wriggles out of her grasp and runs in circles, chasing its tail.

'*She* more like,' Louis says, as they look at him.

Eadie gives him a nudge. 'Oz is a *boy*, Louis!'

'Louis's right!' Chaplin says, confidently. 'I grew up with dogs and *she* is definitely female.'

'No! Valentin had him "done",' Cec says, trying to be polite, as Chaplin laughs.

'She's a girl! I'll prove it!' He holds his hands out as Oz wanders over to him and he scoops the dog up, patting around its belly.

'Solid around the middle . . .'

'He *has* put on a bit of weight recently,' says Cec, guiltily, for she's rather fond of giving the dog treats and scraps.

'That's not weight, Cec!' Louis grins.

'It's puppies!' Chaplin says. 'She's pregnant, Cec!'

The group falls silent for a moment.

'By God!' George says, realisation dawning on him. 'He swapped the dog! He swapped the *bloody dog*!' The room echoes with surprised laughter.

'But that's . . . He *can't* have done!' cries Cec. 'I *know* Oz! I do!' She looks down at her beloved Oz, tries to think when he became livelier, noisier, when he stopped cocking his leg and started squatting. An infection, Valentin had told her, a problem with his leg.

She frowns to herself. *But if this isn't Oz, then the real Oz must still be with Valentin! Loved and looked after, and so this little terrier – and her pups – is a present, along with the wand.*

Cec smiles, remembering the shadows Valentin showed her that first night, the wonders contained within him – and within her too. She wants so much to share it, his impossible *real* self with her new family, but as she glances at her palm and the faint scar of her blood oath, she knows, as she perhaps always has done, she will never tell a single soul.

A little bit of magic that was all Valentin's, for him to use as he saw fit. And her own little bit of magic that is all hers too.

One day, perhaps, she might share hers. *One day. But not yet.*

Cec scoops the dog up, hugging her close, as she grins. 'Well, I love him or her just as he or she is! And I'm sticking with Oz as a name.'

'Good for you, Cec,' George says. 'One other thing that's puzzling me though – how on earth did Valentin get Skarratt to write his confession down?'

Cec chuckles. 'That was me. A little idea I dreamed up, inspired by your father's notebook, Eadie. And Valentin helped. I wasn't sure it would work or, even if it did, how we might get the notebook back, but Mabel, Skarratt's ex-maid and a truly brave soul, helped us get into the house. That's how we managed to get the boxes from his study too. Valentin paid her handsomely for it and set her up at a new place of work. We didn't tell you beforehand about the notebook as we weren't sure we could pull it off.'

'It was quite something!' George says, impressed, and Cec grins.

Harry yawns. 'Sorry!' she says. 'Goodness, what a night! I'm afraid I'll have to turn in.'

'Me too,' says Chaplin. 'I'll take you home, if you like? Help with the crutches?'

'Cec? Do you want to come back with us too?' Harry suggests, getting to her feet. 'You're family now, and I don't think you should be in that apartment on your own, not tonight.'

'Thanks, Harry. Can Oz come too?'

'Ambrose our cat might object, but I'm sure we'll work it out.'

'I should be off as well,' Louis says, stretching himself and nudging Ollie beside him. 'I've finally persuaded Ollie to get a bicycle. We're off to collect it first thing tomorrow, so I, er—'

'Louis is staying with us tonight,' Ollie explains, his eyes shining, and Eadie smiles at them both, a nod of understanding, as they too get to their feet and Louis kisses her on the forehead.

'Oh, before you all go,' Eadie says. 'I quite forgot, in the whirlwind of everything, we had a special guest tonight. Mrs Fearnley, my landlady.'

'And?' Harry asks, hopefully.

'She apologised to me, after the show. Poor Mrs Fearnley. She knows now that Mrs Carnesky lied to her. She was most upset, but she's promised me an extension to the lease, ten or twenty years, however long I want.'

'Then you can stay?' George asks. 'At Regent Street?'

She nods excitedly. 'I still can't believe it!'

'Congratulations!' Louis beams at her. 'I'm so proud of you, Eadie.'

'You too, Louis,' she replies, softly.

The group rises as one, heading out of the door and down the stairs, saying their farewells. All except George.

'I just want to talk to Eadie for a moment,' he says, as Harry smiles knowingly.

'Come on, everyone!' she cries, ushering everyone out before her. 'I'll see you at home,' she says to George. 'Goodnight, Eadie!' and she blows her a kiss, leaving Eadie and George alone on the landing.

George waits until the front door shuts. 'Eadie, look, I wanted to tell you, I've been—'

She interrupts him, taking his hands and looking straight into his eyes. 'I've been thinking too, George. A lot. And—'

She breaks off, blushing. 'I'm sorry, you go first,' she says, suddenly nervous.

'The thing is, Eadie – this evening, the past few months . . . I've *loved* working with you, really I have. And I wanted to thank you, for everything, for all your collaboration and—' He stops, shy suddenly. 'I don't want to stop working with you. Really I don't. I've been thinking and I'm not sure I want to do this "home of magic" in the way I first thought. I love new ideas, experimenting and performing, collaborating with *you* above all – I don't want to run a venue. I'm not a manager! And working with Fintan at the Prince's, seeing all that paperwork – that's not me! What I'm thinking now is a *school* of magic. A summer school, for children. A *city* of magic even, using The Professor's collection he left me in his will. Something *alive and new*. Bringing together everything I've learned, from Valentin and The Professor, from Harry and the Hogarths. From *you*. Animated pictures too. Bringing it all together into something big and interactive, that encourages younger generations, boys and girls, from all backgrounds. D'you see?'

She smiles: George's enthusiasm as infectious as ever. 'I do see. And I think it a most excellent idea. A city of magic. What could be more enchanting?'

'I hoped you'd like it,' he says, bashfully. 'And tonight, Greenhouse and all his business men, I didn't get to spend much time with them but I made the most of it. Greenhouse is quite the convert to living pictures these days! Put it this way, if you're still looking for new investors, you won't have any trouble finding them. And then perhaps, you might recruit more staff? Take the pressure off a bit?'

Eadie is so touched, she doesn't know what to say. She squeezes his hands gently.

'Thank you,' she says softly. 'Was that what you wished to talk to me about?'

'Partly, but also . . .' He frowns as he slips his hands from hers, scratches his head. 'Look, Eadie, before . . . I mean, after Ashton Court.'

Her heart skips a beat.

'I owe you a proper apology. I was on rather a high after the show and, well, with, the champagne and – oh, Eadie! I've felt terrible about it ever since.'

'So have I,' Eadie says, gently placing a hand on George's chest, his heart thrumming underneath. 'I've felt terrible about *that* . . .' she says, pressing gently as he looks at her, wide-eyed. 'And I've tried. I've tried so hard, George, to tell you. To try and explain. I didn't mean to push you away. It was the last thing I wanted. And there's never been a good time to talk to you of late, just you, without other people around. And I didn't know how to say it. Only that I've regretted it so very much, believe me.' She looks deep into his beautiful blue-grey eyes flecked with gold. 'I wanted you to kiss me,' she says, so softly that George isn't sure he heard properly.

'Eadie—' he says, breathlessly.

'George, I was scared. That's the truth. Because we had become such good friends and colleagues and I didn't want to risk any of that. But I wanted you to kiss me. More than anything.'

It takes all of her courage to say it. But there, it is out. She waits, trembling, barely able to breathe, as his mouth slowly curves into a smile.

'Oh, Eadie . . .' he whispers, gazing at her. He lifts his hand and gently brushes her cheek. 'All this time! Might I make a suggestion then?' George smiles and looks deep into her eyes. 'Perhaps we could be scared *together*? You see, the thing is,' he says, 'I've rather fallen in love with you, Eadie Carleton.'

The truth of it floods Eadie with a tidal wave of happiness and relief. She stands for a moment, letting it flow through every cell in her body. The sheer joy of knowing he loves her, that she loves him so very deeply in return.

'Oh, George,' she says, simply. 'I love you too.'

And then she pulls him towards her, and her lips are on his and this time he tastes of champagne and love. Of the new and exciting. Of something wonderful. Of something big and bright and beautiful. Warm and urgent. She pulls him closer, and closer still, lips lingering on his.

'I've wanted to do that again for such a long time,' George whispers as they pull away a little, breath fast and hearts pounding, foreheads still touching.

Eadie smiles, not quite believing he is truly hers. She reaches for him again, she cannot help herself – hands in his hair, bringing his face to hers, faster this time, more urgent, losing herself in him . . .

George reaches for the pins in her hair, gently pulling a couple out until Eadie reaches up, pulling them out herself, as her curls tumble down, a wave of hair falling over her shoulders.

'I've wanted to do that for a long time too.' He smiles, and she laughs, reaching forward to kiss him again, long and lingeringly, revelling in his touch. Her hands reach for his waistcoat, gently unbuttoning it, the warmth of him underneath his white shirt. She draws back a moment. She has never wanted anyone more than she wants him, and it scares her, it does, but it thrills her too, the electricity of him tingling on her skin.

'Will you stay?' she asks, gently drawing a line down his chest with her finger, the words out of her mouth before she's even aware of them. 'Tonight,' she clarifies, as his eyes widen.

'Do you want me to?' he asks, and she grins wickedly at him.

'Eadie Carleton!' he exclaims. 'You are so very full of surprises! By God, I love you . . .'

Eadie laughs. 'I love you too, George,' she says again, and this time the words fit her mouth perfectly. So much easier to say.

She is besotted and breathless as she takes his hand, leading him slowly up the stairs, one by one. And George, as infatuated and enamoured of her as she is with him, follows close behind.

It's dark when Eadie awakes, sheets warm on her bare skin, a faint ache within her. She sleepily reaches out an arm, before looking up and seeing George standing by the window, the moon shining on him through a gap in the curtains.

She smiles as she watches him, moonbeams making his skin glow as if he were luminous. The faint rise and fall of the muscles on his arms. His dishevelled hair. She wonders, briefly, how anyone ever gets anything done when there is such pleasure to be had.

He turns, sees she's awake, and his whole face lights up as she joins him by the crack in the curtains, confident in her naked self in a way she has never even considered before. Barefoot, cold on the floorboards. Skin tingling with goosebumps and the echo of his gentle touch. Drunk on love.

His arm slips around her, and she leans in to him. 'No shooting stars tonight,' he whispers, kissing her on the head, as she takes his hand and leads him back to bed where they curl around each other, warm limbs overlapping.

Such happiness, Eadie thinks, as she softly kisses him. A lifetime of love reaching out ahead.

Sometime later, Eadie is dozing off when George mutters to himself.

'What is it?' Eadie whispers, sleepily.

'Oh, sorry. Nothing,' George replies.

Eadie nudges him. 'It's never nothing with you, George. What is it?'

'It's just . . . I can't stop thinking . . .' he says, softly. 'About Valentin. Not a single one of us had the full picture at any time. Each of us an unknowing accomplice. Cec with that notebook; Chaplin with that little end film; you with the trapdoor. The man in the mirror.'

Eadie rests her head against him. 'He certainly planned it all very neatly.'

'And that last trick,' George says. 'We knew he was going to vanish, but doing it like that on the wrong side of the aisle, an extra twist, just for us. I wonder . . .'

'Go on,' Eadie says.

'That notebook of your father's. Do you still have it?'

'It's in the safe downstairs. Why?'

'I never did get a chance to look at it . . . and I think I'd very much like to.'

He turns to her, eyes glittering, and she laughs. 'What, *now*?' she asks, and he beams at her. 'George Perris, you are quite mad!'

'Come on.' He grins, kissing her. 'Let's put some clothes on.'

Ten minutes later, Eadie has pulled on an old serge gown she sometimes works in, and George has thrown on his trousers and shirt. The lovers stand in Eadie's workshop as she wrestles with the lock on the safe.

'Aha!' she says, pulling out the red leather-bound notebook. She hands it to George, who leafs through it before looking at her, surprised.

'You know there are pages missing?' he says. 'At the end.'

'No!' she says, shocked. 'But that's impossible, it's been locked away!'

George frowns. 'Valentin had this book for a while, didn't he? What did he say to you after he looked through it?'

He hands the book back, and Eadie examines it. The last few pages have been torn out close to the spine, the incomprehensible scribbles and symbols her father had written in India, all gone.

'I can't remember exactly. I can't believe he would have taken pages out!'

'I can't believe he would have taken them for *nothing*.'

'Valentin was here, when I put the book in the safe,' Eadie says. 'I suppose he could have seen the combination over my shoulder. But I can't believe my father really *did* discover anything of importance.'

'But if he had, what then?' George paces up and down for a moment, then stops with a look of shock. He slaps his forehead. 'By God! We've been *played*, Eadie! The rummy old pair of . . .!'

'What? What is it?'

'*The vanishing*. The Professor! He always used to say it was what he most wanted to do. Vanish right in front of you. And he *loved* a practical joke . . .'

'What are you saying?'

'*We saw him*. The Professor. Onstage.'

'George! It was a trick!' Eadie looks at him. 'You can't *really* think—?'

'Yes, Eadie! I do! What if, just *what if* The Professor wasn't dead after all? We all saw him, onstage in the mirror. A double, I thought, someone made up to look like him – but what if it really *was* him? What if, like so many of the best tricks, the simplest explanation is the right one?'

'You're letting your imagination run wild!' Eadie says, trying not to get too carried away herself as George reaches into his pocket and pulls out Valentin's note.

'"You have truly done us proud, both The Professor and me. I meant it when I said I could not bear a long farewell.

For it is, we have always thought, better to go out with a bang." You see, Eadie? "We" have always thought, not "I"! "We"!'

'That's simply a figure of speech! Besides, what about the funeral?'

'No open casket, remember? That death mask on the coffin, a sort of visual confirmation he was inside. Very clever. But what if he *wasn't*? And think, Eadie, *think*, at the end of the show, it was Mrs Gray, The Professor's housekeeper, who Valentin nearly outed from her seat. She must have been in on it too. And the tall man in the row behind her, the man with the beard and glasses. Almost like a disguise, wouldn't you say? And his gait, when he tried to stand, unsteady on his feet, just as The Professor was when getting in and out of his wheelchair . . .'

Eadie ponders for a moment. 'But . . . *why*?'

'To go out with a bang! They fell out, I know, but long ago those two were the best of friends. The mischief they used to get up to! I remember a story The Professor once told me. Years ago, when he was in North Africa – he vanished himself, pretending to have died to get out of a tight spot. Valentin was his accomplice, crying crocodile tears to cover for him. What better way to vanish than to fake one's own death? And taking those pages from your father's notebook, we'll never know the truth of it!'

'But The Professor was ill . . .'

'Undoubtedly. Too ill to perform a full-length show, but not too ill to be an accomplice. They must've been planning it ever since Valentin returned. And The Professor's funeral!

Remember the date? The first of April! By God, we've been well and truly *had*!'

Eadie is lost in thought. *Could it really be true?*

'May I have a look at that note from Valentin?' she asks, and George hands it to her. She reads it and, as she does so, something catches her eye. Puzzled, she holds it up to the light, tilting it first one way, then the other.

'What is it?' he asks.

'A watermark. In the paper. Hard to make out, but I think it says, "Strike all that—?"'

'"Strike all that look upon with marvel,"' George exclaims. 'That's on The Professor's mausoleum at Arnos Vale!'

They look at each other, wide-eyed.

'But if you're right, and The Professor really isn't dead,' Eadie says, thoughtfully, 'then, what's in his mausoleum?'

'Well, there's only one way to find out . . .'

'You can't be serious!'

'Oh, but I am! Don't you see? Everything they did was deliberate, Eadie. *Everything*. Even down to the smallest detail. Like a watermark.'

Eadie relents. 'We should probably wait until morning,' she says.

'Probably,' says George, his face widening into a grin. 'That'd be the *sensible* thing to do.'

They gaze at each other for a moment before Eadie grins back at him. 'Come on then!' she says. 'What are we waiting for?'

A faint glimmer of light is already beginning to reach across the horizon by the time George and Eadie arrive at The

Professor's mausoleum. Eadie's heart pounds with excitement, one hand clasped tightly in George's, the other holding a lantern. She holds it up to the inscription above the entrance, light flickering across the words.

'Strike all that look upon with marvel,' she says, reading out the inscription above the entrance.

George examines the door before giving it a push with his shoulder. A click and the door creaks open. He steps inside first, into the darkness, as Eadie follows.

A gasp from both of them as they see what is inside. *Nothing*. No coffin, anyway. The simple stone space is entirely empty except for two small items in the centre: a hand-tied bunch of creamy-lemon tulips with distinctive pink feathering, still fresh. And one of Valentin's handkerchiefs, neatly folded, embroidered around the edge with red hearts and black spades.

George laughs – he can't help himself. He bows to the two items, giving them a round of applause as Eadie giggles.

'I've remembered where I know that quote from too,' she says. '"Strike all that look upon with marvel." From my school days. It's the end of *A Winter's Tale* when Hermione is restored to life, returning from the dead.'

'The mischievous old devils!' George exclaims.

'Where do you think they went?' Eadie asks.

'No idea. Although there was a place in Wales that The Professor used to sometimes mention. A house on the far west, by the sea – the name escapes me.'

George thinks of them there, The Professor and Valentin, bare feet in wet sand. He chuckles as he looks at the tulips, knowing Mrs Gray must have been in on it too, remembering how she always did seem rather fond of Valentin . . .

A light flickers outside, a night-watchman, and Eadie grabs George's hand as they run out of the mausoleum, breathless and giggling, into the faint glimmerings of the dawn.

On a street corner, somewhere in Totterdown, they stop, catching their breath for a moment, cheeks aching with laughter.

'Is it always going to be like this?' Eadie asks, serious for a moment.

'What, breaking into cemeteries at the crack of dawn?'

She laughs and George delights in having prompted it.

'No. I meant unpredictable. Mad. Glorious!'

'I hope so,' says George, his eyes as full of joy as his heart is with love. 'Life wouldn't be much fun without adventure, would it? Besides, I think we make rather a good team, Miss Carleton.'

'I think so too, Mr Perris,' she says, and he grins, leaning in for a lingering kiss that makes her heart sing.

Eadie's eyes fill with stars; she sees them reflected back at her in George's gaze, and she wants more than anything to preserve this moment, happiness burning bright, a reel of film in her imagination she can play out forever . . .

'Shall we?' he asks, and she nods. And so they run, the two lovers, hand in hand, giggling and breathless. They run over the bridge across the river, through the still-sleeping city, through empty streets and past still-shut shops. They run through deserted squares, and flocks of pigeons. They run past early shift workers, still rubbing the sleep from their eyes, past the docks and ships and boats, the sounds of cranking chains and anchors. And finally, they run, slower now, tired and happy, full of wonder, up the sloping hill to the bright-coloured terraces of Clifton as the morning rises, and to 5 Regent Street, where their new life together is about to begin . . .

Cec sits on the edge of a strange bed in the Perrises' house unable to sleep, excitement from the show still coursing through her veins. It's a small, cosy room, made smaller by bookshelves and paraphernalia. So different to Skarratt's house full of secrets; different too to Valentin's bare rooms.

Oz yawns on the floor and Cec lifts her up onto the bed next to her. She didn't bring much with her, only a small basket of precious items from the theatre she was reluctant to leave behind. She places it on the bed, Oz sniffing at it as Cec reaches inside, laying out the items on the blanket beside her.

Her playing cards. Valentin's walking stick. His wand. The book of butterflies he'd given her, wrapped in one of his trademark handkerchiefs. She smiles as she unfolds it to reveal the book inside.

'Oh, Valentin . . .' Cec sniffs, knowing how much she'll miss him, remembering his words to her before the second half of the show, realising now it was his way of saying goodbye. And that final trick. When he looked back at her, and she had known he was going to do something truly impossible. His last gift to her. A glimpse of what, one day, with hard work and practice, perhaps she might be able to achieve too.

Cec traces the scar of their blood oath on her left palm, as she sniffs again. Absentmindedly, she wipes her nose on her sleeve, a habit she tells herself she really should grow out of, before opening the butterfly book – to find an inscription from Valentin.

Dearest Cecil,
May you spread your wings and always fly free.
All my love,
V x

She smiles as the book falls open; an envelope tucked within its pages. Puzzled, she sees it is addressed to her and she opens it. A note inside, from the bank of Prescott, Dimsdale, Cave, Tugwell and Co in Cornhill, Bristol. A promise to pay Miss Cecily Marsden the grand sum of five thousand pounds.

She cannot believe it. *Five thousand pounds!* Such riches! She turns the note over, thinking it might be a trick of some kind, but Valentin's handwriting is on the back.

Cecil,
    I suggest perhaps you do not spend all of this on fine wine, food and clothes – I hear Miss Carleton is looking for investors in her company, and a wise investment is always a good one.
    V x

Cec laughs with disbelief, a chuckle of love and surprise, before she places the note back inside the basket. She turns her attention back to the book, to the butterflies on the page. Dozens of beautiful images in front of her.

She concentrates, focusing on a single butterfly as she breathes in, holding her breath a moment before slowly releasing it.

Magic only works if you believe in it.

The butterfly, a large blue one, criss-crossed with black veins like lead in stained glass, softly flickers its wings.

Slowly, Cec raises her left hand, the faint scar on her palm feeling warm, as the paper butterfly lifts its wings and flutters up off the page. It circles the room and Oz yips at it, trying to chase it.

But, to Cec's amazement, all the other butterflies on the page start to slowly rise too. Each and every one of them, beating their wings, a cascade of colour, circling silently around the room. Blues and greens, browns and blacks, yellows and oranges. A whole rainbow of butterflies conjured up out of the pages of the book.

Cec gasps and they are gone. Falling back into nothing but ink and paper. She stares in wonder at her left palm, astonished at what she can do, at all the possibilities held within her. A giggle of glee bubbles up inside her and she cannot help but let it out, leaning her head back and chuckling wildly.

This is who I am, she thinks, with absolute clarity, picking Oz up and hugging her tightly. *This is who I've always been.*

She looks up and catches a glimpse of herself in a mirror over the far side of the room. She smiles to her reflection, and the young woman smiles back at her knowingly.

My name is Cecil Marsden, and I am magic.

THE END

Historical note

Eadie, Cec, George, Valentin and the rest do not, of course, exist. They are figments of my imagination and yet each of them has their roots firmly in reality, taking inspiration from a number of real-life performers, photographers, moving picture pioneers and more.

The overlap between magicians and early moving pictures is much bigger and more complex than I imagined when the first inklings *of The Illusions* came to me. The more I learned, the stranger the truth seemed to be – that magicians played a crucial role in developing the language of film, a language we now immerse ourselves in every day. Their sheer inventiveness, bloody mindedness, rivalry, secrecy, ruthlessness and extraordinary egos contrasted with extreme acts of generosity, creativity and collaboration – a heady and contradictory mix that delighted and fascinated me. I fell in love with them; how could you not? The weird and wonderful twists of their lives were far too peculiar to make up – a gift for any writer.

As you no doubt know, the early film scene in the UK was centred around London, Brighton, Bradford and Leeds.

I've cheated and extended this to include Bristol. As a city with a strong history of photography (and the birthplace of William Friese-Greene, a photographer, inventor, and moving pictures pioneer whose legacy is still being fought over) it felt an appropriate place to locate a hitherto unknown, and entirely fictional, branch of early film pioneers.

The real-life counterparts of my fictional characters are well worth investigating. For those of you who might wish to know more, I'd recommend delving into the lives and works of renowned British magician David Devant (whose motto really was 'all done by kindness' – I hope he would not mind me borrowing it), and Britain's equivalent of Georges Méliès, the artist and magician turned filmmaker and special effects pioneer, Walter Booth.

Booth and, in particular, David Devant are the inspiration for George. Devant wrote extensively about his experiences and is celebrated as Britain's greatest magician during what is widely acknowledged as a golden age of magic. He was brilliantly inventive and his greatest tricks, many of which I have borrowed for *The Illusions*, feel as utterly impossible today as they must have done back when he performed them. He was a kind and generous man and ended up being thrown out of the Magic Circle twice for revealing how to perform his tricks. From the moment he first encountered film, in March 1896, he became an ambassador and champion of the medium. Within days, he was screening Robert W Paul's films at the Egyptian Hall in London, Britain's home of magic, where Devant was resident. Just three months after that first encounter, Devant made a short series of four films with Robert W Paul, none of which survive today. A short film of Devant, by Méliès, demonstrating an inexhaustible hat, does thankfully still survive as does a flick-book of a later film, The Incubated Head. I have stolen all of this and more for George.

For Cec, Miss Marion Melville (also known as Mrs Devant) and Adelaide Hermann (born Adele Scarsez in London) were key influences. Marion was an actress and performer who Devant met and fell in love with in a Hall of Mirrors in Margate. They performed together for decades until Devant was forced to retire due to ill health. Adelaide Hermann was a born performer, falling in love with theatre, dance and circus from a young age. Wilful, determined and talented, in the early days of being her husband's on-stage assistant she performed in drag as Mr Alexander. She was brilliantly inventive and with her husband, Alexander Hermann, became hugely successful. One of their acts, Ten Minutes with the Modern Spirits, duplicated the techniques that spiritualists used. After her husband died in 1896, Adelaide continued the act without him, taking the lead to become the star attraction.

Valentin is inspired by various different magicians, amongst them the hugely influential French inventor, magician and storyteller Jean-Eugène Robert-Houdin as well as Howard Thurston and John Nevil Maskelyne. The fiercely competitive world of magic and Skarratt's jealousy in the book are also drawn from real life. Harry Houdini once, allegedly, picked the locks at Devant's establishment in order to steal an idea and, certainly, back-stage bribery was known to have occurred with some performers genuinely employing double-agents to protect their secrets.

Robert W Paul, known as 'the father of British cinema', led a fascinating life. An electrical engineer, he fell into the world of animated photographs almost by accident. An extraordinary inventor, producer, cinematographer and businessman, he was a true moving image pioneer. He first produced animated photographs in 1895 including his most popular film, *Rough Sea at Dover*, and, in 1896 alone, he produced eighty films. Amongst his many achievements, he was one of the first to create a camera on a tripod with a panning head, meaning that the camera itself could be swivelled to follow the action. He produced one of the first-ever colour films in April 1896, filmed the first two-shot film in history, and his comedy short, *The Soldier's Courtship*, was Britain's and, arguably, the world's first fiction film. In his 14-year career in living pictures he produced well over 750 films. Robert and his actress wife Ellen, along with the actress and filmmaker Laura Bayley, helped inspire Eadie. Women undoubtedly played a key role in early film, not just as performers but as stage managers, producers and more. It's only in relatively recent years that their role has, rightly, begun to be re-evaluated. Despite female engineers and photographers being highly active in Britain in the mid-1890s, there is, perhaps surprisingly, no female film-maker in real life who leads as Eadie does. However, over the Channel, in France, the remarkable Alice Guy-Blaché was very much flying the flag. She made her first film in 1896 and became the head of production at Gaumont aged just twenty-three.

Believed to be the first female film-maker, she experimented with sound and colour and pioneered narrative fiction in her films. One further inspiration for Eadie was the female photographer Kate Pragnell, who worked alongside William Friese-Greene before setting up her own business. Pragnell originally trained as an artist in Bristol before turning her hand to photography. In 1896 she was the only female photographer in London to regularly shoot male clients. Hugely successful, she was a fierce champion of other women, hiring and training female-only employees in her studios. After her death in 1905, her business continued under the guiding hand of her business partner and, I suspect, romantic partner too, Alice Stewart.

I should say, and it breaks my heart to do so, that the traumatic incident of Olivia's baby being killed by a stage-prop bottle of milk is also based on a real event. Robert and Ellen Paul's first baby, Robert Newton Paul, was killed in such an accident in 1898 and, distressingly, their second and third children died not long after being born. I can't imagine how on earth they managed to survive this but it is testament to their strength both as individuals and as a couple that, somehow, they did.

Roderick Skarratt, whilst, like all the others, remaining a work of imagination, took inspiration from a range of individuals including the occultist Aleister Crowley, the American writer Charles Fort (the inspiration for the *Fortean Times*), and GA Smith, the Brighton based film-maker, magician and, previously, a mind-reader who claimed telepathy was real. The divide between magicians and mediums did – and still does – run deep. I found it fascinating that Smith had one foot either side of this line whilst also being one of the most inventive film-makers, creating, arguably, one of the first point-of-view shots, and pioneering parallel action onscreen. For Skarratt, I also added a dash of Thomas Edison's ruthlessness and a dollop of HG Wells's somewhat predatory behaviour towards young women.

Disappearances are a key theme in *The Illusions* and, again, there are many mind-boggling real-life inspirations behind it. British magician Charles Morritt was thought to be dead for some years before David Devant came across him in Hexham in Northumberland experimenting with how to vanish a donkey. Bizarrely, this wasn't the first time a British magician had been assumed deceased only to be found alive and well. In 1783, the famous conjurer Philip Breslaw was pronounced dead. A book was produced and promoted as his last legacy, except Breslaw was not dead. He was simply on tour in Newcastle. The most baffling – and undoubtedly tragic – disappearance though is of Louis le Prince, the French-born, Leeds-based early film pioneer who is believed to have recorded the very first true moving pictures before vanishing without a trace. Known to be in debt at the time, and with a brother who owed him a huge sum of money, rumours still abound as to what might have really happened to him. Finally, there's George Drysdale, a young man who faked his own death by leaving his clothes at the side of the Danube before reappearing two years later having spent most of his time in Hungary, teaching English to the son of a Prince.

Like a jackdaw, I have stolen the shiniest bits from these and many other anecdotes and accounts – for it is true that life is sometimes far stranger than fiction.

The Illusions is also a love-letter to theatre. In 1994, aged sixteen – the same age as Cec is – I joined the National Youth Theatre in the design department and my world changed. I loved everything about it – the late nights, the heady rush of excitement that comes from putting on a show, the crazy long hours as opening night loomed ever closer. I loved the smell of paint and hope, I loved eyeing up the beautiful actors, the strange language of backstage, and the fizzy acidic sweetness of Dandelion and Burdock from a vending machine in the dead of night. I have never stopped loving theatre. I wrote an early draft of this book during lockdown when all the theatres went dark and we needed them more than ever.

Finally, a tale to show that things come full circle. In my first year at Bristol University in the late 1990s, a talented young magician came and performed at my halls of residence. He was magnificent – handsome, charming, and utterly delightful with a penchant for velvet. He ran a free workshop afterwards for a small group of us, and showed us how to hypnotise ourselves. It was a glorious, strange, and fascinating night that has lingered long in my memory. That magician's name was Derren Brown.

I have tweaked and changed dates, facts, locations, names, and rehearsal schedules to better fit my story, and compressed time in order to do so. Devant might have worked for years on one of his great illusions, but I've speeded things up considerably in the name of fiction. The Prince's Theatre, as any Bristol historian knows, was actually destroyed in the Blitz but I brought about its demise a little earlier. I believe that dogs were only commonly neutered from around the 1930s but it was too good a twist to leave out. Druidston Haven is a real place and home to The Druidstone, a hotel with cottages and a restaurant, perched on a cliff above a truly glorious stretch of the Pembrokeshire coast. The original building is an old stone house that, funnily enough, was renovated in the late 1890s . . . I think Valentin, Mrs Gray, and The Professor would have had a whale of a time living there.

Finally, as always, I am a storyteller not an historian – any errors or omissions are my fault and mine alone, fiction rather than fact.

All done by kindness.

Acknowledgements

To Sophie 'The Great' Orme for boundless enthusiasm and wisdom. Big thanks to all at Bonnier for support and kindness, particularly Justine, Izzy, Abi, Ellie, Francesca, Clare, Jeff, Jennie, and Mark. You are all ruddy lovely!

To Katie 'lovely' Lumsden, part-time Victorian, writer and editor extraordinaire, for generous advice.

To Anwen, my amazing agent and dearest friend. Dreams can come true!

To the brilliant artist and illustrator Philip Harris for his gorgeous cover design.

In honour of 5 Regent Street and all who sailed in her. Special doffing of caps to Thomas Chalk, Sumika Sakanishi, Dave Wolf, Tony Pitt, and a flamboyant wave of the handkerchief to the one and only Michael. Especial thanks to George Perris for being kind enough to let me steal his name and give it to a Victorian magician.

I am indebted to the marvellous Peter Domankiewicz for advice, information and gossip on all things photography and early film and, particularly, on Kate Pragnell and William Friese-Greene.

To the wonderful Katherine Mills for taking the time to talk to me about magic and mentalism.

To my early readers and champions – Naomi Luland, Rachel Buchanan, Sian Griffith, Polly Shepherd, and Pauline Hyder.

To my 'theatre consultants', my writer twin Hannah Khalil and director extraordinaire Tom Malcolm Wright.

To Stuart Turner for aiding and abetting on all things Bristol.

To Lydia Massiah for her glorious tour of the grounds of Ashton Court and accompanying me around the gardens of Goldney Hall.

To Liv Chapman, Jonathan Davidson, Emma Boniwell and all the Writing West Midlands crew for all their amazing work.

To the Wellcome Collection for their exhibition – Smoke and Mirrors: The Psychology of Magic, the initial inspiration for this story.

To David and in memory of Hedley Todd for their precious family copy of David Devant's *Tricks for Everyone*.

To the Ludlow massive, the Walthamstow crew, my old Bristol Uni pals, and all my other friends and family near and far.

To fellow writers for encouragement and wise words: Rebecca F John, Joanne Burn, Kenny Doyle, Tariq Jordan, Simon Bolton, Jon Bruford, Sara-Jane Arbury, Annie Garthwaite, Stephenjohn Holgate, Jackie Morris, Nicola Davies, and Essie Fox.

To my 'Eadie's – Charlotte Chilton, Jess Laurie, Ali Gardiner, and Rachel B. Curly mafia forever!

To all the booksellers and librarians up and down the country who've been so kind and supportive. Especial thanks to the truly lovely trio of Iran Morris, Ruth Brookes, and Dan Bassett.

Merci bien to Helena Chadderton for all things French! And to Phil and Jane Packer for always knowing what direction to point me in.

In memory of Os, the laziest dog in the world.

Thanks as ever to Rob, for putting up with me.

All done by kindness

The Illusions
Reading Group Questions

1. *The Illusions* is set in 1896, at the very end of the nineteenth century, in a time of great social, scientific and cultural change. How does this impact the novel? How does Liz Hyder explore the changes happening at this point in history?

2. The novel follows multiple characters. Who was your favourite? Who did you feel was the central character?

3. How does the novel examine the position of women at this point in time? In what ways are Eadie and Cec constricted by the roles society wishes to give them?

4. Within the novel, there is both true *magic* and *illusion* – how do these things complement each other? Which of Valentin's tricks do you think were illusion and which were magic?

5. How does the novel look at both the joys and the dangers of illusion?

6. There are various disappearances throughout the novel: characters vanish by running away, by dying, by illusion, by magic. What do you make of this theme? How do these disappearances affect those left behind?

7. Why do you think George's motto is 'All Done by Kindness'?

8. How does the motif of filmmaking and photography complement that of magic and illusion? Where do you think the line was for the Victorians between science and magic?

9. Both Eadie and George are hugely driven to succeed in their chosen careers. In what ways are the two characters different? In what ways are they similar?

10. What did you make of Roderick Skarratt? How did your opinion of him change over the course of the novel? And what about his sister?

11. There are five pairs of siblings in *The Illusions*, all with very different dynamics: Eadie and Louis, George and Harry, Ollie and Alex Hogarth, The Professor and Olivia, Roderick Skarratt and Maria Carnesky. How does the novel look at sibling relationships?

12. In her historical note, Liz Hyder writes that *The Illusions* is a 'love-letter to the theatre'. How does theatre function in the novel, both as a setting and as a theme?

13. What did you make of the ending? Did you see the twist coming?

14. What do you think will happen to the characters after the end of the book?

15. Have you read Liz Hyder's other novel, *The Gifts*, too? If so, what themes do you think *The Gifts* and *The Illusions* have in common?

Hello dear reader!

Thank you so much for reading *The Illusions*! I so hope you enjoyed falling back in time to 1896 and a world of magic and moving images . . .

If you would like to hear more about my books, you can visit www.lizhyder.co.uk and sign up to become part of my free Readers' Club. It only takes a moment to join, there are no catches, Bonnier Books UK will keep your data private and confidential and never pass it on to a third party. I pinky-promise not to spam you with loads of emails too! I'll just get in touch every now and then – every month or so - with news about writing, behind the scenes information, and what other books, films, and music I've been enjoying. And, of course, you're welcome to unsubscribe whenever you want.

If you would like to get involved in a wider conversation about The Illusions, you can find me on both Twitter and Instagram as @LondonBessie or tag me in at #TheIllusions. I love it when readers get in touch!

And, if you wanted to, please feel free to review it on Amazon, Goodreads, any other e-store, or on your own social media.

All done by kindness!

Very best wishes,
Liz H